Snobs

Snobs

A NOVEL BY

JULIAN FELLOWES

Weidenfeld & Nicolson

LONDON

First published in Great Britain in 2004
by Weidenfeld & Nicolson

© 2004 Julian Fellowes

A CIP catalogue record for this book
is available from the British Library.

ISBN 0 297 848763

Typeset by Deltatype Ltd, Birkenhead, Merseyside

Printed in Great Britain by Clays Ltd, St Ives Plc

Weidenfeld & Nicolson

The Orion Publishing Group Ltd
Orion House
5 Upper Saint Martin's Lane
London, WC2H 9EA

To darling Emma and Peregrine, of course,
but also to dearest Micky
without whom this book
would not have been possible

PART ONE

~

Impetuoso-Fiero

ONE

~

I do not know exactly how Edith Lavery came first to be taken up by Isabel Easton. Probably they had a friend in common or sat on some committee together, or perhaps they just went to the same hairdresser. But I can remember that from quite early on, for some reason, Isabel decided that Edith was rather a feather in her cap, someone that little bit special to be fed to her country neighbours in rationed morsels. History was of course to prove her right, although there was no tremendously compelling evidence for this when I first met her. Edith was certainly very pretty then but not as she would be later when she had, as designers say, found her style. She was a type, albeit a superior example of it: the English blonde with large eyes and nice manners.

I had known Isabel Easton since we were children together in Hampshire and we enjoyed one of those pleasant, undemanding friendships that are based entirely on longevity. We had very little in common but we knew few other people who could remember us on our ponies at the age of nine and there was a certain comfort in our occasional encounters. I had gone into the theatre after leaving university and Isabel had married a stockbroker and moved to Sussex so our worlds scarcely crossed, but it was fun for Isabel to have an actor to stay occasionally who had been seen on television (though never, as it happens, by any of her friends) and for me, it was pleasant enough to spend the odd weekend with my old playmate.

I was in Sussex the first time that Edith came down and I can testify to Isabel's enthusiasm for her new friend, later queried by her less generous acquaintance. It was quite genuine: 'Things are going to happen for her. She's got something.' Isabel was fond of using phrases that seemed to imply an inside knowledge of the workings of the world. Some might have said that when Edith climbed out of the car half an hour later, she didn't appear to have got very much beyond her

3

appearance and a rather beguiling, relaxed charm, but I was inclined to agree with our hostess. Looking back, there was a hint of what was to come in the mouth, one of those cut-glass mouths, with the clearly defined, almost chiselled lips that one associates with the film actresses of the forties. And then there was her skin. To the English, skin is, as a rule, the compliment of last resort, to be employed when there is nothing else to praise. Good skin is frequently dwelt on when talking of the plainer members of the Royal Family. Be that as it may, Edith Lavery had the loveliest complexion I have ever seen: cool, clear, pastel colours under layers of flawless wax. I have all my life had a weakness for good-looking people and in retrospect, I think I became Edith's ally in that first moment of admiring her face. At all events, Isabel was destined to become a self-fulfilling prophet for it was she who took Edith to Broughton.

Broughton Hall, indeed the very House of Broughton, was a wounding seam that marbled every aspect of the Eastons' Sussex life. As first Barons and then Earls Broughton and lately, since 1879, Marquesses of Uckfield, the Broughtons had held mighty sway over this particular section of East Sussex for a great deal longer than most potentates of the Home Counties. Until little more than a century ago their neighbours and vassals had mainly consisted of lowly farmers eking a living out of the flat and boggy marshland at the base of the downs but the roads and the railways and the invention of the Saturday-to-Monday had brought the *haute bourgeoisie* flooding to the area in search of *ton*, and, like Byron, the Broughtons awoke to find themselves famous. Before long, the local mark of whether one was 'in' or 'out' was largely based on whether or not one was on their visiting list. In fairness I must say that the family did not seek its celebrity, not at first anyway, but as the major representatives of the *anciens riches* in an upwardly mobile area their power was forced upon them.

They had been lucky in other ways. Two marriages, one to a banker's daughter and the other to the heiress of a large section of San Francisco had steered the family craft through the turbulent seas of the agricultural depression and the Great War. Unlike many such dynasties, they had retained some if not all of their London holdings, and various tricks with property in the sixties had brought them to the comparatively safe shores of Mrs Thatcher's Britain. After that, when the socialists did start to regroup they turned out, happily for the upper classes generally, to have been reborn as *New* Labour and so would prove much more accommodating than their rapacious political forebears. All in all, the Broughtons were the very acme of the 'surviving' English family. They had reached the 1990s with their prestige and, more significantly, their estates practically intact.

Not that any of this was a problem for the Eastons. Far from resenting the family's privileges they positively worshipped them. No, the difficulty was that despite living two miles from Broughton Hall itself, despite Isabel's telling her girlfriends over lunch in Walton Street what luck it was having the house 'practically next door', still, after three and a half years, they had never set foot in it, nor succeeded in meeting one single member of the family.

Of course, David Easton was not the first upper-middle-class Englishman to discover that it is easier to demonstrate a spurious aristocratic background in London than in the country. The problem was that after years of lunches at Brooks's, Saturdays at race-meetings and evenings at Annabel's, mouthing his prejudices against the modern, *mobile* society, he had entirely lost touch with the fact that he was a product of it. It was as if he had forgotten his father had been the managing director of a minor furniture factory in the Midlands and it was with some difficulty that his parents had put him through Ardingly. By the time I met him I think he would have been genuinely surprised not to have found his name in Debrett's. I remember once reading an article in which Roddy Llewellyn was quoted as complaining that he had not been to Eton (as his elder brother had) because it was at Eton that one picked up one's lifelong friends. David happened to be passing my chair. 'Quite right,' he said. 'That's exactly how I feel.' I looked across the room to catch Isabel's eye but I saw at once in her sympathetic nod that she did not want to be in my conspiracy but rather in her husband's.

To an outsider it seems a vital ingredient of many marriages that each partner should support the illusions of the other. Protected, as he had been, by a combination of Isabel's kindness and most London hostesses' indifference to anything beyond their guests' ability to talk and eat the food, it was now bitter indeed to sit at smart dinner tables and be asked about Charles Broughton's trip to Italy or how Caroline's new husband was shaping up and to have to murmur that he didn't really know them. 'But how extraordinary,' would come the answer. 'I thought you were neighbours.' And even in this admission there was a certain dishonesty, for it was not that David did not *really* know them. He did not know them at all.

Once at a cocktail party in Eaton Square he had ventured an opinion about the family only to hear his companion ask, 'But isn't that Charles over there? You must introduce me and we'll see if he remembers where we met.' And David had had to say he felt sick (which was more or less true) and go home and miss the dinner they had all been going on to. Lately he had taken to assuming a slightly dismissive air when they were mentioned. He would stand, loudly silent, on the edge of the discussion as if he, David Easton, preferred *not* to know the Broughtons. As if he had tried them and discovered they were not quite to his taste. Nothing could have been further from the truth. In fairness to David I would say that these frustrated social ambitions were probably as secret from his conscious mind as they were supposed to be from the rest of us. Or so it seemed to me as I watched him zip up his Barbour and whistle for the dogs.

Fittingly perhaps, it was Edith who suggested the visit. Isabel asked us at breakfast on Saturday if there was anything we'd like to do and Edith wondered whether there was a local 'stately' and what about that? She looked across at me.

'I wouldn't mind,' I said.

I saw Isabel glance at David deep in his *Telegraph* at the other end of the table. I knew and understood the Broughton situation and Isabel knew I knew, though, being English, we had naturally never discussed it. As it happens, I had met Charles Broughton, the rather lumpish son and heir, a couple of times in London at those hybrid evenings where Show Business and Society congregate but, like the crossing of two rivers, seldom mingle. These encounters I had kept from Isabel for fear of salting the wound.

'David?' she said.

He turned the pages of his newspaper with a large and insouciant gesture.

'You go if you want to. I've got to drive into Lewes. Sutton's lost the petrol cap of the lawn-mower again. He must eat them.'

'I could do that on Monday.'

'No, no. I want to get some cartridges anyway.' He looked up. 'Honestly, you go.'

There was reproach in his eyes, which Isabel dealt with by pulling a slight face as if her hand was being forced. The truth was they had an unspoken agreement not to visit the house as 'members of the public'. At first David had avoided it because he had expected to know the family quite soon and he did not want to run the risk of meeting them from the wrong side of the cordon. As the months and then years of disappointment had unfolded, not visiting the house had become a kind of principle, as if he did not want to give the Broughtons the satisfaction of seeing him pay good money to see what should, by rights, have been his for nothing. But Isabel was more pragmatic than her husband, as women generally are, and she had grown accustomed to the idea that their position in the 'County' was going to be deferred for a while. Now she was simply curious to see the place that had become a symbol of their lack of social muscle. She did not therefore require much persuading. The three of us packed into her battered Renault and set off.

I asked Edith if she knew Sussex at all.

'Not really. I had a friend in Chichester for a while.'

'The fashionable end.'

'Is it? I didn't know counties had fashionable ends. It sounds rather American. Like good and bad tables in the same restaurant.'

'Do you know America?'

'I spent a few months in Los Angeles after I left school.'

'Why?'

Edith laughed. 'Why not? Why does one go anywhere at seventeen?'

'I don't know why one goes to Los Angeles. Unless it's to become a film star.'

'Maybe I wanted to be a film star.' She smiled at me with what I have since come to recognise as a habitual expression of slight sadness, and I saw that her eyes were not blue as I had at first thought, but a sort of misty grey.

We turned through a pair of monumental stone piers, topped with lead stags' heads, antlers and all, and started down the wide gravel drive. Isabel stopped the car. 'Isn't it marvellous!' she said. The vast mass of Broughton Hall sprawled before us. Edith smiled enthusiastically and we drove on. She did not think the house marvellous, no more did I, although it was in its way impressive. At any rate, it was very large. It seemed to have been designed by an eighteenth-century forerunner of

Albert Speer. The main block, a huge granite cube, was connected to two smaller cubes with stocky and cumbersome colonnades. Unfortunately a nineteenth-century Broughton had stripped the windows of their mullions and replaced them with plate glass so now they gaped, vacant and sightless, across the park. At the four corners of the house squat cupolas had been erected like watch-towers in a concentration camp. All in all, it did not so much complete the view as block it.

The car crunched comfortably to a halt. 'Shall we do the house first or the garden?' Isabel, like a 1960s Soviet military inspector in the heart of NATO, was determined to miss nothing.

Edith shrugged. 'Is there a lot to see inside?'

'Oh, I think so,' said Isabel firmly, striding towards the door marked 'Enter'. It crouched in the embrace of the ponderous horseshoe flight of steps leading up to the *piano nobile*. The rusticated granite swallowed her and we meekly followed.

One of Edith's favourite stories would always be that she first saw Broughton as a paying guest, barred by a red rope from the intimate life of the house. 'Not,' as she would remark with her funny half-laugh, 'that the place has ever had much intimate life.' There are houses with such a sense of the personalities that built them, an all-pervading smell of the lives lived there, that the visitor feels himself a cross between a burglar and a ghost, spying on a private place with hidden secrets. Broughton was not such a house. It had been designed down to the last fender and finial with one single aim: to impress strangers. Consequently its role at the end of the twentieth century had hardly changed at all. The only difference being that now the strangers bought tickets instead of tipping the housekeeper.

For the modern visitor, however, the splendours of the state rooms were deferred, and the cold, dank room by which we entered (later we would know it as the Under Hall) was as welcoming as a deserted stadium. Hard-looking footmen's chairs stood around the walls, conjuring up a vision of endless hours of boredom spent sitting on them, and a long, black table filled the centre of the discoloured stone floor. Apart from four dirty views of Venice, a long way after Canaletto, there were no pictures. Like all the rooms at Broughton, the hall was perfectly enormous, making the three of us feel like the Borrowers.

'Well, they don't believe in the soft sell,' said Edith.

8

From the Under Hall, clutching our guide-books, we climbed the Great Staircase with its carved oak flights clambering up around a burly and rather depressing bronze of a dying slave. At the top, after crossing the wide landing, we came first to the Marble Hall, a vast, double-storeyed space with a balustraded gallery round all four sides at second-floor level. Had we entered by the exterior horseshoe stair this would have been our (intentionally flattening) introduction to the house. From this we progressed to the Saloon, another huge room, this time with heavy mahogany mouldings picked out in gold and walls hung with crimson flock wallpaper.

'Chicken tikka for me,' said Edith.

I laughed. She was quite right. It looked exactly like a gigantic Indian restaurant.

Isabel opened the guide-book and began to read in a geography-mistress voice: 'The Saloon is hung with its original paper, one of the chief glories of Broughton's interior. The gilt side-tables were made for this room by William Kent in seventeen-thirty-nine. The maritime theme of the carved pier glasses was inspired by the appointment of the third earl to the embassy in Portugal in seventeen thirty-seven. The Earl, himself, is commemorated in this, his favourite room in the full-length portrait by Jarvis, which hangs, together with its companion of his countess by Hudson, on either side of the Italian fireplace.'

Edith and I stared at the pictures. The one of Lady Broughton made a little stab at gaiety by posing the heavy-featured young woman on a bank of flowers, a summer hat trailing from her large hand.

'There's a woman at my gym exactly like that,' said Edith. 'She's always trying to sell me Conservative raffle tickets.'

Isabel droned on. 'The cabinet in the centre of the south wall is by Boulle and was a gift from Marie-Josèphe de Saxe, Dauphine of France, to the bride of the fifth earl on the occasion of her marriage. Between the windows ...'

I drifted away to these same, tall windows and looked down into the park. It was one of those hot, sulky days in late August when the trees seem overburdened with leaf and the green upon green of the countryside is stuffy and airless. As I stood there, a man came round the corner of the house. He was wearing tweeds and corduroys despite the weather and one of those tiresome brown felt derbies that Englishmen in the country imagine to be dashing. He looked up and I saw it was

Charles Broughton. He barely glanced at me and looked away, but then he stopped and looked up again. I supposed that he had recognised me and I raised my hand in greeting, which he acknowledged with some slight gesture of his own and went on about his business.

'Who was that?' Edith was standing behind me. She had also abandoned Isabel to her orisons.

'Charles Broughton.'

'A son of the house?'

'The only son of the house, I think.'

'Will he ask us in for tea?'

'I shouldn't think so. I've met him precisely twice.'

Charles did not ask us in for tea and I'm sure he wouldn't have given me another thought if we hadn't run into him on our way back to the car. He was talking to one of the many gardeners who were drifting about the place and happened to finish just as we started back across the forecourt.

'Hello,' he nodded quite amiably. 'What are you doing here?' He had clearly forgotten my name and probably where we had met but he was pleasant enough and stood waiting to be introduced to the others.

Isabel, taken short by this sudden and unexpected propulsion into the Land Where Dreams Come True, fumbled for something to say that would fasten like a fascinating burr inside Charles's brain and result in a close friendship springing up more or less immediately. No inspiration came.

'He's staying with us. We're two miles away,' she said baldly.

'Really? Do you get down often?'

'We're here all the time.'

'Ah,' said Charles. He turned to Edith. 'Are you local, too?'

She smiled. 'Don't worry, I'm quite safe. I live in London.'

He laughed and his fleshy, hearty features looked momentarily quite attractive. He took off his hat and revealed that fair, Rupert Brooke hair, crinkly curls at the nape of the neck, that is so characteristic of the English aristocrat. 'I hope you liked the house.'

Edith smiled and said nothing, leaving Isabel to reel off her silly gleanings from the guide-book.

I stepped in with the pardon. 'We ought to be off. David will be wondering what's happened to us.'

We all smiled and nodded and touched hands, and a few minutes later we were back on the road.

'You never said you knew Charles Broughton,' said Isabel in a flat tone.

'I don't.'

'Well, you never said you'd met him.'

'Didn't I?'

Although, naturally, I knew I hadn't. Isabel drove the rest of the way in silence. Edith turned from the front passenger seat and made a that's-torn-it expression with her mouth. It was clear I had failed and Isabel was noticeably cool to me for the rest of the weekend.

TWO

~

Edith Lavery was the daughter of a successful chartered accountant, himself the grandson of a Jewish immigrant who had arrived in England in 1905 to escape the pogroms of the late, and to Edith's father, unlamented Tsar Nicholas II. I do not think I ever knew the family's original name, Levy, perhaps, or Levin. At any rate, the Edwardian portraitist, Sir John Lavery, was the inspiration for the change, which seemed, and almost certainly was, a good idea at the time. When asked if they were connected to the painter, the Laverys would answer, 'Vaguely, I think,' thus linking themselves with the British establishment without making any disputable claims. It is quite customary for the English, when asked if they have met so-and-so, to say, 'Yes, but they wouldn't remember me,' or 'Well, I've met them but I don't know them,' when they have not met them.

This is because of a subconscious urge on their part to create the comforting illusion that England, or rather the England of the upper-middle and upper classes, is criss-crossed with a million invisible silken threads that weave them together into a brilliant community of rank and grace and exclude everybody else. There is little dishonesty in it for as a rule they understand each other. To an Englishman or woman of a certain background the answer, 'Well, I've met them but they wouldn't remember me' means 'I have not met them.'

Mrs Lavery, Edith's mother, considered herself a bird of quite different feather to her spouse, fond as she was of him. Her own father had been an Indian army colonel but the salient detail was that *his* mother had been the great-niece of a banking baronet. Although kindly in many ways, Mrs Lavery was passionately snobbish to a degree verging on insanity and so her frail connection to this, the very lowest hereditary rank filled her with the warming sense of belonging to that inner circle of rank and privilege where her poor husband must ever be a stranger. Mr Lavery did not, for this reason, resent his wife. Not in the least. On the contrary he was proud of her. She was, after all, a tall, good-looking woman who knew how to dress and if anything he was rather entertained by the idea that the phrase *'noblesse oblige'* (one of Mrs Lavery's favourites) could have the slightest application to his household.

They lived in a large flat in Elm Park Gardens, which was almost at the wrong end of Chelsea and not quite to Mrs Lavery's taste. Still, it was not exactly Fulham nor, worse, Battersea, names that had only recently begun to appear on Mrs Lavery's mental map. She still felt the thrill of the new, like an intrepid explorer pushing ever further from civilization, whenever she was invited for dinner by one of her friends' married children. She listened perkily as they discussed what a good investment the 'toast rack' was or how the children loved Tooting after that poky flat in Marloes Road. It was all Greek to Mrs Lavery. So far as she was concerned she was in Hell until she got back over the river, her own personal Styx, that forever divided the Underworld from Real Life.

The Laverys were not rich but nor were they poor and, having only one child, there was never any need to stint. Edith was sent off to a fashionable nursery school and then Benenden ('No, *not* because of the Princess Royal. We simply looked around and we thought it the *most* inspiring place'.) Mr Lavery would have liked the girl's education to have been continued at university but when Edith's exam results were not good enough, certainly not for anywhere they were interested in sending her, Mrs Lavery was not disappointed. Her great ambition had always been to bring her daughter out.

Stella Lavery had not been a debutante herself. This was something of which she was deeply ashamed. She would seek to conceal it under a lot of laughing references to the fun she'd had as a girl and, if pushed for specifics, she might sigh that her father had taken rather a tumble in the thirties (thereby connecting herself with the Wall Street Crash and echoes of Scott Fitzgerald and Gatsby). Alternatively, fudging her dates, she would blame it on the war. The truth, as Mrs Lavery was forced to admit to herself in the dark night of the soul, was that in the less socially free-wheeling world of the 1950s, there had been clearer demarcation lines between precisely who was in Society and who was not. Stella Lavery's family was not. She envied those of her friends who had met as debutantes with a deep and secret envy that gnawed at her entrails. She even hated them for including her in their reminiscences about Henrietta Tiarks or Miranda Smiley as if they believed that she, Stella Lavery, had 'come out' when they knew, and she knew they knew, she had not. For these reasons she had been determined from the outset that no such gaps would shadow the life of her beloved Edith. (The name Edith incidentally was chosen for its fragrant overtones of a slower, better England and perhaps, half-consciously, to suggest that it was a family name handed down from some Edwardian beauty. It was not.) At all events, the girl was to be propelled into the charmed circle from the first. Since by the nineties Presentation at Court (which might have posed a problem) was a thing of the distant past, all Mrs Lavery had to do was to convince her husband and her daughter that it would be time and money well spent.

They did not need much persuasion. Edith had no concrete plans for how she was to pass her adult life and to delay the decision-making process with a year-long round of parties seemed a pretty good idea. As for Mr Lavery, he enjoyed the vision of his wife and his daughter in the *beau monde* and was perfectly happy to pay for it. Mrs Lavery's carefully tended connections were enough to get Edith onto Peter Townend's list for the opening tea-parties and the girl's own looks won her a place as a model at the Berkeley Dress Show. After that it was plain sailing. Mrs Lavery went to the mothers' lunches and packed her daughter's dresses for balls in the country and on the whole had a wonderful time. Edith quite enjoyed it, too.

The only reservation for Mrs Lavery was that when the Season was over, when the last, winter Charity Balls had finished and the *Tatler* cuttings had been pasted into a scrap-book along with the invitations, nothing much seemed to have changed. Edith had obviously been entertained by the daughters of several peers – including one duke, which was particularly thrilling – indeed, all of these girls had attended Edith's own cocktail party at Claridge's (one of Mrs Lavery's happiest evenings), but the friends who stayed on after the dances had ceased were very like the girls she had brought home from school, the daughters of prosperous, upper-middle-class businessmen. Exactly what Edith was herself in fact. This did not seem right to Mrs Lavery. She had for so long attributed her own failure to reach the dizzying upper echelons of London Society (a group she rather archly labelled 'the Court') to her lack of a proper launch that she had expected great things from her daughter. Perhaps her enthusiasm blinded her to a simple truth: the fact that the Season had opened its arms to her daughter meant it was no longer in the 1980s the exclusive institution it had been in Mrs Lavery's youth.

Edith was aware of her mother's disappointment but while she was certainly not immune, as we would find out, to the charms of rank and fortune, she did not quite see how she was expected to prosecute these intimacies with the daughters of the Great Houses. To start with they all seemed to have known each other from birth and anyway she couldn't help feeling it would be difficult to cater for their pleasures in a flat in Elm Park Gardens. In the end she remained on nodding terms with most of the girls in her year but returned to a very similar groove to the one she had occupied on leaving school.

I learned all this quite soon after first meeting Edith at the Eastons' because it so transpired that she took a job answering the telephone in an estate agent's in Milner Street, just round the corner from where I had a basement flat. I started bumping into her in Peter Jones, or having a sandwich in one of the local pubs, or buying a five-thirty pint of milk in Partridges and gradually, almost without noticing it, we became quite friendly. One day I saw her coming out of the General Trading Company at about one o'clock and I invited her for some lunch.

'Have you seen Isabel lately?' I asked, as we squeezed into a banquette in one of those little Italian places where the waiters shout.

'I had dinner with them both last week.'

'All well?'

It was, or well enough. They were engaged in some school drama about their child. Isabel had discovered dyslexia. I pitied the head-master.

'She asked after you. I said I'd seen you,' said Edith.

I remarked that I didn't think Isabel had as yet forgiven me for failing to tell her I knew Charles Broughton, and Edith laughed. It was then that I heard about her mother. I asked if she'd told Mrs Lavery about our time at Broughton. It so happened that Charles was rather on my mind as that morning I'd seen one of those idiotic magazine articles about eligible bachelors and Charles had led the pack. I blush to say I was rather impressed with the list of his assets.

'Not likely. I wouldn't want to give her any ideas.'

'She must be very susceptible.'

'She certainly is. She'd have me up the aisle before you could say knife.'

'And you don't want to get married?'

Edith looked at me as if I were mad. 'Of course I want to get married.'

'You don't see yourself as a career girl? I thought all women want careers now.' I do not know why I slid into this kind of pompous anti-feminism since it does not in the least reflect my views.

'Well, I don't want to spend the rest of my life answering the telephone in an estate agent's office if that's what you mean.'

I was duly reprimanded. 'That's not quite what I had in mind,' I said.

Edith looked at me indulgently as if it were necessary to take me through my three times table. 'I'm twenty-seven. I have no qualifications and, what is worse, no particular talent. I also have tastes that require, at the very least, eighty thousand a year. When my father dies he will leave what money he has to my mother and I don't anticipate either of them quitting the scene much before 2030. What do you suggest I should do?'

I do not know why but I felt rather muted by this Anita Loos-style practicality emanating from the little rose before me, with her Alice band and her neat, navy blue suit.

'So you intend to marry a rich man?' I asked.

Edith looked at me quizzically. Perhaps she felt she had given away too much, perhaps she was trying to ascertain if I was judging her and if so, whether or not she was coming out ahead. She should have been reassured by what she saw in my eyes for it has always seemed to me that if one can face up early on to what one really wants in life, then there is every chance of avoiding the seemingly inevitable modern disease of mid-life crisis.

'Not necessarily,' she answered, with a trace of defensiveness in her voice. 'It's just that I cannot imagine I would be very happy married to a poor one.'

'I do see that,' I said.

Edith and I did not meet for some time after this luncheon. I was cast in one of those unwatchable American mini-series and I left for Paris and, of all places, Warsaw for some months. The job involved the supremely depressing experience of celebrating Christmas and New

Year in a foreign hotel where they give you cheese for breakfast and all the bread is stale, and when I returned to London in May, I certainly did not feel I had very much advanced my art. On the other hand, I was at least a bit better off than when I left. Quite soon after I arrived home I received a card from Isabel asking me to join their party for the second day of Ascot. She must have forgiven me in my absence. I thought I would have to refuse as I had done nothing about applying for my voucher to the Enclosure but it turned out that my mother (who with such gestures would betray a defiant denial of the work and the life I have chosen) had applied for me. Today, in these more graceless times, it would not be possible for her to apply for someone else, even her own child, but then it was. She had in fact undertaken this annual responsibility in my youth and she proved reluctant to give it up. 'You'll be so sorry if you have to miss something fun,' she would say whenever I objected that I had no plans to attend the meeting. And this time my mother was proved right. I accepted Isabel's offer with the half-smile that the prospect of a day at Ascot always brings to my lips.

Like many famous institutions, the image and the reality of the Royal Enclosure at Ascot bear little or no relation to each other. The very name 'Royal Enclosure' (to say nothing of the glutinous coverage in the lowbrow press) conjures up visions of princes and duchesses, famous beauties and Rand millionaires strolling on manicured lawns in *haute couture*. Of this picture, I can, I suppose, testify to the quality of the lawns. The vast majority of visitors to the Enclosure appear to be middle-aged businessmen from the more expensive suburbs of London. They are accompanied by wives wearing inappropriate outfits, generally in chiffon. What, however, makes this disparity between dream and truth unusual and amusing is the wilfully blind support of the fantasy by the participants themselves. Even those members of Society, or rather those members of the upper-middle and upper classes, who do actually go to the meeting, take a touching delight in dressing and behaving as if they were at the smart and exclusive event the papers talk about. Their women wear just as inappropriate but more becoming fitted suits and swan about greeting each other as if they were at some gathering in the Ranelagh Gardens in 1770. For a day or two every year these working people allow themselves the luxury of pretending that they are part of some vanished leisure class, that the world they mourn and admire and pretend they would have belonged to if it still existed (which as a rule they would not) is alive and well and living near Windsor. Their pretensions are naked and vulnerable and for that reason, to me at least, rather charming. I am always happy to spend one day at Ascot.

David collected me in his Volvo estate and I climbed in to find Edith, whom I had expected, and another couple, the Rattrays. Simon Rattray seemed to work for Strutt and Parker and talked a lot about shooting. His wife, Venetia, talked a little about her children and even less about anything else. We nosed our way down the M4 and through Windsor Great Park until we finally reached the course and David's slightly obscure car park. It was a perennial source of irritation to him that he could not get into Number One and he always vented his annoyance on Isabel as she was pointing out the signs. I never minded; it had become part of Ascot for me (like my father shouting at the tree-lights every Christmas – one of my few really vivid childhood memories), I had after all been with them several times.

Before too long the car was safely on its numbered place and the lunch was unpacked. It was clear that Edith had had no hand in it as it was Isabel and Venetia who assumed control, fussing and clucking and slicing and mixing until the feast was spread in all its glory before our eyes. The men and Edith watched from the safety of the folding chairs, clutching plastic glasses of champagne. As usual, there was a certain poignancy in all this preparation, given the brevity allotted to the food's consumption. We had hardly drawn up our seats to the wobbly table when Isabel, as predictable as David's worry over the car park, looked at her watch. 'We mustn't be long. It's twenty-five to two now.' David nodded and helped himself to strawberries. Nobody needed an explanation. Part of this day, Mass-like in its ritual, was getting to the steps in the Enclosure in time to see the arrival of the Royal house-party from Windsor. And getting there early enough to secure a good vantage point. Edith looked at me and rolled her eyes, but we both obediently gulped down our coffee, pinned on our badges and headed for the course.

We passed the stewards at the entrance, busily dividing the wheat from the tares. Two unfortunates had just been stopped, though whether it was because they didn't have the right badge or were wrongly dressed I do not know. Edith squeezed my arm with one of her secret smiles. I looked down. 'Something funny?'

She shook her head. 'No.'

'Well then.'

'I have a soft spot for getting in where others are held back.'

I laughed. 'You may feel that. Many do. But it is rather low to admit it.'

'Oh dear. Then I'm afraid I'm very low. I must just hope it doesn't hold me back.'

'I don't think it will,' I said.

What was interesting about this exchange was its honesty. Edith looked the perfect archetype of the Sloane Ranger girl she was, but I was beginning to understand that she had a disconcerting awareness of the realities of her life and situation when such girls generally make a show of pretended ignorance of these things. It was not that her sentiments marked her apart. The English, of all classes as it happens, are addicted to exclusivity. Leave three Englishmen in a room and they will invent a rule that prevents a fourth joining them. What made Edith different is that most people, and certainly all toffs, put on a great show of not being aware if it. Any suggestion that there is pleasure in being a guest where the public has to buy tickets, of being allowed through a gate, of being ushered into a room, where the people are turned away, will be met by the aristocrat (or would-be aristocrat) with blank looks and studied lack of comprehension. The practised matron will probably suggest with a slight movement of the eyebrows that the very idea denotes a lack of breeding. The dishonesty in all this is of course breathtaking but, as always with these people, the discipline in their unwavering rules commands a certain respect.

We must have dawdled, as the others were all at the steps, which were fast filling up, and waved to us to join them. A distant roar announced that the carriages were on the way and the footmen or stewards or whatever they are rushed forward to open the gates from the course. Edith nudged me and nodded towards Isabel as the first coach carrying Her Majesty and some dusky premier of an oil-rich state swept through the entrance. Like the other men I took my hat off with a perfectly genuine enthusiasm but I could not ignore the look on Isabel's face. It was the glazed, ecstatic expression of a rabbit before a cobra. She was hypnotised, enraptured. To be included in the Ascot house-party, Isabel, like Pervaneh in *Hassan*, would have faced the Procession of Protracted Death. Or at least she would have considered it. It only goes to show, I suppose, that for all the educated classes' contempt of mass star-worship, they themselves are just as susceptible to fantasy when it is presented in a palatable form.

Actually, the procession that year was a bit disappointing. The Prince of Wales, Isabel's paradigm of perfection, was not there and nor were any of the other princes. The only junior Royal was Zara Phillips, brightly attired in revealing beachwear. Edith had been murmuring irreverent criticisms in my ear, much to the annoyance of Isabel and a woman with blue hair standing next to her, so, rather than continue to spoil their fun, we turned to go when I heard a voice right behind me: 'Hello, how are you?' I looked round and found myself face to face with Charles Broughton. This time there was no awkwardness over names, the best part of the Enclosure being that everyone has to wear a badge with their name written on it. There you will find no fumbling of introductions or pretending that people have already met. Just a cursory glance at the lapel or bosom of the unknown one and all is well. Would that such labelling was compulsory at all social gatherings. Charles's badge proclaimed 'The Earl Broughton' in the distinctive, round handwriting of the well-bred girls of the Ascot Office.

'Hello,' I said. 'You remember Edith Lavery?' I had employed the correct English usage for presenting a person whom one is fairly certain will have been forgotten, but in this instance I was wrong.

'Certainly I do. You're the safe one who lives in London.'

'Well, I hope I'm not as safe as all that.' Edith smiled and, either on her own initiative or on Charles's invitation, took his arm.

The Eastons and the Rattrays were bearing down on us and I could almost see the whites of their eyes when I suggested a visit to the paddock. It seems hard and probably reveals a deep insecurity in me but I felt embarrassed for poor old Isabel in her eagerness, and David's ambition looked nearly malevolent in its intensity. Mercifully, Charles, who was after all quite a polite fellow, nodded a greeting to Isabel that dismissed her but showed at least that he was aware they had been introduced. David, seething, hung back and the three of us headed off towards the paddock where the horses were being paraded before the first race.

Predictably Charles turned out to know quite a lot about horses and before long he was happily engaged in informed chatter on fetlocks and form, none of which interested me in the least, but I was kept amused by observing Edith gazing up at him with fascinated, flattering attention. It is a technique that such women seem to acquire at birth. She was wearing a neat linen suit of a pale bluish colour, I think the correct term is eau-de-nil, with a little pill-box hat tipped forward over her forehead. It made her look frivolous but, in contrast to the Weybridge matrons in their organza frills, unsentimental and chic. It was an outfit that added a dash of wit and humour to her face, which, I was by this stage aware, was extremely beguiling. As she studied her card and made notes against the names with Charles's pencil, I watched him watching her and it was perhaps then that I first became aware of a real possibility that he was attracted to her. Not that this was very surprising. She had all the right attributes. She was pretty and witty and, as she had said herself, safe. She was not of his set, of course, but she lived and spoke like his own people. It is a popular fiction that there is a great difference in manner and manners between the upper-middle and upper classes. The truth is, on a day-to-day level they are in most things identical. Of course the aristocracy's circle of acquaintance is much smaller and so there is invariably with them the sense of the membership of a club. This can result in a tendency to display their social security by means of an off-handed rudeness, which doesn't bother them and upsets almost everybody else. But these things apart (and rudeness is very easily learned) there is little to tell between them in social style. No, Edith Lavery was clearly Charles's kind of girl.

We watched a race or two but I could sense that Edith, in the nicest possible way, was trying to shake me off and so when Charles inevitably suggested tea in White's, I excused myself and went off in search of the others. Edith threw me a grateful look and the pair of them walked away arm in arm.

I found Isabel and David in one of the champagne bars behind the grandstand, drinking warm Pimm's. The caterers had run out of ice. 'Where's Edith?'

'She's gone off to White's with Charles.'

David looked sulky. Poor David. He never did manage to be taken into White's at Ascot, neither in their old tent nor, so far as I am aware, in their new, more space-age accommodation. He would have given an arm to be a member. 'Jolly good,' he said through gritted teeth. 'I wouldn't have minded some tea.'

'I think they were going to meet up with the rest of Charles's party.'

'I'm sure they were.'

Isabel in contrast said nothing but kept sipping at the tepid liquid with its four bits of floating cucumber.

'I said we'd meet up at the car after the second last race.'

'Fine,' David said grimly, and we lapsed into silence. Isabel, to her credit, still looked more interested than irritated as she stared into her unappetising drink.

Edith was already leaning against the locked car when we got there and I could see at once that the day had been a success.

'Where's Charles?' I said.

She nodded towards the grandstand. 'He's gone to find the people he's staying with tonight. He's coming tomorrow and Friday.'

'Good luck to him.'

'Haven't you enjoyed yourself?'

'Oh yes,' I said. 'But not half as much as you.'

She laughed and said nothing, and at that moment David arrived to unlock the vehicle. He did not mention Charles and he was noticeably grumpy with Edith, so it was not as a general announcement but in a whisper that she informed me that Charles had asked her out for dinner the following Tuesday. It was of course more than she could do to keep it to herself.

THREE

~

Edith sat at her dressing table, bathed and sweet-smelling, and prepared to paint on her social face. She hadn't told her mother exactly whom she was dining with and now she pondered why she had not. It would certainly have given Stella a great deal of pleasure. It was probably a fear of this very pleasure that kept her daughter silent. And anyway, at this stage, Edith had not made up her mind whether or not she thought there was any what the magazines call 'future' in it.

Edith Lavery was not in the least promiscuous but, at this point, she was certainly not a virgin. She had, in her time, had several boyfriends. None was serious until she was about twenty-three but then there had been a stockbroker, five years older than her and very good-looking, whom she had made up her mind to accept when he proposed. They went out for about a year, stayed in a lot of house-parties, enjoyed quite a few of the same things, and generally were happy or at least as happy as anyone else. His name was Philip, his mother was fairly grand, there was a little money – enough to start them off in Clapham – and in fact it all seemed fine, so no one was more surprised than Edith when he explained one evening, in halting tones, that he had met someone else and it was all over. For a moment Edith had difficulty making sense of this. Partly because he chose to tell her in San Lorenzo in Beauchamp Place, where the customers on the two neighbouring tables were listening to every word, and partly because she couldn't imagine in all modesty what this 'someone else' could have that she, Edith, didn't. She and Philip liked each other, they were a good-looking pair, they both enjoyed country weekends, they both skied. Where was the difficulty?

At any rate, Philip left and three months later she was invited to his wedding. She went, being very gracious and looking (as she was determined to do) ravishing. The bride was plainer than her, naturally, and rather ordinary really but as Edith watched her gazing up at Philip as if he were God on earth, she had an uncomfortable inkling that this had something to do with what had gone wrong.

After that there had been various walk-outs but not much more. One, an estate agent named George, had lasted about six months but this was only because he was the first competent lover she had experienced and the pleasures he unlocked in her made her wilfully blind to his shortcomings until one day, at Henley (which he had taken her to imagining, rather touchingly, that it was a smart event), while they were lunching in some members' tent, she had looked across the table at him, laughing his loud and gummy laugh, and realised that he really was too frightful. After that it was simply a matter of time.

Her parents had been quite sorry about Philip whom they liked, not in the least sorry about George and, on the whole, without an opinion on the various others who had briefly penetrated Elm Park Gardens, but Edith had begun to notice that the veiled hints and half-joking, half-worried remarks from her mother had been getting more frequent since her twenty-seventh birthday. And for the first time she had started to feel a very far-away, distant echo of panic. Just supposing, for the sake of argument, that no one did ask her to marry them, what would she do?

What *on earth* was she going to do?

But then, she thought as she pulled out the heated rollers and picked up her Mason Pearson brush, everything could change so quickly. Being a woman wasn't like being a man. Men were either born with money or they spent years beavering away at careers to make themselves rich while women . . . women can be poor one day and rich, or at least married to a rich man, the next. It might not be fashionable to admit it but even in this day and age, a woman's life can be utterly transformed by means of the right ring.

It is easy to get the impression from these ruminations that Edith was harshly, even exclusively, mercenary at this time in her life but that would be unjust. And it would have surprised her. If asked whether she was materialistic she would have answered she was practical, if snobbish she would have said she was worldly. After all, she read novels, she went to the cinema, she knew about happiness, she believed in love. But she saw her future career as primarily social (how could she not?) and if it was to be social then how could she have a career worthy of the name without money and position? Of course, by the 1990s, these were supposed to be outmoded ambitions but Edith did not have it in her to rush off and found a keep-fit empire or publish a new magazine. As for any of the professions, she had missed her chance of those ten years before when she left school. And it was no longer unfashionable to want to be affluent. The brown rice and dirndl-skirted generation of her childhood had given way to a brasher, post-Thatcherite world and weren't her dreams, in a way, in tune with that development?

Still, if she was ambitious and reluctantly committed to the idea that it would be a man who would open the golden pathway to fulfilment, it would not be true to say that Edith was fundamentally a snob. Certainly not compared to her mother. She said herself that she liked to be on the inside looking out rather than the other way round, but she was more interested in achievement (or power, to use its less fragrant name) than rank. She wanted to be at the centre of things. She wanted a winner, not a coronet. Within limits. She was not looking for a successful costermonger but she was not really looking for an earl either. Which probably explains why she got one.

She stared at her reflection in the glass. She was wearing a short black dress in wild silk. What her mother would have called 'a little black number', the eternal stand-by of the London Lady. It was well-cut, quite expensive and, apart from a French paste bracelet, she wore no ornament. She looked pretty and snappy with that slight tang of severity a certain kind of Englishman finds intriguing. She was satisfied. Edith was not vain but she was glad, not to say relieved, that she had not been saddled with a plain face. The doorbell rang.

She had entertained the idea that she might simply tell Charles to wait downstairs but then he might think she was concealing something far more compromising than a rather routine father and a snobbish mother so she decided to ask him up but to introduce him in the American way, Christian names only. A modern habit that as a rule she particularly disliked as it withheld the only part of a name that might carry any information. Her mother defeated her as soon as she had taken the field. 'Charles what?' she said, while Kenneth was making them all a drink.

'Broughton.' Charles smiled. Edith saw the penny drop with a silent *boing* but not for nothing had her mother been a life-long admirer of Elizabeth I. The mask remained smiling but immobile.

'And how do you know Edith?'

'We met in Sussex at my parents' house.'

'When I was staying with Isabel and David.'

'Oh, so you know the Eastons?'

Charles nodded, for which Edith was grateful. He was not prepared to say, 'No, I do not know them and we were not introduced at a private party. I met your daughter when she had bought a ticket to see where I live.' This was about the size of it but it would have got the evening off to an odd start. Nevertheless, having escaped this manhole, Edith brought the chat to a fairly rapid conclusion rather than chance her arm a second time. So, far from being nervous, she was actually quite relieved when they settled themselves into the gleaming Porsche that awaited them below.

'I thought we'd go to Annabel's.'

'Now?' She was surprised and spoke before she had edited.

'Is that all right? We don't have to.' Charles looked faintly hurt and she felt mean at dashing what he might have supposed to be a bit of a treat. The thought that he had actually planned an evening for her was rather gratifying.

'Lovely.' She smiled warmly into his open, pleasant, slightly dim face. 'It's just that I've always gone on late. I don't think I've ever had dinner there.'

'I rather like it.'

He drove off and they lapsed into silence until the car pulled up outside the famous basement entrance in Berkeley Square. Charles got out and handed the keys to a doorman. Edith had always been to Annabel's with young men who parked their cars around the square and walked to the club. There was a cosy feeling in the knowledge that she was out with someone who had no need to cut corners. They made their way down the steps and in through the door at the bottom. Charles signed in with a lot of 'good evenin', m'lord' going on all round.

There was practically no one in the bar and seemingly even fewer in the restaurant. The empty dance-floor looked dark and maudlin with its black mirrors reflecting nothing. Charles seemed puzzled at first and then embarrassed. 'You're right. It is too early. I don't think it really picks up until about ten. Do you want to go somewhere else?'

'Not at all,' she said with a brisk smile as she settled into the banquette. 'Now, tell me what to eat.'

She had not yet decided what she thought about Charles but one thing she was quite sure of. This evening was going to be a *great* success if it killed her. The menu provided a few minutes of welcome chat. Charles knew about food and drink, and he was happy to take command, although in fact she had only asked for his help in order to re-establish herself as the helpless underdog like the good, nubile girl she was. The last thing she wanted was for him to start apologising. Experience had taught her that much. But in the event he chose well and the dinner was a good one.

Charles Broughton was not exactly handsome. His nose was too large for that and his lips too thin. But in the candlelight he was not unattractive. He was very what Nanny would call 'distinguished'. He looked so like an English gentleman that he could have come from Central Casting and Edith felt herself being quite drawn to him physically. Much more than she had imagined she would be. She was mildly surprised to realise that she was looking forward to his asking her to dance.

'Do you spend a lot of time in London?' she said.

He shook his head. 'Good Lord no. Little as possible.'

'So you're generally in Sussex?'

'Most of the time. We've got a place in Norfolk as well. I have to get up there from time to time.'

'Funny. I'd thought of you as rather social.'

'Me? You must be joking.' He laughed out loud. 'Why was that?'

'I don't know.' She did know although she was not prepared to say that she had read about him in various social columns. Since he and she had run into each other at Ascot, it all seemed to add up to a rather fun-filled image. It was a mistaken impression that lingered for some time before it was firmly put right.

The truth was that, like most of the human race, Charles went to parties if he was asked and had nothing else to do but he did not have many friends – certainly not many that he had made in the last few years – and he saw himself exclusively as a countryman, helping his father to run the estates and the houses that God had seen fit to entrust to their care. He did not question nor resist his position but neither did he exploit it. If he had ever thought about the issues of inheritance or rank he would only have said that he felt very lucky. He would not have said this aloud, however.

Contrary to Edith's belief, he had not taken her to Annabel's as part of any romantic strategy. The truth was that, without admitting it to himself, he liked to take girls to places where he was known. It put a spin on the dinner that anonymity lacked. It was his turn to speak.

'Have you lived a lot in the country?'

'Not much, really.' Edith realised this was an odd answer even as she said it for she had never, for half an hour, actually 'lived' in the country. Unless one counted boarding school, which of course one couldn't. Still, she liked the country. She'd stayed a lot in the country. She'd walked behind the guns. She'd ridden. It wasn't a total lie. She qualified it: 'My father's business. You know.'

Charles nodded. 'I suppose he has to move about quite a bit.'

Edith shrugged. 'Quite a bit.'

Actually, Kenneth Lavery had had to move about from the London Underground to the same office in the city for the last thirty-two years. He had once had to go New York and once to Rotterdam. That was it. This slight re-shading of the truth was never corrected. Charles was forever thereafter under the impression that Edith's father had been some sort of international whizz-kid, jetting between Hong Kong and Zurich. In creating this false picture, however, Edith had read Charles correctly. There is something much less petit bourgeois about a businessman with permanent jet lag than a stationery drudge buying a ticket for the Piccadilly Line northbound, and Charles did like things just so.

Time had passed and the club was filling.

'Charlie!' Edith looked up to see a pretty brunette in a sharply tailored, sequinned cocktail dress bearing down on them. She was accompanied by, or rather trailing, a whale. He wore a suit that must have taken a bale of worsted and a large spotted tie. When they had made it to the table, Edith noticed the rivulets of sweat that trickled continuously from behind his ears over the fat, red neck.

'Jane. Henry.' Charles stood up and gestured at Edith. 'Do you know Edith Lavery? Henry and Jane Cumnor.' Jane took Edith's hand in a swift and lifeless hold then turned back to Charles as she sat down and poured herself a glass of their wine.

'I'm parched. How are you? What happened to you at Ascot?'

'Nothing happened. I was there.'

'I thought we were all having lunch on Thursday. With the Weatherbys? We hunted and hunted for you before we gave up.

Camilla was bitterly disappointed.' She gave a half-smirk to Edith, ostensibly inviting her to join the joke. In fact, of course, consciously excluding her from it.

'Well, she shouldn't have been. I told her and Anne that I had to have lunch with my parents that day.'

'Needless to say they'd completely forgotten. Anyway, doesn't matter now. By the way, tell me: are you going to Eric and Caroline in August? They swore you were but it seemed so unlike you.'

'Why?'

Jane shrugged with a lazy, sinuous movement of the shoulder. 'I don't know. I thought you hated the heat.'

'I haven't made up my mind. Are you going?'

'We don't know, do we, darling?' She reached across to her puffing husband and kneaded his doughy hand. 'We're so behind with everything at Royton. We've hardly been home since Henry got political. I've a ghastly feeling we might be stuck there all summer.' She again broadened her smile to include Edith.

Edith smiled back. She was quite used to this curious need on the part of the upper-classes to demonstrate that they all know each other and do the same things with the same people. This was perhaps an unusually manic example of the palisade mentality but, looking at Lord Cumnor, aka Henry the Green Engine, it was not difficult to see that Jane had made some severe sacrifices to achieve whatever position she was in command of. It would be hard for her to set it aside, even for a moment, as a thing of little importance.

'Are you very political?' Edith said to Henry, who seemed to be recovering from the effort it had taken him to cross the floor.

'Yes,' he said, and turned back to the others.

Edith had been inclined to feel rather sorry for him but she saw in a moment that he perceived no need to feel sorry for himself. He was quite happy being who he was. Just as he was quite happy to demonstrate that he knew Charles and did not know Edith. Charles, however, was not prepared to have the Cumnors be rude to the girl he had invited for dinner and he consciously and obviously turned the conversation back to her.

'Henry's frightfully serious since he took his seat. What was your latest cause? Organic veg for prisoners?'

'Ha, ha,' said Henry.

Jane came to her husband's aid. 'Don't be beastly. He's done a lot of work for the national diet, haven't you, darling?'

'Which didn't include going on it, I gather,' said Charles.

'You laugh now but they'll come after you when your father snuffs it. You'll see,' said Jane.

'No they won't. Labour will win next time and they'll have the hereditaries out before you can say Jack Robinson.'

'Don't be so pessimistic.' Jane did not want to hear that the world she had pinned all her hopes on was threatened with extinction. 'Anyway, it'd be years before they came up with a formula for the Lords that works better and they won't do anything in a hurry.'

Charles stood up and asked Edith to dance.

She raised her eyes in a half-query as they shambled around the floor, by now crammed with Iranian bankers and their mistresses.

He smiled. 'Henry's all right.'

'Is he a great friend?'

'He's a sort of cousin. I've known him all my life. God, he's fat at the moment, isn't he? He looks like a balloon.'

'How long have they been married?'

He shook his head. 'Four, five years, I suppose.'

'Do they have any children?'

He made a wry shape with his mouth. 'Two girls. Poor old Henry. Setchell's got him drinking port and eating cheese and Christ knows what.'

'Why?'

'To get a boy, of course. To get the bloody boy.'

'What happens if they don't have one?'

Charles frowned. 'There are no brothers. I think some bloke in South Africa gets the title although I'm not sure if he or the girls get the swag. Anyway, they're both quite young. They'll bash on for a while longer, I should think.'

'It could get rather expensive.'

'It certainly could. You never know how long to keep going. Look at the Clanwilliams. Six girls before they called it a day and it's worse nowadays.'

'Why?'

'Why do you think? Even the girls have to go to decent schools.'

They danced in silence for a while with Charles occasionally nodding to various acquaintances on the floor. Edith gratefully recognised two girls from her deb season and flashed brilliant smiles at them. Taking in the identity of her partner, they waved back, allowing her to feel less invisible. By the time they returned to the table, she was beginning to feel that she was really having quite a jolly time.

Henry and Jane had not moved and as they approached, Jane jumped up and seized Charles's hand. 'It's time you danced with me. Henry hates dancing. Come on.' She led Charles back to the floor, leaving Edith alone with her porcine husband.

He smiled vaguely. 'She always says that. I don't really hate dancing at all. Would you like to give it a go?'

Edith shook her head. 'Not unless you're dying to, if you don't mind. I'm exhausted.' The thought of being pressed into that pillow of blubber made her shudder.

He nodded philosophically. Being turned down was obviously not a new experience. 'Do you know Charlie well?'

'No. We just met in the country and then again at Ascot and here I am.'

'Where in the country? Who with?' He perked up a bit at the chance of some more Name Exchange.

'With the Eastons. In Sussex. David and Isabel. Do you know them?' She knew very well he would not. She was right.

'I've known Charlie all my life.'

Edith fished idly in her brain for an answer. 'I don't think I've known anybody all my life. Except my parents,' she added with a laugh.

Henry did not laugh back. 'Oh,' he said.

She tried again. 'Who are Eric and Caroline?'

'Caroline's his sister. I've known her all my life too.' He nodded gently to himself, pleased with these long associations. 'Eric's this chap she's just married.'

'I gather you haven't known him all your life.'

'Never saw him before the wedding.'

'Is he nice?'

'I really couldn't tell you.' Obviously Caroline was guilty of some hideous impropriety in Henry's eyes. Some horrible miscegenation had taken place in this coupling of strangers. Edith felt that she herself was hovering at the borders of a solecism by even talking about the interloper.

31

'Where is Royton?'

This time Henry's face registered surprise rather than distaste. For her not to know where Royton was must surely indicate that she was an eccentric. 'Norfolk.'

'Is it lovely?' Edith was beginning to feel as if she was turning over huge clods of ploughed earth in her effort to keep Henry entertained.

He shrugged and looked round for the bottle to help himself to another glass. 'People seem to think so.'

Edith opened her mouth to try again and then shut it. Not for the last time she was struck by the tyranny of the socially inept. Endless effort is harnessed to a sluggish and boring conversation simply to preserve these dullards from a sense of their inadequacy. The irony being that they are quite impervious to their own shortcomings. If Henry had even noticed things were at all heavy going he would unhesitatingly have blamed it on Edith and the fact that she didn't know anyone interesting. Before the silence had become oppressive Charles and Jane returned and the remainder of the time was spent gossiping about more people that Edith had never met.

'What a lovely evening,' she said, as the car stopped outside her parents' flat. Charles made no attempt to park it so he clearly knew the night would contain no sexual epilogue.

'I'm glad you enjoyed it. I'm sorry we got rather lumbered.'

'Don't be. I liked them,' she lied.

'Did you?' He seemed a bit anxious. 'I'm glad.'

'Henry was telling me about Royton.'

He nodded, back on home territory. 'Yes, they're next door to me up there. That's really why I know them.'

'I thought they were cousins.'

'Well, they are. From a marriage in about eighteen thirty. But I know them because they live next door.'

'It sounds lovely.'

'It is. I'm not sure how good old Henry is at managing it but it is charming. Anyway, there's pots of money so I suppose it doesn't matter too much.' It was easy to see that Charles thought he was *terrifically* good at managing Broughton.

They stared at each other for a moment. Edith realised that she rather wanted him to kiss her. Partly because she wanted to be sure she'd been a success, and partly because she just wanted to kiss him. He leaned forward awkwardly and pressed his mouth against hers. His lips were hard and firmly shut. He sat back. Ah, she thought. More Philip than George. Oh well. What she said was, 'Good night and thank you again. I have so enjoyed it.'

'Good,' he said, and he got out of the car and escorted her across the road to the front door, but he made no attempt to kiss her again as he said good night, nor was there any mention of the next time they would meet. It would be fair to say that, up to that moment, she had not been aware of wanting much more from the evening than the reassurance that Charles found her attractive, liked her company and wanted to see more of her. But now that the ending was proving rather flat, she was filled with a feeling of disappointment, with the sense of a chance lost. This had been a great opportunity and she had blown it without fully understanding why. On the whole, it was with a sense of failure that she crept quietly into her room, trying not to wake the mother who was lying staring at the ceiling two doors down.

She need not have been downcast. She did not know Charles and had misinterpreted his reticence. Because he was generally seen as a prize, she thought he must share this image of himself but this was not so. He felt that it was he, not Edith, on whom the responsibility for the evening lay. He was shy (not rude-shy, really shy) and so, while he could not quite express it, he was very pleased that she had appeared to have enjoyed being with him. In fact, as Charles pushed the key into the lock of his parents' flat in Cadogan Square, it was with a warm sense of an evening well spent. He liked Edith very much. More than he could remember liking any girl. With the respect for hypocrisy that is the due of a hypocritical society, he admired her all the more for pretending to like the Cumnors when it was plain that they, or at least Jane, had been bestial to her all evening. He pushed the door open and stepped inside.

The Uckfields' London flat occupied the ground and first floors of one of those tall, Edwardian Dutch, red brick houses that surround the exclusive, if not exactly bewitching square. It was a pleasant enough place, furnished with that delicately balanced mixture of the comfortable and the grand that his mother had learned from John Fowler and proceeded to make her own. The pictures, from the B-list of the family's collection, were carefully chosen to suggest hereditary importance without overpowering the spaces. The hangings, the ornaments, the very tables and chairs proclaimed the rank of the family but in a modest way. 'This is where we visit,' the artefacts seemed to say, 'but it is not who we are.' Just as no member of the family, not even Caroline, who lived there solidly for four years before her marriage, would ever refer to the place as 'home'. Home was Broughton. 'I'll be in the flat next week', 'I'm going up to the flat', 'Why don't we meet at the flat?' were all very well, but 'I must get home', even at the end of a long London dinner, could only ever mean that the Broughton in question was driving down to Sussex that night. These people may own a house in Chester Square and rent a small cottage in Derbyshire, but you may be pretty sure that 'home' is the one with the grass growing round it. And if no such hide-away exists, then they will make it plain that it is essential to their well-being to escape the smoke and pavements and fly to their rural friends as often as they can, thereby suggesting that while they may spend their lives walking on tarmac or behind a city desk, they will always be country people at heart. It is rare to find an aristocrat who is happier in London – at least, it is rare to find one who admits it.

Charles had his own flat, a jumble of modest rooms on a third floor in Eaton Place but he didn't usually bother with it. Cadogan Square was nicer and more comfortable, and he could pick up any post there and bring it down without a fuss. But perhaps because Broughton was after all the product of many generations' taste, he was always aware of the imprint of his mother whenever he visited her London base. The family's real London headquarters, Broughton House, had been in St James's Square, but it had taken a direct hit in the Blitz and so they were spared the agonising decision of most of their relations as to whether or not it was sensible to abandon the town house at the end of the war. Charles's grandparents had acquired a rather dank flat in Albert Hall Mansions, which his mother had rejected out of hand and it was she who selected and therefore entirely created this apartment as an appropriate setting for the charity work and the entertaining that demanded her presence in the capital from time to time.

As he sat down with a late-night glass of whisky, Charles thought about his mother. He looked at the prettily framed sketch of the seven-year-old Lady Harriet Trevane (as Lady Uckfield was born). It was by Annigoni and was placed on a small *régence* table near the drawing-room chimneypiece. Even as a girl, with a hair-ribbon drooping down among her charcoaled curls, he could detect the familiar, unflinching, cat-like stare. He might as well face facts. His mother would not like Edith. That he knew. If Edith had been presented to his mother as the wife of a friend she might have liked her – if she had taken the smallest notice of her – but Edith would not be welcomed as Charles's girlfriend. Still less, should such a thing ever come to pass, would she be encouraged as Lady Uckfield's ultimate successor, as the one to whom his mother must entrust the house, the position, the very county she had worked so hard on and for so long.

This is not to say that Charles was without sympathy for his mama. On the contrary, he loved her very much and he felt he was right to do so. He saw beyond her public image of studied perfection and he liked what he found there. It pleased Lady Uckfield always to give the impression that everything in life had been handed to her on a plate. This was no truer for her than it is for the rest of the human race but she preferred to be on the receiving end of envy rather than pity and all her life had chosen, in the words of the song, to pack up her troubles in her old kit bag and smile. As a rule, this was not too onerous a choice, since she found her own problems as dull as she found everybody else's, but Charles respected this philosophy and he liked her for it. He did not perhaps fully appreciate the extent to which, in her concerted assumption of the 'brave face', she was only being loyal to the tenets of her kind.

The upper classes are not, as a whole, a complaining lot. As a group they would generally rather not 'go on about it'. A brisk walk and a stiff drink are their chosen methods of recovery whether struck in the heart or the wallet. Much has been written in the tabloid press about their coldness but it is not lack of feeling that marks them apart, rather it is lack of expression of feeling. Naturally they do not see this as a failing in themselves and nor do they admire public emotion in others. They are genuinely bewildered by working-class grief, those bereaved mothers being dragged sobbing and supported into church, those soldiers' widows photographed weeping over 'his last letter'. The very word 'counsellor' sends a shudder of disgust down any truly well-bred spine. What they do not appreciate, of course, is that these tragedies, national and domestic, the war casualties, the random killings, the pile-ups on the M3, offer most ordinary bereaved what is probably their only chance of fleeting celebrity. For once in their lives they can appease that very human craving for some prominence, some public recognition of their plight. The upper classes do not understand this hunger because they do not share it. They are born prominent.

The one arena of his mother's struggles that Charles really knew about was Lady Uckfield's war with his grandmother, the dowager marchioness, who had not been an easy mother-in-law. She was the tall, bony, long-nosed daughter of a duke and so not at all impressed with the pretty little brunette her son had brought home with him. Old Lady Uckfield had been Queen Mary to her daughter-in-law's Lady Elizabeth Bowes-Lyon and the relationship was never warm. Even after her husband's demise and well into Charles's conscious years, the dowager's behaviour continued unchecked and she was still attempting to countermand orders with the housekeeper, instruct the gardeners directly and cancel groceries with a view to replacing them with more 'suitable' items to the day of her largely unlamented death.

That these attempts were not successful, that her power was broken was a direct result of the one real fight between them, the thought of which always made Charles smile. Soon after her dethronement as chatelaine of Broughton, his grandmother had interfered with a new re-hang of the pictures in the saloon while Lady Uckfield was in London. On her return, Lady Uckfield's discovery that her scheme had been abandoned made her so angry that, for the only time in recorded history, she, in modern parlance, lost it. This resulted in a fully fledged screaming match, surely unique in the history of the room in question – at least since the more rollicking days of the eighteenth century. To the enraptured delight of the listening servants, Lady Uckfield denounced her mother-in-law as an ill-mannered, ill-bred, interfering old bitch. 'Ill-bred?' shrieked the dowager, selecting from the list of insults the only one to pierce her carapace. *'Ill-bred!'* and she stalked from the house, determined never to darken its doors again. His mother had told Charles many times that she regretted the incident and it was certainly a relief to her that old Lady Uckfield, having made her point, did eventually return to Broughton for the customary festivals but, even so, the battle had achieved its purpose. Thenceforth the young Marchioness was in charge, and the house, the estate and the village were under no illusions about it.

For these and many other reasons, simple and complicated, Charles admired his mother and the disciplines she lived by. He even admired the way she lived with her husband's stupidity without ever referring to the fact or showing her exasperation. He knew that he, himself, while not quite as slow as his father, was not quick. His mother had guided him well without making him too conscious of his shortcomings but he was aware of them all the same. Because of all this, he would have loved to please her when it came to his choice of a mate. He would have been delighted to arrive at some Scottish stalking party, at some London ball, and find exactly the woman his mother wanted for him. It should have been easy. There must surely have been some peer's daughter, from the old, familiar world Lady Uckfield knew and trusted, who was smart and sharp (for his mother was not a fan of the dowdy, county lady with her wispy hair and her charity shop skirts), and this girl would have made him laugh and he would have felt proud of her and safe, and her arrival would have transformed things.

But, try as he might to find her, somehow she had never turned up. There were nice young women who had done their best but ... never quite *the* one. This was probably because Charles had a central, guiding belief. Like himself, it was simple but it was strong. Namely, that if he could only marry for love, if he could just find the partner who would stimulate him in mind (for he did value the albeit limited activities of his mind) and body, then the life that was mapped out for him would be a good and rewarding one. If, however, he married suitably but misguidedly, then there could be no redemption possible. He did not believe in divorce (not at least for the head of the Broughtons) and therefore, once unhappily married, he would remain so to the grave. He was, in short, much more than he knew, a thoroughly moral, straightforward fellow. Which made it all the more disturbing to him that here was a real possibility of his being drawn to a woman who, while not being ludicrously unsuitable, while not being a pop queen or a drug-running trapeze artist, was nevertheless not what his mother was hoping for.

It was therefore with a hint of melancholy in his heart that, a couple of days later, Charles telephoned Edith and asked her out again.

FOUR

~

To my amusement, it was not long before the fact that Edith and Charles were going about together had begun to attract attention. Gossip columns without a story for the day picked up on it and those tiresome articles in *Tatler* or *Harpers* about what up-to-the-minute people eat at weekends or wear in Paris or do for Christmas started to include Edith as Charles's paramour. The fascination with celebrities was in full swing at that time and since, by definition, there are never enough genuine celebrities to supply the market – even in a much less greedy era than the 1990s – journalists are forced to drag out their tired 'It Girls' and ex-television presenters to fill the gaps. It was ironically Edith's very ordinariness that played into this. Someone saw her as a latter-day Cinderella, the working girl suddenly transported into Dreamland, and wrote an article in one of the Sundays entitled 'The Lavery Discovery', featuring several large and highly coloured photographs. After that, she caught on. At first she was annoyed at being continually described as climbing the social ladder but, gradually, as the original reason for the press interest faded beneath a welter of fashion articles and award ceremonies and invitations onto afternoon television. Edith came to enjoy the attention. The seductive element in being pursued by newshounds is that inevitably one starts to feel that if so many people are interested in one's life, one's life must *ergo* be interesting and Edith wanted to believe this quite as much as anyone else. Of course, inevitably I suppose, it was not long before she began to lose touch with the fact that she was becoming famous for being famous and nothing more. I was at a charity lunch once when she was invited to give some tabloid award and I remember her saying afterwards how *ghastly* the other presenters were, all sports commentators and fashion gurus, and why on earth had they been invited? I pointed out that even a lowly sports commentator has earned his or her own celebrity in a way Edith had not. She smiled but I could see she rather resented me for saying it. She had started at a perilously early stage to believe her own publicity.

These photo-shoots and column inches meant that, slightly mysteriously, she had begun to dress better or more expensively than before. I'm not quite sure how she managed this as I don't think Charles was forking out at that point. Probably she did one of those deals where designers lend you clothes to wear for the night if there's a likelihood of your getting into the papers. Or perhaps Mrs Lavery was stumping up. If she'd had the money, she wouldn't have minded a bit.

I saw much less of Edith during this time. At this distance, I'm not sure if she was still working in Milner Street but I would think she probably was as she was never one for counting her chickens. However, she was obviously less at a loss as to what to do for lunch. But one day the following March, months after she had started seeing Charles, I spotted her in the corner of the Australian having a tuna sandwich and, after buying myself a drink, I walked over to her table. 'Hello,' I said. 'Shall I join you or are you meditating?'

She looked up with a surprised smile. 'Sit. You're just the person I need.' She was distracted and serious and generally rather unlike the cool blonde I was used to.

'What's up, Doc?'

'Are you, by any chance, going to the Eastons' next weekend?'

'No. Should I be?'

'It would be frightfully convenient if you were.'

'Well, I'm not doing anything else. I suppose I could telephone and invite myself. Why?'

'Charles's mother is giving a dinner party at Broughton on Saturday and I want some of my own people at it. I suppose Isabel and David would come?'

'Are you kidding?'

'That's just it. I want you there to calm them down. Charles likes you.'

'Charles doesn't know me.'

'Well, at least he's met you.' I knew what was worrying her. She was tired of being invisible. Of being entirely surrounded by people who automatically assumed that if she were worth knowing they would

39

already know her. She wanted a friend of hers there whom she didn't have to introduce to Charles.

'I'll come if Isabel can put me up.'

She nodded gratefully. 'I'd ask you to stay at Broughton if I could.'

'Isabel would never forgive me. Have you had them over before?'

'No.' I looked surprised and she shrugged. 'I've only ever been down for the night and usually for something specific and you know what they're like ...' I knew. I only had to think of the glint in David's eye at Ascot to know only too well.

'So how's it all going? I keep reading about you in the papers.'

She blushed. Isn't it silly?'

'And I saw you on *This Morning with Richard and Judy*.'

'Christ. Your life must be in serious trouble.'

'I had tonsillitis but anyway I rather like Judy,' I said. 'She always looks harassed and real. I thought you were quite good.'

'Did you?' She seemed astonished. 'I thought I was a total idiot. I don't mind the photographs but whenever I open my mouth, I sound like a complete half-wit. I'm sure they only got me because Tara Palmer-Tomkinson chucked.'

'Did she?'

'I don't know. I'm making it up.'

'Perhaps the answer is not to do any talking.'

'That's what Charles says, but it wouldn't make the smallest difference. They quote you anyway.' This is of course quite true.

'You and Charles make a fetching team. Your mother must be thrilled.'

Edith rolled her eyes. 'She's beside herself. She's afraid she'll find Bobby in the shower and it'll all have been a dream.'

'And will she?'

Edith's face hardened into a worldly mask that seemed more suited to an opera box in the *belle époque* than the Australian at lunchtime. 'No, I don't think so.'

I raised my eyebrows. 'Are congratulations in order?'

'Not yet,' she said firmly, 'but promise me you'll be there on Saturday. Eight o'clock. Black tie.'

'All right. But you must tell Isabel. Do you want me to write to Lady Uckfield?'

'No, no, I'll do all that. Just be there.'

When I telephoned Isabel that evening Edith had already spoken to her and the matter was swiftly arranged. And so, a few days later, I found myself joining the others in the Eastons' drawing room for a drink before we set off. David was being gauche and grumpy to conceal his palpitating excitement at finally being received within the citadel. Isabel was less excited and consequently less afraid of its showing.

'Well, do we think the dinner's in aid of anything?' she said with a giggle as I entered.

'I don't know,' I said. 'Do we?'

David pushed a glass into my hand. His whiskies were always warm, which was rather tiresome. He had read somewhere that gentlemen don't have ice. 'Isabel thinks they're going to announce their engagement.'

The thought had obviously crossed my mind, which would explain why Edith felt she had to have a few people on her own team but nursery training has made me beware of the obvious. 'Wouldn't her parents have been asked?'

'Perhaps they have been.' That was a thought. The image of Stella Lavery walking up to her room to find her bags unpacked and her evening dress laid out warmed my heart. Everyone deserves a few moments when life is Quite Perfect.

'Well, we'll know soon enough,' I said.

Isabel looked at the clock. 'Shouldn't we be off?'

'Not yet. There's plenty of time.' David could afford to mumble his prey now that he was sure of it. 'What about another drink?'

But Isabel won and we set off for our first but (as we were all secretly thinking) probably not our last private visit to Broughton Hall.

The house looked no less forbidding than it had before but the fact that this fortress had been breached made its very chill gratifying. We stood outside the same door and rang the bell.

'I wonder if this is the right entrance,' said Isabel, but before we could ponder further, the door was opened by a butler and we were being escorted upstairs into the Red Saloon. I think I was surprised that the family appeared to use those rooms generally on public show. I had expected to be ushered into some other, sloaney sitting room on the first floor where the portraits and the Louis Quinze furniture would be interlarded with squashy sofas and chintz – that being the usual form on such occasions. I was to learn that I was quite right and the fact that we were having drinks in the Red Saloon and dinner in the State Dining Room should have given the game away at once. At all events, when I walked in and saw Mrs Lavery standing by the fireplace next to the burly figure of Lord Uckfield I knew. Edith had brought it off and we were there to witness her triumph.

Lady Uckfield stepped forward. She was a small, fine-boned, attractive woman who must have been extremely pretty in her youth but at first sight she seemed quite unimposing, even cosy. This always stands out in my mind as the most mistaken in a lifetime of incorrect first impressions. When she spoke her voice was light and bell-like with that tremendously far-back enunciation that one associates with wartime newsreels. 'How terribly sweet you all are to be here,' she sparkled, smiling gaily. 'I know you've come down from London.' She directed this to me. The point being to show us that she had done her homework and she knew precisely who we were.

'How very kind you are to ask us.' I know this game and its responses.

'Not at all. We're *delighted* to see you here.' Lady Uckfield spoke with a kind of intimate urgency, which punctuated everything she said, as if she were sharing a permanent private joke that only you (or whomever she was talking to) would understand. I think of her now as the most socially expert individual I have ever known at all well. She combined a watchmaker's eye for detail with a madam's knowledge of the world. She was also utterly confident. I knew she had been born the prettiest daughter of a rich earl and I supposed then, young as I was, that her confidence was nothing to be wondered at, but I know now that such things do not always follow and I later learned that, like all of us, she had had her share of troubles. Maybe these had made her strong, maybe she was born strong anyway; whatever the reason, by the time I met her she was a complete and invulnerable perfectionist. Every evening I have ever participated in at her invitation has been constructed as carefully as a Cellini salt-cellar. From the species of potato to the arrangement of the cushions nothing was left to chance or others' judgement.

Of course, as soon as she said, 'How lovely it is to welcome some friends of our darling Edith,' I could see that she didn't like her future daughter-in-law. Having said that, 'didn't like' is probably not quite accurate. It was amazing to her that her son should be marrying someone she didn't know or even know of. It was fantastic to her that this girl's friends should not be the children of her friends. *Au fond*, it was extraordinary that Edith had got into the house at all. How had it happened? From thoughts like these, unfortunately for Edith, Lady Uckfield had deduced that Charles had been 'caught' and while she later (much later) qualified this impression, she never really changed it. As a matter of fact I'm not at all sure it wasn't true.

Isabel and I drifted over towards the fireplace. 'Hello, Mrs Lavery,' I said, and Edith's mother turned towards us, revealing in an instant that fatal, diffident graciousness that marks the successful social climber. Their manner invariably conveys to their true equals that the ladder has been pulled up and will never, ever be lowered again. The eager, snobbish Mrs Lavery we had known had gone and been replaced by the Snow Queen. It was as if we were in *Invasion of the Body Snatchers* and we were talking to a pod. Almost reluctantly, sounding every bit as vague about our identities as Lord Uckfield, she introduced us to our host.

He shook our hands in a hearty, blank way. 'Jolly good,' he said. 'Did you have a lot of trouble getting here?'

'We've only come from Ringmer,' said Isabel. 'My husband and I live there.'

'Really?' said Lord Uckfield. 'Was there a lot of traffic on the road? All those bloody people trying to escape the city if there's a glimmer of sun in the forecast. Was it difficult getting out?'

Isabel was about to embark on another long explanation of how she had not come from London, which I spared her. 'I came on the train,' I said.

'Very sensible.' He smiled his expansive, florid smile and nodded us away.

The Marquess of Uckfield was a dull and stupid man but there was, on the whole, no harm in him. He had been spoiled all his life and surrounded by the kind of toadies that such people find comfort in, garnered from the distant strands of their own families as well as on the highways and byways, and so he had no conception of how dull and stupid he really was. His uneducated banalities were greeted as if they had come from Solomon and his unfunny, old jokes were rewarded with gales of breathless laughter. If it is the experience of life that shapes us, is it to be wondered at that men like Lord Uckfield are so signally unshaped? People would speak, even out of his hearing, of his wisdom and judgement when he certainly had neither. The reason for this was that if they could convince themselves they truly believed him to possess these qualities, then they would not have to admit to themselves that they were toadies, which is a powerful motive among the fashionable. And if their outer acquaintance ever expressed doubt as to his Lordship's mental prowess, they could always answer, 'Ah, you wouldn't think that if you really knew him,' thereby giving themselves one mark for being on intimate terms with yet another Great House and a second mark for being a genuine person. He was not ungenerous, just lazy with the fundamental laziness that marks most friendships of the privileged with a dead hand. He had long since decided that pursuing relations with any but sycophants and those members of his own class necessary for his self-image was far too like hard work and he had abandoned the effort, but the decision had been a subconscious one and he still thought of himself as a kind man. In truth, he would always be kind to Edith. He was not in the least admirable but nor was he a snob and anyway, apart from anything else, he was just glad she was so pretty.

I could see the butler in the door catching Lady Uckfield's eye. She nodded, cast her professional glance about the room and walked over to me. 'We're having dinner in a minute,' she said. 'I wonder if you'd like to take in Lady Tenby?' She indicated a stout party of sixty-plus wedged in a chair by the fire. I nodded and muttered and Lady Uckfield continued her rounds. We had been almost the last-comers and I suppose everyone else already had their orders. I walked towards my partner, thinking I might be needed to haul her into an upright position. She looked up and extended a fat, jewelled hand.

'Are you taking me in?' she said. I nodded. 'Googie's so brilliant at organising things. She should have run a hotel chain. Help me up.'

I have always been uncomfortable with the *jejune* pseudo-informality implicit in the upper-class passion for nicknames. Everyone is 'Toffee' or 'Bobo' or 'Snook'. They themselves think the names imply a kind of playfulness, an eternal childhood, fragrant with memories of Nanny and pyjamas warming by the nursery fire, but they are really a simple reaffirmation of insularity, a reminder of shared history that excludes

44

more recent arrivals, yet another way of publicly displaying their intimacy with each other. Certainly the nicknames form an effective fence. A newcomer is often in the position of knowing someone too well to continue to call them Lady So-and-So but not nearly well enough to call them 'Sausage', while to use their actual Christian name is a sure sign within their circle that one doesn't really know them at all. And so the new arrival is forced back from the normal development of friendly intimacy that is customary among acquaintances in other classes.

Dinner had been announced and my partner had lumbered to her feet and was now leaning heavily against me. I could see that for her at least this arm-in-arm procession was more than a self-conscious replay of an Edwardian custom: it was a very necessary service. A few couples ahead of us I could see Lady Uckfield chattering gaily into the face of a shell-shocked Kenneth Lavery. They reminded me of the front benches going through into the Lords to hear the Queen's speech, when the Tory ministers always seem to be filmed frenetically gabbling away to their glum and serious Socialist opposite numbers. Behind them Edith was with Lord Uckfield. She was wearing a black velvet dress, cut low at the neck with long tight sleeves and no jewellery of any sort. The effect was beautiful and *triste* like Juliet in mourning. I suppose she felt it would be tasteless to look too merry.

Lady Tenby followed my glance. 'Very good-looking. No question about that. But who on earth is she?'

I smiled down at her. 'She's a great friend of mine,' I said.

'Oops,' said Lady Tenby, and we continued in silence.

I later learned that the Countess of Tenby was the widowed mother of four daughters and, as Lady Uckfield's second cousin, had always rather hoped to get Charles for one of them. It was not an unreasonable ambition. They were nice girls and quite pleasant of face. Any one of them would probably have made him happy. In the end only the eldest, Lady Daphne, married at all 'well' in their mother's opinion (and he was a younger son), two married routine Hoorays and the youngest and best-looking went to California to live with the founder of a rather sinister sect. The point being that Lady Tenby was not a nasty or an unreasonable woman. She had put in many years work on her daughters for what were to be meagre dividends and now, this evening, she had been invited to witness the triumph of an interloper, a stranger who had stolen into their camp under cover of darkness and made off with the fattest sheep of all. Of course she would smile and congratulate and kiss but then she would go home and say how marvellous Googie and Tigger had been, how nobody would have known they were disappointed, how the girl was, after all, *very* pretty and seemed *fond* of Charles. And forever Edith would be marked as a lucky outsider.

Dinner was delicious, which was a surprise. I had been expecting the usual country house fare dispensed by my parents' generation, more redolent of a girls' prep school than the kitchens of the Ivy but I was not then used to Lady Uckfield's command of detail. I had Lady Tenby on my left and I spent the first course in one of those are-you-an-actor-what-might-I-have-seen-you-in conversations, which are so disheartening, but when the plates were taken away and I was allowed to turn to my companion on my right, I found myself talking to a rather hard-faced but intriguing woman of about my own age who introduced herself as Charles's sister, Caroline.

'So you're an old friend of Edith?' she said.

'I don't know how "old". I've known her about a year and a half.'

'Longer than we have,' she said with a crisp little laugh.

'And do you think you're going to like her?' I asked.

'I don't know,' said Caroline, looking down the table to where Edith was flirting gently with her future father-in-law. 'As a matter of fact I think I might. But is she going to like Charles? That's the question.'

This was of course the question. I followed my neighbour's gaze to where Charles was sitting, his heavy, good-natured face frowning over what was in all probability a rather small intellectual problem being posed by his neighbour. I wondered if Edith had faced up to how thick he really was. Or, for that matter, to how bleak the country can be. Caroline was reading my mind. 'It's frightfully dreary down here, you know. I suppose Edith's ready for all that? Flower shows all summer, freezing pipes all winter. Does she hunt?'

'She rides so she probably could hunt.'

'I don't suppose it matters much. With the antis about to kill it off at any moment.'

'Perhaps she's an anti and doesn't approve. You never know these days.'

'Oh, I doubt Edith is anti-blood sport,' said Caroline carefully. 'She looks quite carnivorous to me.'

46

'What about you? Do you hunt?'

'Heavens no. I hate the country. I don't even go to Hyde Park if I can avoid it.'

'What does your husband do? Or is it common to ask?'

'It is. But I'll answer anyway. Mainly advertising but he also organises charity events.'

I have often thought how simple it must have been to live a hundred years ago when every man one knew was in the army, the navy, the Church, or owned land. These extraordinary jobs one hears about every day, that one never even knew existed, have an unsettling effect on me. Headhunting or working in futures, credit management or people skills, as explanations they all sound as if one were concealing one's true activity. Perhaps a lot of them are. I couldn't think of an appropriate response. 'Does he favour any particular cause?' I said.

'So how do you know Edith?' said Caroline, who was obviously as uninterested in her husband's activities as I was. I explained about the Eastons. 'I wondered what they were doing here. It's funny we haven't met before if they're so near.' I was glad David was too far down the table to hear this. After that we turned to more general topics and I soon learned that Lady Caroline Chase was one of those children of the purple who manage to reject their upbringing in their way of living, their philosophy, their chosen partner and their choice of address and yet take their snobbery with them absolutely intact into their new life. I liked her but she was in her way quite as dismissive as her mother only without, perhaps, Lady Uckfield's armour of moral certainty. To Lady Uckfield her social position was an article of faith; to Caroline it was simply a matter of fact.

The meal progressed with some sort of apple snow for pudding, then the cheese and just when I was expecting our hostess to gather up the women with her and leave us to leaden political discussion and port, I was pleased to see that an unused glass in the nest before me was being filled with champagne. This then was the moment.

Lord Uckfield stood. 'I suppose we all know why we're here tonight.' I suppose we all did, although one or two people looked a bit surprised. Kenneth Lavery, himself, seated next to Lady Uckfield, seemed to be full of wonder as well he might. 'It's to welcome a very charming newcomer into our family.' I looked at Mrs Lavery, glazed with delight on Lord Uckfield's right. Precedence had been set aside for this one night. I do not think I ever saw her seated so advantageously again. 'Shall we raise our glasses? Edith and Charles.' We all stood with a lot of chair scraping and a certain amount of panting from Lady Tenby.

'Edith and Charles!' We drank and sat, while poor Charles, scarlet in the face, attempted some sort of answer in an unnaturally base voice.

'I haven't anything to say, really. Except that I think myself a very lucky man.'

'Hear, hear!' The table was alive with muttered gallantries. I was watching Edith as she gazed at Charles with a kind of fresh-faced, open adoration that reminded me of Elizabeth Taylor in *National Velvet*. When she's given the horse. I don't know if this was a lesson she had learned from her ex-suitor's bride four years previously or if she was simply assuming the most suitable expression to quell criticism or if, for that moment at any rate, she simply adored him. It was probably a mixture of all three. I turned my head and I saw that Lady Uckfield was watching me, a tender, perfectly constructed smile on her pretty cat-face. I looked back at her and she raised her eyebrows slightly before standing and bringing the table once more to its feet. I'm not quite sure what she meant to express by this quizzical look.

Probably Caroline spoke for them all (she certainly spoke for me) when she muttered in a low voice: 'Well, she's done it. I only hope she knows what she's getting into.'

I have not often participated in anything that could remotely be described as a Great Society Event. At any rate, not in an event that garnered much public curiosity. But by then Edith had achieved her status as a minor tabloid heroine and when she did succeed in landing her fish, the journalists who had set her up were only too anxious to reap their rewards. They'd established her as a story and she had not disappointed them. There were consequently offers from *Hello!* and *OK!* – much to Lady Uckfield's hilarity – for exclusive coverage and even though they were of course turned down the level of interest remained high. I do not think Mrs Lavery understood at first why the magazines were not to be allowed their way. I suspect she might have rather liked the idea of Edith and Charles on one of those red-outlined covers surrounded by the noble offspring of Charles's relations but when she had half suggested this to Lady Uckfield, she had been flattened to hear her companion turn to Edith and say, 'Your mother has got a *wicked* sense of humour. She had me quite taken in for a moment.' Naturally, Mrs Lavery then laughed like billyo at the thought that Lady Uckfield might have believed her! And she never mentioned it again. At any rate, for all sorts of reasons, I was curious as well as flattered to be asked to be an usher at what was shaping up to be the Wedding of the Year – or so the newspapers told me.

I received the invitation from Charles, who had written to me in his rather charming, round hand wondering if I would do this for him. It is always hard for an actor to commit in advance to anything social – not least because it is a kind of unwritten law of the theatre that if you accord the slightest importance to anything other than work then you have no talent. I suppose I would have chucked if I had been offered the title role in *Ben Hur* but I was pretty determined to play my part in the Apotheosis of Edith.

Isabel telephoned me the same morning: 'I gather you're an usher,' she said. 'David isn't.' I answered, as I knew I must, that this seemed a bit hard. 'Well, I must say I think it really is. He's in a sulk, which is a great bore and I don't see that there's anything I can do about it.' I said there was absolutely nothing she could do about it and after all, I was the only one of Edith's friends that Charles had even met before the whole thing began. 'I know that and I've said it, but you know David.'

'What about you?'

'What do you mean?'

'Are you going to play any part in it all? I thought Alice might be one of the bridesmaids or something.' Alice was the Eastons' eldest child. She was as plain as a pikestaff but quite amiable withal.

'No.' Isabel's voice was sodden with disappointment. 'Edith tried but apparently there were covens of prior claims and so she's settled for just having tinies. Much nicer really,' she muttered drearily. I could tell she had not finished. 'I was wondering about Charles's night out.'

'What about it?'

'Is he having one?'

'I don't know. I suppose so.'

'But you haven't been asked?'

'No. Should I have been?'

'Well, it's just that David was wondering if he, or both of you, shouldn't do something about organising one ... ' Her voice trailed away.

'Come off it. We hardly know him. What are you thinking of?'

'I dare say you're right.' I wondered if David was in the room with her. 'You might let us know if you are asked.'

David's background anxiety was becoming uncomfortable. He had obviously started on a lifetime's career of dropping Charles's name and he could not face the obloquy of being publicly excluded from his circle of intimates.

'All right,' I said, 'but I'm sure I won't be.'

As it happened, a month later, ten days before the wedding, I was asked. Presumably because of a dropout. A party of twelve was being flown to Paris in a week's time, three days before the Great Event, to dine and stay overnight at the Ritz. I was sent the ticket by bike and all I had to do was to be ready for collection from the flat at the appointed hour. The flight was to take off from the City airport. Instead of telephoning Isabel, I spoke to Edith. 'I've been asked to Charles's shindig.'

'I know. Completely his idea. I think it'll be fun, don't you? I love the Paris Ritz.'

'I suppose David isn't going?'

'No. The thing is Henry Cumnor and Charles's uncle Peter are organising and paying for the whole thing and so he can't have everyone.'

'Fains I tell David.'

'I've told Isabel.' Edith paused. 'As a matter of fact, I do think they're being tiresome. I am fond of Isabel but they want to be such "best friends" all the time. I feel like a heroine out of Angela Brazil. After all, I don't know David well and Charles has hardly met him.'

'My dear,' I said sagely. 'This is only the beginning.'

At three o' clock the following Saturday a capped and uniformed chauffeur rang my basement bell and seized my waiting suitcase to carry it up to the car. I had treated myself to a new one in honour of the elevated company I was about to keep so it was especially irritating when he caught it on the corner of the cellar steps and wrenched one of the handles off. As a result, despite my reckless extravagance, I felt shabby for the entire trip. *Sic transit gloria mundi*, or, I suppose, *sic transit gloria transit*.

Henry Cumnor was already in the car, his corpulence spilling itself across the back seat in vast folds of Turnbull and Asser-shirted flesh, leaving the barest ledge of vacant leather beside him. As I climbed in, I felt like Carrie Fisher squeezing up against Jabba the Hutt. I knew Henry vaguely, as it so happened that we had attended the same school although in different years, and this afforded me a faint protection against his exclusivity, but only faint. At any rate, I knew what to expect as Edith had made quite a funny story out of her 'first date' with Charles.

There was another passenger in the front seat who was cursorily introduced as Tommy Wainwright and whom I recognised as a rising Member of Parliament – if any Tory could be said to be rising at that time. So far as I could remember from those profiles beloved of the Sunday colour sections he was the younger son of a Home Counties peer and was consequently a slightly surprising inclusion in the group on whom Mrs Thatcher had smiled – she not being much in favour of the aristocracy. He was tall, almost lanky, with an amiable, round face and thinning hair that made him look like a kind of trainee old buffer, although, as I would learn, this was not at all the case. He turned, smiled and shook my hand, which placed him three–nil in the courtesy stakes against Henry and we set off.

The talk on the way to the airport was political and I was amused at the contrast between my two companions. Tommy gave his reasons for why the Conservatives had gone so completely down the plug. These were on the whole reasonable and seemed worthy of discussion but Cumnor countered them with a bundle of ridiculous assertions, all smug, all out of date and all apparently received unchewed from his late father (rather like his wardrobe). Feeling that I ought to contribute, I observed that it did not seem to me that the party had been very imaginative in their relationship with the arts.

Cumnor angled his bulk towards me. 'My dear fellow, how many people constitute what you call "the Arts"? We're talking thousands, not hundreds of thousands, not millions. Do you know how many members there are in the TGWU? The plain truth is, whether you like it or not, your "arts" don't matter.' He sat back, having won his point to his own satisfaction.

'Forty million people turn on their televisions every night to find out what they think,' said Tommy. 'What could matter more than that?'

The issue was not important to any of us but I could see that Henry was irritated at Tommy for taking my side, showing that he shared the usual fantasy of the less intelligent members of his class that on every given topic, from port to euthanasia, there is a 'sound' way of thinking and one has only to voice this view to carry the field. Since they are generally only addressing like-minded people, the field is as a rule easy to carry. Tommy Wainwright, in not playing this game, risked creating the impression in Henry's sluggish brain that in some way, ever since Tommy had gone into serious politics, he was 'not quite a gentleman' – the stock response to original thought.

Having arrived at the airport and gone through the procedures, we were shown to a smallish departure gate where we were hailed by the remaining nine of the party. These included Lord Peter Broughton, Lord Uckfield's much younger half-brother, and Caroline's husband, Eric Chase, whom I had met briefly at the engagement dinner. Chase was an unlikely addition to the Broughton clan, being the very definition of a 'Yuppie'. That is to say he was a sleek and belligerent 'executive', whose conversation consisted largely of capitalistic platitudes and references to his membership of Brooks's. His most distinctive feature was an almost pathological rudeness, which made him simultaneously less pathetic and more objectionable although, oddly, he was attractive to women. I cannot imagine why but with the opposite sex (in marked contrast to his own) he undeniably had a good deal of success. I suppose he was handsome in a smooth, over-fed way and his satisfaction with his outward form (as well as, presumably, his dazzling marriage) was demonstrated in a constantly changing wardrobe of over-cut worsteds and tweeds. I later learned that his father had been a manager with British Rail. He made an odd pair with Caroline for politically and philosophically they were streets apart. The plain truth was that he had made a right-wing gesture in marrying her while she had made a left-wing one by marrying him. All this was concealed from them, however, because they seldom talked much when they were alone. It is quite possible in this way for couples often not to discover that they are in profound disagreement over the very fundamentals of life until ten or even twenty years have passed.

Charles strode up with a glass of champagne and a warm smile. For Edith's sake or perhaps for my own he was clearly determined not to let me feel left out of this group who (with the exception of Chase) had all played together in those long-ago nurseries and who he was fearful might be rude to an actor of whom they had never heard. I was touched by his efforts but he needn't have worried. I was not always an actor. I had not only been at school with Cumnor, but I recognised a prep school playmate, a friend from my debbing days and an acquaintance from Cambridge among the others. I also knew that Lord Peter had been engaged at one time to a cousin of my sister-in-law so I did not anticipate much trouble. Such is the world that still exists in a country of sixty million people a century after the Socialists first came to power.

As a further mark of distinction Charles took the seat next to me on the little aeroplane that had been chartered for the event. A raffish steward brought us some more champagne with a tiny bit of caviar squidged onto a slightly tough blini and we settled back.

'This is all very nice,' I said.

'I'm glad you could come.'

'So am I.'

'You were the one who introduced us.'

I laughed. 'In years to come we'll know whether I have earned praise or blame.'

Charles wasn't in joking mood. 'Oh praise. I'd say praise.' He paused. 'Edith thinks you're frightfully intelligent, you know.'

'That's very gratifying.'

He looked down into his drink. 'Of course, she's so bright. You must find that.'

I can't say that I had ever given the matter much thought. Certainly Edith was no Gertrude Stein. Her idea of intellectuality was reading the latest John Mortimer. Still, she was quite funny and in my experience funny people are seldom stupid. 'I'm always pleased to see her, which is probably the same thing,' I said.

He smiled a trifle wryly. 'Well, here's hoping she's always pleased to see me.' I murmured some reassuring nonsense but he was not content to leave it there. He drew in a breath. 'I hope I'm worthy of her,' he said. I suppressed my urge to smile at being trapped in this bit of Frederick Lonsdale dialogue. These were pedestrian sentiments to begin a stag night but they were none the less heartfelt for that. Charles was typical of his kind in that he had no modes of original expression and was almost invariably forced back into cinematic clichés when trying to describe love or hate or anything else not covered by the Jockey Club rules. I said I was sure he would be as worthy as anything and it was Edith who was the lucky one and that he was paying her a great honour, etcetera. I'm usually equal to this sort of thing but I hadn't quite hit the mark this time. He interrupted my encouraging flow. 'It's just that I hope I'm clever enough for her. I don't want her to get bored with me.' He laughed and raised his eyebrows slightly to pass this off as a sort of joke, but I could see he meant it – just as I could see he had a point. Edith was no Einstein but it had already occurred to me that there might come a time when attending race-meetings with a bunch of well-dressed people mouthing received opinions just might not do it for her. I didn't see, however, that there was any useful comment that could be made since I could hardly praise him for his perspicacity.

'Charles,' I said, 'if there's one thing that makes me uncomfortable it's modesty and we'll have no more of it tonight.'

He laughed and the moment was passed.

I love Paris. There are certain cities where you can only have a good time with the help of the residents and there are others where a good time is available to all. Such is Paris, which is just as well given the amount of help one generally gets from the residents. My mother, a poor linguist herself, had been extremely anxious that her children should not suffer as she had suffered, nodding and smiling at French diplomats' wives in a kind of frozen tableau of international goodwill. Consequently, in our early teens we all had one or more school holidays ruined by being sent off to families in the depths of France where, as she had made a ruthless point of checking, we would find no English spoken. As a result of these draconian cruelties we all speak tolerable French, which of course enhances the pleasure of visiting their beautiful capital city.

I had not previously stayed at the Paris Ritz, although I had been there once to a very grand reception, which formed part of a series celebrating a marriage between two spectacularly Faubourg families. It is a great hotel in the sense that it belongs more to that lost era of great hotels, where veiled beauties stood about waiting for their maids to check twenty pieces of luggage before embarking for the Riviera, than to our own eat-and-run epoch. A red, white and gilt palace, sumptuous and yet pretty – quite unlike the modern, Park Lane equivalents got up, as they are, like enormous Maida Vale hairdressing salons. I was thoroughly glad to be there, particularly since I wasn't paying, and even the contemptuous looks the hotel employees cast at my torn and broken luggage could not quench my enthusiasm.

We gathered in the bar, slicked up in our black ties, with that faintly desperate air of the English embarking on a 'good time', and started to tuck into the champagne. Tommy Wainwright came over to me and I asked him if he knew what the plan was for the evening.

He shrugged. 'I imagine we'll have dinner here and then push on to somewhere embarrassing on the Left Bank. Isn't that the form?'

'I expect so. Have you known Charles a long time?'

'We were at Eton together. Then I went out with Caroline for a bit when we were about twenty so we sort of re-met. What about you?'

'I hardly know him. I feel rather a fraud being here. It's just that I introduced him to Edith so I suppose I'm representing her. Just to check that no one tries to put him off the whole idea.'

Wainwright smiled. 'So you're a friend of Edith. How interesting.

We've scarcely met. I must say she's a real beauty. But then she'd have to be to carry off the prize.'

'I imagine there were quite a few noses out of joint when they made the announcement.'

He laughed. 'There certainly were. I think they were all so irritated because none of them knew her. Or none of the ones I know seemed to. Like an outsider winning the Derby. At one point she was starting to sound like a cross between Eliza Doolittle and Rebecca.' I could just imagine and said so. He smiled. 'From the little I know of her, I'm sure she'll do very well.' He nodded over towards the groom. 'He's really smitten, you know. Charming. I like to see it.'

It was a particularly warm evening and the manager had decided to have the tables of the dining room carried out into the little courtyard that lies alongside it. The mellow stone, carefully carved for the seeing eye of César Ritz, and the modest fountain splashing coolly in the darkening night, induced that spirit of contentment, resting on a combination of luxury and beauty, which one would be foolish, whatever one's philosophy, always to resist. God knows it is rare enough. Euro-smart couples sat about, the women in their brilliant jewellery, one with a white poodle, idly barking its unhungry bark. To me it seemed agreeable to watch the rich taking their less controversial pleasures. Unfortunately nothing is perfect and I was seated next to Eric Chase, who proceeded to hijack as much of the arrangement as he could.

'Bring us another bottle,' he said brusquely to the waiter as he sat down. 'And try to get the temperature right this time.' He turned to me. 'We met at my in-laws' house, didn't we?' I nodded. 'You came with those frightful friends of Edith.' I nodded again, since I was certainly not prepared to wreck the evening for the sake of Isabel and David. But like all bullies he was not to be pacified. 'Where on earth did she meet them?'

'I don't really know. I met them because I've known Isabel since we were children.'

'Poor you. Some of this?' Without waiting for an answer he slopped some wine into my glass. 'Well, I'm afraid little Edith'll have to shape up a bit if she wants to bring it off.'

'What do you mean?'

'If she wants to get away with it. As Lady Broughton.' He started to sing, 'There'll be some changes made.'

'Oh, I don't know,' I said. 'Did you find it very difficult to get away with marrying Caroline?' Of course, in a way, this was a mistake and Chase turned to his other neighbour having registered me as an enemy, but I was satisfied to have maintained Edith's honour. Like many aggressive *parvenus* who have climbed the greasy pole, he was under the illusion that the reason people did not point out his social failings was because they were no longer visible. As rude as he was, he could not credit anyone else with politeness. That was his armour. I did not mind crossing him as I had disliked him a good deal on sight and anyway I was not entirely joking when I said I thought I was there as Edith's champion.

The next stage of the evening was quite as embarrassing as anyone could wish. We were transported to Chez Michou in Montmartre, a pocket-handkerchief of a club, where assorted female impersonators mimed to the records of various stars. This was the idea of Lord Peter, who turned out to be, as I think I already vaguely knew, an amiable drunkard with a reputation for being 'quite a card'. Actually we were all pretty drunk by this time, having been at it more or less non-stop since we arrived at the airport in London. Doubtless this helped us enjoy the show, which contained few surprises: Garland, Streisand, a rather compelling Monroe, and an absolutely unlike Rita Hayworth miming to 'Long Ago and Far Away', which Rita herself only mimed to anyway. Drink or no drink, I was beginning to feel the siren call of my bed and I caught Tommy's eye as he made a let's-get-out-of-here gesture towards the door when the compère – or *commère* should it be? – jumped up onto the stage. 'Now, I'd like to introduce our special act for this evening, with our best wishes and congratulations. Ladies and Gentlemen, Miss Edith Lavery!'

I nearly jumped out of my seat as the young man who had given us Monroe reappeared as Edith. An over-made-up Edith with a kind of flashiness she didn't possess, but otherwise astonishingly accurate. Even down to her dress, which could easily have been one of her own. I looked at Charles. He was stunned as were we all. Peter, of course, was grinning like a clown. On the stage the boy/Edith started to sing a song from *Guys and Dolls*. 'Ask me how do I feel, Little me with my quiet upbringing . . .' She wiggled her way across the stage to where Charles sat, still motionless. 'Well, sir, all I can say is if I were a bell I'd be ringing...' At about this moment I realised that this was, in some undefined and complicated way, a terrible insult to Edith. The others started to snicker, as the blonde on the stage frisked and shouted her silly lyrics about striking it lucky. Charles was silent. The performer beckoned him up onto the stage and clearly this was part of what had been pre-arranged but he shook his head and kept his seat, with no change in his expression. The boy/girl looked, puzzled, over to where Peter was sitting with a laughing Eric and a couple of the others. The act was grinding to a halt. In another moment, Peter jumped up onto the stage as her partner and the dance went on. Towards the end, Peter was given a cardboard jewel-box to present to her, which he did, going down on one knee. 'Edith' opened it and started to deck herself out in the glittering gewgaws within. I was reminded of Gillray's cartoon attacks on the actress, Elizabeth Farren, who succeeded in marrying the Earl of Derby in the 1790s. At the bottom of the box was a little coronet, a pantomime walk-down affair, bright with coloured glass. At the last note of the song 'Edith' took it up and planted it on her head.

In fairness to Peter Broughton I'm sure he hadn't quite hoisted in how fantastically offensive the cumulative effect of all this would be to Charles. Certainly the last thing he wanted was for the evening to end as it did. Peter was not one of the cleverest, poor soul, and I remember I thought then that Chase or one of the others must have embellished his original idea of simply having someone impersonate Edith, which, in itself, if 'she' had just sung a love song, could have been quite amusing. As it was, and without I think Peter's really knowing, she was lampooned as a greedy, social-climbing adventuress in front of her bridegroom. Chase and some of the others were applauding loudly. They were sitting behind Charles and so could not see the expression on his face, though for the life of me I can't imagine how they thought he was going to find it funny. But Chase was one of those who insults you and then says, 'Can't you take a joke?' and I suppose he had done this so often he had begun to think these insults really were jokes and that Charles, or anyone who couldn't take them, was simply being dull.

Charles stood up. 'I'm rather tired. I think I'm going back to the hotel,' he said.

Tommy and I volunteered to join him and that was that. We strode off, leaving the others to nurse the failure of Peter's prank.

'Shall we get a taxi?' said Tommy. It was late and the night was perceptibly cooler than it had been but Charles shook his head.

'Is it all right if we walk for a bit? I want some air.' We strode along in silence until he spoke again. 'That was rather unpleasant, wasn't it?'

'Well,' Tommy was placatory, 'I'm sure they didn't mean it to be. I dare say the girl, or boy or whatever she was, misunderstood the brief.'

'It was Peter's fault.'

'Well...'

Charles stopped walking for a minute and stood, looking mutely about him. 'Do you know what really depressed me about that?' We both had some pretty good ideas but naturally said nothing. 'It was because I suddenly realised how absolutely bloody stupid most of the people I know really are. These are supposed to be twelve of my best friends, for God's sake!' He chuckled bitterly. 'I'm embarrassed for them and I'm embarrassed for myself.'

In the end we walked home right across Paris. The others must all have gone to bed by the time we fell through the door in the Place Vendôme. We parted and went to our rooms and I suppose, all in all, the evening must be rated as a flop – particularly considering the planning and the cost – but in some odd and undefined way I found myself feeling rather encouraged by Charles's outburst. My assessment of his brain was not revised but I do not think I had appreciated before that night how thoroughly decent he was. It is not a fashionable quality these days but it seemed to me that Edith's happiness was in safer hands than I had realised.

SIX

When she opened her eyes she knew at once that this was the last morning in her life when she would awake as Edith Lavery. Henceforth, that girl would have gone away and whatever might happen in the future she would not be coming back. Edith attempted to question herself as to what exactly she was feeling. Just as when you are forced into a decision it is often the mouthing of one choice that makes you realise you really want the other, so she wondered if her stomach would tell her that she was making a ghastly mistake simply because this was the day when the whole thing became irrevocable. But her stomach did not wish to play the part of a goat's entrails at Delphi and declined to give an opinion. She felt neither elated nor depressed – simply that there was a lot to do. There was a faint knock on her door and her mother came in carrying a cup of tea.

It is no exaggeration to say that Stella Lavery was so happy on this morning she really felt she might burst, that her heart might stop, exhausted by pumping the feverish blood of satisfied ambition. It is not true to say she would have gladly sacrificed her daughter to a rich marquess's heir if she had thoroughly disliked him, simply that unless he had attacked her with a knife it was not physically possible that she *could* dislike him. Actually, I don't think she had given Charles *qua* Charles much thought. He was pleasant, well-mannered, not bad-looking. That, to coin a phrase, was all she knew and all she needed to know. That, and the fact that after tomorrow her daughter would be the Countess Broughton.

It had been a source of the faintest irritation to Stella that her daughter's title was not to be Countess *of* Broughton, which she thought more romantic, and it seemed to her tiresome of the first Broughton to receive the earldom not to have asked for the 'of.' After all, the Cholmondeleys had done so and so had the Balfours when they were presented with their titles. True there was a village called Cholmondeley and somewhere in Scotland called Balfour but was there not a place called Broughton? Surely there must be one somewhere? Still, allowing the fact that 'you can't have everything' she had grown used to the form and now gained a good deal of pleasure correcting her friends. After all, the blessed 'of' would come, with the marquessate, all in good time.

'Good morning, darling.' She whispered the words, gently conveying, as she thought, great tenderness. This was a moment when she knew it behoved her to feel some nostalgia and regret at losing the child of her heart. The fact remained, however, that, notwithstanding the very real and deep joy Edith had given her mother over the years, this morning Mrs Lavery was as happy as a sandboy. Not only was she gaining a son, as the saying goes, but, as she saw it, a whole new position in the firmament. Gates as rusty as the ones at Ham, locked after the departure of the last Stuart king, were everywhere springing open before her. Or so it seemed. Stella Lavery was not a complete fool. She did realise that it was up to her to make a success of this opportunity, that if some of the people she was going to meet, most particularly Lady Uckfield, could be induced to like her, could actually want her friendship, then she could turn herself into Edith's asset rather than being (as she very secretly and reluctantly suspected) her liability. She also knew enough to go slowly. Never must there be the slightest scent about her of a beast of prey in pursuit of its quarry. Softly, quietly, mutual interests must be unearthed, books must be lent, dressmakers must be suggested. In her mind, on this dizzy morning, were shining images, holographs of elegant pleasure, showing her tucking into a light lunch with Lady Uckfield before they rushed off together to their shared milliner, pulling on their gloves as they waved for a taxi . . .

''Morning, Mummy.' Edith was by this time used to the dream-reverie in which her mother seemed to exist. She did not grudge her the pleasure this marriage brought, although she hoped it had not been a contributory factor, pushing her into the torrent that Edith felt whirling her towards the coronet. 'Is it raining?'

'No, it's heavenly. Now, there's no need to rush. It's just after half past eight. The hairdresser will be here at ten, then we've got two hours before we have to be at St Margaret's. I'll make some breakfast while you have a bath and if I were you I'd just get into your undies and stick on a dressing gown. Then you can stay in that until everything's ready.'

'I'm not madly hungry.'

'Well, you must have something. Or you'll feel sick.'

Edith nodded and started to get up, sipping her tea as she did so. It was one of those moments when she was acutely aware of every movement of her body, even of the muscles in her face. Each word seemed to come from some other source than her own brain. She felt drugged, but in a bright, unsleepy way. No, not drugged, dazed – or even hypnotised. Am I hypnotised? she thought. Have I been mesmerised by all those unquestioned values I have sucked down since I was three? Have I lost myself in other people's ambitions? But then she thought of Charles, who was a nice man who loved her and of whom, by this time, she really was very fond, and of course, she thought of Broughton and of Feltham, the family's other estate in Norfolk, and most of all she thought of the flat in which she was now standing and the job in the estate agent's in Milner Street and the opportunities the one life offered and the exhausted, negligible opportunities of the other, and so thinking she threw back her head and strode towards the bathroom. Her father was just coming out. He smiled a rather wistful smile.

'Everything all right, Princess?' he said and she knew, even as he spoke, that he would probably have to stop calling her Princess, that it sounded suburban, and she made a resolution there and then that she would not let him stop calling her Princess. It was a resolution she broke almost at once.

'Fine. How about you?'

'Fine.'

The wedding was going to cost Kenneth Lavery a great deal of money. Although less than it might have done, as Lady Uckfield had been given permission for the reception to be held in St James's Palace. Nevertheless, and even because of this, the Laverys had both been determined that they would carry the entire bill for the rest. They had even eschewed the modern, rather charmless custom of expecting the bridesmaids' parents to pay for their dresses. Edith was, after all, their only daughter and they did not want there to be any suspicion that she came from a family which could not afford to pay its way. Mrs Lavery, living as she was a plot from a Barbara Cartland novel, had even wondered if they were not expected to make some sort of dowry settlement on Edith but although her husband had touched on this with Lord Uckfield it had not been taken up. Probably because the Uckfields did not want to embroil themselves in any corresponding legal entitlement. After all, as Lady Uckfield had pointed out before turning out the light, nowadays one could never be sure these things were *for ever*. Edith was grateful to her parents for ensuring she entered Broughton with her head held high, although again she was conscious of yet another of the million threads that pinned her, like Gulliver, to the ground.

She lay back in the bath and tried to conjure up her favourite mental image of herself presiding over charity boards, raising money for the disabled, curtseying to various Royalties before escorting them to her box on gala nights, visiting the sick in the village – she stopped. Do people still visit the sick in the village? She realised she had unconsciously clad herself in a crinoline in her daydreams. And she thought of Lady Uckfield and of what a model daughter-in-law she was going to be, how the day would come when they would all bless the hour that Edith came into their lives.

*   *   *

I arrived at St Margaret's at about twenty past ten to be handed my white carnation, stripped of course of the fern that the florist had so painstakingly arranged with it, and my list for the front pews. It was the expected combination of duchesses and nannies, with places marked for the tenants and staff at Broughton and, behind them, the tenants and staff at Feltham. From the Reigning Family we were to get the Princess Royal and the Kents, all of them, but not the Prince of Wales (a bit of a disappointment for Lady Uckfield, a tragedy for Mrs Lavery) as he was on a goodwill junket somewhere in the South Seas. Nor were we to welcome the Queen. I don't know why as I believe Her Majesty and Lady Uckfield got on well. Needless to say, I was not deputed to usher any of them, this honour going to Lord Peter Broughton, who nodded to me as I came in. I had not seen him since leaving Chez Michou as we had been given a choice of return flights and, having no City deadline to meet, I was still in bed when most of the party had set off. I had written to thank him and Henry but I had obviously said nothing of the debacle.

'I got your letter. You shouldn't have bothered.' The English always say you shouldn't have bothered to thank them when, of all races on earth, they are the most unforgiving when one does not. I smiled in reply. He pulled a face. 'God, I had a head the next day! I was in a meeting by eleven. I do not think I gave it my best.'

I couldn't remember what he did. Something financial, I assumed, although I have noticed of late that the brain standard of the City has been rising in inverse ratio to the fall of its social status. I wonder where this is going to leave people like Peter Broughton. 'You were very kind to lay it all on,' I said.

He nodded in turn, slightly awkwardly. 'I'm afraid Charles was a bit shirty.' I shrugged. 'The thing is, it seemed the most frightfully funny idea, d'you see? Henry and I went over with photographs and things and we'd even borrowed one of Edith's frocks ... She thought it'd be terrifically funny too, d'you see? She was a great sport about it, she even told Charles not to be silly ...' He tailed off rather lamely. Good for Edith, I thought, to come out of that ghastliness ahead. I hardly needed to point out that had she seen the act she would have been less sanguine. We could be sure that Charles had not told her exactly what he had found so offensive.

'I expect the boy doing it misunderstood his brief,' I said, borrowing Tommy Wainwright's line.

Lord Peter nodded furiously. 'That's it, exactly. I think the song was wrong, that was the trouble. That and Eric's idea of the jewel-box. I can see that wasn't too clever.'

I nodded, unsurprised at Eric's complicity. It was interesting, though predictable I suppose, that Edith's first enemy in the Broughton household should be someone of considerably lower rank than herself, who had made an infinitely greater leap in catching at his bride. 'I should forget about it,' I said. 'I'm sure Charles has.' I was actually sure that Charles had not, although I was pretty certain he would never refer to the incident again.

Of course, Edith made a lovely bride and the collection of familiar Royal and Society faces on the Broughton side of the aisle put a glamorous spin into the whole business, which I, for one, thoroughly enjoyed. Even the sermon seemed quite interesting. The Lavery side of the church was inevitably rather over-shadowed but Edith had managed to attract one or two of her new, media-friendly friends and her mother, desperate to keep face, had written to her third cousin, the present baronet, introducing herself and enclosing an invitation to the wedding. Consequently, this very ordinary solicitor who lived in an old vicarage near Swindon (the family's modest pile had gone two generations before), suddenly found himself in the front pew of a London wedding, staring at what seemed to be half the Royal Family a few feet away. Actually, because of St Margaret's custom of keeping an empty pew for the Speaker on the right-hand side of the aisle, this necessitated a kind of half-backwards squint but he soon got the hang of it. At any rate, he was delighted to be there and so was his ugly wife, although she, understanding these things better than her husband, retained an air of having done the Laverys a favour in agreeing to come. Which was, of course, quite true.

We had all been given special stickers to park on the gravel at the edge of the Mall so it was easier than usual to get to the reception. I had never got past the tables in the lower gallery of the Palace where, in those days, you could collect your badge for Ascot, so I was curious, as we stood in a long, slowly-moving, drinkless queue, to see what the state rooms had in store. We shuffled up the great staircase, past a suitably dissolute full-length of Charles II, through a small ante-room, sumptuously lined with dark tapestry, where we were at last given a glass of the inevitable champagne, and then into the first of the three huge, red, white and gold apartments. In the receiving line it was not Mrs Lavery, whom I had met many times, but Lady Uckfield who greeted me by name and to my surprise offered me a cheek to kiss.

'I saw you beavering away in church,' she said, using her habitual tone of sharing a naughty secret that only I would understand. 'What a happy day.'

'We've been jolly lucky with the weather.'

'I think we're jolly lucky all round.' With that she dismissed me by angling me towards her husband, who, needless to say, hadn't a clue who I was, and having shaken his hand, I wandered off into the throng. It was clear that Lady Uckfield was making an effort to be agreeable to me but it wasn't all that obvious as to why. Probably she wanted to make sure that the only friend of Edith's that Charles liked at all would be her ally. She meant to subvert any attempts of Edith's to set up a 'rival court' right from the start. This would ensure that if anyone had to do any adjusting it would be Edith, not her. I would not hazard a guess as to how conscious this was but I am fairly sure it was so. Just as I am sure that she was successful and that we all played our parts. From the start I was very taken by Lady Uckfield's ability to combine the kittenish with the autocratic and I do not think that where she was concerned I was ever a very useful friend for Edith.

I had hardly spoken to the bride in the line and I didn't really expect to get much of a chance to talk to her as I murmured and nodded my way through various chattering and kissing groups. David and Isabel were there of course, but I could see that they had not come to St James's Palace in order to spend their time talking to me so I let them get on with it and wandered into another huge, scarlet and gilded chamber, at right angles to the first. Large, full-length portraits, mostly of Stuarts, hung on chains against the stretched damask. I stopped beneath one, which, from the half-shut eyes and luscious *décolletage* I had taken for Nell Gwyn (who may not have been a Stuart but certainly served under them) so I was surprised to see from the plaque on the frame that the melting beauty was Mary of Modena, Queen of James VII and II.

Edith's voice behind me made me jump. 'What do you think of the show so far?'

'There's nothing like starting at the top,' I said.

'It seems rather fitting that my wedding should be celebrated in a Royal palace, traditional seat of the arranged marriage.'

I looked up at the heaving, painted bosom of the queen. 'I shouldn't think this one was very hard to arrange.'

Edith laughed. We were almost alone in the room for a minute and I had time to marvel at her beauty, now reaching the years of its zenith. She had chosen a dress in the style of the 1870s, with wide flounces and a bustle behind. It was of ivory silk with a tiny self-patterned sprig of flowers. What I assume was someone's mother's lace fell from her thick blonde hair, held there by a light, dazzling tiara, fashioned for a young girl, like a glistening diamond-studded cobweb, not one of those heavy metal plates made for dowagers to sport at the opera, which always look as if they belong in a Marx Brothers comedy. I imagine it was part of the Broughton trove.

'You'll come and visit us?' she said.

'If I'm asked.'

We stared at each other for a moment. 'We're going to Rome for a week, then on to Caroline and Eric in Mallorca.'

'That sounds nice.'

'Yes, it does, doesn't it? I'm not supposed to know but I do. I like Rome. I don't really know Mallorca. I gather Caroline takes a villa every year there so obviously they enjoy it.' She laughed again rather mirthlessly.

There didn't seem to be anything more to say as I wasn't prepared to comment on her melancholy outburst. The last thing I believe in is the deathbed confession. In this case she'd made her bed and was already lying on it. All that was left was to shut her eyes. Anyway, I can't say I was worried. Presumably, many brides, or grooms too for that matter, have a slight what-have-I-done? feeling at the reception.

I kissed her. 'Good luck,' I said. 'Telephone me when you get back.'

'I'm not going yet.'

'No, but I won't have another chance to talk to you.'

And so it proved. Charles came to fetch her to parade her past yet more of his unknown relations and I was left alone again. I wandered into the throne room, which opened out of the end of the first room we had entered. More red, more gilt, this time as a background for a splendid canopied and embroidered throne, and more paintings in chains, these ones Hanoverians. I was admiring the chimneypiece when a fat, red-faced man in his sixties nodded to me. We talked for a while about a painting of George IV by Lawrence that hung in the room, whether it was the original or a copy and so on, when he suddenly leaned towards me conspiratorially. 'Tell me,' he whispered hoarsely, 'are you a friend of the girl or are you one of us?'

I must confess I was momentarily stumped for words.

'Both, I hope,' said Lady Uckfield, approaching at a brisk pace.

I nodded to her for getting me off the hook and she introduced me to my companion, who turned out to be called Sir William Fartley, which nearly made me laugh out loud. He sauntered away as Lady Uckfield took my arm and strolled us both across to the windows.

'I hope you'll come down and see us again soon,' she said. 'I know Charles would like it.'

This was to tell me that Charles was prepared to have me as a friend and also to let me know that they, the family, saw no threat in my friendship with Edith. I thanked her and said I should be delighted. 'I don't suppose you shoot?'

'As a matter of fact I do.'

She was quite surprised. 'Do you? I thought theatre people never shot. I thought they were always terrific antis.'

I shrugged. 'Better death on the wing than in an abattoir is my feeling.'

'What a relief! I was thinking we were going to have to scratch around for some writers and talkers to amuse you. I know Edith thinks you're terribly bright.'

'That's nice.'

'But if you shoot you won't mind normal people.'

'Like Sir William Fartley. Can't wait.'

She laughed and pulled a face. 'Silly old fool but he only lives three miles away so there's nothing I can do.'

I commented inwardly that he was further away than the Eastons, that there were probably two or three hundred people a similar distance from Broughton who would cry out for an invitation and would never receive one but naturally I said nothing.

Lady Uckfield patted my hand. 'Seriously. You must come. I'll see to it.'

'I'd love to, but only if you promise not to ask any writers or talkers. I don't want to lose face in front of Edith.'

She smiled her conspiratorial smile and was gone about her duties.

It was all over quite soon after that. The lucky pair went off to change and we followed them out as a shining barouche landau carried them away. This rather mawkish detail had been specially arranged by Edith's father with the mistaken idea that it would lend glamour to the occasion. At any rate, when we all turned back we found that the Palace had been locked against us. The authorities had decreed that the day was over and there was nothing more to do but go home.

SEVEN

~

To Edith, as much as to anyone else who knew it, one of the oddest aspects of her marriage, at least in the context of the 1990s, was that she had never slept with Charles before their wedding night. It sounds quite remarkable but the fact remains that it was so. At first she had resisted his advances as she knew that he was definitely the type who did not respect in the morning the easy conquest of the night before and several dates had to have taken place before it was sufficiently established that she was a 'nice girl'. This went on for two or three months but when she had decided that it was just about safe to yield she found to her puzzlement that Charles seemed to have accepted the pattern of their relationship and that he did not apparently want more. He would kiss her, of course, and embrace her but without the deadly urgency that she had come to expect in these moments. Once when they were lying on the sofa in her parents' flat (Kenneth and Stella were in Brighton for the weekend) she had casually allowed her hand to slide across the front of his trousers but although she could feel a perfectly satisfactory erection beneath the fabric the gesture made him jump so sharply that she did not repeat it. And after he had asked her to marry him there didn't seem much point. After all, she wanted him whether or not they 'suited' between the sheets but, if they did not, might he be put off? So when, a few weeks before the wedding, he had suggested that they 'get away together' for a weekend she had murmured that she thought it better to wait, now it was so near, and not 'spoil it'. Charles had accepted this because although, being a man of his generation he had acquired a certain amount of sexual experience, deep in his subconscious he still believed that bride-material should enter the wedding-chamber chaste. Of course, Edith was not chaste in this sense but she decided that, if questioned, she would refer to 'an incident' when she had been very young which she didn't want to talk about. In actual fact she never had to as Charles seemed to be satisfied with the fact that this was *their* first time together and sensibly refused to enter into a competition with her past.

He had booked a room in the Hyde Park Hotel in Knightsbridge. The world knows that this establishment now forms part of the Mandarin chain and so, technically, the old name is defunct but the upper classes are slow to alter accepted nomenclature. To them it will be the Hyde Park Hotel at least until their children are in late middle age. The plan was to spend the wedding night there and then fly to Rome at noon the following day. Accordingly the barouche swept them up St James's, down Piccadilly past the Ritz, over Hyde Park Corner, and turned round in front of the Bowater House entrance to the park to deposit them on the steps of the hotel. As they bowled along, passers-by, tourists and Anglo-Saxons alike, turned to smile and even wave. Probably the connection between carriages and Royal occasions is fixed in the public Pavlovian consciousness. So that she might be undisap-pointing and because the brilliance of her new state filled her brain with a cloud of sparkling lights, Edith waved tentatively back. Charles, on the other hand, looked straight ahead as if somehow his candidacy for officer material was in question. She understood why. Charles was saddled with that most tedious of all English aristocratic affectations, the need to create the illusion that you are completely unaware of any of your privileges. That cool insouciance, so chic in theory so crashingly boring in practice, was to ruin many occasions in the future for the pair as Edith suspected, looking at the frozen profile beside her. But this time at least the drive did not last long, certainly not long enough for Edith. Barely fifteen minutes after they had left the reception they were in the foyer of the hotel. It was still only about half past five and Edith wasn't absolutely clear what happened next.

She thought of suggesting that they stay downstairs and have some tea but since this would betray a total lack of urgency to be alone with Charles (that she was afraid she was feeling) she rejected the idea. They were shown into the Bridal Suite, which they had not requested but was theirs anyway – the difference in price being compliments of the management, following the age-old principle 'To them that hath shall be given' – and there they found their luggage as well as flowers and fruit and more of the bottomless supply of champagne. Then the door shut and they were alone. Married. They stared at each other in silence.

Edith felt a slight tremor of panic as the reality of seeing this man more or less every day for the remainder of her life hit her. What on earth were they going to talk about?

Charles pointed at the bottle. 'Shall I open this?' he said.

'Honestly I don't think I could. I'm swimming in it already.' She paused. 'I think I'll have a bath.'

She started to undress as casually as she could with Charles lying on the bed watching her but at the last moment her nerve failed and, still with her bra and pants on, she snatched her dressing gown out of her suitcase and dashed into the bathroom.

When she came out, half an hour later, Charles was still lying on the bed, reading a newspaper. He had taken off his coat, waistcoat and tie as well as his shoes and socks, and something about the slightly studied relaxation of his pose told Edith that her hour had come. She strolled over to the bed and lay down next to him, naked beneath the gown, and pretended to read the paper over his shoulder.

'Happy?' he said, without raising his eyes.

'Mmm,' she replied, wondering how long it was going to take him to get to it. Now that the moment was here, she was suddenly rather anxious. She felt the need to reassure herself about the physical attraction between them. This, after all, was the side of their relationship that had nothing to do with ambition or even shared interest. It was the sexual conjunction that, at this point at least, she was determined was going to be the only one she would know for the rest of her natural life.

After what seemed an eternity, Charles folded the paper and turned to her. With a deadly earnestness and in absolute silence (which lasted throughout), he started to kiss her as he inexpertly unfastened her dressing gown. She responded as well as she could, trying not to lead. This time when she touched his penis, although he still started like a frightened colt, he didn't actually pull away. And so they lay there, fondling each other through their garments until Charles deemed a suitable period had passed and then he sat up, still in absolute silence, and removed his shirt, trousers and underpants. Edith shrugged off the gown and waited. Charles had quite a good figure, in that he was muscled and covered without being fat, but he had one of those English bodies, white, faintly freckled skin, with a little ginger pubic hair around his groin and none on his chest. His beaky nose and crinkly, public-school hair looked somehow odd on top of an undressed body, as if he had been born in a double-breasted suit and being nude was too raw to be natural. In truth, he seemed more skinned than naked.

Still without a word he turned back to her, the same furious intensity in his face, and, avoiding direct eye contact, he started to kiss her while he planted his right hand against her vagina. Once it was in place, he began to massage her with a kind of dry pumping action, which reminded her of someone blowing up a lilo. She groaned a bit by way of encouragement. He didn't seem to need more as suddenly he heaved himself over between her legs, fumbled himself into her, thrust away a few times – no more than six at the outside – and then, with a terrific gasp to tell her that it was *now* (which she countered with some cries and pants of her own), he collapsed on top of her. The whole business, from the moment he folded the paper, had taken perhaps eight minutes. Ah, thought Edith.

'Thank you, darling.' One of Charles's more irritating habits was always to thank Edith after sex, as if she had just brought him a cup of tea. Of course, at this point, she did not know it was habitual.

She thought of responding, 'Oh, but thank *you*,' then decided it was too like people waving at each other through a hotel door so she settled for simply saying, 'Darling . . .' in a sort of misty way and kissing him on the neck. He had rolled off her by now and she was feeling a bit chilly lying there but moving seemed the wrong thing as this was all constituting a 'very important moment' for Charles and she had no intention of spoiling it. She did not allow herself any review of the love-making – if that was what they had just been through. It was, after all, early days, and she was beginning to suspect that Charles, for all his *savoir faire* with waiters, was not very confident when it came to the more private areas. At least he seemed to feel that something momentous had taken place, even if her body had never left the station, so the episode surely rated as a success rather than a failure. That said, she did catch herself briefly hoping that things would improve with practice.

They dined in the hotel, more to avoid being spotted and congratulated by any of their friends (who never dine in hotels except with Americans who are staying there) than for any particular enthusiasm for the *cuisine de la maison* and then went to bed around eleven. They had a repeat performance of the afternoon's activity and then rolled over to sleep. Edith stared at the ceiling, contemplating the oddness of life. Here she was with this man, whom she hardly knew when she really thought about it, asleep, naked, beside her. She pondered that central truth, which must have struck many brides from Marie Antoinette to Wallis Simpson, that whatever the political, social or financial advantages of a great marriage, there comes a moment when everyone leaves the room and you are left alone with a stranger who has the legal right to copulate with you. She was not at all sure that she had fully negotiated this simple fact until then.

The thought had not left her when she awoke – the first time for a good long while that she had awakened next to anyone – and she was rather relieved when Charles made it clear, slightly sheepishly, that he was not a 'morning man'. Things eased when they began to discuss the wedding, the various near-dramas, which guests they disliked, who was unhappily married, who was going broke. Of course, thought Edith, this is what we're going to talk about, the things we've done together, and the longer we're married, the more shared experiences we'll have to discuss. She was just comforting herself with these ruminations when Charles lapsed into silence. Not for the last time, he had run dry. There was a knock at the door. A waiter came in wheeling a trolley of breakfast.

'Good morning, my lord,' he said to Charles and then, as he approached the bed with a tray, 'Good morning, my lady.'

Oh well, thought Edith, things could be worse.

Given the fact that their first hours together had not been an overwhelming thrill, it was perhaps a little surprising that the trip to Rome, by contrast, went very well. They stayed at the Hotel de la Ville, quite near the top of the Spanish Steps, and just down from the Villa Medici. Rome is a very beautiful city anyway and this was of course Edith's first experience of being milady'd and contessa'd everywhere she went, which was amusing (though she knew enough not to show it) and a solid reminder of why she was in this spot. The food was delicious and there was plenty to see and consequently to talk about and so as they sat in the Piazza Navona eating under the stars or strolled down the fountain-decked walks of the Villa d'Este out at Tivoli, Edith began to feel that she had after all made a good choice and that the rich and rewarding life of her imaginings really did lie ahead.

During their stay Charles started to talk about Broughton and

Feltham in an affectionate, detailed way that was new to her. Perhaps he had thought that before she had actually, so to speak, *become* a Broughton she would not be interested. He loved his homes and his cares and since this was all fitting in along the lines of her pre-nuptial fantasies, she loved him for it. She was able to respond to his enthusiasm with an unfeigned enthusiasm of her own. To her delight, she discovered that he was a bit rusty on the history of the family itself. Here was her task! She saw herself lovingly cataloguing the furniture and pictures, entertaining ancient aunts and writing up memoirs of long, hot Edwardian summers at Broughton, bringing down and cleaning forgotten pictures in the attics of some particularly amusing ancestor. She was interested in both history and gossip – what could be better qualifications? It is true that the sex did not improve dramatically and the format never varied but once Charles was less nervous with her it did at least take a bit longer. Altogether, as they boarded the aeroplane for Madrid, the first leg of their journey to Mallorca, Edith and Charles were able to stare into each other's eyes in a deliberate imitation of two people who were as 'happy as newly-weds'.

EIGHT

~

At Palma, where they surged out of the ticket hall surrounded by what looked and sounded like the entire supporters' club of Wolverhampton Wanderers, they were hailed by a wrinkled cockney with a face like beaten leather and red nylon shorts. He was, he explained, Eric's 'driver' and had come to take them to the villa. Charles was slightly put out at not being met in person – Edith would learn that like many apparently easy-going grandees his insecurity manifested itself if he ever felt that he was being treated like an 'ordinary person' despite his often saying that this was exactly what he wanted. She, herself, was simply glad to be out of the airport and in a car and gradually her relief transmitted itself to him. In the end he forgave the Chases for staying at home: the drive consisted of two and a half hours of dry scrub and shanties as they crossed the centre of the island. Edith had never visited Mallorca before and had not known what to expect. But she realised on looking out of the car window that the images in her mind had consisted of various combinations of Monte Carlo and Blackpool, not the scratch farming and dust of the plains of Salamanca. As they approached Calaratjada, however, the huge concrete hotels of her imaginings began to materialise together with the crowds – mainly respectable but with the hovering hint of kiss-me-quick hats – and all the sights and smells of the Beach Holiday made their familiar and comforting appearance.

The villa itself was a large, white, modern affair constructed around a kind of hill/courtyard, with vast tiled terraces looking out across the bay. There was a private jetty, which was apparently more for swimming than for tethering boats, and meant that there was no need for the villa's inhabitants to use the crowded, sandy beach that launched the tourist swimmers into the sea from a point a few hundred yards to the left of their position. Across the water, the smart houses of the

Mallorcin could be glimpsed through their modest curtaining of trees and beyond there was the wide, blue ocean. Edith and Charles stood admiring the view, as a pin-figure far below them on the jetty waved and started to run up the steps. A few minutes later Caroline appeared. They were kissed and congratulated and, in turn, they admired the villa.

'Isn't it fabulous? It belongs to some client of Eric's so we've got a frightfully good rate. It's far cheaper than the one we had last year and it's twice the size. Needless to say, we're being used as an absolute boarding-house all summer long.'

Charles frowned slightly. 'I thought it was just going to be us this week.'

'I know. So did I. But then Peter rang because this was the only week he could do. And Jane and Henry suddenly said they could come after all. And then one of Eric's business people appeared with his wife.' Caroline momentarily wrinkled her nose. 'Apparently Eric had asked them and forgotten all about it. Wasn't it frightful? Anyway, they're here now and they seem to have forgiven us.'

'You mean they're all here now? This week?'

'This minute. They're coming up to change for dinner even as we speak. Has anyone shown you your room? You've got the best one so you mustn't grumble.'

Charles threw himself on the bed in what Edith could only describe as a 'pet'. 'Christ! I don't know why we didn't just go to Trafalgar Square and set up a tent.'

Edith lay down next to him. 'Oh, darling, it doesn't matter. I'm sure everyone just does what they want anyway. We'll be able to push off by ourselves.' Actually she was feeling rather guilty as when Caroline was speaking she, Edith, suddenly realised that she was rather relieved to discover it wasn't just going to be the four of them after all. From what she knew of him she didn't like Eric much, Caroline she found rather intimidating and she had to admit that she was feeling just the teeniest bit talked-out with Charles. 'It'll be much easier later when we've done more together,' she said to herself but it was with a faintly sinking feeling that she realised she could already predict what his opinion would be on more or less any given topic. As a sort of private game with herself, she had begun to introduce odd items into the conversation, like psycho synthesis or the Dalai Lama, in the hope of catching herself out and being surprised by something he said. So far she hadn't dropped a point.

They met the rest of the party when they assembled that evening on the top terrace. Edith had been nervous of Caroline during the courting months for the simple reason that Caroline was a good deal more intelligent than Charles, and Edith was half afraid that she would try to put him, if not off her, at least on his guard. This may well have been true but Caroline, snobbish and egocentric as she was, was not essentially bad-hearted. Now that Edith was her sister-in-law she was determined to get on with her and she was equally determined that Charles, of whom she was extremely, if rather parentally, fond, should have a happy stay. All this Edith saw in the genuine smiles and the slightly touching arrangements of festive nibbles and champagne on ice as they walked across the sitting room and out through the glass doors to join the others. All the women wore expensive cocktail, rather than evening, frocks and all the men were in open-necked shirts. They looked oddly mismatched, like a bad hand in Happy Families. Jane Cumnor was the most over-dressed in strapless black moiré, but she held no threat any more for Edith who was quite content in off-the-shoulder cotton. Since they had last met properly she had breached Jane's citadel and Edith was anyway the prettier woman. Their relationship had subtly altered overnight, a fact of which Jane was quite as aware as Edith. She sidled over to plant a lipsticky kiss on the cheek of the bride. Henry lumbered across and pushed his face against hers. In his brightly coloured summer clothes he resembled a nineteenth-century bathing-machine. Edith wondered if his shirt might suddenly open to reveal a timorous swimmer in stripes. Caroline raised her glass: 'Welcome to the family.'

'Yes,' said Eric, who was standing behind the others nearer the edge of the terrace. 'Well done, Edith.'

The others noticed but ignored his tone and raised their glasses to the name, making the salutation sound more normal. Edith smiled and she and Charles drank their thanks and everyone sat down.

The moonlit sea glittered behind their heads as they sprawled and chattered on their cushioned wicker, champagne in their hands, the women in their *couture* dresses, diamonds twinkling in their ears. As she lay there, curled up against the squashy Liberty prints, more spectator than participant, Edith found herself warmed by the enveloping luxury of privilege. All the years of her growing up she had wanted not just to avoid being a have-not but to be an emphatic *have* and now, at last, just at the moment when she had begun to face the possibility of failure, here she was, living her dream. This gaggle of lords and millionaires was a sample of her set from now on, this exotic setting the first of many. Just as a driver can see distant mountains across a desert far before him and then realise that he is up in those very mountains without being aware of their coming nearer, so Edith pondered with wonder her progress from the respectable *haut bourgeois* life of Elm Park Gardens and Milner Street to this cross between an American soap-opera and a novel by Laclos.

The first evening passed uneventfully enough. Edith knew everyone there except for a lacklustre blonde who seemed to have come with Peter and Eric's friends, the Watsons. Of these the husband, Bob, was dull and rather common but the wife, Annette, though also common, was pretty and funny and Edith warmed to her. She had been a model and an actress in the early eighties before her marriage and was full of hilarious anecdotes about various Roman epics and Spanish westerns she had appeared in. She babbled away through dinner, which was served in the loggia/dining room that opened onto the courtyard, and saved Edith from the Name Exchange, which she knew was all she could expect from the others.

Charles was more non-committal about their fellow guests. 'Well, she's got plenty to say for herself, I'll give her that,' was his only comment as he turned the light out.

'I like her. She's funny.'

'Don't speak too soon.' In some mysterious way she felt reprimanded, although his tone had not been angry, and it was with a vague feeling of apprehension, like a child who expects a beating the next day, that Edith lay back on the pillow. Nor was her thought-train interrupted before sleep set in as it was the first night, since their marriage, that they did not make love.

The next morning Edith woke late and found herself alone. With a delicious, almost tangible sense of well-being she rang for breakfast as she had been bidden to do and settled back into her habitual review of the life that lay ahead. The maid arrived with her tray and told her that the others had already eaten and were down on the jetty so as soon as she was ready she put on a bathing suit, took up a towel and set off down the steep paved stairs that were cut into the rock below the villa. She could see the Chases, the Cumnors and Charles, but there was no sign of the rest of the party. On the jetty itself she waved a hello to everyone, spread out her towel and lay down, letting the soft, woolly warmth of the southern sun wash over her body. Charles threw himself down next to her, spraying her with drops of sea and gave her a salty kiss. 'Good morning, darling.' She smiled and kissed him back.

'What shall we do today? Just lie here and drink up the sun?'

Caroline answered her. 'We thought we might go into Calaratjada for lunch and then the Franks have asked us for tea. You're all included.'

'Who are the Franks?'

'They're this rather extraordinary family who are fearfully rich and they have a collection of sculpture that apparently must not be missed.'

'Why are they so rich and how do you know them?'

'To the first, God knows. Something to do with Franco so we'd better not ask, and to the second, we don't, but Mummy's godmother to one of their nephews in Rome and she let them know we were going to be here.'

Edith lay back and closed her eyes. This great network, this web that reached far beyond national boundaries, that crossed seas and mountain ranges, need not threaten her any more because now she was part of it. And soon, in Vienna or Dublin or Rome, people would be saying, 'I saw Edith Broughton when I was in London. She says they might be in New York in September...' and this would be greeted by some member of the Inner Circle saying, 'Edith? How is she?' or better still, 'I'm so mad about Edith. Aren't you?' and thus would be excluded all those other people in all those rooms in Vienna or Dublin or Rome who did *not* know Edith Broughton; and they would feel the poorer and the more middle-class for it, which would have been the intention of the name-droppers who would then go away satisfied that they had once again asserted their caste. In all this Edith would play her part by being the kind of person it is hard to meet unless you are in her set. And just for a moment on this particular morning, with the sun caressing her eyelids and the children shouting on the distant beach, Edith pondered the ultimate purpose of this endless raising and lowering of barriers.

There was a terrific thud near her and she opened her eyes to see the awe-inspiring sight of Henry Cumnor stretching out to sunbathe. If anything he looked even larger without his clothes, like a seaside postcard captioned 'Where's my little willy?'

'What about the others? We can't all go to these wretched people, can we?' He spoke undirected, straight up into the air, so that he should not have the inconvenience of moving more than his lips.

Caroline shrugged. 'I don't see why not. I said there were lots of us.' She had that curiously English upper-class belief that whatever the occasion, however much people have put themselves out, even when, as now, total strangers extend their hospitality as a duty, still she, Lady Caroline Chase, was doing them a favour. It is impossible for such people to conceive that they have not necessarily honoured a house by entering it. Consequently, because of this sense of having blessed her hosts by her presence, Caroline made no effort whatsoever with anyone outside her own crowd and despite being an intelligent woman could be a crushingly boring guest. Something of which neither she nor the many others of her kind who are just like her have any suspicion. 'We'll ask them when they come down,' she said.

'How long are they staying?' said Jane, propping herself up on her elbows and reaching for the oil.

'Who? Peter or the others?'

'Oh, not darling Peter. "Bob" and "Annette".' Jane spoke their names in inverted commas, distancing herself from them to make it clear to her listeners that she did not consider them as ordinary members of the house-party but rather as strange specimens of an alien culture. This was carefully judged.

'Tuesday or Wednesday, I think.' Caroline looked over to Eric who nodded and wrinkled his nose. He was quite clear about which team he wished to be on.

'Crikey,' said Henry. 'Who's in the listening chair this evening?' They all laughed.

Edith felt an irresistible urge to tear up her membership of the Club. 'Is this Annette you're talking about?' she said in a tone of feigned disbelief. 'How funny you are. I really like her.'

Henry was unfazed. 'Well, you can sit next to her at dinner. I hope you're ready to discuss her film career *ad nauseam*.'

Edith smiled. 'Why? What would you rather talk about? The people you all know in Shropshire?' She lay back with her smile still intact and her eyes closed, relishing the awkward silence like a naughty schoolgirl.

'I'm not often *in* Shropshire, actually.' Henry rolled away from her, bloated and breathless, like a beached whale far from the water.

'I'm going for a swim,' said Charles.

They lunched late on paella with too much squid in it in an open-air restaurant overlooking the harbour with its bobbing flotilla of yachts and then set off in two cars for the Franks's house, which lay outside the town on the edge of the sea and appeared to be entirely surrounded, on the land-locked frontier at any rate, by a high stone wall, topped with broken glass. The gates were not gates but rather iron doors, which swung open automatically when they identified themselves and then clanged shut, only just missing the rear fender of the second vehicle. 'Well, they're obviously not expecting two cars,' said Annette with a laugh.

Undaunted, Caroline, who was driving the first car with Edith, Annette and Henry, ploughed on through the enormous, empty pleasure gardens. Tantalising glimpses through the trees of Henry Moores and Giacomettis flashed past until rounding a huge clump of rhododendra they came to a fork in the road. One led apparently up to a nineteenth-century castle that was perched on the highest point of the estate, which Edith had assumed was their destination, while the other, incredibly, pointed the way to another house, as large as the first only modern, which had been built at the water's edge. It was too low, with its balconies thrusting out barely higher than the waves, to be seen from the road.

'Which one do we go to?' said Edith.

'The bottom one. Mrs Frank likes to be near the sea.'

'What happens up on the hill?'

Caroline looked suitably vague. 'I think it's mainly for the grandchildren.'

'Blimey O'Reilly,' said Annette and Edith noted with interest that no one else would acknowledge the strangeness, the orgiastic luxury that they were witnessing. She was beginning to understand it is a point of honour in that world that one must never be overawed by any display of wealth, no matter how fabulous. To register that riches on any scale are not routine, even mundane, is to risk being 'middle-class' – a sector of society to which many of them spend most of their lives proving to no one in particular that they do not belong. There are exceptions to this rule. It is possible to exclaim, 'How simply lovely!' but it is done in such a way as to show generosity rather than awe on the part of the speaker. Better yet, 'My dear, how *grand!*' This in a tone to show that the decoration, menu, whatever, is excessive and verging perilously close to vulgar. Lady Uckfield was particularly adept at crushing with smiling enthusiasm. These are hard skills for the novice though and Edith did well not to attempt them.

A white-coated footman took the party through the gleaming marble rooms out on to the terrace where Mrs Frank, a sun-beaten, robust figure, reclined in a brightly coloured cotton sarong, chunky bracelets bouncing and rattling against her sinewy, masculine arms. She waved them all over towards her.

Caroline took charge. 'How do you do?' she said lazily. 'I'm Caroline Chase.'

She started to indicate the other members of the party, deliberately pausing a fraction of a second before the three non-Broughton guests, Bob, Annette and Peter's girl, as if to demonstrate to Mrs Frank that they were not in the first circle and she need not therefore bother with them. Mrs Frank took the signal and welcomed the outsiders with a perceptibly cooler smiling nod than the one she reserved for the principals.

'You must be the bride,' she said, rising and taking Edith by the arm to lead them back into the house. Edith smelled the strong musk of her scent and watched the leathery creases move around the thin, scarlet-greased mouth. 'How are you enjoying Mallorca?'

'We only arrived last night. It seems lovely so far.' She smiled back into the glassy, bored eyes of her grinning hostess.

'You must let us entertain you while you're here. Tell me, how is darling Googie?'

'She's fine. She and Tigger are in Scotland.' As the words came out, Edith realised that this was the first time she had spoken these ludicrous nicknames out loud. Before her marriage she had privately determined to address her in-laws as Harriet and John, but already the unspoken urgings of intimacy, of club-membership, which rippled through Mrs Frank, had made her break her vow because the truth was that whatever she might say to her friends, she did not want to be the 'foreign' daughter-in-law. She did not want people to sympathise with Lady

Uckfield that Charles had not done better. She wanted her mother-in-law to be congratulated on her, Edith's, brilliance, on her taste, on her charm, on her entertaining. And so Edith learned the first lesson of why England has had no revolutions, of what has emasculated so many careers from Edward IV's queen to Ramsay MacDonald. Namely that the way to deal with a troublesome outsider is to let him in, to make him a convert with a convert's zeal and in no time he will be *plus Catholique que le Pape*. Learning this lesson did not reduce Edith's resentment of the forces that taught it to her but she had another heady moment of realising she was now a member of the Gang. It made her feel powerful. She turned and smiled at Charles.

A tour of the sculptures had been planned and the party set off. As they came out of the front door they were approached by a young, rather stringy woman, a reduced, ferret-sized version of Mrs Frank. She had obviously just been playing tennis and carried a slightly oversized racket in front of her, covering her face, half shield half fan. Their hostess introduced her as her niece, Tina. Unlike her aunt the girl was painfully shy. She fell into step with them as she was quite clearly commanded to do but mutely, only muttering miserable, whispered answers if she was directly addressed.

They passed a swimming pool, cut into a small cliff above the sea, and Edith heard Annette asking about the terracotta vases that surrounded it, apparently continually filling it with faintly steaming water.

'They are Roman,' said Tina almost inaudibly. 'My uncle had them brought up from a wreck off the coast near here.'

'And now they're plumbed in?'

'What is "plumbed in" excuse me?'

Charles cut off Annette rather irritably. 'She means that now they're used to feed the pool.'

'Yes. With sea water.'

'Sea water? *Warmed* sea water?'

Tina nodded. 'It's much better for you, no? We have another pool with clear water but I think this is good, no?'

Annette was silent for a while. She was clearly beginning to agree with the others – that she was out of her depth. The group had stopped on a terrace dripping with bougainvillea where a large male torso by Rodin stood on a marble plinth. They murmured and admired. Mrs Frank turned to Caroline and started to enquire about various mutual friends. She appeared to resent the fact that she had not been asked to Charles's wedding, as many of her queries ended by an assumption that 'they must have been at the reception', and time and again Caroline was forced to admit that they had been. The names rippled out as they climbed from terrace to terrace, against the deep azure blue of the Mediterranean sky. Had they seen the Esterhazys? the Polignacs? the Devonshires? the Metternichs? the Frescobaldis? Names torn from history books, names that Edith knew from studies of Philip II of Spain, or the Risorgimento, or the French Revolution, or the Congress of Vienna. And yet here they were, stripped of any real significance. They had simply become court cards, rich court cards, in the game of Name Exchange. These were high stakes indeed and Edith noticed with some amusement that Jane Cumnor and Eric had dropped back with Tina, no doubt anxious to avoid the left-out feeling that it pleased them to inflict on others. Caroline and Charles were unfazed. It was clear that whatever the extent of the Frank millions they could match name for name and top them too. And so the afternoon passed in a litany of duchesses intoned against a background of art enshrined by money. An hour and three quarters after setting out they were back at the modern palace-by-the-sea.

On the terrace a tea had been set out 'English-style', that is to say 'American-hotel-style' and three white-coated footmen waited to serve it. Mrs Frank led them to their chairs. Peter's girl, Bob and Annette were thoroughly squashed by this time and secretly longing to regain the villa and turn this flattening experience into a funny story. Eric brought up the rear, red-faced with his exertions and clearly irritated that his social ignorance had excluded him from the conversation that had revolved around his wife for most of the afternoon. He dumped down onto a *chaise* next to Edith and seized a proffered cup.

Mrs Frank turned her attention back to the bride. 'Tell me, was Hilary Weston at the wedding? Someone said she was stuck in Canada.'

Eric looked up with a snort. 'No good asking Edith, is it, old girl? You'll have to wait until she's done a bit more training.'

Edith ignored him. By some merciful providence it so happened that she had spoken to Mrs Weston for quite a time at the reception. She thanked her patron saint as she spoke chattily across Eric making no reference to him. 'No, she was there. Galen was in Florida and couldn't get back. I suppose that's what they were thinking of.'

Mrs Frank nodded, casting a slightly strange look at Eric. 'She does so much! I feel like a sloth when I think of her.' She moved on. Edith had passed.

Eric lay back and looked at her: 'Well done. Ten out of ten.'

She stared back at him, holding every inch of gained ground. 'Do you know Hilary?'

'I know her as well as you do,' said Eric, and stood up to join Caroline at the other end of the terrace. This interchange was oddly refreshing to Edith because it established beyond any doubt that Eric was her enemy in the family circle. There was no pretence necessary any longer and, best of all, in their first round, Edith had won.

She was singing in the shower when Charles came in to change for dinner later that evening. He smiled. 'You seem very happy. Did you enjoy yourself today? What a collection! What a place!' Even in these circles amazement is not forbidden in private between consenting adults and Charles clearly felt he had been unimpressed for long enough.

'I'll say. And yes, I am happy.' She turned off the tap and kissed him, standing there wet and naked.

The next few minutes, indeed the rest of the evening, were as agreeable as any she had known with Charles and it was with a sense of victory and well-being that she climbed into bed that night.

Charles turned to her. 'I gather the Franks want to give us a dinner before we go.'

She pulled a slight face. 'Oh dear. I suppose we have to?'

'Come on, darling,' said Charles. 'It's good of them and they're not that bad.'

'The old girl's not that bad but the niece is a nightmare.'

He laughed. 'I thought she was rather sweet. We must be kind.'

Edith propped herself up on her elbows beside him. 'Why is it that when someone like Annette is talkative and funny you all cold-shoulder her and wrinkle your noses behind her back and yet with Tina Frank, who must be the most boring and inconsequential young woman I have ever met, you make excuses and pretend that she's a dear?'

'I don't know what you mean.'

'Yes, you do, Charles.' She felt oddly confident, almost breezy. For the first time since her marriage she began to sense that she really was Lady Broughton. She had managed things well and according to the ancient tradition she was 'entitled to her own opinions'. She continued, smilingly severe. 'You know very well. And I'll tell you the answer. Annette does not know the people we know and Tina does and Tina has a hundred million besides. I don't know, darling, doesn't it ever make you wonder? Just a bit?' Edith was feeling her oats. She smiled at her husband quizzically, shaking her head slightly, imagining how charming her hair must look, rippling against her neck.

Charles stared at her. 'Who are all these people that you and Tina Frank know?' he said sourly and turned out the light.

PART TWO

~

Forte-Piano

NINE

~

I did not see a great deal of Edith in the months after she had returned from her honeymoon although they were in London from time to time. She did not apparently care for her mother-in-law's lair in Cadogan Square but they used Charles's little flat in Eaton Place and occasionally they would come up for a party or a show. I ran into them at a couple of dinners and I was asked for a drink with a few others in their tiny second-floor sitting room one day in October but there wasn't much of an opportunity for talk. Edith looked happy enough and had already begun to acquire that patina of the privileged, the faint, touch-me-not aura of *luxe* that marks such people apart from us mortals, and I was amused to trace the beginnings of an *hauteur* starting to obliterate the lucky girl from Fulham.

I didn't see them at all in the build-up to Christmas and I was just beginning to feel myself drifting out of their circle when I received a letter tucked into a card, not from Edith but from Charles, asking me for a day's shooting in January. It was to be a Friday so I was asked for dinner and the night on the Thursday and, since nothing further was specified, I was presumably intended to vanish after the shoot to make way for the arrival of Saturday's guests. The lateness of the invitation meant that someone had chucked, but it was no less attractive for that and I knew (for once) that I was going to be free on the date in question. I had already been booked to be villain-of-the-week in one of those endless boy-and-girl-detective series, which was due to start five days after the date proposed so I wrote back accepting and received, almost by return, directions by road or rail. These told me which train to be on if that was how I would be travelling or alternatively to arrive at the house at about six o'clock.

I enjoy shooting. This I know is as difficult for one's kind-hearted London theatrical friends to understand as it is easy for the country-bred fraternity but I do not propose to launch into a defence of blood sports since I have never encountered anyone of either opinion who could be swayed. While I must say that there does not seem much logic in people gaily eating battery-processed food and objecting to conservation-conscious game-keepers, still I accept that there is not necessarily a logical basis for all or even any of one's feelings. At all events, at that time in my life, most of my sport had been of the country shoot variety and so it was with a sense of pleasurable anticipation that I set off for what promised to be a real, Edwardian *Grand Battu*.

I knew the way well enough, as I had often been down for weekends with the Eastons, but getting out of London to the South can be a nightmare and so I was in the habit of leaving time for hold-ups. On this occasion, I had not allowed for the fact that I was making the journey on Thursday instead of Friday and so, after a comparatively free run, I arrived at Broughton not much after half past five. The butler who went by the unlikely name of Jago told me that Lady Uckfield and Lady Broughton were in the yellow drawing room finishing a committee meeting of some sort.

Having no desire to join in – the committees one is forced to attend are bad enough – I settled into a surprisingly comfortable velvet-and-gilt William Kent armchair in the Marble Hall. I didn't have very long to wait before the door opened to release some of the members, muttering fawning farewells to Edith who was in the process of showing them out. She broke away.

'Hello,' she said. 'I didn't know you were here.'

'I'm rather early so I thought I'd wait instead of coming in to spoil your fun.'

She sagged her shoulders with a comic sigh. 'Some fun!' she said. 'Come and have a cup of stewed tea.' Ignoring the nods and smiles of the departing ones, she led the way back into the room. They did not object to this treatment. Far from it. The net result of her cutting them in order to greet me was simply to make them include me in their deferential smiles as they sidled towards the staircase. I imagine they thought that I too had been touched by the golden wand.

The remaining members of the committee, the usual collection of provincial intellectuals, tightly permed councillors and farmers mad with boredom, were in the final stages of leaving. Some of them had that dilatory manner of collecting their things together, which betrays a resolve to 'catch' somebody before they go. The prey that most of the lingerers were after was, of course, Lady Uckfield, who was ensconced in a pretty, buttoned chair by the chimneypiece, surrounded by admirers. A few of the aspirants, disconcerted by the competition, made do with five minutes of Edith and left. I approached my hostess, who rose to greet me with a kiss, which was a kind of signal to the entourage that the audience was over.

'Goodbye, Lady Uckfield,' said a black councillor in a baggy artist's smock, 'and thank you.'

'No, thank *you.*' Lady Uckfield spoke with her usual intimate urgency. 'I gather you're doing the most *marvellous* things down in Cramney. I hear it's simply *buzzing.* I can't *wait* to come and see for myself.'

Her companion beamed, shedding his Socialism on the spot. 'We will be most glad to see you there.' He retreated, wreathed in smiles.

'Where's Cramney?' I said.

Lady Uckfield shrugged. 'Some ghastly little place in Kent. Do you want some tea?'

By the time I made it to my room, my things had been unpacked and my evening shirt, tie, socks and cummerbund lay waiting for me. There was, however, no sign of my clean underpants. I hunted around through various drawers and was just in the process of searching under the bed when I heard a voice behind me. 'What *can* you be looking for?' I turned and saw Tommy Wainwright standing in the doorway that connected my room, aka the Garden Room, with its larger neighbour, the Rose Velvet Room, where Tommy was billeted. Actually, despite these impressive titles, the chambers themselves were rather small, having been squeezed into a sort of mezzanine floor at one side of the house. They had been created by the architect as part of an arrangement to provide a score of secondary bedrooms while only messing up one end facade of the house. Consequently, despite the fragrant names, these chambers overlooked the stable yard, had eight-foot ceilings, and faced north.

We hunted around for my missing undergarment for a bit, then gave up, abandoning it to its fate. Presumably, to this day, a rather old pair of pants is still wedged at the back of some drawer in the Garden Room of Broughton Hall. Tommy retreated to his chamber and returned with a small bottle of Scotch and two tooth glasses. 'Essential equipment for hotels and house-parties,' he said, and poured us both a slug.

'Are they mean with the booze?' I asked. I have often been surprised at the fantastic discomfort and deprivation the grand English are prepared to put their friends (and total strangers) through, particularly in my youth. I've been shown into bathrooms that could just about manage a cold squirt of brown water, bedrooms with doors that don't shut, blankets like tissue, and pillows like rocks. I have driven an hour cross-country to lunch with some grand relations of my father, who gave me one sausage, two small potatoes and twenty-eight peas. Once, during a house-party for a ball in Hampshire, I was so cold that I ended up piling all my clothes, with two threadbare towels, onto the bed and then holding all this together with a worn square of Turkish carpet – the only bit of floor-covering in the room. When my hostess woke me the next day, she made no comment on the fact that I was sleeping in a sort of webbing sarcophagus and clearly could not have been less interested in whether I had ever shut my eyes. When one thinks of the Edwardians who revelled in luxury it seems odd that their grandchildren should be so impervious to it. Recently I have detected that the comfort demanded by new money is effecting a slow improvement in the houses of the *anciens riches* but, heavens, what a time it's taken.

Tommy shook his head in answer to my question. 'No, no. They're not mean at all. Not a bit of it. Lord U chucks it down everyone's throat. It's just too complicated to try and get a dressing drink.'

We sat and gossiped for a bit and I asked if Tommy had seen a lot of the Broughtons.

He shook his head. 'Not really. They're always down here. I must say, I'm quite surprised that Edith is content to coddle the village and give away prizes without taking a breather but the fact is they're hardly in London at all.'

I too found this slightly unlikely. Particularly as the young couple were still living in the big house with Charles's parents. There had been plans to renovate one of the farm houses when they were first married and I asked Tommy if he knew how it was coming along.

'I'm not sure they're going on with that,' he said. 'I gather they've gone off the idea.'

'Really?'

'I know. It's funny, isn't it? She wants to stay here and her in-laws are delighted so Brook Farm will probably be finished quickly and let.'

'Do they have a flat in the house, then?'

'Not as such. Some sort of upstairs sitting room for Edith and Charles has his study, of course. But that's it. Rather like one of those American soap-operas, when they're all worth a hundred million and they still cram together in one house with a big staircase.'

I shook my head. 'I suppose Charles likes the set-up here but it seems rather tiresome for a bride.'

Just as Charles, like all his breed, was not immune to the sense of getting 'special' treatment wherever he went – in fact, as Edith had already observed, he resented its being withheld from him – so I could understand that, after a lifetime of pretending he was unaware of the extraordinary baroque surroundings of his life, it would be hard actually to give them up.

The English upper-classes have a deep, subconscious need to read their difference in the artefacts about them. Nothing is more depressing (or less convincing) to them than the attempt to claim some rank or position, some family background, some genealogical distinction, without the requisite acquaintance and props. They would not dream of decorating a bed sitting room in Putney without the odd watercolour of a grandmother in a crinoline, two or three decent antiques and preferably a relic of a privileged childhood. These things are a kind of sign language that tell the visitor where in the class system the owner places him or herself. But, above all things, the real marker for them, the absolute litmus test, is whether or not a family has retained its house and its estates. Or a respectable proportion of them. You may overhear a nobleman explaining to some American visitor that money is not important in England, that people can stay in Society without a bean, that land is 'more of a liability, these days', but in his heart, he does not believe any of these things. He knows that the family that has lost everything but its coronet, those duchesses in small houses near Cheyne Walk, those viscounts with little flats in Ebury Street, lined as they may be with portraits and pictures of the old place ('It's some sort of farmers' training college, nowadays'), these people are all *déclassé* to their own kind. It goes without saying that this consciousness of the need for the materialisation of rank is as unspoken as the Masonic ritual.

Of course, the Broughton position was an unusually solid one. Few were the families in the 1990s that held their sway and the day would dawn when Charles would enter Broughton Hall as its owner. Still, listening to Tommy, I suspected he might have dreaded the possibility that people, awe-struck as they shook his hand in the Marble Hall, could make the mistake, on finding him at home in a chintz-decorated farmhouse sitting room, of thinking that he was an Ordinary Person. In this, however, I was wrong.

Tommy shook his head. 'No, Charles wouldn't mind. Not now he's used to the idea.' He paused for thought and then decided against it. 'Oh, well. I must get changed.'

We assembled for dinner in the drawing room that the family generally used, a pretty apartment on the garden front, much less cumbrous than the adjacent Red Saloon where we had gathered for the engagement dinner. There were a few vaguely familiar faces besides Tommy. Peter Broughton was there, though apparently without his dreary blonde. Old Lady Tenby's eldest daughter, Daphne, now married to the rather dim second son of a Midlands earl, was talking to Caroline Chase in the corner. They looked up and smiled carefully across the room. Filled with trepidation, I looked around for Eric and saw him scoffing whisky as he lectured some poor old boy on the present state of the City. The listener stood looking into Eric's red face with all the pleasure of a rabbit caught in the headlights of an oncoming car.

'What would you like to drink?' Lady Uckfield stood by my elbow and sent Jago off to fetch a glass of Scotch and water. She followed my glance. 'Heavens! Eric seems to be making very large small talk.'

I smiled. 'Who is the lucky recipient of his confidences?'

'Poor dear Henri de Montalambert.'

For some reason or other, I knew that the Duc de Montalambert was a relation of the Broughtons by marriage. His was not a particularly smart dukedom by French standards (they, having so many more than we do, can afford to grade them) since it had only been given by Louis XVIII in 1820, but a marriage in the 1890s to the heiress of a Cincinnati steel king, had placed the family up there alongside the Trémouilles and the Uzès. Lady Uckfield had referred to him in the manner in which one speaks of an old family friend, but since she always disguised her true feelings about anyone, even from herself, I was, as usual, unable to gauge the true degree of intimacy. 'He looks a bit dazed,' I said.

She nodded with a suppressed giggle. 'I can't imagine what he's making of it all. He hardly speaks a word of English. Never mind. Eric won't notice.' She accepted my laugh as tribute and then rebuked me for it. 'Now, you're not to make me unkind.'

'How long is Monsieur de Montalambert staying?'

Lady Uckfield pulled a face. 'All three days. What are we to do? I'm still at *où est la plume de ma tante*, and Tigger can hardly manage *encore*. Henri married a cousin of ours thirty years ago and I doubt if we've exchanged as many words since.'

'Is there an English-speaking *duchesse*, then?'

'There was. But since she was deaf and is dead, she cannot help us now. I don't suppose you speak French?'

'I do a bit,' I said with a sinking heart. In my mind's eye, I could see the re-shuffling of place cards and the endless, sticky translated conversation that lay ahead.

She caught my look. 'Cheer up, you'll have Edith between you.' She darted one of her flirtatious, birdlike glances at me. 'How do you find our bride?'

'She's looking very well,' I said. 'In fact, I've never seen her prettier.'

'Yes, she does look well.' Lady Uckfield hesitated for a fraction of a second. 'I only hope she finds it amusing down here. She's been the most marvellous success, you know. The trouble is they all love her so much that it's frightfully hard not to rope her into sharing all the wretched duties. I'm afraid I've been rather selfish in unloading the cares of state.'

'Knowing Edith, I bet she enjoys all that. It's a step up on answering a telephone in Milner Street.'

Lady Uckfield smiled. 'Well, as long as it is.'

'She seems to have given up London so you must be doing something right.'

'Yes,' she said briskly. 'If they're happy, that's the main thing, isn't it?'

She drifted away to greet some new arrivals. It struck me that I had missed some nuance in the coiled recesses of Lady Uckfield's perfectly ordered mind.

The dinner, as predicted, was rather leaden. I had Daphne Boling-broke, Lady Tenby's coolly pleasant daughter, on my right, so I was all right for the first course but behind me I could hear Edith struggling gamely with M. de Montalambert on her other side and, in truth, I found it quite hard to concentrate on my own conversation. The trouble was that Edith's French and her neighbour's English were more or less on a par. That is, terrible but not so non-existent as to preclude all effort. It would have been simpler if neither had commanded a word of the other's language but they had, alas, just enough vocabulary to be utterly confusing. Edith kept maundering on about bits of Paris being so *'bon'* and London being *'épouvantable'* with M. de Montalambert alternately looking completely blank or, worse, when he thought he had understood her observation, answering with a swirling torrent of French of which Edith could barely catch more than the first word or two.

The courses changed and I turned to rescue Edith from her travails but M. de Montalambert declined to obey the English regulations and refused to give her up. Instead, grasping at the slight improvement in communication that my moderate French offered him, he launched into a passionate denunciation of the French government, which had reference, in some mystifying way that was quite lost on me, to Louis XVIII's minister, the Duc Decazes.

'What are we talking about?' said Edith softly under the apparently unstoppable Gallic flow.

'God knows. The French Restoration, I think.'

'Crikey.'

In truth, we were both completely worn out by this time and longing for a reprieve but the Duc resolutely ignored Lady Uckfield on his left and she, needless to say, could not have been more delighted to set aside the conventions this once.

The Duc paused and smiled. I sensed a change of topic. Perversely, having discovered that my French was better than Edith's, he decided it was time to demonstrate his grasp of English. 'You like sex?' he said pleasantly. 'You find you come often?'

At exactly this moment Edith was drinking some of her water and so of course did a massive nose trick. Seizing her napkin, she tried vainly to pass it off as a fit of coughing. To my right I could feel Daphne shaking with silent laughter. A desperate schoolroom hysteria was enveloping the table.

'I think,' said Lady Uckfield, who sensed the whiff of civic unrest, 'that Henri is asking if you are familiar with Sussex.' She spoke firmly, like a schoolmistress with a rowdy troop of children, but inevitably her statement gave rise to another terrible wave of giggles among us all. Edith was literally red in the face and almost weeping in her attempts to control her mirth.

At this point Charles looked up. He had naturally missed everything. 'Darling,' he said, 'do you know what I've done with my other gun sleeve? Richard wants to borrow it tomorrow and I cannot think where it is.'

His words achieved what his mother's had failed to do. They fell like a heavy fire-blanket on the burgeoning hilarity and effectively stifled it. There was a flat pause before Edith spoke. 'You lent it to Billy Westbrook,' she said. And as she turned back to her tiresome neighbour, she caught my eye. It was at that moment, hearing Edith's patient answer and sensing her weariness, that I began to realise her bargain had perhaps not been an easy one.

I was up early the next day, but when I arrived in the dining room, most of the house-party was already there, munching away at the splendid, *fin de siècle* breakfast that was spread out in silver chafing dishes along the sideboard. I helped myself to various cholesterol-rich preparations and took my plate over to an empty chair next to Tommy.

'Do we draw numbers, or do they just tell us where to stand?' I asked.

'Numbers. Charles has got a frightfully swanky silver thing with numbered spills in it. We do it when we assemble in the hall. The great thing is not to draw the place next to Eric.'

I could think of any number of reasons to follow this advice but from Tommy's expression, I gathered that simple self-preservation was the main one. As it happened, I was only one away from Chase, with the hapless M. de Montalambert between us. I could see his face fall when he pulled his number, although it might have been simply because he dreaded another Pound-versus-Euro lecture. I had Peter Broughton on my right. There were eight guns in all and of these four had loaders, so what with wives, dogs etcetera, we made quite a party as we stepped out to be stowed into the team of Range Rovers that waited on the gravel.

Edith, I noticed, was not among us. The reason for this I discovered after the third drive when she appeared with thermoses of delicious *bouillon* laced with vodka (or plain for the virtuous). 'Can I come and stand by you, or will I put you off?' she asked.

'Come, by all means. I can't be put off. I miss alone or accompanied. Won't Charles mind?'

'No. He's much happier with George. He says I talk too much.'

They were driving a high wood, quite a way from the house and the guns were placed in a semi-circle around the base. I had originally drawn the number two, so now, on the fourth drive of the morning, I was in position eight and at the end of the line. Edith and I pottered across the field to the numbered stick that beckoned me, and there we waited.

'Do you really enjoy this?' she said, moving over and leaning against the post-and-rail fence.

'Certainly I do. I wouldn't be here if I didn't.'

'I thought you might have accepted to study me in my splendour.'

'You're right. I might have done. But, as it happens, I do enjoy it. It was kind of you to get Charles to ask me.'

'Oh, it wasn't my idea.' She paused. 'I mean, of course, I'm perfectly thrilled you accepted, but it was Googie who proposed you.' She had long ceased to notice that she used her in-laws' tiresome nicknames.

'Then it was kind of her.'

'Googie is seldom kind for no reason.'

'Well, I can't imagine what her reason could be.' The whistle sounded so I loaded my gun and stared at the tops of the trees. If anything, my turning away from Edith seemed to relax her.

'She's worried about me. She thinks I'm bored and you'll cheer me up. She imagines that you're a good influence.'

'I can't think why.'

'She thinks you'll remind me how lucky I am.'

'And aren't you?' Edith made a wry face and stretched along the fence. 'Oh dear,' I said. 'Don't tell me you're bored already.'

'Yes.'

I sighed slightly. I cannot pretend the idea of Edith's discovering that kind hearts mean more than coronets and simple faith than Norman blood was exactly surprising. I suppose I'd thought it was bound to happen sooner or later but even bearing the previous evening in mind, this really did seem unreasonably early. Like most of her friends, I hoped that by the time she had made the time-honoured discovery that you can only sleep in one bed or eat one meal at a time she would have children to give her a genuine and unfeigned interest in her new life. And after all, whatever one might say of Charles, he did have a kind heart and, I would have thought, a pretty simple faith. I could feel an admonishing spirit rising in me as I spoke.

'What exactly are you bored with? Charles? Or the life? Or just the country? What?'

She didn't answer and my attention was taken by an extremely high bird heading my way. I vainly lifted my gun and blasted away. The pheasant flew merrily on.

'I must say,' I continued, becoming slightly more conciliatory, 'it seems a bit rough to be starting your married life under the same roof as your parents-in-law – capacious as that roof may be.'

'It isn't that. They offered us Brook Farm.'

'Why didn't you take it?'

Edith shrugged. 'I don't know. It seemed rather – poky.'

Of course, it was suddenly quite clear that the real problem was she was bored to sobs with her husband. Her life was just about acceptable in the magnificent surroundings of Broughton Hall where there were people to talk to and where there was always the heady wine of envy in others' eyes to drink but to be alone with Charles in a farmhouse . . . That was out of the question.

'If you're so bored, why don't you spend more time in London? We never see you there, now.'

Edith stared at her green Wellington boots. 'I don't know. The flat's tiny and Charles hates it so. And it's always such a bloody production.'

'Couldn't you sneak up on your own?'

Edith stared at me. 'No, I don't think so. I don't think I should, do you?'

I stared back for a moment. 'No,' I said.

So that was it. She had barely been married eight months and already her husband bored her to death. On top of that she was afraid of starting up a life in London because she knew that, without a shadow of a doubt, it would engulf her entirely and at once. She was at least sufficiently honourable about the Faustian pact she had made to wish to keep it.

I smiled. 'Well, to quote Nanny: you *would* do it,' I said. She nodded rather grimly. 'Whom do you see down here? Not much of Isabel, I'll be bound.'

She pulled a face. 'No. Not too much, I'm afraid. I've been made to feel that I've failed David. He keeps dropping hints about shooting for one thing and I simply haven't dared tell them you were coming today.'

'Won't Charles have him?'

'Oh, it's not that. I mean he would if I asked him but, you know, it's just a different crowd whether they like it or not. And David can be a bit ... ' she paused, 'naff.'

Poor David! That it should come to this! All those years of Ascot and Brooks's and drinks at the Turf! And the end of it was that Edith was embarrassed by him. Harsh world. I was not completely complicit, although of course I knew what she meant.

'You'll have to tell him I was here. I'm not having Isabel finding out and thinking we're in league against her.' Edith nodded. 'What about this "different crowd"? Are they fun?'

She sighed, idly scratching a bit of dried mud from her Barbour. 'Terrific. I know almost everything there is to know about estate planning. I could list the parts of a horse in my sleep. And what I haven't learned about running a charity is, believe me, not worth knowing.'

'You must get about a bit, though. Isn't that quite interesting?'

'Oh, it is! Did you know that in Italy the bowl of water in front of your place is to dip your fruit in, not your fingers? Or that in America you must never discuss acreage? Or that in Spain it is the crudest social solecism to use a knife when eating an egg however it may be cooked?' She paused for breath.

'I didn't know about the egg,' I said. She was silent for a while and I had another go at a bird passing overhead. 'There must be some of them you like.'

'I suppose so.'

'What about the family? Do they know how bored you are?'

'Googie, yes. Not darling old Tigger, of course. He's much too dense to notice anything that doesn't hit him over the head. Caroline, I think.'

'And Charles?'

Edith looked up at the woods above us for a moment. 'The thing is, he finds it all so riveting that he is quite sure that, as I get into it, I will too. He sees it as a "period of adjustment".'

'That sounds very sensible to me.' Of course, as I said these words, I realised I was failing her by taking Charles's part. But I couldn't, for the life of me, think of any other line to take. The simple fact remained that she had married a man who was, through no fault of his own, much duller than she was, for the purpose of her own social advancement. That was the deal she had made. No amount of fretting was going to make Charles witty and dynamic, and I already doubted that Edith was prepared to rejoin the mortals on the tier from which she had so lately risen. She had that common twenty-first-century desire, namely to have her cake and her half penny too. 'Surely there must be a lot to do? Didn't you have great schemes of combing the attics and re-writing the guide book?'

'There really isn't anything in the attics except for a lot of Victorian furniture. Googie rescued all the good stuff years ago. And the librarian got rather ratty when I suggested putting a bit more about the family into the book.' She yawned. 'Anyway, Tigger and Charles were so completely uninterested. They think it's rather common to know too much. It was a bit disheartening in the end.'

'Then you'll have to find something else to take up. I can't believe you're short of offers from the local charities.' Even as I spoke I knew I was sounding more and more like a German governess but the truth was I felt like one, watching this spoiled beauty pouting against the fence.

She sighed drearily. 'So I suppose you're saying I've just got to tough it out?'

'Well, haven't you?'

She caught my eye as the whistle blew. The drive was over and we headed back to the Range Rovers. There we were distracted by a certain amount of fuss and suppressed rage, which appeared to have been caused by Eric Chase firing more or less directly at M. de Montalam-bert's nose. Eric was, of course, wildly indignant at the very suggestion, while the other side was muttering a collection of extraordinary French phrases, some of which were quite unfamiliar to me. I was appealed to as an independent witness but, needless to say, chatting to Edith, I had missed the whole thing.

Caroline listened to my protestations and nodded her approval. 'Quite right,' she said, blandly. 'I should stay out of it if I were you.'

I wasn't absolutely sure as to what she was referring.

After tea, I was just getting into my car at that slightly awkward moment when one lot of guests leaves and the next contingent draws up, when Charles followed me out across the gravel and came up to the driving window. I wound it down, wondering what I'd forgotten as I'd already done all my goodbyes, tips and signing. 'I meant to tell you,' he said, 'we've had an offer from a film company. My father's a bit blank. It's your neck of the woods. What do you think we ought to do?'

'They want to make a film at Broughton?'

'I don't know if it's a real film or one of those television things, but yes. What are they like? Is it safe?'

As a general rule, speaking as an actor, I wouldn't let a film unit within a mile of my house, under any circumstances, but it is nevertheless true that they are fairly reliable when they are dealing with anything that might qualify as 'historic'. Of course, whether or not it is worth it rather depends, like everything else in life, on what one is getting out of it. The best I could do was give Charles the name of an agency who might know the form for negotiating with film companies and suggest that he did what they told him.

He thanked me and nodded. 'We must stipulate you as part of the contract,' he said with a smile, as I drove away.

TEN

~

Oddly enough, and in sharp contrast to most of my Show Business acquaintance in similar circumstances, Charles kept his word. The film in question was one of those made-for-television pieces, which gather together as many fashionable actors as are short of money at the time, and run for three interminable hours on Sunday nights.

It was supposed to be the story of the Gunning sisters, an obscure pair of Irish beauties who arrived in London in 1750, took it by storm and married respectively the Earl of Coventry and the Duke of Hamilton. As it happened, the Hamilton marriage was unhappy – a situation rectified by the early death of the Duke – but the widowed Duchess went on, with some panache, to marry her long-term admirer, Colonel John Campbell, himself the heir to the dukedom of Argyll.

This was clearly the stuff of which pseudo-historical mini-series are made. Broughton was to double as both Hamilton Palace (demolished in the twenties) and Inverary (which I suppose was too far from London. Either that or the present Duke of Argyll didn't relish the prospect). In addition, various interiors would be employed for the vanished splendours of Georgian London.

It was to be directed by an Englishman named Christopher Twist, who had enjoyed some success with a couple of zany pieces at the end of the sixties when that style was in vogue and who was still eking out a living on the scraps of his earlier reputation. I knew the casting director, who had been kind to me in the past and I assumed it was due to her that I had been summoned for the quite reasonable part of Walter Creevey (a gossip of the period who had been written up as the double Duchess's confidant, although I don't believe there was much factual evidence of their friendship) but as soon as I had sat down Twist gave the game away. 'I gather you're a close friend of the Earl of Broughton,' he said.

I suppose anyone who lives in Hollywood may be forgiven for falling into American ways as, unlike many other peoples of the globe, Los Angelinos do not appreciate any code but their own. I was nevertheless slightly irritated, not by the misnaming of Charles's title, nor by the clumsiness of referring to his rank in full, but by that most intrusive phrase, 'close friend'. In my experience, anyone who says they are a 'close friend' of some celebrity has generally a slight acquaintance at best. Just as 'sources close to the Royal Couple' in a newspaper means gossip from the outermost circle of Royal hangers-on. 'I know him,' I said.

Twist wasn't put off. 'Well, he thinks very highly of you,' he continued. He had that odd, mid-Atlantic manner of speech that reminds one of a television chat show where every trivial remark is supposed (a) to denote a caring soul and (b) to bring all reasonable conjecture on the subject to an end.

'That's nice,' I said.

'So,' he lay back in his chair, stretching his legs and revealing a pair of cowboy boots covered in frightful Red Indian patterns, 'tell me a little about yourself.'

It is hard for anyone who is not an actor to comprehend fully the level of depression into which one is plunged by this question, when the credits of one's feeble career must be dragged out and displayed like the tawdry contents of a salesman's battered suitcase. I shall consequently pass over it and say that I was given the job. This was not because of the 'little about myself' that I had told but because Twist did not want to start on the wrong side of Lady Uckfield, who had apparently, I later learned, been most resolute in my cause.

As soon as my agent had confirmed that I was hired for the full eight weeks of the movie – which would involve six weeks in or around Broughton – I telephoned Edith.

'But how perfectly thrilling! Of course you'll stay with us.'

It is always nice to be asked but I had already resolved that I would not stay at Broughton itself. I could foresee a certain amount of awkwardness being generated by my being friendly with the family as it was. Had I stayed with them, in a short time I would have separated myself from the actual 'making' of the film entirely.

'You are kind. I don't think you could stand me for six weeks.'

'Don't be silly. Of course we could.'

'I shan't be so unreasonable as to put you to the test.'

Edith understood this kind of talk well enough to know that she had been turned down and the invitation was not repeated. I told her that I would be at the unit hotel, a converted country house just outside Uckfield, but that we would obviously be seeing a lot of each other. I must confess that after my little taster at the shooting party, I felt a slightly ghoulish curiosity to see her and Charles on their home ground. Perhaps at the back of my mind was a faint glimmering of *Schaden-freude* – that terrible pleasure we feel at our friends' ill-fortune – although I hope not. But I had witnessed Edith's accession to Dreamland and I'm afraid there is always a kind of pleasurable self-justification in others' disappointment in the world's blessings. It is the consolation prize of failure.

Two or three weeks passed. I went for my fittings at Bermans and Wig Creations, occasionally bumping into others in the cast. The Gunnings themselves were to be played by a couple of American blondes on 'hiatus' from a Hollywood cop series. The product was consequently doomed from the start so far as any artistic standards were concerned. I do not wish to sound snobbish here. There are many roles that should unquestionably be filled by American blondes. I only mean to imply that the casting of Louanne Peters and Jane Darnell meant that the producers had entirely abandoned the idea of trying for any kind of truthful representation of eighteenth-century London in favour of viewing figures. One cannot blame them, I suppose, or at least one would not if only they would ever admit what they have done. As it is, the rest of the cast has to sit in endless restaurants on location hearing how hard they've tried to get the right candlesticks or mob-caps when they know as well as you do that the central characters do not and will not bear the slightest semblance of reality. Actors laugh together as they 'take the money and run' but it is disheartening all the same. At any rate I was glad to learn that the sisters' mother, Mrs Gunning, was to be played by an actress called Bella Stevens with whom I had once shared a cottage in Northampton during early rep days after leaving drama school, and it was pleasant to renew a friendship that we had made no effort to maintain during the interim.

A strange and perhaps unique feature of theatrical lives is the depth of involvement one forms with people when working together, only to return home and literally never bother to pick up the telephone to contact them again. Weeks of tearful intimacies, to say nothing of sexual liaisons, are lightly discarded without a backward glance. It is inevitable in that the nature of the work generates intimacy and the number of jobs makes the support of all such relationships impossible. But it is strange nevertheless to contemplate how many people are walking the streets of London who know a great deal more about you than anyone in your immediate family.

Conversely, nothing is more agreeable than the renewal of such a friendship after several years' interlude, as there is no need for the preamble to intimacy. It is already in place. One may immediately pick it up, like a piece of unfinished tapestry, where one left off ten years before. So it was with Bella. She was a ferociously strong personality, with a dark, almost satanic face, a cross between Joan Crawford and the *commedia dell'arte*, but this went along with a kind heart, a witty if promiscuous tongue and a genius for cookery. The repertory company we had worked in – she as leading lady, me as assistant stage manager – had been unusually chaotic even by the standards of the time, run as it was by an amiable, alcoholic cynic who slept through most rehearsals and all performances, and we consequently had a good many shared horror stories to laugh about.

Soon after I had arrived in my hotel room, while I was still reeling from the obligatory brown and orange colour scheme, the telephone rang. It was Bella. I agreed to meet her in the bar in an hour. She was sitting at a table with a companion she introduced to me as Simon Russell, an actor of whom I had more or less heard, who had landed the good part (if any parts in these epics may be defined in such terms) of Colonel John Campbell, faithful lover of our principal heroine and eventually, in the last five minutes of the film, Duke of Argyll.

Physical beauty is a subject that many skirt around and almost everyone attempts to down-play thereby demonstrating some sound moral stance, but it remains one of the glories of human existence. Of course, there are many people who are attractive without being beautiful just as there are beauties who bore, and the danger of beauty in the very young is that it can make the business of life seem deceptively easy. All this I am fully aware of. I know too, however, that of the four great gifts that the fairies may or may not bring to the christening – Brains, Birth, Beauty and Money – it is Beauty that makes locked doors spring open at a touch. Whether it is for a job interview, a place at a dining table, a brilliant promotion or a lift on the motorway, everyone, regardless of their sex or their sexual proclivity, would always rather deal with a good-looking face. And no one is more aware of this than the Beauties themselves. They have a power they simultaneously respect and take for granted. Despite the moralists who tut about its transience, it is generally a power that is never completely lost. One can usually trace in the wrinkled lines of a nonagenarian, stooped and leaning on a stick, the style and confidence that turned heads in a ballroom in 1929.

Simon Russell was without question the most beautiful man I have ever seen. I do not call him handsome for the word implies some kind of masculine confining of the concept of beauty, a rugged state of alluring imperfection. Russell's face had none of this. It was quite simply perfect. Thick waving blond locks fell forward, half shading large, startlingly blue eyes. A chiselled, statue's nose (I have always disliked my nose, and so am rather nose-conscious), and a modelled, girlish mouth framing even, if marginally sharp, teeth completed the picture. Nor did the perfection end there. Instead of the weedy build that one associates with the Blond Toff school of actors, Russell was possessed of an athlete's body, muscular and trim. He was in short a magnificent specimen. Sometimes it seems the Gods grow bored with marring their handiwork and allow someone through without a hitch and Russell was such a one. If he had a fault, and really one had to search for it, I suppose his legs were a little too short for his size. I later learned that this tiny detail, this fleck of dust against the rainbow, caused him hours of mental anguish daily, revealing the paranoia and ingratitude of the human race.

The three of us, having decided to avoid both the director and the hotel dining room, found ourselves some time later ensconced in the booth table of a curious restaurant in Uckfield decorated with, of all odd choices, a Wild West motif. It was a pleasant evening and a heartening start to the job. Simon was good company, one of the lovely things about the lucky being that they are so easy to be with. He was married with three children, a boy and two girls, about whom we heard (and would continue to hear) a great deal, and he talked of himself and his triumphs in that relaxed unselfconscious way that only the deeply egocentric can manage. Still, he was funny and pleasant and charming, and he toned well with Bella's more frenetic volubility. He was also patently a colossal flirt. No interchange with another mortal, from our waitress to a man we stopped to ask for directions, escaped the beam of his arc lamp smile. Everyone, no matter how mean or meagre, had to be roped to his chariot. I enjoyed watching him at work enormously.

'I don't think I can manage six weeks in the room I've got,' said Bella. 'I thought there must have been some mistake. It's the size of a drawer and the lavatory is in a sort of wardrobe.' She waved her hand for another bottle.

It is a truism that the collective noun for actors is 'a grumble'. They are never happier than when they can have a really good whinge about the conditions under which they're working, sleeping, changing. There is the old joke about the actor who, after five years of unemployment, at the point of suicide, is given a starring film role opposite Julia Roberts and when asked if it's really true replies: 'Yes. And the best thing is, I've got tomorrow off.' Nevertheless, even I, who care little about such things, felt daunted by the prospect of six weeks of orange and brown wallpaper and it was at this moment that the idea of the three of us sharing a cottage took shape. It was a risk, of course, and we resolved to make it a week-by-week arrangement, but it would be a great saving on expenses and generally a considerable improvement on our present situation. 'The only thing is,' said Bella, 'I've been asking around. Practically everything near here is part of the Broughton estate and I gather they're not keen on short-term rentals. They have an absolute embargo on holiday lets.'

'Couldn't the film people pull some string?' Simon smiled the gentle smile of one for whom an inconvenient status quo can always be overcome. 'They must be making quite a lot out of us. Who's the location manager? Someone must be on good terms with them. At least at this stage.'

Since we were starting on the film the next day and it was bound to be revealed quite early on that I knew the family, I cut in. 'I know them,' I said. 'I don't know if there's anything to let, but I can certainly ask.'

Bella was pleased and unsurprised at this turn of events. She had known my double life of old and, being unsnobbish, did not feel any attitude to it was called for. I could see, however, from the headlight-glare of Simon's eyes as he turned to me with a chariot-roping smile, that I had risen quantifiably in his estimation.

The next morning I'd barely arrived on the set, a ballroom scene in the Red Saloon where Charles and Edith had received us at the engagement dinner, when my cover, if I had one, was blown. Most of the principals had assembled in their not-very-accurate costumes when Lady Uckfield came in. 'Ah, Marchioness,' said Twist with what I suppose he thought a courtly bow. Not a glimmer of a wince could I trace in her even, smiling features as, portentously, like the local mayor in a Midlands manufactory, he started to introduce her to the cast. Spying me, she broke away, kissed me on both cheeks and led me over to the window. For most of the unit, in that one second, I was a marked man and it took me several weeks of production to regain the slightest credibility as an actor.

'Edith tells me you won't come and stay with us.'

'You are kind but honestly not. I think I'd get muddled about which team I was on.'

She laughed and answered, with a cursory glance round the room, 'I do hope not.' I smiled. 'So where are you going to stay? You can't seriously mean to stick it out in the local pub?'

I thought of those sad brochures on my hotel dressing-table welcoming me to the 'country house splendours of Notley Park', and shook my head. 'I don't think so.'

'Thank goodness for that.'

'As a matter of fact, three of us were wondering if there was anywhere on the estate we might be able to hire. What do you think? It doesn't have to be sumptuous. So long as there are three bedrooms and hot water.'

'Which three?'

I nodded towards Bella, laced into burgundy velvet, who was talking to Simon. He was in pale blue silk, with lace at his throat and wrists, and a wig, which, unlike those of most of the extras, did not look as if it had been removed from a body in the Thames but rather framed his face with even more of the abundant, fair curls he boasted in life. He caught our glance, looked over to us and smiled.

Lady Uckfield smiled carefully back. 'Heavens, what a beauty.'

'He's our love interest.'

'I can well believe it.' She turned back to me. 'I'm sure we can fix up something. You could probably have Brook Farm if you don't mind pretty minimal furnishing. I'll ask Charles to sort it out. Come to dinner tonight and bring the other two. For vetting,' she added crisply, as she moved off. 'About eight and don't change.'

'You're sure this is all right?' said Bella for the twelfth time, as we crunched to a halt outside the front entrance.

'I'm sure.'

She wriggled out of the car. 'God, I've brought nothing but dungarees and sweaters.' Actually she looked quite saucy in a black outfit with big earrings, like a French singer in some politically subversive *bôite*.

Simon was considerably cooler as we approached the great horseshoe stair. He was one of those actors, who come if not in battalions at least not singly, who play aristocrats so often on television that they end by believing in themselves as one. He had worn almost every uniform, gone over the top in almost every conflict, ridden to hounds and danced till he dropped in epic serial after epic serial, and now in some way he believed that he was indeed the sort of person who gets his shoes from Lobb's and his hats from Lock's, that somehow he would be a member of White's if they only knew about him, that he was, in short, a member of the *gratin*. He would lounge around Fulham sitting rooms making disparaging remarks about junior members of the Royal Family with the air of one who would rather not tell all he knows. Not that there was much difference between him and David Easton down the road. It was just that he had been less in the country and so was still unaware that it is a harder act to bring off out of London.

Of course, what neither Simon nor David ever really grasped was that the key to these people is their familiarity with one another. Most of them are unable to receive anyone as 'one of their own' who is not either known to them from early youth or at the very least known to one of their circle. They cannot accept that they would not have come across, at least at one remove, anyone who was entitled to be included in their set. The best that all those grinning racing-drivers and cockney actors can hope for as they glow in the pews at Royal weddings is the position of unofficial court jester, a service that may be dispensed with at any time. Simon was insufficiently familiar with the great world to understand this and so he maintained throughout the evening a kind of swagger, which was presumably supposed to demonstrate to the company that he was always dining in large stately homes all over the country. Needless to say, they were neither deceived nor interested.

There were only the four of them at home when we were ushered by Jago into the family drawing room and when we walked in they were all silent and reading. I thought, although I could not be sure, that I detected a rather torpid atmosphere. Lady Uckfield came over to greet us. Receiving Bella's gushings, she led her instantly to her husband with whom, she could see straight away, Bella was going to be a great hit. When she turned back to us, Simon had already forged over to Charles to ask him about the possibilities of Brook Farm and I watched as Charles almost jumped at the ferocity of this full frontal attack, but he recovered his ground. In fact, he was nodding with an amiable half-smile after a while so I assumed that all would be well. Edith, I noticed, after acknowledging me, had not risen and had returned to her book. I watched Simon eyeing her but she would not be included and after he had tried throwing a few remarks sideways, he gave up for the moment and returned to dazzling her husband.

Lady Uckfield brought me some whisky and water, my evening drink, without being asked, which was flattering. Her glance followed mine. 'Charles seems to think Brook Farm will be fine if you're really serious. He'll have Mr Roberts go over it in the morning. We must have it ready for next month at the latest anyway so it'll be good to have a spurt at it. You could move in the day after tomorrow if you don't mind a bit of work going on around you all. I hope this means we'll be seeing a lot of you.'

'Much too much, I have no doubt.' I hesitated for a moment. 'Wasn't Brook Farm being done up for Charles and Edith?'

Lady Uckfield nodded. 'Yes. But they've changed their minds.' She caught my eye. 'Too lovely for Tigger and me,' she said firmly.

I nodded. 'Lovely,' I said.

Poor Charles had rather a dry time of it at dinner. Bella was having a great success with Lord Uckfield, telling him raucous and unsuitable stories to his obvious delight, and he was not inclined to include anyone else in their exchanges, while Simon was giving the same treatment – though more decorously – to Lady Uckfield at the other end. Edith certainly seemed to have very little to say to her husband though, as it happens, she didn't appear to have much to say to anybody. I saw her watching Simon as he sprayed her mother-in-law with wit and charm.

He had of course met his match in Lady Uckfield who was not to be caught in such a frail net as his but I must say this for him: he clearly knew he was outranked, something that in all the time I knew him he was seldom conscious of.

'Your actor friend seems very confident,' said Edith.

'Why are you so grumpy this evening? What's the matter with you?'

'Nothing. I'm not grumpy. Although I am rather miffed that you turned us down for these two. Do you really think you'll enjoy sharing with them?' She was speaking half under her breath as if to excite curiosity while remaining audible. I found it rather tiresome.

'I don't see why not.'

She looked at Simon again, sharply. 'Googie's taken a great shine to him, I must say. She announced at tea that she'd let Brook Farm to the handsomest man she'd ever seen. I was rather surprised.'

'Were you?' I said.

We were both looking across at Russell as he laughed and flirted with our hostess. The candlelight reflected in his hair, which he constantly tossed back, like a restless stallion. His eyes, darker than by day, shone like two sharply-cut sapphires. I looked back at Edith. She was beautiful too, of course, as a general rule by far the most beautiful at this table but this evening I was aware of how much of her animation had gone. I remembered her twinkling away at Lord Uckfield when her engagement was announced but her flickering secret smile had been replaced by something grander and more resolute. It was not a becoming alteration.

'He is handsome, I suppose,' she said dismissively. 'But actors are such girls about their looks. I can't take a man seriously who worries about eye-drops and mascara.'

I turned to her. 'Who's asking you to take him seriously?' I said.

Edith returned to her plate.

~

ELEVEN

The Countess Broughton lay brooding in her bath, occasionally wriggling her body to disperse the hot water trickling from the tap that she operated expertly with her toes. Soon Mary would be bringing up her breakfast and would be surprised to find her in the bathroom. She was breaking the routine that had already somehow contrived to become established in her cabined life. Even Charles had looked startled when she had rolled out of bed and started to run the water. 'Are you having your bath, now?' he said, watching her like a puzzled puppy. Hardly daring to question her actions, and yet, as ever, fearful of change.

'Yes. Why shouldn't I?'

'No reason. No reason.' Charles was not a fighter. 'You normally have it after your breakfast, that's all.'

'I know. And this morning I'm having it before my breakfast. All right?'

'Yes. Yes. Of course.' He raised his voice, as she moved into the bathroom and started to clean her teeth. 'I'm going up to Brook Farm with Roberts. Do you want to come?'

'Not really.'

'We can look over what has to be done. I don't think much, if they only want it for a few weeks. It seems an odd idea to me. Wouldn't they be better off in a hotel?'

'Well, obviously they don't think so.'

'No. No, I suppose they don't. Well then. Did you like the other two?'

'I hardly spoke to them. Your parents didn't give me much of a look in.'

Charles laughed. 'I must say that Bella gave the Guv'nor a pretty good evening. I can see him wandering up to Brook Farm to see if she wants a cup of sugar. Russell looks a bit of a smoothy to me.'

'Googie seemed very taken with him.'

But Charles had said all he wanted to say. Leaving his wife to her novel arrangements, he pushed off into his dressing room.

Whatever he may have sounded like, he didn't object in the least to letting the farmhouse. Far from it. It gave him an excuse to gee up its completion and now that Edith had gone off the idea of living there he was anxious to hurry up and get the place rented and dealt with. Its empty, pretty rooms, which they had discussed together in such detail just after their marriage, were a reproach to him, a bewildering reminder of his failure to – what? To understand? But what was it he was supposed to be understanding? One minute, they seemed to be having such fun 'setting up home'. He would puzzle obediently over little squares of wallpaper and swatches of fabric (although he couldn't have cared less which she chose) and they would refer coyly to one of the bedrooms possibly being 'useful' later on, as they planned a better bathroom for it than the room might reasonably have expected. Then the next moment it all seemed somehow . . . Charles was aware of his wife's dissatisfaction. He was sufficiently anxious as to her well-being not to wish to ignore any signs of her unhappiness but he couldn't see where it had come from. What had changed? Certainly, he was completely stumped when it came to progressing the situation. He offered to spend more time in London but, no, that was not the answer. He invited her to take more of a role in running the house shop and the visitors' centre but, no, she thought she'd be treading on his mother's toes. In the end, he had hoped that doing up Brook Farm and perhaps generating a social life down in Sussex that was separate from his parents' might do the trick but one day Edith had suddenly decided that she didn't want to leave the main house after all and then he had really come to a full stop. 'I just can't quite see us sitting there staring at each other, can you?' she said lightly. These words struck a low and sombre note in Charles's heart because of course this was exactly what he had envisaged. The two of them, possibly eating at the kitchen table or with trays on their laps in the little library, watching television, chatting over the day's dramas . . .

Charles's real difficulty, as he would freely admit (to himself, at least) was that he just couldn't see what was wrong with their life. He couldn't grasp what was wrong with seeing the same people and having the same conversations and doing the same things month after month, year after year. His annual round had always been circumscribed by the usual demands: shooting until the end of January, hunting on until March, a bit of time in London, then perhaps a trip away, fishing somewhere and up to Scotland for some stalking. What could be the matter with that? Well, obviously something was the matter with it, but he couldn't see it. And quite what he was supposed to do next to please this wife whom he loved but who bit his head off at the slightest provocation was a serious conundrum to him. A conundrum he was unlikely to solve that morning, he thought, as he put on his tweed jacket and started downstairs for breakfast with his father in the dining room.

Meanwhile, Edith lay back silently in the warm water, listening to his footsteps clattering on the polished wood of the great staircase. She knew she was a worry to Charles, but in some odd and undefined way, she thought he deserved a bit of worry. And this morning, more than usual, she was disturbed and yet she hardly knew why. It was as if some kind of creeping rot had infiltrated itself behind the grand structure of her life and could only be detected by the faintest, acrid smell in the most sensitive of nostrils. There was a knock at the bedroom door and Mary came in with the tray. 'Milady?'

'I'm in here, Mary. Just leave it.'

'Are you all right, Milady?' Mary's voice, hovering discreetly near the open bathroom door, was tinged with worry occasioned, presumably, by this fractional alteration of routine.

'I'm fine, Mary. Thank you. Just leave the tray. I'll be straight out.'

'Very good, Milady.'

Edith listened to the maid bustling about in the bedroom until the door closed and she heard the footsteps retreating along the corridor.

How ordinary her life seemed to her. Today it seemed to be drenched in a kind of grey ordinariness that suffused the atmosphere of these stuffy, chintz-filled rooms and hovered like a mist above the waters of the bath. And yet, how recently these details – these Miladys, these echoing footsteps on polished floors, these male breakfasts far below, sparkling with silver dishes, these lace-covered trays glistening with exquisite china – how sweet to the senses these touches had been. In those early days at Broughton how much pleasure had she derived simply from the monograms on her linen, from the damask-covered bergères in her room, from the Derby figures on her desk, from the telephone with its buttons for 'stables' and 'kitchen', from the footman, Robert, blushing with nervousness when he came to collect her emptied luggage, from the swans on the lake, from the very trees in the park.

She was a princess in fairyland. And how quickly she had learned the tricks of graciousness, of being showily unaware of her setting, of making people ill at ease with her studied relaxation. She delighted in the Eastons' discomfort in their triumph, as they found themselves at the Broughton table (at last!) surrounded by people all of whom knew each other and none of whom knew them. She had quite consciously imitated some of the tricks of the late Princess of Wales in the way she perfected her warm and delightful manner for the village, that combination of undisappointing celebrity and studied informality that was guaranteed to win all hearts. She would glow and gush as she was escorted round the new playgroup facilities or as she gave away prizes at the flower show, winning new friends, disarming old critics. What fun it was to catch the children shyly glancing at her and to disarm them with a sudden, winning smile and then to follow it up with a sunbeam directed at the mothers. But then again it was so easy . . .

With a low groan, she pulled herself out of the water, shut off the tap, pulled out the plug and sloped through into her bedroom to pick at her breakfast. Mary had tidied her bed and lit the fire – the *dernier cri* of luxury, particularly in September – and her tray, as pretty as ever, had been left on the table in the middle of the room. Nestling among the charming flowered china were her letters, appeals, thank-yous, invitations to boring parties in the country, which they would be going to, and amusing parties in London, which they would not. She flicked through them idly as she bit into a piece of toast, mid-brown with its crusts carefully removed. Mary had tidied her clothes, a tweed skirt, a cotton shirt, a jersey with a rabbit motif. She would wear these things, with some pearls and some not very sensible shoes, as a costume for the endless part that she found herself playing. She thought of her day: some errands, the librarian, Mr Cook, to luncheon ('luncheon' – she even thought in the language of her role), a committee meeting in the village to discuss the summer show, a cousin of Googie's for tea. It was a dreary prospect.

But although she had already decided that resuming a London life would not be sensible for her, Edith had not at this point fully articulated her objections to it. She would murmur that it was a 'bad idea' without specifics. She explained these feelings to herself with observations on how 'left out' Charles would feel with her friends. After all, his London acquaintance was tremendously similar to the people they spent their time with in Sussex. And anyway it was true, or sort of true, when she told people how much he hated London and that (at this stage at least) she too had 'come to the end of it'. Still, she was aware that she was talking about being in London with Charles. There was already a potentially fatal sense that it might be more amusing, and therefore more dangerous, to be in the capital on her own. Even so, it was only occasionally, and then in a very faint voice, that she actually admitted to herself she was ready to take a lover.

Edith prided herself on having become, more or less instantly, a Great Lady, on obeying all the rules of her new life as one born to it. Of course, by this time, she had pretty well lost touch with the fact that she was *not* born to it. She had succumbed to her mother's self-image, and now imagined, in some mysterious way, that she had grown up in the Gentry and simply married into the Nobility. This was completely untrue but as an argument it had the supreme merit of allowing her to feel less grateful to Charles than she had formerly felt obliged.

Inevitably, part of her newly acquired rank was the morality it brought with it. She had proudly discarded the last traces of middle-class fastidiousness and assumed, without a struggle, the cold, hard-headed values that were the other facet of the Great World whose cause she had espoused. She had rapidly become one of those flawlessly-dressed women who lunch together and say things like: 'Why did he make such a fuss? The two boys were definitely his', or 'Stupid woman, it would have blown over in a year or two', or 'Oh, she doesn't mind a bit. Her lover's just moved here from Paris', and they lower their voices conspiratorially, half hoping to be overheard, as they bite into a leaf of radicchio. She had acquired the pretended horror of publicity and the genuine horror of scandal that are the hallmarks of Charles's class. And yet there was something truly felt even in these stock attitudes. Edith did not admire scandal. Above all, she did not admire people who had 'brought it off', and then 'made a mess of it'. She had brought it off and she had every intention of dying in the saddle.

And yet ... and yet ... with all these thoughts floating through her brain, she took another bite of toast and decided that perhaps she would, after all, go down with Charles to see Brook Farm.

*   *   *

She did not need to tell me later that she had gone on the tour of inspection, as I was watching from one of the windows on the Garden Front when they set off. It was our second day in the house and we were having one of those bitty, unsatisfactory mornings of being filmed coming out of doors and walking up and down corridors. All very useful to get the feel of a costume, of course, or to make friends with the cameraman, but not exactly demanding. Bella was sitting next to me on the window seat, laced into a brown travelling outfit this time, busily engaged in rolling a rather meagre cigarette, this habit being the last obvious trace of her earlier, sixties bohemianism. Simon was with us but not in costume as he was not called that day. He was simply one of those actors who cannot stay away from the set, who would rather be called for a one-minute pick-up shot and spend the day waiting in make-up, than actually take some time off.

'Where are they going?' said Bella, as we watched the pair of them strike off across the park.

'Charles said he'd look over the farmhouse for us, and see if anything needed doing.'

'How long before we can move in, do you think?'

I shrugged. 'Straight away, I gather. If we don't mind roughing it a bit.'

'God knows I'd sleep on a mountain side rather than spend another night in that hotel,' said Bella with a wry laugh as she held a flame to her apparently non-inflammable, little smoke.

Simon took another look at the departing figures below. 'I think I might go up there with them. I can tell him if he's fussing unnecessarily. After all, we want to get in tonight if we can.' He nodded and walked off down the corridor. Bella and I watched him go in silence. She spoke first.

'Off he goes. To break more hearts.'

'Don't you like him?'

She bent down to concentrate harder on her dingy little fag. 'What's not to like? I just get a bit worn out with all that charm.'

'I shouldn't think Charles would notice it,' I said.

'Maybe not. But she will. And judging by last night I'm not sure she'll like it much. I hope he doesn't bugger things up before we've even moved in.'

He didn't. Or not enough to prevent us taking up residence that night. We had broken for lunch and were sitting at a rickety caterers' table on the gravel in front of the house, making the best of our cardboard lunch, when Simon returned in triumph, dancing and punching the air as he spoke. 'We're in!'

'When?'

'Today.'

'What about the hotel?'

'All done. I've given them notice for the three of us and told them we'll be back to pack and pay as quickly as we can. They're making so much money out of the film they didn't complain too much.' He beamed. 'Edith and Charles have asked us back for supper tonight so we don't have to worry about any shopping.'

'But how very generous of Edith and Charles.' Bella let the unaccustomed names linger on her tongue with a conspiratorial half-smile at me. I could see that Simon was destined to give her a great deal of amusement.

It was of course rather a bore to have to return to Broughton for the second evening running and make more polite conversation with 'Tigger' and 'Googie'. Bella and I confessed later that we had each privately thought of chucking. I would imagine that Simon had no such scruples. But in the event we came independently to the conclusion that it would have been a churlish return for what was both a favour and a dramatic improvement in our lot, so once again, shortly after eight o'clock, we crunched our car to a halt and made for the front door.

Simon was a changed man. The night before, his general braggadocio (unbeknownst to him, of course) had betrayed his social unease even to the unobservant. He had dropped names that had no kudos and spoken of social events that had either no currency value or with which he was clearly completely unfamiliar. In the end it was hard to resist a twinge of sympathy for his gaucheness despite the success he was having with his hostess. Like many actors, or civilians for that matter, he had been caught out by the need to demonstrate his right to belong in a world that he had long claimed as his own but seldom, if ever, penetrated. Tonight, however, he was free. He had that glow that distinguishes the insecure egomaniac when they find that their doubts were ill-founded and that they are *liked*. It was hard to avoid catching Bella's smiling eye as we made our way up to the family drawing room, with Simon trailing his hand along the gleaming banister and chattering amiabilities to the butler all the way, very much the Friend of the Family. Once there, we witnessed him greeting both Lord and, particularly, Lady Uckfield as Old Pals.

Of course, one of the basic truths of life is that, as a general rule, the world takes you at your own estimation. Just as the inexperienced hostess will tremble over her guest list, pondering endlessly whether or not she dare invite some grandee or media personality she hardly knows, only to discover in later years that nobody usually questions anyone's 'right' to send them an invitation. If they want to go, they will accept. If they don't, they won't. So, now, it would not have occurred to Lord Uckfield to ponder whether or not Simon Russell was his social equal. He appeared to consider himself so, and that, coupled to the fact that his role in Lord Uckfield's life consisted of eating dinners and telling funny stories, more than justified his amiability and relaxation in the peer's eyes. Just so are many social careers, particularly in London, constructed. Simon was no different to the art-dealers and opera-enthusiasts that are taken up by the various duchesses of our day, whose grinning images, sandwiched between media personalities and the wives of the heirs to great fortunes, are glimpsed in magazines. Of course, such people, like Simon, are generally unaware that beneath the superficial acceptance that their charm and easy manner can gain for them, their grand hosts do not seriously consider them to belong to their world. It is sad to watch the 'walker-favourite' of a great family arrive, after years of drawing-room service, at a public event – a wedding, say, or, worse, a memorial – only to find that they are placed in the back pew between the local MP and the central heating duct, while half-known and much disliked grandees are shown up to the front. Such is life. Or such, at least, are the values of this life. Something that Simon Russell was quite ignorant of, and Lady Uckfield knew very well indeed.

What interested me this evening, however, was not Lady Uckfield's response to Simon, which was predictably one of careful amusement, but Edith's. The sulks and rather affected hostility of the previous night had gone and been replaced by a mannered silence. She was looking more beautiful than she had been the evening before, in a black skirt and cream silk top, with some pearls at her throat and another string wound round her wrist in a chunky tangle. For want of a better word, she looked sexier than I had seen her since her marriage. She had not abandoned her cold *hauteur*, which I truly believe was already unconscious, but as we walked in, she looked up from the sofa with the kind of measured glance that I have learned from experience generally indicates that a woman means business.

Looking back, I am forced to conclude that Edith's plan to stay in the country in order to keep out of trouble was a poor one. Like some bored colonial wife in a hill station in India, the lack of sympathetic companions only really served to throw into advantageously high relief anyone who did make it to the outpost. I am not sure that if she and Charles had flung themselves into the whirl of parties, charities and all the other rubbish so eagerly awaiting them in London, that her virtue would have been in graver danger. I suspect it would have been quite the contrary. Society has the great merit of blunting the dullness of one's partner. The couple that never talk to each other never discover how little they have in common. Companionship, like retirement in the middle classes, can so often bring divorce in its wake. One thing I am sure of: in London, Edith would never have been attracted to Simon Russell. He was astonishingly good-looking as I have said, but in truth the trailer was better than the feature. He could talk and he was a really expert flirt, a joy to watch in action in fact, but when the chips were down and the doors were closed there was not much substance there. I do not mean to imply that I disliked him. On the contrary, I was extremely fond of him. And he could discuss mortgages or Europe or Madonna as well as anyone, but then couldn't Charles (at least the first two)? Of the *feu sacré*, that holy, charismatic flame that makes the world seem well lost for love, Simon had none at all. Or none that was discernible to me.

'Tell me, Mr Russell, what sort of acting do you like best?' This was Lady Uckfield. She was always careful to address strangers, especially those younger than herself as 'Mr' and 'Miss' or by their correct title. The main reason for this, indeed the reason for her whole vocabulary, was to underpin her image of herself as a miraculous survival of the

Edwardian age in modern England. She liked to think that in her behaviour and manner people had a chance to see how things were done in the days when they were done *properly*. How matters would have been managed by Lady Desborough or the Countess of Dudley or the Marchioness of Salisbury or any of the other forgotten *fin de siècle* beauties who made their lives their art, which consequently perished with them. As part of this carefully studied performance, everything she touched was credited with uniqueness. She would speak of 'receipts' and 'luncheon' as she made a special point of her Irish ham ('dry and delicious and quite *unfindable* in England') or her French cherries ('I'm simply *stuffing* myself with them') or her yellow, American paper ('I find I just can't *write* without it'). The fun of this approach was that all her guests were blackmailed, on the principle of the Emperor's New Clothes, into agreeing that they could perceive an enormous difference in everything that was set before them, thus reinforcing the very prejudices that had made them lie. Actually, the food was always good and well-chosen so I was as craven as the rest in pretending to discern huge shades of taste between different types of asparagus or whatever the challenge of the day might be. And anyway, the more I came to know Lady Uckfield the more I came to admire the completeness of her self-image. She never took time off from being the ultra-charming but ultra-fastidious marchioness of the long Edwardian Summer. Never. I am sure that if she were going in for a potentially fatal operation, she would be fussing about the make of the surgeon's scissors.

Edith never understood the strength of her mother-in-law's chosen path. She thought her a fuss-pot and a pain in the neck. But Lady Uckfield had a self-discipline that would have kept Edith out of trouble. She did not know what it was to be bored – or rather, to admit to herself that she was bored. The fact she was married to a man who hadn't a quarter of her brain had never disturbed her conscious mind for half a second. Her road was chosen and she would make a success of it without pity or remorse. In our sloppy century, one must at least respect, if not revere, such moral resolution. And, after all, to borrow a phrase from Trollope, when all was said and done, 'her lines had fallen in pleasant places'.

The other reason that Lady Uckfield called Simon 'Mr Russell' of course, was to stop him calling her 'Googie'.

'Well, I like being employed,' he said in answer to her question. 'I don't know that there's much more to it than that.'

'Don't you want to be a great film star?' To an actor, this is an unfair question. They all want to be great film stars but it is something that, by universal unspoken agreement, they are not supposed to admit to.

Simon fell back on the stock reply. 'I think I just want to do good work.' He looked awkward as he said it although there was, to be fair, more truth in this than one might suppose. Or rather, it would be true to say he wanted to be admired for doing good work, which is not quite the same thing. But how else was he to answer her? Obviously, he wanted to be a great film star, just as Lady Uckfield had supposed. But while he knew this, he also knew not to reveal it.

'And will you always be an actor?' Here Lady Uckfield unconsciously exposed her own prejudices and put Simon even more securely in his place. It is a question often asked and yet I cannot for the life of me imagine people saying, 'And will you always be a doctor? Will you always be an accountant?' The reason is simple: try as they might they cannot see acting as a 'real' job. There is a distinction to be made here between the middle classes, who in some mysterious way are often affronted by the choice of acting as a career – as if one was choosing to live off immoral earnings – and the upper classes, who are usually only too delighted for one to be having a jolly time. But neither group can envisage actually staying with it. Perhaps because, despite quite a large number of posh actors in recent years, very few seem to make it through into the top strata of the profession. This may be because of prejudice, or lack of temperament, or simply because the road is too thorny for those with financial options, but the result is that while almost every aristocrat knows someone whose younger son or daughter has had a 'go at the stage' almost none of them know one who has succeeded. It can't be encouraging.

'Will you always be a marchioness?' said Edith from her place on the sofa, without raising her eyes.

Lady Uckfield glanced at her daughter-in-law for a moment. She quite understood the significance of Edith's weighing in on Simon's behalf. But she turned it back with a laugh. 'These days, my dear, who knows?' The smile became general and although I could not resist exchanging a quick look with Bella, we set about the business of being guests.

Simon, delighted to have acquired so attractive a champion, joined Edith on the sofa and was soon regaling her with Tales of the Film Set in his most engaging fashion.

Within minutes he was sparkling like the Regent Street Christmas lights. I watched Edith as she laughed and answered and flicked her hair about and laughed again, and watching her, I became aware that Charles, half talking to his mother across the room, was watching too. We both knew that we were looking at a more animated Edith than we had either of us seen in many moons and I knew that, above all things, I must be careful not to catch his eye or I would become complicit in a knowledge that would ultimately bring him great unhappiness. When he glanced towards me, I looked away and joined Bella, who was, needless to say, telling some *risqué* story about being stranded overnight in a garage to a fascinated Tigger.

Once into the dining room, the evening was undemanding and pleasant enough. The food was excellent as usual and I noticed that the servants had begun to assume towards me that slightly ingratiating manner that is their usual defence in the case of 'regulars'. Having ascertained that you will be back, all servants who view their position as a career will abandon the (no doubt great but inevitably temporary) pleasure of assuming a patronising air and snubbing you on behalf of their masters. Instead they adopt a kind of respectful chumminess that will ensure large tips and a good mention for them if they come up in conversation. This pat-a-cake is usually accepted. I have known many people who should know better to feel flattered at being made a fuss of by the staff of the grand. They believe this intimacy will bring them many opportunities in the future of demonstrating their familiarity with a Great House that may be denied to other guests. They will enjoy these moments a good deal. Properly handled, the relationship soon develops into a mutual, if slightly glutinous, admiration society. At any rate, on this occasion I disappointed myself by feeling quite warmed by deference as we made our way back to the car. Bella and I chatted on the way home, both of us relieved that the evening was over and yet pleased that it had been easier than we had anticipated. Reaching Brook Farm, we loitered outside as Simon went in and started to turn on the lights.

'So he's made another conquest after all,' said Bella.

I nodded. 'Thank goodness really,' I said. 'After last night, I thought I might find myself keeping the peace.'

'Oh, I don't think that's going to be your role at all,' said Bella with a half-smile.

I raised an admonishing finger. 'Don't make scandal. We're all getting on very well and this is a cushy job. Let us look no further than that.'

Bella laughed. 'Maybe. But you haven't noticed one thing.' I raised my eyebrows quizzically. 'He hasn't spoken a word since we left the party.'

She was right. I think I had noticed but had forced the knowledge out. For when someone as eager for approval, as hungry for status, as ready for the world to know of his adventures as Simon Russell, spends the evening basking in the intimate glow of a young and beautiful countess and feels no need to brag about it, then it is generally because the story has only just begun.

And so it proved.

TWELVE

~

I was perhaps not as observant as I might have been around this period as it so happened that some time before beginning the film at Broughton I had met the girl whom I was going to marry. She does not play much of a part in Edith's story and so I shall try to be as brief as possible. There was nothing particularly unusual in our meeting. It was at a cocktail party in Eaton Terrace given by a friend of my uncle's and, as it happened, her mother's that neither of us had especially wanted to attend. I was introduced to her quite soon after she arrived (with said mother) and more or less at once decided that this was my future wife. Her name was Adela FitzGerald, her father was an Irish baronet, one of the *earliest* creations as she was wont to point out crisply from time to time. She was tall, good-looking and business-like, and I saw at once that this was someone with whom I could feasibly be happy for the rest of my life. I was consequently very taken up for the next few months trying to persuade her of this truth, which seemed manifestly self-evident to me but was not, I must confess, so immediately apparent to her. Quite why one makes one's choice in these matters is a mystery to me as much now, happily married as I am, as then when I was chasing after someone I hardly knew. I had spent many years trying and failing to find the right partner and it seems rather illogical that I should have been satisfied on the instant but I was. Nor have I had any cause to regret my decision since.

I concealed Adela from my acquaintance for a while. When you are approaching forty everyone is apt to make a great fuss over any companion you are seen out with more than once – well-meaning friends kill many romances in the bud – and so I thought I would keep quiet until I knew if there was 'anything in it'. However, in the end, I felt there was and so I introduced her around. My society friends and to a much greater extent my family were relieved that I had chosen from my old world rather than my new. My theatrical friends – more generous if more casual of heart as a rule – were just relieved that I'd found somebody.

We were nearly at the end of the shoot when I suggested that Adela might like to come down to Sussex one Friday, watch a bit of the filming and stay two nights at the farmhouse. This was to be arranged, to Bella's delighted hilarity, quite properly, with me giving up my room and sleeping on the sofa. Adela accordingly drove down on the appointed night in her rather battered green Mini, was introduced to the other two over a merry and, thanks to Bella, delicious dinner and promised to join us on the set the following day when she had done a bit of shopping.

The next morning, before she had arrived, Edith came stalking me. We were filming in a rose garden, which was at the end of a short avenue leading away from one side of the house. The scene had originally been scheduled for the first week but had been endlessly delayed, I forget why, and so here we were, shooting it in mid-October. However, the luck of our (fearful) producers held and the day dawned as bright and hot as any in late June. I was almost irritated that their improvidence should have been so rewarded. It was a long sequence, involving Elizabeth Gunning (the fiercest American, Louanne) and Campbell (Simon) in a love duet, which was ultimately interrupted by Creevey (me). I was therefore sitting and reading, waiting my turn on the edge of the proceedings and I must say enjoying the location when Edith came into view.

'What's this I hear? You're a very dark horse.' I nodded that I was. 'Is it serious?' I observed that since I was already established as a dark horse it wasn't very likely that she'd know anything about it if it wasn't. 'Is she an actress?'

'Certainly not.'

'There's no need to sound so indignant. Why shouldn't she be?'

'Well, she isn't. She works in Christie's.'

Edith pulled a face. 'Not one of those earl's nieces at the front desk who sound so superior and then never know the answer to anything you ask them?'

'Exactly. Except she's not an earl's niece, she's a baronet's daughter.'

'What's her name?'

'Adela FitzGerald.'

'Well, you do disappoint me.' She threw herself down on a bank near to my folding chair. There were other empty chairs near so I felt no guilt.

'I can't think why.'

'You, my artist friend, to sink to a suitable match.'

'I'm not sure I'm prepared to listen to that from you. Anyway, surely the point is whether the suitability is an incidental detail or the primary motive.'

Edith blushed faintly and was silent. The first assistant signalled to us to be quiet and the cameras started to roll on Simon and the deadly Louanne. She pouted her way into the best position before the lens. We had all more or less reconciled ourselves to Jane Darnell, who was playing Lady Coventry. She was inept but there was no malice in her and she didn't appear to think much more of her chances of impersonating an eighteenth-century Irish beauty than we did. She was only really interested in collecting horse-brasses to take back to her Laurel Canyon home. Louanne Peters was an entirely different matter. Not only was she convinced that she was possessed of a seriously remarkable talent but her egotism nearly ranked as mental illness. She would talk of her successes and her looks, her lovers and her earning capacity by the hour, and always without asking a single question of her unwilling listeners. At first one was inclined to think that it must be some sort of complicated joke and that she was waiting for us all to call her on it, to burst out laughing, to hold up our hands and shout, 'Enough! We give in!' Only it wasn't and she wasn't. Simon loathed her, which didn't help their rather underwritten love scenes.

The shot finished, releasing Simon and Louanne, just as Adela came striding down the avenue towards us. In her corduroy knee breeches and fisherman's sweater, her long hair held back with a briskly tied silk scarf, she was the very antithesis of Louanne's synthetic charms and, for a moment, she showed Edith's carefully painted face in a slightly unfavourable light. She was so . . . healthy. But then again, of course, I was in love with her.

Edith stood up in greeting. 'Adela, how lovely to meet you at last. I'm Edith Broughton.'

'But I'm thrilled to meet you too!'

The girls exchanged their guarded greetings. That they were guarded was for two principal reasons, neither of which meant that there was the smallest romantic rivalry between them. Edith was not then and never had been in the least interested in me in that way. No, on her side it was the annoyance of having to surrender a confidant who has done good service and who will never be quite so useful married as he has been single. If you marry late there are many who feel this, even if those that love you attempt to control it. Added to which, just as happily married friends drive us all mad by their insistence that the married state is the only possible one, so do one's unhappily married acquaintance see it as their mission to turn all and sundry back from the church door. This stance is often used, half jokingly, as a means of insulting their partner in public. 'Get married! What on earth do you want to do that for?' one hears jocularly at a dinner party, and from further down the table comes a sour look from a lip-biting spouse. Ominously, this was a position that Edith, quite unconsciously I'm sure, was nudging into.

On Adela's side the guardedness was more subtle. She knew of course exactly who Edith was and, until meeting me, had been inclined to take the other point of view about the new Lady Broughton – that Charles, whom she had met a few times on the circuit, had been 'caught.' I had brought her at least to the point of suspending her judgement but in Edith's tone of greeting Adela had detected, with some justification, the faintest note of graciousness. Edith the Aristocrat welcoming this nice little actor's girlfriend. These things are hard to gauge correctly but it is true that Edith had developed a rather grand manner by this time so she may have been tempted into this dangerous area. Understandably, Adela, while previously prepared by me not to snub Edith, was damned if she was going to be patronised by her.

To make matters worse, just at this moment Charles arrived to see what was going on. He recognised Adela and I think in revenge (although she would have denied it) she lost no time in leading him into a conversation about several people that they both knew but Edith did not. In short she used Edith's dreaded Name Exchange against her. I suppose I should have felt indignant for one or the other of them but these things have a way of sorting themselves out without help from outsiders and anyway I could see that Adela had a point. I don't think I expected, even then, that she and Edith would ever be particularly close. Adela was too near what Edith wished to be (certainly so far as her past went) and while Adela was not a snob as a general rule, she was not above putting the likes of Edith in their place. I used to call it her

'Vicereine Mode.' All in all I could see that the best I might hope for was a kind of mutual tolerance. On this particular morning, before things could get sticky, Charles offered to show Adela the stables and with a nod towards me they set off. Edith watched them go.

'That's who should have married Charles.'

'Well, she's going to marry me.'

'No, I mean that's the kind of girl who would have made him happy. Giving out prizes, running the WVS. Can't you see it?'

'If that had been the kind of girl he wanted to marry, he would have married one. Lord knows there were plenty to choose from.'

'That doesn't sound very complimentary to your beloved.'

'You are talking of her obvious characteristics, which are, as you rightly observe, those of her time and her class. Her unusual qualities, of which you know nothing, are at the root of why she has chosen to marry an impoverished actor with a basement flat and not a rich earl.'

'Well, we'll have to watch our Ps and Qs around her.'

I wasn't having that. 'Don't make us into two teams, my dear. If you do, I warn you I'm on hers not yours.'

'Ouch.'

'Anyway, who says Charles should have married anyone but you?'

Edith said nothing but lay back and stared at the sky.

'You two look very intense.' Simon appeared, stripped of his embroidered coat, more romantic than ever in his flapping linen sleeves. He threw himself down on the bank next to Edith with a gay disregard of his costume. I could see his dresser sucking his teeth in the background but Simon was playing Byron to Edith's Caroline Lamb and he was not going to let a detail like grass stains deflect him. 'Where's Adela? Wasn't she here?'

'She's gone off to see the stables with Charles,' I said.

'To catch up on old times,' added Edith dryly.

Simon laughed. 'Lawks,' he said. 'We'd better be on our best behaviour when those two get together.'

'Don't start that,' said Edith. 'I've just been ticked off.'

Simon gave a comic guilty look in my direction but actually I was rather interested that his social confidence had grown sound enough to attempt this kind of joke. I suppose I was faintly annoyed that Adela was being equated with Charles under some kind of 'dull nob' label by them both, but when I saw Edith smile and mutter to Simon under her breath I realised at once what a clever flirt he was. For by including me in his observation he had contrived to take the threat out of what was nevertheless a deliberate complicity, a shared joke with Edith, which excluded Charles. I saw then that Adela and I were quite irrelevant to his purposes.

It transpired that this weekend, Edith, in a spirit of revenge as well as generosity, and quite against Charles's will, had invited the very Bob and Annette who had been staying with the Chases during the Mallorcin honeymoon. She had done this partly to see Annette again (who had, of course, kept up a lively correspondence with her new and eminent pal), partly to annoy Charles, partly to annoy Googie, and mainly to annoy Eric Chase who was down at Broughton with Caroline. She thought it would infuriate him to have this pair introduced to his parents-in-law as 'friends of Eric' as if they were typical of his crowd. She was correct. It did.

Simon, Adela and I had been asked for dinner, Bella having taken off for a few days in London, so at eight that night we found ourselves joining this motley throng in the family drawing room. The mis-matched group promised a strangely disparate evening and in fact, Adela initially got the wrong end of the stick and spent the first hour assuming that Eric was something to do with the film and not the family. The more names he dropped the more she was confirmed in her opinion until finally he referred to 'my father-in-law, Tigger', in red-faced exasperation. Even then she looked over to me for a second opinion.

Lady Uckfield's responses on the other hand were calculatedly, and deliberately, disappointing to Edith. She made a great fuss of Bob and Annette all weekend and simultaneously managed to convey, with a sort of discreet gush, what a relief it was to her to find a kindred spirit in Adela, which was, I think, meant as a compliment to me.

It reassured her that, having taken an actor into her circle, he should turn out to be her sort after all. She found it fitting that her friends should marry people she had more or less heard of. As it happened she knew one of Adela's aunts quite well and had come out the same year as her mother, all of which was as it should be in her quaintly ordered world. Obviously, it was exactly this security blanket that Charles's choice of Edith had withheld and it was hard not to suspect a touch of spite towards her daughter-in-law in the liveliness with which Lady

Uckfield took up my intended. Adela, naturally, blossomed under the attention, still only half aware of the games being played around her. I found Edith in one of the windows, staring grumpily at the ill-assorted party. She nodded at my beloved. 'What did I tell you? She's perfect.'

'I know.' I followed her gaze and saw that it had shifted from the cosy scene on the sofa to a far corner where Caroline Chase was listening absorbedly to Simon, apparently, as always, in full flow. Between the groups Charles wandered rather disconsolately, offering refills. 'Poor old Charles. Who's got him at dinner?' The question was more impertinent than I had meant but I suppose I wasn't thinking. At any rate, instead of reprimanding me as she should have, Edith shrugged.

'Who knows? We've got the most ghastly evening ahead.' I looked enquiringly. 'Bob and Annette Watson are taking us all out.'

'That's very nice of them. Why on earth should they?'

Edith did not share my view of things. 'That's not all. They've booked us into Fairburn Hall. Googie's in fits. She's thrilled, of course. She's been dying to see what they've done with it since the de Marneys left and she's never dared admit it.'

Her lack of gratitude at the Watsons' invitation did not surprise me. The plan was, naturally, a frightful prospect to the Broughtons and their ilk. In England one of the saddest mistakes a social climber can make is excessive generosity. It's odd really for what could be more charming? To arrive with presents and treats, to gather up whole house-parties and take them out on the town – what could be nicer than this? And yet these courteous acts are as clear a signal to the Insiders that the would-be benefactor is a newcomer to their world as if they had worn a sign on their hat. Of all these solecisms, that of offering to take people 'out' in the country is perhaps the worst. The English upper-classes do not as a rule leave their houses in the country in the evening except to go to other people's houses. They might be tempted by a country house opera or even the occasional play with a picnic attached, but if they want to eat in a restaurant they do it in the week and in London. Nor do they ever go to 'country house hotels' unless it is on a pilgrimage of personal curiosity. They might visit one because 'I used to spend my summers here when it belonged to my Aunt Ursula', but they would never, on pain of death, book in for dinner or a weekend. One of the saddest aspects of these places is that the gentility promised in the brochures can never, by its very nature, be reflected in the guests.

The Watsons, anxious to ingratiate themselves with Lady Uckfield and to become Broughton 'regulars' had hit on the sure way to render themselves ridiculous to their hostess for ever, as well as providing her with a welcome new source of funny stories. For this privilege they would pay a great deal of money.

Fairburn Hall was a large and ugly house on the other side of Uckfield. It had belonged for several centuries to the ancient if low-achieving family of de Marney, who had finally managed a baronetcy by befriending, of all people, Lloyd George. The de Marney of a particularly unfortunate architectural period in the 1850s had encased a blameless Queen Anne manor house in a hideous, neo-gothic shell, studded with bas-reliefs of the family's triumphant, historical moments. These apparently were few and as a result rather nebulous and un-sourced scenes of 'Gerald de Marney welcoming Queen Eleanor to Fairburn', or 'Philip de Marney taking the colours at Edgehill' gave rise to great hilarity among the Broughtons. I need hardly say there was no love lost between the families and never had been. Technically the de Marneys were the older family and had consequently always tried to assume a lordly manner towards their neighbours. This was absurd of them as the Broughtons, whether the de Marneys liked it or not, were much richer and much grander as they had been for the previous three centuries. A couple of years before this, the current incumbent, Sir Robert de Marney, had given up the unequal struggle, sold Fairburn on a long lease to a large group of 'Leisure Hotels' and moved with his family into the dower house four miles away.

'Do you think we ought to be *veiled*?' whispered Lady Uckfield, as we climbed out of the cars. She turned to me. 'It was always the vilest house in the world. My mother-in-law used to swear they'd muddled up the plans with Lewes prison and got the wrong one.'

The entrance was through a wide semi-conservatory, with stone flags and odd, quasi-armorial grills at the window, like a rather grand bank. Through this one came into a cumbrous entrance hall. Thick, square Victorian columns stood everywhere, but the decision in the rebuilding not to raise the original ceiling height of the old house gave it the look of some central German under-vault, making one feel like a caryatid. The de Marney crest in loud colours was on every wall and an ornate family tree, framed in gilt, hung over the gas-log fire. Lady Uckfield stared at it. 'They've got the wrong branch,' she said happily.

An immensely important head waiter came towards us and mistaking Bob Watson's nervous enquiry about the reservation for the general tone of the party he attempted a very superior air as he ushered us into what he referred to as the 'withdrawing room'. He was soon disabused.

'What a horrid colour!' said Lady Uckfield, ignoring the chair he was indicating and plumping down onto a sofa instead. 'Too sad, as this was really the only room that was nice at all. It was the music room in the old days although they were tone deaf to a man!' She laughed pleasantly, as the crushed waiter tried to salvage his position by fawning over her for her choice of 'aperitif'.

'I think Lady Uckfield would like some champagne,' said Bob loudly, and one or two lacquered heads in the corners of the room looked round. He, in his turn, wanted to get some mileage out of bringing such a distinguished group to this, as he imagined, smart venue and I can't say I blamed him. Heaven knows he was going to pay dearly for it. His tone further flattened the attendant who was sufficiently familiar with the area to realise by now the extent of his initial *faux pas*. The party was becoming uncomfortable and Charles and Caroline exchanged a quick, edgy look. I found myself longing to defend Bob and his kindness of spirit, but I knew I would be fighting insuperable odds and, coward-like, I seized one of the huge, leather-bound menus when they arrived and hid behind it until the wine was brought with a great flurry of silver and glass and linen. At this moment, to everyone's amazement except possibly Caroline's, Eric leaned forward, plucked a bottle out of its silver-plated, ice-lined nest and spoke, not to Bob but to the waiter:

'Haven't you got any of the ninety-two?'

The waiter shook his head with murmured apologies. Just as Bob's timorousness had at first made us all worthless so far as he was concerned, now Lady Uckfield's presence made us all fine folk indeed.

Eric glowed at his deference. 'Then you shouldn't say it's ninety-two, should you?' He dropped the bottle back into its holder and sat back as the waiter poured.

Across the group Edith caught my eyes and rolled hers.

Bob was fumbling. He knew he faced a bill of something in the region of seven or eight hundred pounds and already the mixture of suppressed giggles and secret smiles was telling him that, mysteriously, his treat was making him not eminent but ridiculous. This was doubly irritating to him as his wife had tried to talk him out of it and had suggested, instead, asking the Broughtons and the Uckfields to dinner at the Ivy in London (which would, of course, have been perfectly acceptable to them).

Charles came to his aid. 'This is delicious,' he said firmly, sipping his wine and looking towards the rest of us.

'Absolutely lovely,' said Adela, and I nodded away.

Actually, it was quite nice but too cold. However, Simon, on this dangerous evening, had clearly decided to go for broke. Once and for all he was determined to shake off the concept that he was in any sense overawed by the present company.

'Would it be a great bore if I have a whisky?' he said.

'Good idea,' said Eric. 'Me, too.'

The careful cruelty of this was that Bob had already ordered three bottles opened, which the rest of us could not now possibly finish. He was foundering. His wine had been rejected, he had been insulted and yet somehow he had to go on as if everything was going swimmingly. 'Of course!' he smiled broadly. 'What about you, Edith?'

Edith sank back into the over-stuffed, chintz-covered chair and stared her pellucid stare. I could see her gaze trailing over Charles, who was giving her an admonishing look, imploring her to behave. Poor man. These were his wife's friends and yet it was he who was having to work to save the evening. Behind him, Simon stood beaming at her. 'I wouldn't mind some vodka,' she said. Simon half winked, and they both caught in their smiles before they spilled over into impropriety.

'Fine,' said Bob in a lacklustre voice. He looked around for more trouble but Caroline, with a deliberate gesture, reached across Eric to help herself to a large glass of champagne. The battle-lines were forming.

The food was predictably pretentious, with bonfires going at practically every table. Inadequate portions arranged like cocktail hats followed each other in blank, tasteless succession, fussed over by suspiciously French waiters. The maître d' would not, by this time, leave us alone and kept dashing up for a review of the current course until Simon finally suggested he might like to take a seat to save himself the bother. Of course we all laughed and of course he was never seen again. In truth the dinner itself was the least awful part of the evening because of Simon. He certainly was on very funny form that night. He could match Annette's stories without challenging her and the pair of them did keep things going. Even Lady Uckfield gave in to the prevailing mood and chuckled away as she toyed with her unsatisfactory and costly dishes.

Charles, on the other hand, was more or less in hell the entire time. He was not quick enough to get the point of most of the anecdotes, let alone tell his own. These were not his kind of people and unusually for him (for he seldom risked the possibility) he was outnumbered. Unlike his father he was not a flirt, unlike his mother he had very little sense of humour. Caroline tried to rescue him once or twice but she was in a dark mood of her own and in the end it was Adela who got him onto the business of improving the shoot at Feltham. He had apparently only restarted it three years before after a long gap and the topic released some of the pent-up flow within him, but even this had a limited success for when Simon was telling a story about some production he'd been in where the stage manager had filled the bath with boiling instead of cold water, he paused for the punch line and into the silence came Charles's voice: 'The great thing is to leave a wide enough headland of kale, which of course some of the farmers are reluctant to do ... '

Simon laughed. 'Well, obviously Charles is fascinated,' he said. He meant it pleasantly enough, I think, and all would probably have passed on if Edith had not spoken up at that moment: 'Oh, Charles for God's sake, shut up about your bloody shoot.'

I imagine she thought that in some way this would be a joke too and we would all smile but it came out wrong. Her voice was harsh and I suppose unloving in a way that, particularly in the presence of Charles's parents as we were, made a strange and embarrassing tremor at the table. I saw Annette catch Bob's eye as I felt Adela nudge my foot.

Charles looked up, hurt rather than angry, like a puppy who has been smacked for some other dog's pee. 'Am I being very boring?' he said.

There was a faint pause and then Eric, either misguidedly thinking to be amusing or, more probably in his case, just in order to be unkind, said, 'Yes, you are. Better have some more to drink.' He started to pour wine into Charles's glass but Charles shook his head.

'Actually, I don't know why but I'm terribly tired.' He turned his harassed eyes to Bob. 'Would you forgive me if I skipped the coffee and headed on home?'

Bob knew by now, long before he had reached for his plastic, that the evening had been the most crashing flop and so he shook his head merrily. 'Of course not! You go. We'll be fine.'

Charles smiled wanly and stood up. 'Well then, I think I will be off if I may. We've lots of cars, haven't we? Will you be all right, darling?'

Now it was perfectly plain to everyone present that Edith ought to have jumped to her feet, said that she, too, was tired and left with her husband. Normally this is exactly what she would have done but this evening some kind of devilry had got into her. Or maybe it was simple lust. At any rate, she neither moved nor spoke and it was Simon's voice that broke the silence:

'Don't worry about Edith. I'll bring her home.'

Charles looked at him and for a second they were what the Americans call 'eyeballing' each other. It might seem that Charles, rich and titled as he was, and really not that bad-looking in his 1930s-ish way, held all the aces, which of course in the long view he did, but Simon Russell, feeling successful and busy and as handsome as a man can be, bristled or rather shone with charismatic confidence that night. To all the onlookers at the table Charles paled before him and I at least felt a pang of real pity for this man who had everything. Obviously, looking back, I know that Simon had the confidence of a man in love whose love is returned and Charles conversely had the fear of a man facing ruin but even without that knowledge the figure of Russell, clad in his waisted blue velvet coat, eyes and hair aglow, looked like the embodiment of some unconquerable force in a mythological painting. I say this that one may perhaps be less hard and more forgiving of Edith. Having taken in the tableau for a moment, it was Lady Uckfield who spoke.

'That's very kind of you, Mr Russell. Are you sure?' She broke the mood further by rising and forcing the company to their feet. 'Am I leading the ladies out? Or do we all go through together, here?'

Even in this supreme moment of face-saving she could not resist pointing up the fact that she thought this place quite extraordinary and so, presumably, not governed by the normal rules of her existence. I have said before that I came to admire Lady Uckfield a good deal and this was one of the moments that underpinned my view of her. She had witnessed her son made a fool of, she had seen him dismissed by his wife, she was well aware of the danger in the air from Simon's offer and yet she would not have revealed any of these things for worlds. She would have cut out her tongue rather than give anyone the impression that she thought it a bad idea for Edith to travel home alone in the dark with Simon. And yet she would have given one hundred thousand pounds then and there to have Russell removed from her sight for ever. If Edith had only had her mother-in-law's control, there would have been no scandal of any kind, then or later.

Back in the horrible 'withdrawing room' Lady Uckfield beckoned to me to sit beside her. If she felt uneasy, she did not betray it with the slightest flicker. 'You must let me congratulate you on your choice.'

'You're pleased for me, then.'

'Well, as your friend I'm pleased but as a hostess I'm *furious*.' I smiled because she spoke the truth. She would forgive me the inconvenience of ceasing to be a single man but only because of the 'rightness' of the thing. 'When will you be married?' I explained that while I had every reason to believe I would be successful, it was not all quite settled yet. I imagined it would be five or six months. 'And what about children? Have you thought about that? I'm an old woman so I can ask.'

I shrugged. 'I don't know really. We both want them but I can't help feeling that the timing is rather up to the wife, isn't it? After all, my bit's rather easy.'

Lady Uckfield laughed. 'It certainly is. But don't wait too long. I hope Charles and Edith don't.' She looked me in the eye as she said this because of course we both knew that they had already waited too long. If Edith was now fretting over some golden head in the nursery or indeed if she was simply big with child, none of the threatened nightmare would be happening.

'I quite agree,' I said.

THIRTEEN

~

I had wondered, when Simon made his offer to escort Edith home, whether his plot would be foiled by finding that he had to take various others with them, but as soon as I emerged from the house with Adela I saw that this would not be the case: the whole back seat of his car was stuffed with a pair of chairs and what looked like an assortment of gardening tools. By my side I could feel Lady Uckfield taking in the same fact. My guess is that she had intended to join her daughter-in-law in the shabby Cortina, but, if so, it was not to be. I offered her and Lord Uckfield a place in Adela's Mini and, with a glance at Eric, who had brought some sort of Tonka Toy/Range Rover, they accepted. Lady Uckfield and I squeezed into the back seat, leaving Lord Uckfield and Adela in front. Eric gestured to them impatiently but in her sublime way Lady Uckfield affected not to notice. We drove off, leaving Bob and Annette to the tender mercies of Eric's red-faced driving.

'I hope he isn't stopped,' said Lord Uckfield.

Lady Uckfield made a slight *moue* with her mouth. 'Oh well,' she said.

We travelled in silence for a bit, all, I imagine, thinking of Simon and Edith whose car was nowhere in sight.

Lady Uckfield spoke again. 'Aren't those places too extraordinary? Who do you think goes to them?'

'Isn't it these whad'y'a call "yuppies"?' Lord Uckfield spoke in inverted commas, pleased to be so up to the minute.

'Well, it can't only be yuppies. Are there enough of them? There can't be that many round here. Americans too, I suppose. So sad, really.'

'Oh, I don't know,' said Adela. 'I'd rather see them as hotels than council offices or pulled down altogether.'

'I suppose so.' Lady Uckfield nodded doubtfully. In truth, she'd rather have seen them filled with the same well-mannered, rich people who'd lived in all these houses a hundred years ago. Even the ones whom, like the de Marneys, she disliked. For her there was no merit in the changes the twentieth century had wrought. Time had blurred her memory so that like the old recalling only the sunny days of childhood, she could think of nothing harsh or mean in the England of her beginnings. I found her views interesting. Even if her vision of the past was not quite as inaccurate or outlandish as Jeremy Paxman would have it, still Lady Uckfield's beliefs were rare by the closing years of the twentieth century. She had that absolute faith in the judgement of her own kind, seldom seen since 1914. No doubt it was common enough before then, which must have made Edwardian society such a philosophically relaxing place to be. If one were an aristocrat.

*   *   *

Simon made a show of fuss in getting out his car keys so that the other Broughton cars had all pulled away as he started the motor. He turned to look at Edith. She hugged her coat around her and leaned back against the window. They were two games players, with equal hands, and now at last they were alone with intent. 'With intent' because something in the nature of Edith's rudeness to Charles, something in the brashness of Simon's offer of a lift, had signalled to both of them that the fun was about to begin. Looking at Simon's roguish smile, the slightly crooked crease by the side of his mouth where his beard was beginning to push through, Edith felt a tremor of sexual excitement shiver through her body. She was startled by the immediacy of her own lust. She had been with men who had attracted her, she remembered enjoying making love with George and there had been a time, admittedly mostly before her marriage, when she had relished the thought of being alone with Charles, but she was sharply aware that this was something rather different. Looking into Simon's dark blue eyes, she realised she simply and absolutely wanted to be naked with him. She wanted to feel his hard, nude body against and inside hers. She felt hot and faintly uncomfortable. The terrifying, exhilarating thrill of her principles deserting her rippled through her stomach. 'Hadn't we better get going?' she said.

Simon was watching her carefully. Her blonde hair fell over her grey-blue eyes and she pushed it out of the way with a slightly petulant gesture. Her lips had not shut again after she spoke but stayed moist and parted with her white teeth just visible in the darkness. He too was excited but not in quite the same way as she. He had made love to a good many pretty women in his time and it was not the thought of the sexual delights to come that aroused him. It was the certain and confirmed knowledge of her attraction to him.

He was intensely aware of his own beauty. What is more he respected and enjoyed it as he sensed, quite rightly, that it was the core of his power. It was this simple truth that was at the epicentre of his flirtatious charm. From everyone, friend or foe, man or woman, he needed to eke out some response to his own physical desirability. Only then, in the warm glow of these aliens' admiration could he relax and be happy. The more threatening the situation, the more necessary it became to be wanted and wanted physically. He spent his life throwing out smouldering looks, laughing mysteriously, winking and twinkling at strangers solely in order to reassure himself that he was in control. Needless to say, he left behind a bewildered trail of wounded, who had responded for weeks or even months to clear signs of sexual and romantic interest only to find, once they were captive, that he had no more need of their love than if they had been trees in the field.

He did not trouble himself much over his search for constant reassurance. He simply expected his looks to break down all barriers, even if he did glimpse dimly that this is not the behaviour of a securely-based personality. In a way, this lack of faith in his other qualities meant that his vanity was closely entwined with a kind of modesty. He had no real respect for his own intellect, and socially, for all his bravado, he knew he could be clumsily inept. Given these reasons, it was probably inevitable that his bourgeois yearnings coupled to his compulsion to inflame desire should have led him to Edith. The irony being that she saw in him some kind of escape from the Broughton life, while he, conversely, saw her as the entrée to it. At this stage of the proceedings however these truths were concealed from them both. They were, in short, enraptured with each other.

Lust, that state commonly known as 'being in love', is a kind of madness. It is a distortion of reality so remarkable that it should, by rights, enable most of us to understand the other forms of lunacy with the sympathy of fellow-sufferers. And yet as we all know, it is a madness that, however ferocious, seldom, if ever, lasts. Nor, contrary to the popular teaching on the subject, does lust usually give way to a 'deeper and more meaningful love'. There are exceptions of course. Some spouses 'love' forever. But, as a rule, if the couple is truly well matched, it gives way to a warm and interdependent friendship enriched with physical attraction. Should they be ill-assorted it simply fades into boredom or, if they have the misfortune to be married in the interim, dull hatred. But, paradoxically, mad and suffering as one is in the heat of the flame, few of us are glad as we feel passion slip away. How many of us, re-meeting objects of desire who once burned a scar through seasons and even years, whose voices on the telephone could start up flights of butterflies, whose slightest expression could set off a peal of tremulous sexual bells in our vitals, search our inner selves in vain for the least attraction to the face before us? How many of us, having cried bitter, rancid tears over a failed love, are actually disappointed when we discover, seeing the adored one again, that all trace of their power over us is gone? How often one has resisted the freedom-giving knowledge that they have actually begun to irritate us as that seems like the worst kind of disloyalty to our own dreams. No, while most people have been at their unhappiest when in love, it is nevertheless the state the human being yearns for above all.

It was not that Edith really saw Simon as any solid part of her future life, entranced as she was. But she had long forgotten her early irritation with his flirtatious verbosity and now she loved to listen to his trials, to his hopes, to his dreams – as much as anything because she loved watching the way his mouth moved – and then, wonderful looking as he was, he made her feel so warm and so wanted. She liked physically to be near him, to let his arm brush her sleeve, his hand graze hers, but she thought no further than that. Or had not up to this moment. Unfortunately for her, he had come into her life at a time of wretched *ennui*. Before her marriage, yawning over her estate agent's telephone, she had dreamed of all the variety that her new life would bring her but she had not allowed for the fact that within months that new life would have acquired a sameness all its own. And so she was bored and, having expected nothing but excitement in the fulfilment of her social pretensions, she thought boredom more terrible than it is.

Slowly but inexorably she had allowed her residual affection for Charles to be driven out by his inability to interest her. Although, somewhere in her brain, Edith was aware that she need not have. If, like her mother-in-law before her, she had early on faced and dealt with the limitations of her husband then there could have been fondness between them. If she had ceased to look to him for her amusement, then she might have relied on him only for those things he could have given her: loyalty, security, even love in his unimaginative way. But, just as she had never really faced within herself that she had deliberately married a man she did not love for his position, so she could not now accept the responsibility for the fact that she was living with a man who was duller and stupider than she. It seemed to Edith to be Charles's fault that her life was so dreary, it was Charles's fault that they did not have a vivid round in London, it was Charles's fault that she dreaded their times together more than the hours she spent alone. Added to which she had already slid into that dangerous option, open only to those with high-profile, 'public' lives, of playing the part of the happy and gracious wife to an adoring crowd, which must always serve to throw the frigid inertia of her life at home into sharp relief. As popular as she was with the villagers, with her charities, with the estate workers, she had even begun to think that this happy and elegant woman she saw reflected in their eyes (and in the local press) was some kind of real truth and that it must be Charles's fault that he did not respond to her as her adoring, provincial fans did.

Not that she had any substantial taste for danger. She had accepted Simon's offer of a ride home as much to irritate her mother-in-law as anything else. She was, in fact, surprised if anything at the strength of her physical attraction to him when they found themselves, as they now did for the first time, alone and in the dark. But what took her even more unawares was an aerated sense of the raising of her spirits and with it that heady flavour of unexplored potential. This, she suddenly knew in a blinding flash of revelation, was the very thing she had most missed since her marriage. For months now there had seemed to be no open-endedness about her existence. All the decisions had been taken and must now be lived with. And yet here she was, looking at the corduroy of Simon's trousers stretched over the muscles of his thigh, and sensing a delicious awareness that there were still unplanned-for possibilities between her and death.

*　　*　　*

The Uckfields asked us in for a drink when we arrived at Broughton. I think they might have preferred us just to head for home but we accepted, partly out of politeness but also from that ghoulish sense that we all feel when we suspect an evening is not yet quite over. We were (or rather I was) still curious as to whether Charles really had gone to bed, how long it would take Simon and Edith to get home, how Lady Uckfield would behave – any number, in fact, of the different aspects of the case still to be revealed.

Charles was in the drawing room. He had hardly touched the whisky on the table beside his chair and was, I suspect, staring into mid-air until he heard our step. At any rate he seemed to be very puzzled by the women's magazine he had snatched up as we came in. He fetched Scotches for his father and me and some water for Adela (her customary, somewhat lacklustre late-night refreshment) and we all sat down. We had not been there long before the unmistakable sounds of Eric on the staircase told us that the Range Rover at least was back. The four of them came into the room.

'Where's Edith?' said Eric brightly, happy of course to see that she was not back and that therefore he might score some points off her.

'I hope they haven't broken down,' said Adela firmly.

'Oh dear. Might they have?' said Lady Uckfield.

Under silent instruction from Adela, I nodded. 'Simon's car is the most frightful wreck. I do hope not.'

Lady Uckfield recognised instantly that this was a life raft that she could rope to her decks in case of future need. She was not exactly grateful. For her to register gratitude she would have had first to admit to herself that there was anything wrong. But she was noticeably warm as she joined Adela on the sofa and started to question her about her aunt.

Eric had another try. 'They took forever before they even started the car,' he said. 'We were loaded up and out of the gates before I heard the engine.' But the initiative had slipped from him. The later the errant couple were, the more the family could hide behind fear of a breakdown or an accident. All other possible reasons for lateness had by this means been painlessly obviated.

As the conversation became more general and people flopped down into the various chairs and sofas around the room, Charles came up and asked me if I would join him in his office. I forget his excuse, some book or picture he had been meaning to show me, the usual sort of thing, but we both knew that he simply wanted to talk to me alone. I nodded and followed him out, uncomfortably aware of Chase's slightly quizzical smile, and we started down a corridor to the left. I wasn't looking forward to the interview as I had begun to feel responsible for the mayhem that even then I was only just starting to admit might be looming. I had after all been the one to introduce Simon to them. Had I not been in the film I am quite sure he would never have penetrated the charmed circle of the family.

Charles's office, its door sporting one of those 'private' notices that give one such pleasure to set aside, was a smallish corner room some distance away from the drawing and dining rooms used by the family. It was an extension of the main library, still on the principal floor, and so had handsome cornices and door cases and, by day, a fine view across the park from both of its tall windows. A pair of double doors would have connected it to the larger room if they were opened, which, as the library was one of the rooms on the public tour, they seldom if ever were. The fireplace was a delicate one of some kind of pinkish marble and the walls themselves had been covered with crimson damask that stretched from dado to ceiling. Against it stood high, glazed bookcases that looked as if they had been made for the room. A portrait of some female forebear, painted in a costume for a fancy-dress ball, hung over the chimneypiece, the gilded frame and the marble shelf below stuffed with a mass of invitations, snapshots, notes, postcards – the usual paper chaos with which the upper classes demonstrate their ease with their elegant surroundings.

'This is very nice,' I said. 'Where's Edith's sitting room? Is it next door?'

Charles shook his head. 'Upstairs,' he muttered. 'Quite near our bedroom.'

He stared at me mutely and rather than return his anguished glance, I started to peer at the spines of the books in the cases round the room. *Can You Forgive Her?* by Trollope caught my eye and gave me a disloyal inner smile. *He Knew He Was Right* by the same author sobered me up. I don't know that I had then any real understanding of Charles's capacity for jealousy, since I had no true knowledge of his capacity for emotion. The fact that someone is not particularly intelligent is no guide in these things. People may be stupid and extremely complicated just as they can be clever and incapable of deep feeling.

'What do you think?' I heard him say and for a moment I wondered if I was being asked my opinion of some unusual book but catching sight of Charles's face, I thought this was probably not the case. Just to be safe I answered with a question:

'What do you mean?'

'What are they up to?'

He was gruff and tweedy in his manner and I realised that we were embarking on what is called a 'man-to-man' talk. I shuddered at the prospect. Apart from anything else I am a firm believer in the 'least said soonest mended' school of marital harmony – a belief incidentally quite unshaken by marriage itself.

'Oh, Charles, come on,' I said warmly, implying that they couldn't possibly be 'up to' anything. I am not sure whether I was being dishonest in taking this tack. I rather think not. It seems naive but although, looking back, it is clear that Edith and Simon were drawn to each other from the second day, I don't know that their mutual attraction had really impinged itself on me much before that evening.

'You come on,' said Charles, more sharply than usual.

'Look,' I was very conciliatory, 'if you're asking me if I know anything, I don't. If you're asking if I think anything, I don't either. Much. I think they like each other, that's all. Is that so terrible? Haven't you ever wanted to flirt with anyone since you were married?'

'No,' said Charles, slumping into a Chippendale chair, and resting his elbows on a charming and untidy partner's desk. His let his head fall forward into his hands as he spoke and started to push his fingers through his hair. He was posing for a statue of misery. I felt wrong-footed in that I had judged badly to think that warm reassurance would do the trick and yet I didn't want to lead the way into a different level of intimacy, which Charles, whom after all I did not even then know well, might regard as an impertinence. I felt sorry for the fellow and wished to find a way to lighten rather than increase his load. My detached ruminations were interrupted by a sigh from the desk.

'She doesn't love me, you see.' He spoke to a pile of papers beneath his face but since the remark was presumably addressed to me, I tried to assess the correct level of response.

Of course, what made this doubly hard was that Charles's statement, bald as it was, was essentially true. There was no question in my mind but that Edith did not then love him. She did not desire him (which of course I only surmised at that time), she did not enjoy his company, she did not share his interests, she did not like most of his friends. I do not think, then or later, that she ever actually *dis*liked him but I could hardly say that in answer to Charles's cry of pain. I was silent, which I suppose was in itself a tacit agreement, and Charles looked up. I cannot say how moved I was by the terrible suffering in his simple, county face. His narrow eyes were reddening with tears, which had already begun to run down his large and bony nose. His hair, normally as sleek as a 1930s advertisement for unguent, was ruffled and untidy and sticking up in awkward little spikes. Great grief can be worn charmingly by a beauty and I have seen a lot of gracious dignity at funerals in my time but it is my experience that when grief is becoming it is also suspect. Real unhappiness is ugly and wounding and scarring to the soul. I blush to recall that I was surprised that Charles – nice, bluff Charles with his shooting and his hedgerows and his dogs – had a heart that could be broken. But he had and I was there to witness its breaking.

Before I could say anything there was a sound from the corridor outside. 'Charles?' It was Lady Uckfield. Rather than commit, even in a moment of emotional tension such as this, the social solecism of knocking at a sitting-room door (an action that, with white-gloved butlers, always plays so prominent a part in inaccurate television period drama) she contrived to wrestle with the door knob as if it would have been easier to get into the Ark of the Covenant. At any rate, having given us both enough time to dress had we so needed let alone dry our tears, she opened the door and came into the room. 'Ah, Charles,' she smiled easily into her son's face, ignoring the Fall of Rome that was written there, 'Edith's back. They got stuck getting out of the town. Too boring.' She nodded towards me. 'Your friend's gone straight on up to the farm.' Charles nodded his thanks in a kind of daze and started back towards the drawing room. I would have followed but Lady Uckfield, with an almost imperceptible pressure on my arm, held me back.

'We'd better be off, too.' I said. 'Where's Bob? I must thank him for dinner.'

'He's gone to bed,' she replied. 'Your nice Adela said thank you.' We were silent. She stood by the fireplace, idly fingering the pasteboard squares that summoned her child to various festivities. There was only one light on in the farthest corner of the room, a glass and ormolu desk lamp, which threw longish shadows about her and in the half-light grooved her face cruelly. For once she looked her years. The glamorous veil of her manner was momentarily lifted and a tired, worried woman in late middle-age was revealed to the naked eye.

'Well, this is a pretty kettle of fish,' she said, not looking up from the invitation to a wedding on which I could see a tick and 'Acc' in Edith's loose scrawl.

'Oh, I don't know,' I replied. My position was an awkward one for, after all, I was in that house as a friend of Edith. It behoved me to be loyal to her and yet I did think she had behaved foolishly. I was not, if you like, 'on her side' while finding it unsuitable that I should be on anyone else's.

'Well, I do.' She paused while I looked up in answer to her acid tone. 'It's worse than you think. Eric was by his car when they arrived. He saw them kissing.'

I was for a moment what a cockney friend of mine would call gobsmacked. I had thought we had been fringing around slight improprieties brought on by Edith's tedium. I had expected a little chat about Edith 'bucking up'. Of course, I suspected at once that Eric was not 'by his car' when they drove up but was quite consciously concealed somewhere near the entrance that he might not miss this Heaven-sent chance to nail Edith, whom, by this stage, he absolutely detested. Much more than I had realised. At any rate, whatever the truth of his motive, he had not lied about what he had seen. For old times' sake I tried to dig Edith out of the hole she had buried herself in. 'Oh, surely, she was just kissing him goodnight.'

'She was kissing him passionately. His hand was inside her shirt and hers was out of sight beneath the dashboard.' Lady Uckfield spoke with the dead-pan delivery of a policeman giving evidence in the County Court. I stared at her in silence. My first instinct was to apologise for being there at all and run for it. Certainly I could think of nothing more to say. Lady Uckfield continued. 'It is the greatest pity that it should have been Eric who saw them. He is quite incapable of keeping anything to himself and anyway I have a suspicion he is not overly fond of Edith. He has already told Caroline who told me. She will try to keep him quiet but I imagine she will fail.' What interested me most about all this was Lady Uckfield's manner. I had grown used to her passionate, half-whispered intimacy when she shared with you the day's headlines or your place at dinner. Now she really did have a secret to impart and all her girlish urgency was gone. She might have been an officer in the WVS addressing a group of recruits. 'I suppose we may hope that things have not progressed any further but I'm not sure what difference that makes anyway.'

'Will you tell Charles?'

She looked up startled. 'Of course not. Do you think I'm mad?' She relaxed again. Her shock at being thought unworldly was past. She dropped the card and strolled over to the window. 'He'll find out, though.'

'How?' I asked, meaning to imply that I too would be silent.

She smiled sadly. 'Probably because Edith will tell him. At any rate, someone will.' There was nothing I could profitably add to this since she was unquestionably right. Edith in her boredom was just ripe for succumbing to that fatal desire to 'bring things to a head' that so many married couples these days seem to indulge in. In sharp contrast to their great-grandparents who expended all their energy in trying to stop things coming to a head at any cost. My silence felt clumsy but I didn't in truth know exactly why Lady Uckfield was telling me any of this. For all her pseudo-intimacy she never usually imparted anything even faintly private, let alone potentially scandalous. She must have caught this question from my manner for she answered it without being asked: 'I want you to do something for me.'

'Of course.'

'I want you to tell the boy Simon to leave her alone.'

'Well . . .' Woe betide the man who accepts this kind of commission readily. Whatever opinion I might have of Simon's character or morals, I was hardly in a position to act the wise uncle with him.

Lady Uckfield drove full tilt at my hesitation. Her voice resumed more of its normal glib, light tone as the words gushed forth. 'She's bored. That's all there is to it. She's bored and she ought to get up to London more. She ought to see more of her friends. Or have a baby. Or get a job. That's what she needs. As for this boy . . .' She shrugged. 'He's handsome, he's charming and, above all, he's *here*. One does these things when one is settling into a new life. They mean nothing. The nuisance is that Eric saw her. He will almost certainly tell and it's our job to make sure no one can corroborate his story.'

I began to see things by her light. Of course, it was all a silly nonsense that was only horrid because it could hurt Charles if he found out. Yes, it was a pity that Eric had seen them. That was the pity. Her charming, even voice beat back the threat of anarchy and storm that had seemed to envelop us for a moment and returned us to the shore. 'I'll do my best,' I said.

'Of course you will, and the film's nearly over anyway. Too sad to be losing you,' she added hastily, remembering herself, 'but all the same...'

I nodded and she started towards the door. Her work was done. She had acted to contain the damage and that had necessitated taking me into her confidence. But I was already her ally. Things might have been worse.

'Lady Uckfield,' I said. She stopped and turned, her hand still resting on the gleaming door knob. 'Don't be too hard on Edith.'

'Of course not,' she laughed. 'You may not believe it but I was young once too, you know.' Then she was gone and I knew beyond a shadow of a doubt that she hated her daughter-in-law as fiercely as she would have hated any woman who had made her only son cry.

FOURTEEN

~

'What on earth was going on?' said Adela as soon as we drove away from the front of the house.

'What do you mean?'

'Well, first of all you two slope off and everyone looks haunted. Then Eric vanishes. Brief calm and then suddenly we're into farce with people running in and out of doors with stricken faces. I, meanwhile, am sitting there throughout with Lord Uckfield who's trying to explain something about trout farming. What happened to you? I thought I was going to have to ring and ask for a bed.' I told her everything of course and we drove on in silence for a while. Adela broke it. 'What can you possibly say to Simon? Unhand this lady? Won't he hit you on the nose?'

'I shouldn't think so. He doesn't look the type.'

'Well?'

I didn't really have an answer for her as I also could not quite envisage how to play this most embarrassing of scenes. And by what right was I even to open my mouth on the subject?

Adela gave me my motive. 'I suppose you'll just have to do your best for poor old Edith. It'll be a shame if she buggers it up after all that effort. And for such a nothing.'

We arrived at the farmhouse to find Simon sitting at the kitchen table nursing a glass of wine. His mood and the mere fact that he had not gone to bed seemed to suggest the desire for an unburdening talk although he could not have guessed that I already knew what he had to unburden. This was a worrying sign. We had already discovered, Bella and I, that Simon liked to talk of his romances, despite an almost constant stream of doting references to his children and their mother languishing at home. I did not then realise that for him the fame abroad was quite as pleasurable as the deed itself and this is a most dangerous characteristic in a married lover of married women. Adela went straight up to her room and I took Simon's proffered drink with a heavy heart. We sat in silence for a moment or two. At last he could curb his impatience no longer. 'Good evening?' he said.

I nodded in a half-hearted fashion. 'Quite. I thought the dinner was pretty filthy. Poor old Bob. He blenched visibly at the bill.' There was another silence. I suppose neither of us was clear about how to get on to the subject that was uppermost in both our minds. This time I tried the opener. 'You didn't come in.'

Simon shook his head. 'There was a bit of an awkwardness with that frightful brother-in-law when we got back. I thought I'd better just hop it.'

So that was it. No wonder Simon wanted to talk about it. Eric had made his presence known. The chances of his keeping his secret were statistically reduced to zero. Eric had made a scene. This, in my experience, generally happens when people want to make a scene. 'I heard about that,' I said.

Simon looked up. 'Oh? Who from? Not from Edith?'

I shook my head. 'From Charles's mother.'

I could see that this was a bit of a facer – as well it might be – but at the same time, while the flushed embarrassment of discovery was spreading over Simon's features, it brought in its wake, in the shy smile that he threw at me, a certain ominous delight in being the central figure in what I soon perceived he saw as a romantic drama. My heart sank even further at the realisation that with his actor's perverse pleasure in crisis, Simon would soon be all set to enjoy this chance of notoriety. 'Does Charles know?'

'Not when I left. Should he? Is there anything to know?'

Simon was not to be had so easily. He laughed gently and shrugged as he helped himself to another tot. I looked as paternal as I could. 'Don't start making a mess, Simon.' But still he only smiled and winked at me with that infuriating sexual confidence of the never-refused who think moral laws are designed for lesser mortals. My only recourse seemed to be some sort of appeal to his better nature. 'Edith is an old friend of mine.'

'I know.'

'And I don't want to see her made unhappy.'

'She's unhappy now.'

There was some truth in this, though much less than either he or Edith knew. 'She's not half as unhappy as she's going to be if you start making some silly little scandal for no better reason than that she's here and you're bored.' Again he smiled and shrugged. Of course I was on a hiding to nothing as few things could have given Simon more pleasure than to be begged to avert the arc-light of his fatal charm from some tender victim. Here was I, pleading with the Great Lord to have pity on a poor damsel. He was thrilled. I tried a new and faintly dishonourable tack. 'What about your wife?'

'What about her?'

'Won't she be upset?'

This, to my delight, did at last make him slightly uncomfortable – or at least irritated. 'Who's going to tell her? You won't.' This was obviously true as far as it went and for a moment I did wonder if I wasn't over-reacting when I heard a knock on the glass behind me. I turned and to my complete amazement I saw Edith, in an Hermès scarf loosely knotted on her chin, rapping at the window and begging, like Cathy Earnshaw, to be let in from the night. Simon, however, was no Heathcliff and it was I, not he, who jumped up to open the back door.

'What the hell are you doing here?' I said, but she pushed past me and sauntered over to the Aga to warm her hands.

'Don't you scold me as well. I've had enough for one night I can assure you.'

'Does Charles know?'

'Of course. Eric told him.'

'But does he know you're here? And why are you here, for God's sake? Don't make everything worse than it is.'

All this time Simon had neither moved nor spoken. Now, very deliberately he rose from his chair, put down his glass, walked over to Edith and slowly, for my benefit I assume, enfolded her in his arms and bent his head to kiss her with the slow, moist, hungry motion of a modern film star in close-up. He looked as if he were eating her tongue. For a moment I watched their two blond heads rocking against each other and behind them, like the ghosts in Richard III's tent, I saw Charles and his mother and the wretched Mrs Lavery whose dreams were being incinerated in a farmhouse kitchen in Sussex as I stood there. And behind them, the more distant figures of the Cumnors, and old Lady Tenby and her daughters, and all those others who would be enthralled and secretly (or not so secretly) delighted at the ruin that was being encompassed by these two silly people.

'Well?' said Adela, whom I had promised I would report to before turning in. She rolled over in bed, blinking herself into concentration.

'Hopeless,' I said.

'Wouldn't he listen?'

'He's loving it, I'm afraid. Anyway, I didn't say that much. I was just getting started when Edith turned up. She's down there now.'

Adela was quiet for a second. 'Oh,' she said. And then: 'So it is hopeless. Poor Charles.' And she rolled back into her pillow, pulling the covers up around her face.

Some time after this I proposed and was accepted. It was rather a tense period for me, I must confess, as I was inspected by an endless series of my intended's disapproving relations, most of whom were seriously unnerved by the thought of their beloved Adela relying on a stage career in future. 'Well, all I can say is *good luck* with that artistic temperament,' was the advice she received from a particularly unpleasant aunt. After a couple of months of this sort of thing, I was anxious to end the waiting. We decided to be married in April and, since it is a notoriously unpredictable month, to have a London ceremony. As Adela remarked, 'Country weddings can be such muddy affairs.' It was a 'Society Event', I suppose, though not quite on the scale of the Broughtons, but even so, anyone who has ever played a central part in a large wedding, let alone a large London wedding with all the paraphernalia it involves, will understand that I had very little time to worry about Edith and her *ménage* in the months that led up to it. I had asked the Uckfields and the Broughtons and, to my mother-in-law's delight, they had all four accepted. I was comforted by this, in the thick of the chaos of my nuptials, as I assumed it meant that the trouble had passed and the nonsense of an autumn night had been forgotten. Then, about two weeks before the wedding itself, I had a telephone call from Edith. 'Have you invited Simon?' she said.

I understood at once that she was anxious lest there might be an awkwardness and I was able to reassure her. 'No, I haven't. You're all right.' I laughed mildly, so that that hideous evening might be turned the sooner into a shared joke between us.

'Could you?' she said.

The smile left my face, the straw my clutch. 'No, I could not,' I said tersely.

'Why not?'

'You know very well why not.'

There was a pause at the other end of the line. 'Can I ask you a favour?' I didn't answer this as I dreaded to hear it. I was not spared. 'Could we possibly borrow your flat while you're away?'

'No.'

Edith's voice was cold and definite. 'No. Well, I'm sorry to have bothered you.'

'Edith, darling,' I said. This is the kind of thing that always happens just when one is entirely engrossed in some other large event. The night before crucial exams is invariably the moment that the parents of one's friends choose to die or go to prison. 'Of course you can't see Simon here. How could I possibly do that to Charles? Or to Simon's wretched wife for that matter? Don't be insane, darling, please. I beg you.'

But she was not to be won. With some perfunctory formula words she slid away and the line went dead.

I told Adela and she was not surprised. 'He thinks she can get him into things. That she can open doors. He's Johnny-on-the-make.'

'I don't know how interested he is in all that.'

'He's interested. He wants to be at the Head Table, that one. You'll see.'

'Well, I don't know how much poor old Edith can fix it for him.'

Adela smiled, a trifle coldly I thought. 'She can't. She'll be lucky to get a table in the St James's Club when all this is finished. Stupid fool.'

It was Adela who nudged me to look towards the door when, as we were standing to receive the line of our guests, the footman announced in ringing tones: 'The Marquess and Marchioness of Uckfield and the Earl Broughton,' rolling the words lovingly around his tongue like delicious sweets. The three of them entered.

'Where's Edith?' I said.

Charles shrugged faintly and we let it go. I was, in truth, rather touched that the Uckfields had made the effort to come. As a general rule, such people are long on friendship on their own terms but short on doing anything on yours. I don't actually think Lord Uckfield had any idea why he had been forced to dress up and sacrifice a perfectly good afternoon when he might have been watching racing on the box, but Lady Uckfield, I believe, liked me by this time and also, I suspect, wished to establish a beachhead on Edith's only pre-marriage friend that had made the transition into her new life. They were ushered on through into the reception and we turned back to the unending line of old nannies and relations from the shires.

It is not possible to speak to anyone properly at your own wedding – certainly not at a smart wedding where it is out of the question that the company should do anything as middle class or sensible as sit down to eat. The bride and groom are passed round, like one of those endless trays of nibbling things, for a few words here or there, justifying those overnight journeys down from Scotland or those flights from Paris and New York. Still, Charles did manage to seize me for a moment. 'Can we have lunch when you get back?' he said. I nodded and smiled but avoided discussing the matter since the beginning of one marriage seems a poor place to ruminate over the probable end of another. I must confess I was flattered that by this time Charles obviously thought of me as his friend as well as Edith's, flattered but also vindicated for I certainly was on Charles's side, if sides there must be. Of course, I knew well enough that I was not one of Charles's close pals, but I had the merit of being able to discuss his wife with some real experience of her, which most of his friends, since they had never met her before the engagement, could not.

Adela and I spent a delightful fortnight in Venice and when we got back to the flat we found, along with further piles of wedding presents from Peter Jones and the General Trading Company, a letter from Charles suggesting that I meet him at his club the following Thursday. I accepted. Charles's club was inevitably White's and I accordingly found myself outside its familiar Adamesque entrance at one o'clock on the appointed day.

Of the three smart clubs whose charming eighteenth-century facades dominate St James's, White's is, I would guess most people are agreed, the smartest. It boasts few sleek City *arrivistes* even among its younger members, perhaps because there is still enough of the *gratin* left to supply its needs, perhaps because the air is too thin for lesser mortals to breathe and after one or two visits they decide to try for something a little less rich. Having said that, I have always enjoyed White's. I would no more wish to be a member than I would apply to sponsor a polo team but one of the virtues of the English upper-class (and it is only fair to give some credit, alert as I am to their vices) is that when they are gathered together in familiar, congenial surroundings, they are a most relaxed and pleasant bunch. They've all known each other since they could first breathe and, when there is no one near to criticize them for it, they revel in this familiarity of the extended family. At their best, alone together and in a 'safe house', they are polite and unafraid, a charming combination.

I gave my name and asked for Charles at the mahogany booth in the entrance hall but 'his Lordship' had not yet arrived and I was invited to sit and wait for him. Not here the nodding through of strangers into the inner sanctums. But I had hardly had time to read the latest bulletins from the tickertape machine (alas now gone) before Charles clapped me on the shoulder. 'My dear fellow, forgive me. I got stuck.' We went on through the staircase hall to the little bar, where Charles ordered dry sherry for us both. He was looking a good deal more like his old self, I was happy to see, smartly dressed and neatly coiffed. His crinkly, blond hair in smooth Marcel waves, a tie of some educational or military significance at his throat. 'So, how are you? Busy, I hope.'

I wasn't frightfully, as it happens, but there was a chance of one or two things coming up so I hadn't yet reached the desperate stage that is the occupational hazard of Equity membership. I muttered away about Adela, the flat, Venice and so on but of course Charles was aching to get started. 'How are things with you?' I asked.

As if in answer he put down his drink. 'Let's go up and get a table,' he muttered, and we started up the staircase.

The dining room of the club is a grand, undisappointing chamber with a high gilded ceiling and long windows overlooking St James's. Against its damask-covered walls hang full-length portraits of erstwhile grandee members, the whole emanating that characteristic of aristocratic solidity that Charles correctly, if subconsciously, believed the mainstay both of his personality and his way of life. We gave our orders as we came in and found ourselves a table for two on the wall away from the windows.

'I think Edith's left me.' The statement was so bald that for a moment I suspected I'd misheard.

'What do you mean "you think"?' I didn't quite see how one could be mistaken about such things.

He cleared his throat. 'Well, perhaps I should say she thinks she's left me.' He raised his eyebrows. I suppose the only way that he felt he could have this conversation at all was by distancing the whole business. As if we were exchanging a piece of gossip about someone else. 'She telephoned this morning. She's rented a flat in Ebury Street. Apparently the idea is for them to set up there together.'

I think the phrase is 'the universe reeled'. My first response, rather unworthily, was that I couldn't believe Edith would be this stupid before the scandal had forced her hand. 'What did she say?'

'Just that they're in love. She's been very unhappy. Nobody's fault, blah, blah, blah ... You know. What you'd expect.'

At that moment my potted shrimps arrived, closely followed by Charles's avocado. I tried to use the silence to collect my thoughts but for the life of me I couldn't think of anything sensible to say. I chose badly. 'Who else knows?'

'You sound like my mother.'

At the mention of her name I yearned for Lady Uckfield to take the helm and steer everyone out of this ghastly mess. Not for her, be she never so young, a rented flat in Ebury Street shared with a married actor. 'Does your mother know?'

'She doesn't know all the details. Edith telephoned me a few days ago. When I sent round the note to you. I've been rather incommunicado since then. I don't see that there's much to be gained in facing the storm if the storm itself can be avoided.'

In my mind's eye I could see the articles in the very pages that had taken Edith up as Charles's intended and covered the wedding in such loving, glutinous detail barely two years before. I know, only too well, the high moral tone those raddled alcoholic journalists love to take when they choose to discuss the low lives of the *haut monde*. And Edith had made herself their creature, had willingly allowed herself to become a columnist's toy, something I knew would give them every licence to tear her in pieces now.

'Can it be avoided?' I asked.

'I don't know. That's where I need your help.'

Naturally my heart sank at the sound of these words. All of this was happening too close to me. I yearned to get back into the outer circle of this family's world. How little Americans know when they disparage acquaintanceship in favour of real, true friendship. It is in acquaintance-ship, bringing with it as it does delicious dinners, comfortable weekends, gossip shared in picturesque surroundings, but no real intimacy, no responsibility, that the greatest charm of social intercourse lies. I am an observer. It troubles me to be forced into the role of participant.

'You'd take her back then?'

Charles looked almost puzzled by the question. 'What do you mean? She's my wife.'

It is hard to explain quite why I found these words so moving but I did. It sounds odd to write it in our tawdry era but at that moment I was aware I was in the presence of a good man, a man whose word could be trusted, a man whose morality was more than fashion. What could Edith possibly have found in the embrace of her tinsel lover that was worth more than this solid, unquestioning commitment? He looked almost embarrassed by his noble declaration.

'I just want you to talk to her.'

'Well, I assumed you didn't want me to kidnap her.' I put down my glass. 'But what can I say? I think she's quite mad.' Charles smiled. 'But I don't imagine that my telling her that will make much odds if she doesn't listen to you or her mother.'

Poor Mrs Lavery! This news would bring hara-kiri in its wake.

'I know that but . . .' Charles paused. 'I mean, you know the world that this Simon chap operates in. I don't mean to be, well, rude, but is it the sort of world that Edith would like? Has she thought about all that?'

Now this was quite a complicated question, certainly more complicated than Charles was aware. Nobody knows who is going to like the stage world. Adela took to it like a duck to water and never had a moment's difficulty synthesising it with her other, more traditional, social group. She found she liked the feast-or-famine, crisis-ridden, siege mentality of the whole thing. To others, my mother-in-law for instance, the people of the stage seem simply awful, a sleazy crowd of oiks, all plastered in make-up, falling in and out of other people's beds, and getting drunk in restaurants. There is a good deal of truth in this picture, too. Charles was of the latter school. It quite amused him to know an actor socially but it was no accident that the only one he did know had grown up in fairly traditional circumstances. If he came to us for a drink it was fun for him to see people he recognised from various television series but he had no desire to befriend them. This was one of his main difficulties throughout the whole affair. He found it impossible to understand how Edith, having known his world from the inside, a world that if nothing else is elegant and rooted in charming settings, could have deliberately renounced it for an environment as alluring to him as Cardboard City.

Of course, the danger of the stage world, even for those initially drawn to its glitter, is that there is always a risk that one may grow out of it. It is the choice of high colour over more muted shades in terms of one's daily drama and for many there comes a time when the sobbing in the dressing room, the anti-director cabals, the midnight telephone calls of reassurance, simply become an adolescent bore. Some actors slake this sense of growing emptiness by the discovery of a 'cause' and try to put their need for daily trouble and strife to some use. Nothing is easier than to raise a crowd of furiously indignant actors who will happily protest at almost anything. But causes are a taste not shared by all, certainly not much by the pragmatic. Besides, there is a risk, not always avoided by some quite famous stage names, of attaching oneself to so many noble struggles against injustice that the weight of one's contribution finally becomes rather flimsy. All in all, the most effective antidote to the palling pleasures of stage gossip is simply to become very successful. Then the money and the status that fame brings are pleasant enough in themselves and lead to a rather broader life willy nilly. Which thought brought me back to the question of Edith's adjustment to her new existence. I attempted to answer honestly.

'I think it would depend on how well Simon does.'

Charles shook his head impatiently. 'I'm not saying she'd mind moving in with Jude Law but how successful is this fellow? I've never heard of him. Edith's used to living high on the hog, you know.'

I knew. 'It's difficult to say. He's started picking up some good parts. He might easily get the lead in a series and then he'd be up and running.'

'But he might not.'

This was certainly true. People in the outside world talk of actors being 'successful', which roughly means stars that they have heard of, or 'unsuccessful', which means the bottom 60 per cent who never really make a decent living. You do not need to be a mathematician to work out that there is a large group in between these two, doing quite well, earning reasonable amounts, known within the business, any one of whom can be picked for a new television show and have their fortunes transformed, as the papers like to put it, 'overnight'. This is the trap of the stage life. It is easy to give up something if you are failing, almost impossible to do so if you are almost succeeding. Simon Russell was definitely in this category.

I bought some time as our main course arrived. 'The trouble is, Charles, what argument could I employ that would make any difference? As I have just told you, I think she's quite crazy but she's a grown woman. To give up what you've offered her in order to go and live with an actor of moderate talent and even more moderate means is beyond comprehension to me. But she already knows all this and so I don't know what I could add to it that would be helpful.'

'I suppose she loves him. I suppose it's sex.' He bit the word out of the air and two men on the next table glanced briefly in our direction.

'It might be sex,' I said. 'But I'm not at all sure that she loves him.'

Charles frowned disapprovingly. 'I can't quite follow you there,' he said, and turned his attention to the bones of his lamb chops, which he began to scrape fiercely, apparently anxious to retrieve every last morsel of edible matter.

It was clear Charles was not prepared to admit that his wife could differentiate between these elements, that she might be able to indulge her body without involving her heart. I loved him for it.

We didn't say much more. All I knew was that by the time I was back in Piccadilly strolling down the Ritz arcade towards Green Park Underground station I had agreed to telephone Edith and attempt to 'reason' with her.

FIFTEEN

~

As it happened Edith sounded quite eager to meet, 'so long as you don't start to lecture me.' I shouldn't have been surprised. Freud has some special word for this 'compulsion to reveal' that undermines us all. She longed to discuss everything with someone who knew all the characters involved and given that she would expect some sympathy from her listener, I was probably in a category of one. We decided on a cheap and cheerful little restaurant in Milner Street, alas long gone now, a victim of the developers, that we had occasionally used during her estate agency days. When I arrived I found her already seated in a separate booth in the corner. She wore a scarf tied tightly and pulled forward over her brow. It was all quite exciting.

'I suppose Charles has put you up to this?' she said. I nodded since I supposed he had. 'How is he?'

'How do you think?'

'Poor darling.'

'Indeed.'

She wrinkled her nose crossly. 'Now you're not to make me feel like a beast.'

'But I think you are a beast.' We were interrupted, perhaps just in time, by the arrival of the waitress. Of course it was easy to see that Edith was enjoying the whole adventure tremendously. 'How's Simon?' I said.

'Oh, terribly well. He's having lunch with his new agent. Apparently she thinks he's the natural successor to Simon McCorkindale.'

'And that's good, is it?'

'Very good,' she said crisply with an admonishing glance. 'At any rate, it's much better than his last agent who always seemed to think he was lucky to get a job.'

'Is he working now?'

'He's about to do a play in Bromley. A revival of *Rebecca*. Apparently they're hoping it might come into the West End.'

'Edith, it'll be a cold day in hell when a revival of *Rebecca* comes into London from Bromley.'

'Well, that's what they've told him.'

'They say such things for two reasons. One is to tempt you into being in it, and two, so that you have something slightly less pathetic to tell your friends when they ask you what you're doing. This is my world, remember.'

She nodded slightly. 'I imagine that's why Charles has chosen you to talk to me. You're to take the gilt off the gingerbread and show me the dingy lowlife that lies beneath. He's given up trying to remind me of the glories of Broughton although I dare say I've got all that to look forward to when Googie gets in on the act.' She shivered in mock dread.

I felt rather slighted. 'I don't see why I shouldn't remind you of the glories of Broughton,' I said. She shrugged. Suddenly I was irritated by her air of insouciance. I knew, better than most, the effort that had gone into netting Charles and I was damned if I was going to witness Edith playing the part of a jaded aristocrat coming to the end of an arranged marriage. 'Come off it,' I said, driving back the waitress who was approaching with our first courses. 'You loved it. You loved every minute of it. All those cringing shop assistants and sucking-up hairdressers. All that "yes, milady, no, milady". You'll miss it, you know.'

She shook her head. 'No, I won't. You know better than anyone that I didn't grow up with it.'

'It's precisely because you didn't grow up with it that you'll miss it so severely.' I sighed. 'You're in for a terrific setting down, I'm afraid.'

'You don't sound afraid,' she said. 'You sound thrilled.' She took a sip of her Perrier as the plates were laid before us. 'And if Simon becomes a star? What then? Aren't more people interested in meeting a star than some boring old lord?'

It was then that I perceived that Edith, in the full flush of something akin to love, had made two tremendous miscalculations. Firstly, in weighing up the relative merits of aristocracy and stardom she had assumed that the benefits that would accrue to her, as partner, would be roughly equivalent. In fact, nothing could be further from the truth.

The wife of an earl is, after all, a genuine countess. When people meet her it is not solely because they see her as a route to her husband. Better still, if the family she has married into still possesses its estates, as the Broughtons did, then the landed peer offers his wife a mini-kingdom where she may reign as queen. On the other hand, the wife of a star is ... his wife. Nothing more. If she is cultivated by people it is usually only so that they may ingratiate themselves with her husband. He has no land where she may reign. His kingdom is the studio or the stage where she has no place and where in fact, on her rare visits, she is in the way, an unprofessional among working people. She is excluded from the shared jokes between her husband and his workmates, she holds no interest even for his agent except as a method of controlling him. At dinner her opinions only irritate the other professionals present. Finally and worst of all, while a divorced peeress faces the world and the search for a new husband with a dented but legal title, the divorced wife of a star has returned absolutely to square one. As many Hollywood wives have had to learn before now.

Edith's second miscalculation was simpler. The comparison was false. Charles was a lord. Simon was not a star. Nor was he, in my opinion, very likely to become one. I felt myself becoming caustic. 'What makes you think so well of Simon's prospects?'

'You're very acid this morning. Anyway,' she looked at me with a real expression of appeal and I felt myself softening a little, 'the simple fact is I love him. I don't know whether he's worth it, perhaps he isn't, but I do. And there we are. You wouldn't want me to deny the first genuine feeling I've ever had, would you?'

Part of me wanted to scream yes into her stupid ear but I could see that was not what the moment called for. Poor Edith. She was probably right when she said this passion for Simon was the first real emotion she had ever felt. That was precisely why she knew so little of what she was going through. She never guessed that after a year, however lovely the sex might be, it would no longer obscure from her the life they were leading together. Besides, I knew the strength of the ambition that lurked below Edith's placid surface. Modern psychology constantly harps on the dangers of suppressing one's true sexual nature. It seems to me that it is quite as dangerous to give one's sexual nature free rein and suppress one's worldly aims. Edith was, *au fond*, the ambitious child of an ambitious mother. Quite unconsciously, she had begun to defend her defection by assuming Simon's eventual stardom and wealth. In her mind's eye she already saw herself at a premiere in white fox (or whatever the glamour equivalent is in these ecological days), blowing a kiss to the waiting crowds and sweeping into a stretch limo with a motorcycle escort.

'Darling Edith,' I tried a softer tone, 'I'm not here to lecture you on your morals. I just want to be sure you understand that the likelihood of Simon being able to give you anything approximate to the life you have tasted since your marriage is more or less nil.'

'Well, hurrah for that,' said Edith.

We were done. For the rest of lunch we gossiped about various topics. Moving into the stage world she had of course crossed paths with a few people I knew so we had a new field for our malice. As we were leaving she asked after Adela. I said she was well. 'And madly disapproving, I suppose?'

'Well, she'd hardly be madly approving. Who is?'

'She should have married Charles. She'd have stuck to him through thick and thin.'

'Am I supposed to think badly of her for that?'

She smiled and ruffled my hair. 'You've earned your living in chaos and married into the system. I've been imprisoned in the system. Can you blame me if I yearn for a bit of chaos?'

We parted amicably enough. I telephoned Charles who was grateful and sounded more resigned, I thought. At any rate about a week later it hit the papers so the chance of sorting everything quietly was gone. Adela laid Nigel Dempster's column before my breakfast eyes and I studied the laughing, bosomy picture of Edith that had been selected. There was a more sombre one of Charles and a perfectly terrible 'cad' shot of Simon, which was presumably a still from some television show. It was clear from the illustrations and the headline – 'the Countess and the Showboy' that Dempster had already chosen his side. In fairness to him, both pragmatism and decency seemed (for once) to favour the same team and I couldn't see Edith picking up many supporters.

The story itself was a moderately accurate account of the meeting at Broughton with a dignified quote from Simon's wife that did her credit.

'Really!' Adela was always curiously unforgiving about this sort of mess. 'Stupid fools!'

I don't know why she was so offended when people appeared to let their hearts rule their heads. After all, she had chosen to marry me, which her mother, for one, had thought a choice reckless to the point of lunacy.

'Why are you so cross?' I said. 'I think it's all jolly sad.'

'Sad for Charles and for that wretched woman with her children. Not sad for them. They're just wreckers.'

Once Dempster had opened the floodgates, Edith was predictably savaged by those very journalists who had taken such pains to ingratiate themselves with her as a bride only months earlier. The timing didn't help. It was during the period of disenchantment with John Major's government, when New Labour was performing the Dance of the Seven Veils before an increasingly bewitched electorate, and this tale of high corruption suited the public mood exactly. So there were critical columns from Lynda Lee-Potter on the right and snide disparagement from *Private Eye* on the left. Edith the self-made success story had been replaced by Edith the Social Climber to end all, her greedy, grasping ways apparently a reflection of the heartless society Mrs Thatcher had created. Like the Hamilton scandal or the Spencer divorce, it was soon clear that the actual events and personalities had ceased to have much significance and instead it was simply what the papers decided they stood for that counted. Predictably, it was a nightmare for the Uckfields, who were completely of that school where a respectable woman's name only appears in print three times: hatch, match and despatch – that is to say, when she is born, when she marries and when she dies. Finding their daughter-in-law criticised in column headlines was like being stripped naked and whipped in a public square and if it was ghastly for them it was really horrible for Charles. Slightly illogically, since the press was already limbering up for the Blairocracy that was then in training, they decided that Charles, despite being a worthless aristocrat, was the innocent party (probably because there was no other way of telling the story) but even so, to see his wife's adultery gloated over in newsprint and magazines was a kind of martyrdom for him. The more they telephoned Broughton, urging him to tell 'his side', the more invaded and violated Charles felt. The truth was his horror of scandal was not an affectation but a deeply-held belief and here he was in the middle of one. He was being punished and he hadn't done anything wrong. This at least was Charles's view of the whole hideous episode and I do not think it was unjust.

After this circus had been played out for some weeks, it transpired that I had accepted an invitation for both of us to a supper party at the home of an actress I knew who had recently played Simon's mother in a television thriller. I thought there was every likelihood that the lovers might be there.

Adela was very cool when I told her. 'Well, I'm not going to flounce out of the room or cut her dead if that's what you're worried about.'

'I'm not worried. I'm just telling you they might have been invited. I think it's desirable to avoid publicly taking sides.'

'You need have no fear on that score,' she said witheringly. 'However,' she added, giving an unusually searching look in the glass and picking up her lipstick in real earnest, 'I'm not going to kiss her and wish her every happiness either.'

As it happened, I was right and Edith and Simon were on the guest list for that evening. Edith told me later she hadn't really wanted to go as they had been out every night since the scandal broke but Simon was insistent. He suffered from that common illusion among disappointed actors that it is good to be 'seen' at things. The truth is that it is good to be employed. Whether one is seen at parties is immaterial. However, he had acquired a newsworthy mistress and he probably wanted to get some mileage out of her. If I'm honest and at this distance, I suspect Simon was sorry it had not all been managed without her leaving Charles. That said, since the breach had happened, he would have wanted to profit from the publicity.

Simon Russell was one of those actors whose initial progress had seemed to point inexorably toward a stardom that, somehow, the years had never quite delivered. In the early days he had been given the lead in a series opposite a popular female star but the show had failed. Then he had landed a good part in a Hollywood sequel, which had died at the box office. And gradually the spotlight had shifted and slid away to those newer, younger, blonder men who seemed to arrive in such limitless supply. He was good – or good enough – and, as I have said, wonderful looking, especially when well photographed, and it could all still have happened for him but, by the point of our story, there was no time to lose. And now, most unexpectedly, his private life had put him into print. Edith had made him a topic.

As for his wife and children, I think it would be wrong to say he didn't worry about them. He did. As much as he was able. She, Deirdre, had done her best for him and he really loved the kids, but I suppose it had all become a bit dreary over the last few years and so terribly the same. Besides, it was obvious when you saw them together (which we did a couple of times during the early days of the filming at Broughton) that Deirdre had ceased to think of him as a romantic figure and had begun to treat him more and more as a kind of overgrown, recalcitrant boy. He wanted worship and what he got was someone telling him to eat his greens. Of course, I wasn't sure how much unmixed adoration he would be able to count on from Edith. Or for how long.

*　　*　　*

'Darling, please . . . we *must* go . . .' It was quite unconscious but Simon had fallen into the habit of dealing with Edith in a wheedling tone, a cross between a lounge lizard and a travelling salesman. 'I hate to be naff but you have to get used to the idea that I earn my living. I'm not Charles swanning around giving orders at the Home Farm. I have to be out there. I have to remind people that I exist.'

She sat before the little dressing table in their dreary bedroom, frowning with concentration as she studied her reflection. It did seem rather naff really. Edith was hating her black celebrity. Every time some 'friend' rang her with the news that yet another journalist had taken a swipe at her ('I thought I ought to tell you, darling, before you read it unawares,' the voice would gloat), her heart would sink anew. She wanted fame in a way but fame that brought status and conferred glamour, not this awful washing of dirty linen. She even caught herself feeling sorry for her parents-in-law when she thought of the papers that were probably being edited by Charles or the servants before the Uckfields could set eyes on them. Poor Charles . . . how was he coping with it all, poor dear? And these frightful parties that Simon kept wanting to take her to. Could it be so necessary to keep chatting up these weird representatives from another planet? She had been too long a Broughton to be able to throw off (easily anyway) the notion that Simon's crowd was a sort of joke – useful to enliven a party but not quite right for every day.

'Why?' she said.

He watched her painting her face with care and artistry. He knew what she was thinking but he didn't much care. If she wanted to go back among her old world rather than spend all their time in his, well, that was fine so far as he was concerned. In fact, he was becoming the teeniest bit impatient to get started on some of her gang. She had introduced him to a few Fulham Sloanes, but that wasn't what he had in mind as her contribution at all. Where she dreamed of shepherding him past the Press into his trailer on the Universal lot, he saw himself in tweeds, a gun on his arm, a welcome guest at other houses in the Broughton mould where he would flirt with other great ladies and be taken up by other great families. All of this his alliance with Edith would bring about. He did not grasp, perhaps because she did not yet either, that the great world was preparing to shut its doors on little Edith. From now on she would be condemned to the company of a few divorced wives of younger sons, eking out their alimony selling ugly jewellery or writing gossip columns for unread giveaway magazines.

She put down her mascara. 'Who is this woman tonight, anyway?'

'Fiona Grey.'

'Never heard of her. Have I met her?'

'No, I don't think so but you do know her. She was the girl in the film about the confidence trickster. When he fell off the train. On television last week. Michael Redgrave was the policeman.'

'Never heard of him, either.' Simon winced. 'She must be a thousand.'

'She's about seventy.' Actually Simon was very flattered to have been invited by Miss Grey. For this was the other side of his schizophrenic ambition. While part of him wanted Edith to get him into the world of the 'nobs', the rest of him, in almost direct contradiction, longed to be taken seriously as an actor, by the kind of actors that other actors take seriously, and just such a one was Fiona Grey. She had played Juliet opposite Gielgud in her youth and Lady Teazle opposite Olivier. Now, when she appeared on television it was usually some sort of an event – a series directed by Peter Hall or written by Melvyn Bragg – and she was invariably mentioned lovingly in English stars' autobiographies.

Theatre folk are much given to making claims for the classlessness of their world but the truth is that there is a rigidly structured class system within the business. It is only classless in the sense that this system is based on different values to that of the outside world. Birth may mean nothing but success is all. And not just success but the right kind of success. Simon Russell was acutely aware that, even when he had tasted his little helping of fame, he had never come close to doing work that was 'rated' by his fellow members of Equity and, secretly, it pained him.

When actors tell television interviewers that they don't mind what the critics say so long as the public enjoys what they do they are lying. Few actors care anything for the public's opinion when set against the verdict of the critics and their peers. To be valued and given status behind the proscenium arch is their goal. If it can be accompanied by public adulation, fame and money – so much the better. At the core of the business is a clique whose pre-eminence in 'correct' work is unassailable, and Simon had ever longed to be included in it. The stars and directors, the writers and designers who count among this number patronise all but the most tumultuous public stardom. Their names may be linked to many causes, their interview manner and (certainly) their clothes may seem like a rejection of distinction, but the fact remains they form an elite whose exclusivity rivals that of the *noblesse d'épée* at the court of Versailles. Simon ached to be a member of this golden group who always get good reviews from *Time Out* and are never off the list at BAFTA.

His dreams were not realistic. On this particular evening, for example, he'd only been invited because he was in the papers. Despite their high-sounding principles, these players share one characteristic with their Hollywood brethren: they love to be with famous people. If they lunch with Labour politicians, they like them to be front bench Labour politicians, if they march in a cause, they like to march next to Ian McKellen or Anita Roddick, not some obscure enthusiast from Harlow. But if Miss Grey had taken Simon up because he was In The News, she was incurious about his talent.

*   *   *

The party was in a house in Hampstead, which seemed to Edith to have taken about a year to get to and which, from the street anyway, did not appear to be worth the effort. Inside, every trace of the labourer, whose domestic arrangements it was designed to house in the 1890s, had been swept away in a sea of gleaming wooden floors and concealed lighting. There were knots of earnest discussion in the large living room, which opened off the hall, but the loudest noise was, inevitably, coming from the kitchen downstairs. Adela and I were standing by the stove, surrounded by bowls of pulses and pasta interlarded with strange creatures from the deep, when they came in. I felt Adela nudge me with her elbow as she went on talking animatedly to the unemployed designer we had got stuck with.

Our hostess advanced to Simon and kissed him, staring at Edith throughout. 'Now first you must have a drink and then you must let me introduce you. Do you know David Samson?' She indicated a famous comedy star who had planted himself at her elbow almost as soon as the couple had appeared. Edith smiled and took his hand only to find that hers had been raised to his hoary lips.

'Lady Broughton.' His fruity and familiar tones rolled the name round his tongue, savouring its flavour. He spoke loudly enough for bystanders to turn in curiosity and connect Simon and Edith with the stories they had read or vaguely heard of. There was a faint buzz of awareness. Edith received Samson's adulation coldly, I thought, with a murmured, 'Edith. Please.' Samson was not to be put off. He drew her arm through his and prepared to wheel her about the room. He turned to an inquisitive group nearby, booming out, 'Do you know the Countess of Broughton?'

Edith, needless to say, was in hell.

I would have rescued her earlier but Adela restrained me. I wonder if she didn't take a malicious pleasure in seeing Edith exhibited like a captive in a Roman Triumph. Adela had never endangered her footing in the old camp when she ventured into this new one and I suppose it was hard for her not to feel a tremor of victory. Simon came up to us, beaming. There are some who shudder at the thought of being an 'item' in the news. There are, conversely, others who cannot live without it. Simon was on the latter team. As the half-curious eyes followed him about the room, he was in his element. We broke away, leaving Adela to work over a rather grim-faced casting director on my behalf.

'How are you getting on?' I asked.

'Fine,' said Simon. 'Great.'

'So what happens next?'

'What do you mean?'

'Well, divorce, marriage, statements to the press?'

Simon raised his hands and eyebrows. 'Woah!' he cried with a spangled laugh. 'You sound like my mother.' It is easy to forget that even people like Simon have mothers. Some decent widow of a civil servant sitting in a flat in Leatherhead wondering what on earth was going on. He made me rather cross.

'You do know that you've got in very deep here? You do see that a lot of people are very upset about all this?'

He stroked my cheek. 'Oh well,' he said.

Of course, Adela enjoyed the whole evening hugely. Quite as much as Edith detested it, paraded round the rooms, as she was, like a sacred cow. Adela watched her struggling for small talk with these people who were so remarkably like ordinary people – the very people, in fact, that Edith had spent her twenties trying to escape from forever. The irony of all this was that, for all her hatred of the world of the Name Exchange, Edith had grown used to the comforting snugness of its limited membership. Suddenly she was back in open country where nobody seemed to know anyone she'd ever met. She felt something akin to panic. What did one talk about to people with whom one had no interest and no acquaintance in common? After her time in Broughtonland, she had forgotten.

'Well, I hope she's enjoying herself.' Adela snuggled down into her coat as we started the long trek south.

'Do you?'

'Well, really! What has she done? And to leave without producing a child! So when the door shuts it's shut for ever. What a fool!'

I was still capable of being shocked by my wife's intense worldliness that lived so happily alongside her great, and I knew quite genuine, kindness.

'Isn't it better that there aren't any children?'

'Better for whom? Better for Charles and Googie. Not for her. To produce the heir is the only effective second act for a first wife. Think of Consuelo Vanderbilt's triumph when she returned to hated Blenheim as the mother of the new duke. There'll be none of that for little Edith.' She sighed wearily. 'As for him!'

'I thought you rather liked him.'

'He's pleasant enough in his silly, blond way but hardly the craft to be entrusted with the cargo of life's happiness. What is she thinking of?'

*   *   *

Similar thoughts were flickering somewhere at the back of Edith's brain at just that moment as they too sped back towards what she regarded as

Civilisation. She was conscious of a kind of dull disappointment deep in her vitals. She had just been to another 'show business party' and as the phrase echoed through her brain she remembered the image it used to conjure up: vivid actresses, over made-up beauties in sequinned *haute couture*, intense, Jewish writers lecturing groups in the corners of the room, singers helping out a drunken pianist and, all the time, glassy laughter slashing the air ... In fact, when she thought about it, she realised that the whole scene had been taken, more or less unchewed, from *All About Eve*. It seemed to have so little to do with this pack of suburbanites, eating health food and talking about their holidays in Greece.

Nor did she care for their fascination with her as the envoy of a different, and obviously disapproved of, world. She was not indifferent to the glamour of the stage but she had started to see that the quality of glamour as such was no longer rated by the fashionable thespians themselves. To make matters worse, she felt that she had entered this strange arena not as a star (which privately she had counted on) but as a freak.

'What a ghastly bunch! Who were those people?'

Simon never answered these questions, which were in truth more or less rhetorical. They both knew that what Edith was pointing out was that she found theatre folk 'common', though she would never quite say it. Simon, partly because he was not interested in whether they were common or not because it wasn't relevant, and partly because he suspected (deep in his heart) that by her standards he was pretty common himself, never rose to this one. 'I had a good time,' he said.

'You didn't have some frightful man with a voice like a bowl of fruit salad slobbering over your hand all evening. Are all your parties going to be like that?'

'Are all your parties going to consist of six Sloane Rangers and someone who lost money in Lloyd's? Because, if so, I'll take the fruit salad. Any day of the week.'

They drove home in silence.

SIXTEEN

~

It happened that I was in the Fulham Road late one afternoon running various errands and Adela had asked me to look in on Colefax and Fowler to collect some braid she had ordered a few weeks before. Normally I would have refused the commission since at that time (unlike today) all the assistants there seemed to have taken a degree in Higher Rudeness, but she insisted and in fact I was dealt with by a pleasant enough woman. Even though, as Adela had expected, the order had still not arrived, she did seem quite sorry about it.

At any rate, I was just receiving my token apology together with the standard assurances that it would be in next week when I glanced back towards the street and there, leafing idly through the racks of samples, was Edith's mother. I had last seen Mrs Lavery almost exactly two years before, around the time of the festivities of the wedding. It moved me now to think of that victorious figure, trembling with satisfied ambition in the Red Saloon at Broughton, as I looked at this lost and broken soul. She stared glassily at the huge flapping areas of pattern as they waved past her face but she saw nothing. Nothing, that is, except the ruin of all her dreams, which clearly played endlessly like a cursed tableau in her brain.

'Hello, Mrs Lavery,' I said.

She turned to me, gathered the knowledge of who I was from some distant mental shelf and nodded a greeting. 'Hello,' she answered in a hollow, frigid tone.

I learned later that she blamed me for introducing Simon to the Broughton family. With some justice, I suppose. It is customary nowadays for people to shrug off guilt in this sort of thing by saying 'it would have happened anyway' but I am not at all convinced by this argument. Most of our lives are not the fulfilling of some inexorable design laid down at birth but rather the sum total of a series of random events. If Edith had never met Simon – or not met him until after she'd had a child – I think it quite unlikely that the whole thing would have happened. However, she had met him. And it did happen. And, when all is said and done, I had introduced them.

'Have you seen anything of Edith lately?' I said. The sense of her daughter's Banquo-like presence in the room, of her daughter's story, was making us both uncomfortable. It seemed easier to normalise the situation by talking about it.

'Not very much, no.' She shook her head. 'But she . . .' she hesitated, '*they* are coming to dinner tonight. I dare say I shall catch up then.'

I nodded. 'Well, give her my love.'

But Mrs Lavery was not quite prepared to let me go. 'You know him, I gather. This new fellow.'

'Simon? Yes, I know him. Not very well but we were in a film together. Down at Broughton. That's how they met.'

'Yes.' She stared at the floor for a moment. 'And is he nice?'

I was rather touched at this. Mrs Lavery was trying to force herself to be a Good Mother and to concentrate on the timeless values in assessing her daughter's new beau when we both knew that if Simon had been the nicest man in Europe he could never have repaid what had been lost with Charles. 'Very nice,' I said. 'In his way.'

'I don't suppose you've seen much of Charles? Since all the – business happened?'

'I have, in fact. I had lunch with him the other day.'

Mrs Lavery was surprised. I suppose in her romantic imaginings of her son-in-law's world she had erected much fiercer divisions than in fact exist. Also my admission gave the impression that I might not have encouraged Edith in her folly. She softened noticeably. By this time she had convinced herself, of course, that her affection for Charles was genuine and based entirely on his qualities as a man. It wasn't but I don't know that it was any the less felt for that. 'How is he? I'd love to see him but . . .' She trailed off miserably.

'Oh, you know. I'm sure he'd love to see you,' I lied. 'He's still pretty cast down.'

'Well, he would be.' She sighed wearily and without hope. 'I'd better get going. They're coming at eight and I haven't done a thing.'

And she left the shop, her shoulders stooping as she pulled at the heavy door. When I had last seen her she had resembled a character from some frothy Coward comedy. Now she looked like Mother Courage.

*　　*　　*

Simon was oddly nervous as they turned right off the King's Road down the Vale towards Elm Park Gardens. He'd been fiddling with his tie every time they stopped at a light and as they drew closer, he started picking at his nails. Edith could feel herself tensing with irritation. She couldn't decide if he was apprehensive because he thought her parents were much grander than they in fact were – or if he was nervous of his role as a Wrecker of Marital Bliss. Either way she just wished he'd relax, as the evening promised to be quite sticky enough as it was.

'What is the matter with you?'

Simon just smiled and shook his head. He himself was not exactly clear as to why he had such butterflies although it was true he did think that the Laverys were smarter than they were. He had a very unclear idea of the nuances of London Society and, since he had no knowledge of the Inner Circle whatever, he was unaware of the extent to which Edith had been an outsider at the time of her marriage. Since he still thought of his new mistress as fearfully smart he imagined her background was correspondingly impressive. But that was not actually the source of his unease on this particular evening. Probably it was the more ordinary complaint that this formalisation of their relationship, this presentation to the parents, seemed to set some sort of seal of finality on what had originally been nothing more than a flirtation. He had not really, even now, faced that he was heading into the realms of 'divorce' and 'division of property' and 'maintenance' and 'custody' and all sorts of other depressing words and phrases and yet that is what suddenly seemed to loom ahead. He supposed that in some perhaps roundabout way Mr Lavery was going to ask him about his 'intentions' and it struck him that he didn't really have any intentions – not absolutely fixed ones anyway. But then he glanced across at Edith and she did look very lovely when he thought about it and he was aware of how much prettier her profile was than Deirdre's, who had always looked just a little gormless from sideways on and he thought that after all he could do worse. And thus mollified and heartened he got out of the car.

Mrs Lavery had confided in her husband about her meeting in

Colefax. The words of the conversation had gone round and round her head until she had tried to spin them into a skein of hope. Even as she cooked for her daughter's lover she shouted through to the drawing room, 'What do you think he meant by "cast down" exactly?'

Kenneth Lavery was almost as unhappy as his wife over the turn events had taken but for more honourable motives. He hated to see his beloved 'Princess' involved in a public scandal. He hated to witness his wife's despair. And he was not insensible to the fact that his daughter had thrown away a position of power from which she might have achieved fine things and run instead to a place barely within decent society. He had been proud of his daughter as a Great Lady and he was saddened by her fall. Having said that, he was a good deal more philosophical about the nature of Edith's folly than his wife. Unlike her he had never deluded himself that Edith's marriage was going to make all that much of a difference in his own life.

'I think he meant what he said. Charles is cast down. Of course he's cast down. His wife has just gone off with another man. What would you expect him to be?'

Stella Lavery stuck her head round the door. 'I just meant that it sounds as if Charles still hasn't got used to the idea. I wondered if there was any point in perhaps getting in touch with him...?' Her voice trailed away, as her husband started to shake his head slowly but firmly from side to side.

'My dear, it is not Charles who decided to end the marriage. It doesn't matter what he thinks. He is not to blame for this. Nor do I think it fair to start trying to stir him up. Maybe he is getting over her, maybe he isn't. Either way it will not help him to have his hopes revived by you. He is a nice man and our daughter has behaved badly to him. It is fitting for us to keep out of his way.' So saying he returned to the television.

His wife did not resent this treatment by her husband because in her heart she agreed with it. Try as she might to affect some sort of modern tolerance the fact remained that she was deeply, deeply ashamed of Edith's behaviour. As long as she could remember she had imagined herself perfectly suited for a Great Role in the public life of England. She would daydream as she watched those ladies-in-waiting hovering behind the Queen in Parliament, all dressed in their fifties Hartnell frocks, and she had thought how well she, Stella Lavery, would have acquitted herself as Duchess of Grafton or Countess of Airlie if fate had only called her. She would have served well, she knew, even if, like the little mermaid, every step had been taken on knives. And all this fantasy had been passed on to her daughter who had, miraculously, made it come true. But now, instead of hearing that Edith had been asked to chair the Red Cross or to join the household of one of the princesses, the telephone had rung to tell her that it was all over. That her dream was in ruins. And at the bottom of this pit of slime into which she had been hurled was the bitter gall of knowing that all over London people were tut-tutting and saying that after all Charles had married beneath him, that Edith was a little nobody who just couldn't 'handle it' and that he should have stuck to his own kind.

The doorbell went but before they could get to it Edith had let herself in and was calling to them through the flat. As the lovers entered the drawing room, she hurried to kiss her father. He gave her an affectionate squeeze and she knew he at least would be no trouble as she led him over to be introduced to Simon. One glance at the frozen statue of her mother framed in the doorway, however, told her all she needed to know about the evening to come.

Mrs Lavery advanced stiffly and extended a hand. But she could not smile and in a way it was almost a relief that, as soon as Kenneth had left them to fetch some drinks, she dispensed with Simon's inept attempts at small talk and launched straight into the heart of the matter. 'You will understand that this is all very difficult for us, Mr Russell.' She deliberately ignored his attempts to make her call him Simon and in this there was a certain similarity to the way her idol, Lady Uckfield, would have managed the meeting. The latter would have been much cosier, of course. 'We are both very fond of our son-in-law. So you will forgive us if we don't fall on your neck.'

Simon smiled, crinkling up his eyes in a way that was usually effective. 'Neck-falling is quite optional, I assure you,' he muttered gaily.

Mrs Lavery did not return his smile. It wasn't that she was immune to physical attraction. She could see well enough that Simon was one of the handsomest men she had ever encountered but in her eyes his beauty was the explanation of her daughter's ruin. Nothing less. At that moment she could cheerfully have taken a knife and cut the features from his face if it would have turned Edith back from her chosen course. 'My daughter was,' she paused, '*is* married to a fine man. Obviously you've thought about what you're doing but it's hard for us to see her break her vows without a pang.'

'It wouldn't have cost you much of a pang if I was leaving Simon for Charles,' said Edith.

Now this was completely true. So true in fact that it made Mr Lavery smile momentarily as he came back in with a tray of glasses, but Edith was forgetting that Mrs Lavery had cast herself in the part of Hecuba, the Noble Widow. In Stella's shattered mind she and Googie Uckfield were two high-born victims in a cosmic disaster (she talked *of* Lady Uckfield as Googie but not yet *to* her. Now, she thought tearfully, she would never have the chance). There was no room for irony in her suffering. She looked at her daughter with brimming eyes.

'How little you know me,' she said, and retreated majestically into the kitchen. Edith, her father and Simon stared at each other.

'Well, I suppose we all knew it was going to be a rough night,' said Mr Lavery, tucking into his whisky.

Later, sitting round the oval reproduction table in the flat's modest dining room, the four of them did contrive some quasi-normal conversation. Mr Lavery questioned Simon about acting and Simon questioned Mr Lavery about business and Mrs Lavery fetched the food and removed the plates and made elaborately courteous remarks all evening. She had that uniquely English talent of demonstrating, through her scrupulously polite manner, just how awful she thought the company. She could leave a roomful crushed and rejected and yet congratulate herself on behaving perfectly. It is of course of all forms of rudeness the most offensive as it leaves no room for rebuttal. Even at the height of hostility the Moral High Ground is never abandoned.

Edith watched the three familiar faces and tried to question herself as to what was really taking place. Was this the cementing of a new alliance that would shape her future life? Would these three people be her companions through twenty Christmases to come? Would Simon and her mother build their bridges and talk about the children and come to share private jokes? Handsome as Simon was and strong as her desire for him remained, she was struck this evening by the dreariness of them all.

She had lived the last two years in the front rank of English life and on reflection she was surprised to discover how normal it had become for her to do so – until, that is, she had removed herself from it. While she had been at Broughton she had been oppressed by the lack of event, by the emptiness of her daily round. Now that she had left it, however, hardly a day passed when at least one of her acquaintance from her life with Charles was not in the newspaper. And when she thought about it, having at the time complained ceaselessly that they never did anything, she remembered dinner after dinner where she had sat opposite some faintly famous face from the Cabinet or the opera or simply the gossip columns. Bored to sobs as she was by Googie and Tigger, she had become used to hearing political and Royal chat days or even weeks before it hit the headlines. She was accustomed to knowing the details of the private lives of the great before they became common knowledge – if indeed they ever did. She and Charles had not spent a great deal of time staying away but now her memory reminded her of three or four shooting parties during the winter and a couple of house parties in the summer. She knew Blenheim by this time and Houghton and Arundel and Scone. She had lost the sense of these places' historicity. They had become the homes of her circle. In this she was almost being honest – as honest certainly as those born to the class to which she had so briefly belonged. Edith had learned well all the tricks of aristocratic irreverence. She would stride like the best of them into a dazzling great hall by Vanbrugh, lined with full length van Dycks, and curse the M25 as she threw her handbag into a Hepplewhite chair. By this stage, she understood how to make that statement of solidarity. 'This wonderful room is ordinary to me,' their actions say, 'because it is my natural habitat. I belong here even if you do not.'

Now, it seemed to her, looking at Kenneth and Stella with their framed flower prints from Peter Jones, their pseudo-Regency furniture, their Jane Churchill print curtains, that her membership of that club where she could curl up in an armchair in the long library at Wilton and leaf through Vogue, hugging a vodka and tonic, had been revoked without reference to her. In a rare moment of clarity she understood that in choosing this actor, far from making a wild bohemian statement, she had in fact returned to her own country. That Simon was far more of a piece with Stella and her faraway baronet cousin or Kenneth and his business friends than Charles had ever been. This world, where, as a general rule, one laughed and cried alongside the obscure – this was her real world. The world in which she had grown up and where she would now again live. Charles and Broughton and the Name Exchange only touched her people tangentially. They were, whatever her mother might like to think, an entirely different tribe.

'Phew!' said Simon, as they pulled away from the curb and headed back towards the King's Road. Edith nodded. They had survived. That was the main thing. She had taken the first step in explaining to her mother that her dream-life was over. Simon winked at her. 'We're alive,' he said. For a moment they rode on in silence. 'Do you want to go straight home?'

'As opposed to?'

'Well, we could go on somewhere.'

'Where?'

Simon made a slight pout. 'What about Annabel's?'

Edith was rather surprised. 'Are you a member?'

He shook his head, a little petulantly, she thought. 'No, of course I'm not. But you can get us in.'

Edith wasn't at all sure that she could get them in. Charles was the member, after all, and although they had been together fairly frequently and they certainly knew her at the club she wasn't clear as to where that left her. Nor was she convinced that it was a good idea. There were bound to be people there from Charles's set. 'I don't know,' she said.

'Come on. Charles is in Sussex and you can't run away from being seen all the time. We've got our life, too, I suppose.'

This time, unlike her excursions with Charles, they parked in the square and walked to the entrance steps. Simon had only been once before and was grinning like a madman as they descended. Edith was less certain of herself and the moment they had entered the corridor hall she knew she had been right. This was a Mistake. The club servant in charge greeted her affably enough. 'Lady Broughton,' he paused to take in Simon, 'are you meeting someone? Can I tell them you're here?'

Edith felt herself blushing. 'Well, we're not actually. I just wondered if we could come in for a moment.'

Again the answer was scrupulously polite. 'I didn't know you were a member, milady.'

'Well, I'm not. I mean, Charles – Lord Broughton – is and I just thought . . .' She tailed off in the face of the regretful smile on the face of the attendant.

'I'm very sorry, milady . . .'

If fate had been kind that would have been it but at that precise moment the door pushed open and with a sinking heart Edith heard the shrill tones of Jane Cumnor. Turning, she smiled straight into the huge, sweating face of Henry as he lumbered in, puffing with the effort of clambering down the basement steps. For a fraction of a second Jane was silent as she took in Edith and, of course, Simon. Then her smile returned.

'Edith! How lovely!' She kissed her coldly on both cheeks. 'Aren't you going to introduce us?'

'Simon Russell. Lord and Lady Cumnor.' She didn't really know why she hadn't used their Christian names. Could it be that she felt the need to impress Simon? After the evening they had just spent?

Jane gave her a slightly old-fashioned look. 'Are you coming in?'

For a moment Edith was going to say that they were in fact leaving when Simon spoke. 'They won't let us. Apparently you have to be a full member.' He didn't really understand the enormity of his betrayal of Edith in this. He simply wanted to get inside the club and so far as he could see, here were two people who could manage it for them.

But Henry was not to be caught. Sensing what was coming he nodded briskly. 'Edith,' he said, and strode on past her down the corridor towards the bar.

Jane smiled wanly. 'What a bore for you,' she murmured. 'I'm not a member either. I, um, I suppose I could go after Henry if you want ...' She tailed away to demonstrate how very much she did not wish to carry out her own suggestion and Edith let her go.

'No, no,' she said. 'It couldn't matter less. We're late anyway. I don't know why we looked in.' She kissed Jane perfunctorily with Simon twinkling away by her side, still hoping to be taken in and still missing what was going on. And then they were alone again. The attendant, ever impeccably polite, was anxious to bring about a satisfactory conclusion. 'I am sorry, Lady Broughton ...'

Edith nodded. 'We're just off,' she said.

They were outside the door and at the bottom of the steps when a voice hailed them from above. 'Edith?' They looked up and there was the lanky figure of Tommy Wainwright descending towards them. 'Fancy meeting you.' He smiled affably enough and shook Simon's hand. His wife, Arabella, a cooler customer entirely than her husband, was silent. 'Are you going already?' said Tommy.

'Yes,' said Edith. But before she could stop him Simon was having another shot at completing his evening in the way he had planned.

'Edith thought she could get us in but she can't,' he said, thereby giving Arabella Wainwright a funny story and a parable of Edith's fall all in one phrase.

Tommy smiled. 'Then you must let me.'

'Really, it doesn't matter,' protested Edith.

'Come on,' said Simon.

Arabella murmured gently, 'If she doesn't want to . . .' It was quite clear that she was no more anxious than Jane Cumnor to be seen escorting Edith Broughton and her new lover into Annabel's but Tommy was made of stouter stuff. A few minutes later he had equipped them all with drinks and they were seated at the foot of a giant Buddha in the little red smoking room to one side of the bar. Simon saw Arabella as a challenge and they had hardly sat down before he was inviting her to dance. Perhaps because being seen dancing with an unknown was preferable to being spotted in Edith's company, she accepted and Tommy and Edith were left alone.

'How've you been?'

Edith shrugged. 'You know.'

'I do.' He smiled at her quite kindly. 'You mustn't let the newspaper nonsense get to you. I should know, in my job. Today's scandal really is tomorrow's budgie paper. People forget more or less everything.'

Edith nodded. She knew well enough that while this is a general truth, it is seldom a personal one. She had been touched by scandal and inasmuch as she would ever feature in the papers again once it was all over, there would always be a small paragraph referring to her separation from Charles until the end of her life. 'Have you seen Charles?' she said.

Tommy nodded. 'I saw him in White's last week. We had a drink together.'

'How is he?'

'Not very chipper but I suppose he'll manage.' Edith felt a sudden pang of nostalgia for Tommy and White's and even Jane Cumnor, whom she had nodded to across the bar but had not attempted to join. Six months ago she would have sat with Tommy and ranged over the up-to-date stories of their mutual acquaintance and whatever she might say about all that now, it would have made her feel rather cosy. But on this evening there didn't seem to be any point. It wasn't her world any more and they both knew it. As for Charles. Poor old Charles. What had he done to deserve this? He'd just been dull company. That's all. Nothing worse than that. And then Simon returned and, much to Arabella's relief, led Edith away to the dance floor.

She was silent in the car although she smiled at Simon to allay his fears that she might be angry about something when she really wasn't. As she put the key into the lock of the Ebury Street front door Simon allowed the arm that had enclosed her waist to slip down to her buttocks, which he caressed gently as they walked through the little hall and stopped outside the door to the flat. Edith could feel a tingling sensation start to warm her at the base of her stomach. Simon leaned forward and kissed the back of her neck, his tongue licking her softly between his parted lips. They were hardly inside the door before she was kissing him in a strong, fierce way, and running her hands over his body and down to his crotch. She felt his large, hard penis pushing against her. 'Darling,' he said with the anticipatory smile of a man who understands and enjoys his work.

They made love three times that night at Edith's insistence. Simon had never known her throw herself into it with quite such abandon before. She mounted him and pushed herself down, forcing as much of him into her as she could. Because it was suddenly quite clear to her that this was the decision she had made. When she came home with Charles the evening was over as they shut the door. When she went out with Simon the evening was something that had to be endured until they could be alone together again. Fate had given her the choice between her private and her public life. Neither man, it seemed, could provide her with both. Well, she thought as she lay back watching the dawn and listening to Simon snoring gently beside her, she had chosen private fulfilment over public splendour and she was glad of her choice. Glad, that is, in the night, when she lay naked and satisfied and far from the world.

It was in the morning that she had to make up her mind all over again.

PART THREE

Dolente-Energico

~

I did not see Edith for some months after this. In the autumn I was given the part of a villain in one of those series that are optimistically described as 'family viewing' because no one can decide into which category they really fall. At any rate, it was shot on location in Hampshire and I was consequently a good deal out of London for some time. I took a cottage in Itchen Abbas and Adela joined me when she could. Some time in November we discovered she was pregnant and the thought that my life was about to take yet another quantum leap rather drove all other considerations from my mind. We purchased books by the dozen to learn more about our new condition and spent the evenings looking up why Adela kept tasting metal filings or feeling back pains. Actually this was pretty fruitless as the answer to more or less everything we asked was 'the cause of this is not yet known'. However, we were kept quite merrily occupied.

Of Edith, Simon and Charles we had little news. The papers had dropped them as there did not appear to be any signs of divorce and presumably they were all saving the second half of the story for when it came to court. Once I wrote to Charles because I had seen, in some obscure art magazine, that a Broughton portrait was up for sale and I thought he, or some relation, might be interested. Naturally I also imparted our news and I received, almost by return, quite a touching letter wishing us well. 'How right you are not to wait too long,' he wrote. 'Being married is all very well but it's having a child that makes a real family. I envy you that.' I do not necessarily agree with this view but I took it, correctly I think, as a comment on his own marital disappointments. He concluded by asking us to get in touch when we were back in circulation and I thought I would. I felt that by this time Charles and I had gone through enough together to qualify as friends even by English standards and the potential awkwardness of attempting to prosecute friendships with the Mighty no longer seemed to apply. I was interested that he had not mentioned Edith and indeed we had no news of her from any quarter. Gossip confirmed that she and Simon were still together and that, either because his notoriety had paid off or just conceivably because of his talent, he had landed a running part in some police series. I had made up my mind that I would also contact her when I returned to London, as I was determined not to be cast in the role of someone who drops their friends when their status diminishes, but in actual fact it was not I but my spouse who renewed our links.

We had not been back in London long when Adela received an invitation from a cousin to attend Hardy Amies's spring dress show. The relation in question, Louisa Shaw, was in the household of a junior member of the Royal Family and either for this reason or (more probably) because she was an occasional purchaser she had got onto the various lists to be invited to these glittering events, always with jolly good seats. She and Adela had been friends from childhood and consequently she allowed my wife to share her good fortune on a regular basis.

Unbeknownst to us as Adela and Louisa made their plans, it so happened that our old familiar, Annette Watson, was also a Hardy Amies customer. She had been, as I have said, something of a screen beauty of the Lesley-Ann Down vintage and she had always provided willing fodder to the photographers at bashes where there was a scarcity of celebrities but now she figured on the pages of the glossy magazines wearing *couture*, which naturally made her a welcome guest at these galas. Annette, in fact, was doing quite well by this stage, largely because, against all predictions, the dreary Bob had gone from well-off to extremely rich during the heady nineties. I seem to recall that his success was somehow connected to the 'dot.com' revolution although I cannot remember exactly what he did, if I ever knew. Anyway, whatever it was he obviously did it profitably. In the two or three years since the Watsons had been Eric's embarrassing guests in Mallorca they had consolidated their social position and, in London at any rate, they had gathered up quite a satisfactory address book. They had not penetrated Lady Uckfield's charmed circle on any level but they were on good terms with a couple of the more disreputable young marchionesses and the 'It' girls who were busy on the London scene at this time. Annette had even been pictured in *Hello* shopping with the Duchess of York. On the whole, she was satisfied.

A good part of that satisfaction was because she was now in a position to refuse the Chases' invitations, which had become more pressing of late. Caroline Chase, of course, cared little one way or the other, but Eric's shadowy dealings on the outer fringes of what he optimistically described as 'Business Skills and Public Relations' had been badly hit by the recession. These skills, it seems, were among the first economies in the newly hard-pressed companies that had bloomed so fast and were now looking as if they would wither as quickly. Eric felt that a helping hand from Bob Watson might make all the difference. Indeed it might have, I suppose, but perhaps because of that terrible dinner at Fairburn, the hand was withheld. The Chases, or Eric anyway, had ceased to be necessary to the social game-plan of the Watsons. Apart from anything else Eric was not expected to be around all that much longer. It was known that they were living on Caroline's money and questions were beginning to be asked among her circle as to how long this would go on. Particularly as there were no children to confuse the issue. To Caroline's set, there did not seem to be much logic in being married to someone who was common *and* poor. Although I reject these people's values in many areas, when dealing with someone as abrasive as Chase I must confess to understanding them.

It is pleasant to record that one friend who had not dropped Edith and automatically taken Charles's side in order to keep in with the Broughtons was this same Annette Watson. For Edith had paid a severe penalty for her chosen path. Actually I didn't much blame most of their crowd. They had been Charles's friends to begin with and Edith certainly had behaved badly. But this was not the real reason that they flocked to the Broughton banner. To a man they would have remained on Charles's team if he'd beaten Edith while keeping a string of chorus girls in the attic. However, I suppose one must concede that in this particular instance it was hard to argue with them. At any rate, Annette, partly because she knew she held few charms for Charles or his mother and partly because she really did like Edith, had stuck by her pal and one of the invitations she'd proffered was to accompany her to the Hardy Amies afternoon show and have some lunch beforehand.

*   *   *

Edith had never been to the first-floor restaurant of the Meridien in Piccadilly, which had recently been subjected to an exhaustive 'renovation'. The dining room was formed out of the old terrace, which had been glazed and palmed and marble-floored and generally made into a home from home for all those natives of Los Angeles who were now, hopefully, going to flock through the newly re-opened doors. Edith picked her way among the tables, following Annette's waving hand. She was smartly dressed in a snappy winter suit, complete with pearls and a brooch. She had surprised herself by being tempted to wear a hat. She didn't, but the costume, as it stood, was perhaps an expression of a part of her life that had been suppressed for a time beneath the T-shirts and sequins, apparently the only two options of Simon's crowd. Even he had commented on her outfit as he lay on a sofa happily reading the next day's scenes: 'Heavens, very smart! You look like your mother-in-law!' But she hadn't risen. Maybe, subconsciously, she'd felt complimented.

Annette kissed her and ordered glasses of champagne for them both. It was not long before they had moved from the customary greetings to the real business. 'So, when do you make your next move?'

'Move?' said Edith.

'Well. The divorce. Are you getting on with it?'

Edith shifted slightly uncomfortably. 'Not really. Not yet.'

'Why not?'

She shrugged. 'I suppose I – we – rather feel that we might as well wait out the two years and do it with a minimum of fuss. Otherwise it means such a palaver . . .'

'Two years!' Annette laughed. 'Oh, I don't think Charles is going to be happy waiting two years.'

'Why not?'

Annette stared at her. 'Darling, you must know the race is on.'

Edith was surprised to find that her stomach lurched. 'What do you mean?'

'My dear, as soon as the news was out he was absolutely pounced on. How could he not be? You haven't even had a child so there's nothing to hold them back.'

Edith felt herself growing irritated. How dare this woman know more about her husband than she did? 'I don't think he's seeing anyone particularly.'

'Then you think wrong.' Annette took a sip to punctuate her pause. 'You remember Clarissa Marlowe?'

Edith laughed and breathed easily again. The Honourable Clarissa Marlowe, great-granddaughter of a courtier who had been raised to a lowly barony in the 1920s, was a second cousin of Charles's through their mothers. She was a hearty, healthy brunette, good in the saddle and helpful at sticky dinner parties. She worked as an up-market receptionist in a dubious property company, thereby lending it some respectability, and she lived in a flat with her sister just off the Old Brompton Road. A classic member of the Alice Band Brigade and, Edith thought comfortably, not at all Charles's type.

'Don't be silly. She's his cousin. She's just chumming him.'

Annette raised her eyebrows. 'Well, she chummed him to the West Indies for a week just before Christmas and she spent the New Year at Broughton.'

There was no denying that this was a blow. In fact Edith was astonished at its severity. What had she thought? That Charles would stay single for ever? She had been gone for eight months now and he was only human. As she conjured up the image of Clarissa, Edith felt herself washed with a tide of rage towards this blameless, county girl. In truth she had always rather liked Clarissa, who put herself out to be useful and laughed at Edith's funny stories and had never been one of those relations who persisted in treating her as a tiresome foreigner. When she thought about it she supposed that his cousin had always had rather a soft spot for Charles. With a sinking heart she recognised Clarissa for what she was, the sort of girl men like Charles marry.

'Oh,' she said.

The waiter had arrived to hand them enormous, leather-bound menus in ungrammatical French. He retreated with a murmur of guttural Rs.

'Cheer up, darling,' said Annette with a piercing look. 'Tell me about Simon. Is he well?'

'Oh yes,' said Edith, bracing herself again. 'Very. He's got a series that goes on until June and then, with any luck, starts again in December.'

'How marvellous! What is it?'

'Oh, you know,' said Edith, trying to decide between liver and seared tuna. 'Some detective police thing. He's the nice side-kick who keeps missing the point.' She finally fixed on kidneys with a salad.

'Well done him,' said Annette. 'Who else is in it? Do you go on the set and everything?'

Edith appreciated Annette's efforts at enthusiasm. It was kind of her. 'Not really, no. Sometimes. So I can put a face to the stories. It puts him off a bit.'

The truth was that, try as she might, she had found that she just could not get really involved in Simon's work. There were parts of it she quite liked, first nights and a few (very few) of the parties and meeting people one knew from television. She was quite interested in reading scripts and then comparing them to the finished product but most of it, well . . . At the beginning she had gone down to the location a few times but, honestly, it was *so* monotonous. They just seemed to say the same three lines to each other from a thousand angles until she ended up in the make-up room, gossiping to the girls. If she was really honest she couldn't understand why Simon made such a song and dance about it all. Most of it seemed to be pretty straightforward. You learned the lines, they trained the camera onto you and you said the lines. She was quite able to see that some people could do it and some couldn't, but fretting about it didn't seem to help. She never noticed that Simon was much better in the parts he had sweated over than in the ones that he did off the top of his head. One thing she had grasped since our lunch together in those early days – there wasn't really a place for her down on the set. After her initial forays she would roll up once or twice, or stay on location for a weekend, so that she could say hello to the other members of the cast and crew and leave it at that. It seemed to be the best way to play it.

'Give him my love,' said Annette. They locked eyes for a moment and to Edith's relief the waiter reappeared at this precise moment to take their orders. That done, they shifted their ground back to more general topics.

＊　　＊　　＊

Louisa rang our basement bell promptly at a quarter to one. They had decided to lunch at home as they were going on to Fortnum's for tea after the show. Adela, at five months, had only recently stopped feeling sick and was sorely in need of a Treat. I was to give them a lift to Savile

Row on my way to a wig fitting in Old Burlington Street. I liked Adela's cousin. The daughter of an Anglo-Irish landowner, she had that slightly fey, unjudgemental quality of her tribe, so unlike their English counterparts, that made her easy company for anyone, despite her tweeds and sensible shoes. She was also a natural spinster for whom, I suspected, a lifetime of Royal service was going to have to do the work of husband and children. Of course, she was thrilled by the idea of the impending baby and I could see before Adela asked me that she was classic godmother material.

The traffic was not heavy and accordingly it was no later than a quarter to three when the two of them climbed the staircase of Hardy Amies's headquarters and entered the large, first-floor salon overlooking Savile Row itself, where the collection was to be displayed.

There is no real benefit in getting to these things early as all the seats are clearly and unarguably allocated but they had enough to gossip about to pass the time and so, once they had been ushered to two seats labelled, in a flowing hand; 'Lady Louisa Shaw & Friend', they were soon so engrossed in their own soap-opera that they were oblivious to the rest of the fast-filling room. They were seated well, at the foot of the catwalk on the short side of the room near the door from the staircase and therefore had a full view not only of the length of the catwalk but also of most of the rest of the seating. So Adela was quite surprised, on looking up as the lights were turned on to signify that the show was about to begin, to see Edith Broughton tucked into the far corner, in the back row, opposite the door where the models make their entrance. It seemed odd that Edith had not said hello, since she must have brushed past them to get to her seat and even now, while looking at Adela, she made no real sign of recognition. I am afraid that one could have read in this the treatment that Edith had had to endure over the previous months but at any rate Adela, for whom even the vestige of any kind of feud is anathema, immediately smiled and waved, and Edith, relieved perhaps, waved back.

The conversation was beginning to die away in anticipation when there was a slight confusion at the door. Adela turned in time to see one of the princesses enter the room, followed by Lady Uckfield. Smiling their apologies, they made their way to two seats reserved for them near the foot of the catwalk beyond my wife and Louisa, in the front row. They were in their places before Adela looked back to where Edith sat, her eyes fixed on her mother-in-law. The contrast between the state of the two women was not lost on Adela and it must have seemed vividly clear to Edith. She sat in the back row, with her over-made-up friend, about to look at clothes she could not seriously entertain a thought of buying. Two rows before her sat the woman she might herself have been, with a member of the Royal Family, envied by more or less every other woman present. The music started, a selection of Copacabana rock, which seemed a surprising choice given the age of the majority of the clients. Adela glanced down at her programme for the description of the first presentation. Three models appeared, the numbers of their dresses displayed on plastic discs in their elegant hands, and the show had begun.

It was a lively hour with the audience chatting relentlessly as each ensemble was paraded before them. 'Lovely for Spain', 'What an odd colour, I wonder if they do it in cream', 'Pretty dress, wrong model', and other similar phrases would ring out, quite audibly, as the girls sailed imperviously by. From time to time a little fun was added by a model dropping her number disc (I gather these have since been abandoned, perhaps for this reason) or one might stumble in a graceful spin but these were rare breaks in the super-smooth operation. Still, Adela was distracted. Every time she glanced over to where Edith sat, she could see that her gaze was not on the catwalk but on the back of her mother-in-law's head, still blithely unaware of Edith's presence, as she scribbled on her programme and exchanged whispers with her august companion.

The collection was presented and the company, notes jotted and images fixed, rose to go. A way was made for the Royal Highness to pass, with Lady Uckfield following on. With proper diffidence Adela did not draw attention to herself but it so happened that the princess recognised Louisa at the same moment that Lady Uckfield saw my wife. Accordingly she was presented, made her curtsey, and for a few moments the crowd fell deferentially back to leave them in a foursome. They were chatting quite amiably about which frocks they had preferred when Adela caught sight of Edith edging towards them through the thinning crush. These situations are hard. Though I say it myself, Adela is not one to shirk a difficult task, but what was the point of spoiling Lady Uckfield's afternoon or placing her in an invidious position as regards her companion? Her daughter-in-law was a figure of scandal and this was a public place stuffed with journalists. Judas-like, Adela opted for Damage Containment, and catching Lady Uckfield's eye nodded slightly in the direction of Edith's advancing figure. Lady Uckfield, demonstrating the skill that ran the Empire, became aware of her daughter-in-law's presence without so much as a flicker of recognition. Even Adela would have been hard put to it to deny that her immediate departure was simply fortuitous, had it not been for the conspiratorial squeeze of her arm by the older woman. In a moment princess and attendant were gone, leaving Adela to introduce Edith as she drew alongside a slightly bemused Louisa.

They talked for a while with Edith asking about me and Adela rather pointedly not asking about Simon and then they parted. Though not before Edith had observed brightly, 'My dear mother-in-law looks well.'

'Very well, I gather,' said Adela.

Edith laughed. 'How funny to think one has turned into an awkward relation! Oh well. She can't avoid me entirely. She might as well get used to the idea that I do still live in London, whether she likes it or not.'

'I don't think she was avoiding you. She just didn't see you,' said Adela, adding lamely, 'I never thought to say anything . . .'

'No,' said Edith. 'Why would you?'

And so they parted, Adela and Louisa to Fortnum's and then back to the flat to tell me every detail, Edith to Ebury Street and Simon, who was in a rage because one of his speeches had been cut from tomorrow's scene. He suspected his co-star, whom he was already beginning actively to dislike, and his brain was so full of this particular injustice that he had very little time for Edith's narrative. I doubt she told him much anyway. Only that she'd seen Googie but Googie hadn't seen her. In truth, beyond lesser horrors like the evening at Annabel's, this had been the starkest illustration so far of the extent of her fall and she could not yet talk about it without beginning to feel slightly ill.

I knew enough from Adela's account to understand that Edith must be going through a pretty rough time however happy she was with Simon and I resolved to telephone her and buy her a decent lunch. But before I got around to it, I was surprised to receive an invitation from Isabel Easton to go down to Sussex for the weekend. The envelope was in fact addressed to Adela. Isabel had apparently learned her lessons well and grasped that the upper classes only ever address an envelope to the female part of a couple. Why? Who knows? At any rate it was Adela who read it first and she who suggested we accept. Adela was only mildly fond of Isabel and she didn't like David much so I suspected at once that she had an ulterior motive.

'We might give Charles a ring when we're there,' she said, so I didn't have to wait long to know what it was.

I don't think I had stayed with the Eastons since that time, three years before, when we had all been summoned to Broughton to witness Edith's triumph. I had seen them in London so the gap was not obvious and, looking back, I'm not sure why I had got out of the habit of going there. Perhaps the fact that Edith and I had become friends over their heads had made an awkwardness between us. I'm not sure. At any rate I was quite glad to find myself and my wife, a couple of Friday nights later, back in their familiar, GTC drawing room of frilled tables and chintz sofas and over-stuffed cushions. We had unpacked and bathed and been given a pre-dinner drink, but not much more than this before the real reason for our invitation became clear.

'Are you going to go over to Broughton while you're here?' said David.

I looked at Adela. 'I don't know. I don't know if they're there. We thought we might give them a ring.'

'Good,' said David. 'Good.' He paused. 'Give our love to Charles when you speak to him, anyway.'

And there it was. I should have guessed. After all, what a situation they were in! For years they had been driven nearly mad by their inability to get onto any sort of terms with the local family. Then, miracle of miracles, their friend marries the heir. They start to inch their way into the County. They are just beginning to make a little headway with the Sir William Fartleys of this world when, bang, a scandal erupts. Suddenly Edith, their friend, the woman they first invited down to these parts (for one may be sure they had made no secret of the role they had played), runs off with an actor, disgraces the family, lets down poor, darling Charles. Exeunt David and Isabel Easton.

I think one would have to be very hard-hearted indeed not to feel some sympathy for them, poor things, even if their goal was a worthless one. It is easy to laugh at the pretensions of others – particularly when their ambitions are trivial – but most of us have a thorny path of it in some area of our lives, which is not worth the importance we give it. I suppose it is hard to live in a small society and to be obliged to accept that one is excluded from the first rank of that little group. This is what drives so many socially minded people back to the towns where the game is more fluid and up for grabs. On top of which the Eastons had come, at least in their own minds, so near the prize . . .

David continued. 'I'm afraid the simple truth is that our dear Edith has behaved most fearfully badly.'

We all, including Isabel, greeted this with a slight silence. Even Adela (who, I knew, most thoroughly agreed with this assessment) seemed reluctant to weigh in with David in Edith's absence. 'I don't know,' I said.

'Really!' David was quite indignant. 'I'm surprised to hear you defending her.'

'I'm not defending her exactly,' I said. 'I'm just saying that one doesn't "know". One never knows anything about other people's lives. Not really.'

This is a truism but it isn't completely true. One does know about other people's lives. And I, in fact, knew quite a lot about Edith's and Charles's lives but, even if I was guilty of a certain dishonesty, there was some truth in what I said. I am not convinced that one ever knows quite enough to come down with a full condemnation.

Isabel entered with her peace-making hat. 'I think all David means is that we felt so sorry for poor Charles. He didn't seem to deserve any of it. Not from where we were sitting anyway.'

We all agreed with this but it was nevertheless perfectly obvious that David hoped to be able to ditch Edith and by demonstrating his indignation to someone who would report it to the Broughton household, he believed he would earn points and end up back on their list. Or on their list, full stop, since he wrongly thought he had penetrated the citadel during Edith's reign. In this I think he was mistaken for two reasons. The first was that he was simply not Charles's cup of tea. The English upper classes are, as a rule, not amused by upper-middle-class facsimiles of themselves. This brand of *arriviste* has all the dreariness of the familiar with none of the cosiness of the intimate. On the whole, if they are to fraternise outside their set they choose artists or singers or people who will make them laugh. But the second reason was more personal to Charles. I had a feeling that he would not admire David for attempting to abandon Edith and her cause, however he, Charles, had been treated.

At any rate, following both David's urgings and Adela's original suggestion, I did indeed telephone Broughton that night. Jago, the butler, answered and told me that Charles was in London but when I was about to sign off there was the sound of an extension being lifted and Lady Uckfield came on the line.

'How are you?' she said. 'I ran into your pretty wife the other day.' I said I knew. 'Is there any chance of seeing you down here in the future? I do hope so.' She spoke with the intimate urgency, with that voice of a Girl With A Secret, that I had come to associate with, and enjoy about, her social manner.

'In actual fact we are here. Staying with the Eastons. I just rang to see if Charles was down.'

'Well, he should be back tomorrow night. What are you doing for dinner? I don't suppose you can get away?' She made the heartless request without the glimmer of a qualm. Did she know that David would give his life's blood to be included among her intimates? Probably.

'Not really,' I said.

Her tone became even more conspiratorial. 'Can't you talk?'

'Not really,' I said again, glancing over to where David stood by the fireplace watching me like a sparrow hawk.

'What about tea? Surely you can manage that?'

'I should think so,' I answered, still rather non-committally.

'And bring your nice wife.' She rang off.

David was bitterly disappointed that the call had not resulted in the general invitation that had been his unspoken plan. He suggested rather grumpily ringing back and asking the Uckfields to dinner instead but Isabel, always more reasonable, prevented him. 'I expect they want to have a bit of a chat about Edith and everything. Who can blame them?' In conclusion, deciding perhaps that since he had asked us down to re-establish relations with the Great House there wasn't much point in preventing us from doing so, he agreed that we should go for tea but carry with us an invitation for a drink on the Sunday morning.

~

EIGHTEEN

There were about six or seven people staying the weekend, which was par for the course with the Broughtons. I recognised Lady Tenby, who nodded at me quite pleasantly and a cousin of the family whom I had met with Charles and Edith in London a couple of times. I did not then know that there was any special significance in Clarissa Marlowe's presence but we did both notice that she was very proprietary in her manner, worrying about whether we were comfortable or had a sandwich or whatever and I suppose in retrospect that marked her out from an ordinary guest. The others, men in corduroys and sweaters, girls in skirts and walking shoes, barely looked up from their respective tasks, reading, gossiping, stroking the dogs, making toast at the glowing fire, as we came in.

The Uckfields, by contrast, could not have been more solicitous. They asked our news, chatted about the dress show, discussed some film they had seen me in, fetched crumpets, topped up tea-cups until it must have been as plain to the other occupants of the room as it was to us that we were about to figure in some Master Plan. The normal manner one has come to expect from hosts and fellow guests alike in an English country house is a state of moderately amiable lack of interest. The guests loaf about, reading magazines, going for walks, having baths, writing letters, without making any great social demands on each other. Only when eating – and even then only really at dinner – are they expected to 'perform'. This lack of effort, this business of people barely raising their heads from their books to acknowledge one's entry into a room, may seem rude to the foreigner (indeed it is rude), but I must confess it brings with it a certain relaxation. They make no effort to be polite to you and you therefore are not required to make any effort to be polite to them. In fact, when a great fuss is made of someone in a house party it is almost invariably because they have been recognised as an 'outsider' or at the very least someone with a terminal illness on whom extra energy must be expended. For everyone to jump to their feet and gush is therefore more or less an insult to the recipient.

Adela and I, however, did not read any kind of social 'set-down' in the lathering we were receiving. We simply understood that a favour was about to be asked. Consequently, when Lady Uckfield wondered if I would like to see her sitting room, which had just been decorated and which, apparently, we had discussed at some time in the past, I got to my feet at once. My wife was included in the invitation but something in Lady Uckfield's manner told her that what was wanted was me on my own and since we were both dying to know what was going on, she opted to stay with Lord Uckfield and have some more tea to precipitate the expected intimacy.

The sitting room in question was quite far from the rooms I knew and was situated in one of the wings, separated from the main block by a curving corridor from which the windows looked across the park. Once reached it was revealed as a charming and elegant nest, displaying Lady Uckfield's sure touch for *gemüchtlich*, fussy grandeur. It was quite a large room, with walls upholstered in rose damask and pretty chairs covered in delightful chintzes. Little japanned bureaux, painted bookcases and delicate inlaid tables stood about, all littered with the debris of the aristocratic rich, flowers, bits of Meissen, pretty lamps, miniatures, bowls of dried lavender, enamelled candlesticks, small paintings on carved stands, and, of course, on her main desk (a handsome, ormolu-mounted *bureau plat*, which sat sideways to the wall), a mass of papers and invitations and official requests. A day bed upholstered in buttoned moiré was placed at right angles to the little fire, which twinkled and crackled in the leaded and polished grate. Above the mantelshelf, where china figures and snuff-boxes jostled with chewed dog toys, a knitted rabbit and postcards from friends in Barbados and San Francisco, was a pastel by Greuze of an earlier Lady Broughton. It was, in other words, the definitive HQ of a Great Lady.

'How nicely you've done it,' I said.

But Lady Uckfield had forgotten on what excuse she had brought me here and just waved me to the armchair on the other side of the fire from the day bed as she sat down with a grave expression.

'Have you seen Edith lately?'

'Not lately, no. Not since Adela saw her at the dress show.'

'I see,' she said. She was silent for a moment. In truth I had never before seen her uncomfortable but that is certainly what she was at this moment.

'How's Charles?'

She answered with a shrug of the mouth. 'I want to ask you something. I know that Edith is still with what's-his-name. Does she intend to marry him?'

I was rather taken aback. 'I don't know. He isn't divorced yet – I'm not even sure he's started the whole process.'

She nodded to herself. 'Charles has told me she's planning to wait the two years and go for a non-contested separation.' She paused and I sort of nodded back. This was news to me but it didn't seem such a bad idea, if only because it would hardly be headlines by that time. 'The thing is, Tigger and I are not behind this plan . . .'

She hesitated, more awkward than I had ever seen her. 'We feel that the sooner Charles can draw a line under the whole thing and start his life afresh, the better for him. We hate the idea of everything dragging on and on and his never really feeling that anything's over.' She looked at me quizzically. 'You do see what we mean?'

'I suppose I do.'

'You may not know it but it has cut him up most dreadfully. He's not a great one for showing his feelings but he was in the most frightful state, I can tell you.'

I nodded. I had only to think of that scene in his study when he had cried in front of me to believe this implicitly. Charles was one of those men, much less rare than modern women's magazines would have us believe, who make their choice in marriage and then never question it. They do not ration the commitment they give their wives because it never occurs to them that they will have to regroup their emotions before death separates them – and even then they tend to assume that it will be the husband who will go first. I do not necessarily think that he would have been incapable of infidelity. On some farming convention in America, during some shooting party in Scotland, who knows what could happen? But I would say that he would have been incapable of instigating the end of his own marriage. Having chosen Edith, he had given her all the love of which he was capable and, as a natural sequitur, all the trust. Neither of these would have been very interesting in their quality but they would have been given in great quantity. Of that I am sure. No, I was not surprised to hear that he had been in 'a frightful state'.

Lady Uckfield had not finished. 'We are so desperately hoping he can rebuild his life and we really feel that he has a chance of that now.'

'Has he met someone else?'

She inclined her head to one side without answering and I knew he had. Or that they hoped he had. Minutes later I had worked out it was probably Clarissa.

'The point is if he was free he could plan in those terms. Now he can't. The past is pulling and pulling at him until I don't believe he can think straight.'

Now this was an intriguing choice of phrase. In what way was Charles not 'thinking straight'? She watched me, waiting for some acknowledgement.

'How can I help?' I said. I wanted to find out what Lady Uckfield had in store for me. I knew it would be something big because it is an absolute truth that for a woman of her type to discuss any aspect of the intimate life of her family with anyone other than a life-long, contemporary friend of similar rank (and that only rarely) was a kind of torture. Whether she liked me or not was irrelevant. This interview was agony for her.

'Can you talk to Edith? Can you ask her if she'll let Charles divorce her now? Of course, in the past that would have been an uncomfortable way round but do people think like that these days? I don't believe they do – and you must assure her that it would make no difference to the settlement. None at all.' She was gushing to cover her own embarrassment. And no wonder. This was a vulgar request if ever I heard one. Perhaps the only vulgar thing I ever knew to issue from her lips. My surprise must have shown on my face. 'You must think this a very tiresome commission.'

'I don't know that tiresome is the word I'd have chosen.' My tone was a little severe but Lady Uckfield was enough of a lady to know that she had transgressed her own code. She took the reprimand gracefully as one who deserved it.

'Of course, it's an awful thing to ask.'

'You do Edith an injustice,' I said. 'She wouldn't think about the money.' This was true. I do not think it ever occurred to Edith to take anything off Charles beyond a few thousand to give her a breathing space. It was enough that he had paid the rent in Ebury Street and left her able to cash cheques in this interim. What Lady Uckfield did not understand was that Edith was fully conscious of having behaved badly. People like the Uckfields can be slow, indeed unable, to realise that 'honour' is not a perquisite of their own class. They have heard so often about the materialism of the middle classes and the grace and self-sacrifice of their own kind that they have come to believe these two fictions equally.

She raised her eyebrows slightly. 'I suppose that might be true.'

'It is true,' I said. 'You do not like Edith and because you don't like her you underestimate her.'

At this she unbent slightly. She did not deny what I had said and when she answered me she spoke with a slight smile. 'You are right to defend her. You first came to this house as her friend – and you are right to defend her.'

'I will tell Edith what you've said but I really cannot do much more than that.'

'You see, we can't have Charles bringing a case and her contesting it or challenging it in any way. We must know that won't happen. You see that?'

'Of course I do.' Which I did. 'But I can't advise her. She wouldn't listen to me if I tried.'

'You'll tell me what she says?'

I nodded. Our interview was over. We stood and had almost left the room when Lady Uckfield clearly felt impelled to convince me further of the urgency of her request.

'You see, Charles is so dreadfully unhappy. It can't go on, can it? It's so terrible for us. Seeing him like this.'

In answer I put my arm round her shoulders and gave her a squeeze. It was considerably more intimate an action than anything I had attempted before. Perhaps it was a sign that we were somehow bonded by this awful mess of tears and waste. At any rate, she didn't object. Nor did she assume that faintly perceptible stiffness that her kind of English women use at such a moment to demonstrate that some unwarranted liberty has been taken.

We went back to the drawing room where Adela, in an effort to escape from Tigger's meticulously outlined plans for the South Wood, was attempting to teach one of the dogs to balance a biscuit on its nose.

She looked up when we came in and, since she was burning to hear what had happened (as I was to tell it), we made our excuses fairly soon after that. We still had the awful burden of David's invitation to impart but, since it was the price by which we had bought our tea, we knew it had to be done. Lady Uckfield followed us down to the Under Hall so it was easier than it might have been.

'David and Isabel,' I started. She looked quizzical so I clarified, 'Easton. Our hosts.' She nodded. This interchange alone would have been enough to have depressed David for months. 'They wondered if you'd like to bring your party over for a drink tomorrow morning?' It was done.

Lady Uckfield smiled briskly. 'But how *very* kind. I'm afraid we're too many for that. But do thank them.' Her customary urgent intimacy was back as she rejected an invitation I knew well enough would never be accepted. But she surprised me by continuing. 'Why don't you come back here instead – and bring them?'

This was kindness above and beyond the call of duty. Feeling guilty at the thought of David's delight had he but known, I shook my head. 'I think that's rather a bore for you, isn't it? Let's leave it for another time.'

But Lady Uckfield, to my further bewilderment, was insistent. 'No, please. Do come.' She smiled. 'Charles will be back. I know he'd love to see you.'

At the time, I didn't understand what she hoped to achieve by bringing us together with Charles. It seemed if anything a risk to her plans, for if I had confided her mission to her son, I am certain he would have been furious. But later I realised that she wanted me to see Charles in his misery for this would be her justification and might motivate me more than ever to carry out her wishes. It is possible too that she believed that by allowing us to bring our friends to Broughton we would be even more tightly strapped to the family carriage. 'Don't feel you have to,' said Adela, but we could protest no more and so, bidding her goodbye until the morrow, we set off to deliver our happy message to a delighted David and a less enthralled but pleasantly surprised Isabel.

Charles was waiting for us in the drawing room when we reappeared the next day or so it seemed. He bounded out of his chair, kissed Adela on both cheeks and almost wrung my hand. He wasn't able to say much more than how pleased he was to see us, as his mother approached to normalise the situation and lead us over to the drinks cupboard, cunningly inserted behind a dummy door that had originally been constructed to balance the door that led, through an ante-room, to the dining room. Tigger stood there in his role as Mine Host, dispensing Bloody Marys. He presented one to his wife. She wrinkled her nose fractionally. 'Not enough Tabasco, the wrong vodka – and you've forgotten the lime juice.' I was waiting for a bowl of fresh limes to be rung for when to my surprise Lord Uckfield took down a plastic bottle of lime juice cordial and sloshed a great measure into the jug. I was about to request one without this ingredient then thought better of it and took what I was given. Naturally enough, it was delicious.

'How do you think he's looking?' said my hostess.

She knew well enough that Charles looked perfectly terrible. His face was tired and lumpy. His skin, which normally shone with the kind of uncomplicated health redolent of grouse moors and hunting fields, looked sallow and almost dirty. His hair hung in unsorted tendrils down his neck.

'Not great,' I said.

She nodded. 'You do see why I felt I had to ask your help?'

She drifted away without referring again to our curious interview of the previous day. To be honest and in her defence I could see why, as a mother, she had been driven to pretty desperate measures. Clearly her son was dying by inches before her eyes. What puzzled me was this hinted-at, burgeoning romance that promised new life and happiness. He really did not look like one who has found his True Love, even though Clarissa was in his eye-line. There were some other pre-lunch drinkers and she was again playing the hostess, leading people here and there and introducing them but, so far as I could tell, without exciting any special interest in her cousin's heart.

The house-guests were as surly as they had been the previous day and I saw a couple of them being grudgingly yoked to David and Isabel. One, Viscount Bohun, who had been out for a walk the day before, I had met occasionally in London. His youngest sister had been a vague friend of mine at one time and I had always suspected him then of being mentally sub-normal – or at least as near sub-normal as one can be without actually risking clinical classification – so I had been quite surprised to read somewhere that he had married a pretty girl with a respectable job in publishing. Remembering this, I was curious to see the new Lady Bohun, she who had made this unholy contract. She was easy to spot. Her shining hair swept back flawlessly under a velvet band, her nose tilted in the air, she was being as grand and as difficult with a foundering David as it is possible to be without actually resorting to insults. The poor man struggled on, hopefully dropping names and references, all of which were courteously spurned, until I could almost see the sweat popping out on his brow. I can only hope that such petty victories were worth the terrible sacrifice of her life that she had made. Bohun himself had caught the wretched Adela and was telling her some interminable story, which he kept punctuating with a shrill and unprovoked laugh. I could see her checking the exits.

Charles approached and touched me on the elbow. 'So how are you? How was your filming?'

'OK. How about you?'

He gestured towards a window seat where, untroubled by the others, we might perch and be a little alone. He stared out over the gardens for a moment in silence. 'Oh, I'm fine.' He smiled rather wryly. 'Well, quite fine.'

He didn't look it but I nodded. 'I'm glad.'

'Mummy said you were over here yesterday.'

'We came for tea.'

'I expect they wanted to talk to you about, you know, the mess.'

'A bit.'

'What did they say?' I wasn't really prepared to betray Lady Uckfield to her son. Apart from anything else, although I thought her request had been intrusive and improper, I did not question the honesty of her motives. Her child looked like hell. Of course she wanted to bring things to an end, what mother wouldn't? I couldn't blame her for that so I shrugged. Charles continued. 'They're very keen to hurry everything on. They want me to "put it all behind me"'.

'And shouldn't you?'

He stared back out of the window. It was early May and the flowers that were springing into life all over the lovingly tended terraces should have looked fresh and gay but there had been a cloudburst that morning and instead they all seemed rather soggy and careworn. Beyond the ha-ha, the trees in the park were in leaf but still light, their first foliage so much more subtle in its colours than the thick lushness of high summer.

'They packed me off to Jamaica in November with Clarissa and some friends of hers.'

'Was it fun?' I found Clarissa who was busying herself with refills. Charles followed my glance.

'Poor old Clarissa. Yes. Quite fun. I like Jamaica. Well, Ocho Rios anyway. Have you ever been?' I shook my head. 'My dear old mother's trying to make a match for me. She doesn't want to take her chances on the open market a second time.' He laughed.

'I suppose she just wants you to be happy,' I said.

He looked at me. 'It isn't quite that. You see, she does want me to be happy but this time she wants me to be happy in a way she understands. She fears the unknown. Edith was the unknown. She thinks she's working for my happiness but more than that she is anxious to prevent a repetition. There are to be no more strangers at Broughton. Edith and Eric have been quite enough.'

'Well, I can see her point so far as Eric's concerned,' I said, and we both laughed.

I looked back at Clarissa who was beginning to cast slightly nervous looks in our direction as if she sensed that our conversation would bode her no good. I felt sorry for her. She was a nice girl and she would have made a success of all this – far more of a success probably than the wretched Edith ever could. Why shouldn't she have a go at making Charles happy? But even as I entertained such thoughts, I knew the whole thing was a figment of Lady Uckfield's imagination and destined to remain so.

'Have you seen Edith lately?' he asked.

I was struck again by the common error, into which I have often fallen, certainly with Charles, of assuming that stupid people are spared deep feeling. Not that Charles was exactly stupid. He was simply incapable of original thought. But I knew now that he was more than capable of great love. It is endlessly fascinating to speculate on the reasons for love's choices. I liked Edith and I had since I met her. I enjoyed her beauty and her low-key self-mockery and her naturally cool manner, but I could not pretend to understand how she had become so great a love object for this Young Man Who Had Everything. Her greatest merit as company, after all, was her sense of irony, which Charles was not capable of appreciating or even understanding. In my way I was as puzzled as Lady Uckfield as to why he had not chosen someone of his own sort who would have known the ropes and the other members of his world, who would have chaired her charities and ridden her horses and bossed the village around without a qualm, certainly with none of the suppressed sense of self-ridicule that underlay so much of Edith's role-playing. At all events, there it was. Charles had fallen in love with Edith Lavery and he loved her with a disinterested heart. The blow she had dealt to his self-esteem and indeed to his life had obviously been critical but it was quite clear from the look he turned to me that he loved her still.

'Adela saw her the other day at something.'

'How was she?'

'Well, I think.' This was a thorny path, if you like. I did not want to say she had looked rather down in case it stirred up hopes in his breast that were doomed to disappointment, nor did I care to say she was bursting with happiness as that would be needlessly painful. It would also be, from what I could gather from Adela, untrue.

'Will you be seeing her soon?'

'I thought I might give her lunch.'

'Tell her – tell her I'll do whatever she wants. You know. I'll fit in.' I nodded. 'And give her my love,' he said.

Predictably David had not enjoyed his sojourn in Valhalla. As so often in such cases, the realisation of the dream brings resentment in its wake. Perhaps because, in their imaginings, David and his like see themselves as inner members of the Charmed Circle, chums of half the peerage, swapping stories about childhood friends and making plans to share a villa in Tuscany. Inevitably, the reality of these attempts at intermingling tends to make them bitter and irritated as they find themselves snubbed as aliens by those very people they have spent their adult life admiring and emulating.

'I must say,' he muttered as he climbed into the back seat of my car, 'I found those Bohuns pretty hard going. Do you know them?'

'I used to know him a bit.'

'Really? I don't know what I thought of him.'

I smiled. 'He's a half-wit. What's she like?'

'Quite difficult, I'd say.'

Isabel nodded. 'Diana Bohun has made a hard bargain and her only compensation is the envy of strangers. I wonder how long she'll bear it.

No doubt in five years we'll read that she's run off with the local doctor.'

Adela shook her head. 'No, we won't. I knew her when she came out. She'd stay with Hitler if he brought her a title and a house.'

Isabel raised her eyebrows. 'I think I'd rather have Hitler.'

I was interested in this exchange because, even as they ridiculed the pitiful hypocrisy of Diana Bohun, I was well aware that Adela and David and even Isabel, whatever they might say, fundamentally approved of her pact with the devil. Perhaps none of them would have been prepared to marry someone who actually repulsed them, but nevertheless those girls in their acquaintance who had done so (and I could name at least seven in my own address book) were not despicable figures to them unless they reneged on their bargain. To the members of this world this was Edith's real crime. Not marrying Charles without loving him, but leaving him for love of someone else. To them, her folly was in abandoning the false values she had endorsed with her marriage and in attempting to return to the timeless virtues. Her decision was unworldly, it was not *mondaine*. Americans may affect to admire this in their fiction if not in their lives but their British counterparts, at least among the upper-middle and upper classes do not. In the States, the Abdication story, for example, is portrayed as The World Well Lost For Love while the English, of a certain type anyway, see it only as childish, irresponsible and absurd.

And it was by these standards that Edith had been judged and found wanting.

NINETEEN

~

Here was a hard task. On the one hand I had a commission from Lady Uckfield, which I had sworn to carry out, to ask Edith to allow herself to be divorced at once, on the other, I had been made fully aware during our time at Broughton that Charles was still in love with his wife.

'So what are you going to say?' said Adela on the day when I had arranged to meet Edith for lunch. Naturally I had told my wife all. I don't know that I had been sworn to secrecy but even if I had been I never feel it includes one's spouse except in the most exceptional cases. Nothing can be more irritating than attempting to live intimately with a Keeper of Secrets.

'What Lady Uckfield wants me to say, I suppose.'

'Don't tell me you're going to promote the cause of that wretched Marlowe girl?'

I shook my head. 'No, I'll keep off that. I'll tell her they want it to be over, that's all.'

Adela pondered. 'Tell her Lady Uckfield wants it to be over. That'll be nearer the mark.' Considering her prejudice, I thought this was commendably just.

I had arranged to meet Edith at the Caprice. At lunchtime particularly it seems to combine a sense of clean, business-like lines with a whiff of glamour, which I thought would be an appropriate and undepressing setting for our proposed conversation. I arrived to find that I had been allotted the table at the far end of the restaurant away from the bar. This was by chance but it could not have been more suitable. I ordered a glass of champagne to cheer myself up and waited for my guest.

Edith was glad of my choice of venue. Simon was working a lot these days and earning quite respectable sums but what with his mortgage and his wife and the general financial backlog that any actor has to pay off when things start to roll again, he was not one for much West End entertaining unless it was at someone else's expense. Edith could have managed it as she had been given no real guidelines as to how much she could spend but she was reluctant to use Charles's money for inessentials. She had been known to interpret this term fairly widely but somehow to take Simon out for treats on her husband's money didn't seem quite cricket. And then the bore was she had no money of her own – something that had come to seem quite strange to her, so far had she travelled from the world of her girlhood. At all events she was always glad to have an excuse to dress up and go out.

We kissed and chatted and ordered, knowing as we did so that there was a conversation of some substance to come, but by mutual consent we waited until our first courses, bang bang chicken for me and some hot *hors d'oeuvres* for Edith, were on the table. The waiter filled our glasses and retreated and we knew that we had a little while to ourselves.

'We saw David and Isabel last weekend,' I opened. 'We stayed with them in fact.'

'How are they?'

'All right. David's quite busy though I never really know what with.' I paused. 'We all went over to Broughton for a drink.'

Edith took a bite of something in thin batter. 'David must have enjoyed that.'

'He didn't much. He was stuck with Diana Bohun. He kept trying to impress her, which I don't think was very successful.'

'I should say not. She cut me dead the other day in Peter Jones.' She continued to eat and drink with some gusto but she would not give me the slightest help with my task. With an inward sigh I soldiered on.

'Lady Uckfield was there.'

'So I imagined. How is dear old "Googie"?' She was of course being ironic although not uncomfortably bitter. The tiresome nickname had once again gone into inverted commas as it had been in the first weeks of her marriage. And there was the recognition of a barrier there, a deep divide, which now separated the existences of her former mother-in-law and herself.

'Very well. I think. Of course, she wanted to talk about you.'

'There's no "of course" about it. As a matter of fact, I'm rather surprised. Googie is not one for discussing the family troubles. You should feel very flattered.'

'I think she felt that I might be of some use.'

Edith nodded. The penny was dropping and she began to understand that this talk might be leading to deeper waters than she had come prepared for. 'Ah,' she said.

'She told me you were planning to wait the two years.' Edith looked at me in a non-committal way. 'It's not what they want. They want Charles to divorce you now. Straight away. She needs to know what you would think about that.'

I had said it and there was some relief. The words were out. Edith stopped eating and laid her fork down gently on the plate. Very deliberately she sipped her wine as if she were savouring each separate droplet. I suppose the point was it had come. The End of Her Marriage. I am not sure to what extent she had truly accepted that this was where her romance with Simon had brought her until this moment. Though I must say her voice was quite calm when she spoke. 'You mean they want Charles to divorce me for adultery. Citing Simon.'

I nodded. 'I suppose so. I don't think it really works like that these days but I would guess that's the general idea. We didn't actually talk details. If he were to divorce you now it would have to be for a reason, or has that finished? I'm not too sure.'

'I can't say it seems very gentlemanly.'

'It wasn't very ladylike going off with a married actor.'

She nodded and resumed her eating. 'So what do you want from me? What am I to say?'

'I think they feel they have to know that if the divorce does go ahead now you won't suddenly try to fight it. It won't interest you but it won't make any difference, you know, to the money.'

She looked at me rather sadly. 'I don't want any money. Not much anyway. Less than Charles would give me tomorrow if I asked him.'

'I know,' I said. 'I told Lady Uckfield that.'

'Anyway,' she added after a pause, 'it's not a generous offer. Nowadays there isn't a "guilty party". It never does make any difference financially. Didn't you realise that?' I shook my head. 'Well, I bet "Googie" does.' We continued eating in silence for a while. The waiter returned, took away our plates and came back with salmon fishcakes and a bowl of *pommes allumettes*. But the subject remained there on the table like a weeping centrepiece. It was Edith who introduced the character we were both thinking of. 'What does Charles say about all this? I assume he was there. Did you talk to him?'

'Yes, I talked to him.' While theoretically correct, my answer was a lie, for Charles had not been there when Lady Uckfield was sketching out her plans, which is what Edith had meant by her question. I very much doubted he would have allowed his mother to talk as she did had he been. I corrected myself, suddenly oppressed by my implied deception. 'Actually he wasn't there when I was talking to his mother but we went back the next day.'

'And?'

'He says he'll abide by your decision. Whatever you want to do.'

'That sounds more like him. Poor old Charles,' said Edith. 'How was he?'

I had dreaded this. If I could have said that he was looking fine and dandy I would have. I had come to feel, like Lady Uckfield, that it was time to call a halt to this unsuccessful experiment in miscegenation. The problem was he had not looked fine and dandy. 'OK,' I said. 'I don't think all of this has done him much good.'

'No.' She helped herself to some more chips. 'Was Clarissa down there?'

I nodded and Edith was silent. I was about to tell her to discount whatever she had heard, that it was a rumour inspired by Lady Uckfield's ambitions and nothing else, but I was silent. What was the point? She had to let Charles go and where was the good in slowing up her decision? For the rest of lunch we chatted about Simon and acting and Isabel and buying a flat, but as we were leaving Edith reopened the topic.

'Let me think about it.' She smiled slightly. 'Of course, we both know that I'll do what I'm asked but let me think about it. I'll telephone you.'

* * *

Edith Broughton did not go home – or rather she did not return to Ebury Street – at once. It was a crisp, sunny, spring day, when everything seems as clear as a cut-out, cold and bright as a jewel. She was warmly dressed and so, once past the Ritz, she turned left into the Green Park. She strolled down the path, past Wimborne House, past the restored, statue decorated splendour of Spencer House, past the Italianate magnificence of Bridgewater House until she stopped and looked up at Lancaster House, the golden pile, built and occupied for many years by the mighty Dukes of Sutherland. Their duchesses had dominated London Society, one after another, summoning the great and the good of the different eras to ascend the giant, gilded staircase in the grandest of all grand London halls to pay court to each other's wealth and power.

It struck Edith then that she would have enjoyed that older, simpler world when these houses had held sway over the capital. When the Guests and the Spencers and the Egertons and the Leveson-Gowers had lived their ordained lives under these teeming roofs instead of the charitable organisations and government departments and Greek shipping magnates who occupied them now. Forgetting for the moment that she, Edith Lavery, would have had the greatest difficulty in penetrating even the outermost fringe of this golden troupe in any period but our own, she saw herself in her crinoline, never questioning her own happiness and, consequently, being happy. And as she did so, she was struck by how similar her fantasies of the old, pre-Great War world were to those fantasies about her coming life as Lady Broughton, which she had entertained while lying in the bath just before her wedding. How simple things were to be, how the villagers and tenants were going to love her, how the family would bless the day she had come among them! She found herself smiling wistfully as the dream image of herself as the Great Social Force of Twenty-First Century Society receded before her inner gaze, swathed in mist, tearfully waving goodbye.

Pondering this, it seemed at first to her troubled brain that her mother had been wrong and the media had been right all along, that these dreams and ambitions were outmoded, that no one nowadays wants titles and rank and inherited power, that these are the days of the self-made man, of talent, of creativity. But then, looking about at the office workers and sweepers and job interviewees who loitered near her in the park, she was struck by the dishonesty of the media pundits of our time. Was there one here who would not change places with Charles if they could? Was it not possible that the small screen gurus praised meritocracy because it was the only class system that would accord them the highest rank? Even if unearned riches and position had no moral merit, even if they embodied the Dream That Dare Not Speak Its Name, it was still a dream that figured in plenty of people's fantasies. And she had casually discarded it.

Then she thought again with puzzled wonderment of her own supposed unhappiness with Charles. Why exactly had she been so unhappy? When she tried to think back to their time together, she kept remembering those pretty rooms at Broughton and the servants and the park and her work in the village. The only discomforts she could recall were things like packing the car and standing behind Charles at a shoot in the rain. Were these so terrible? And if she thought of Charles, himself, it was with a rather intimate affection. She remembered him swearing at fellow motorists or farting in his sleep and it provoked in her a kind of nostalgic warmth. There was no trace of relief at his passing. If only there had been. Instead she found herself worrying about his loneliness. It pained her to think he was suffering. And increasingly she asked herself what exactly was this personal fulfilment for which so much disruption had been necessary? Was it sexual? Was she admitting that she had done all this because of Simon's cock? Or was it simply to do with boredom? But if it was, how much less bored was she now, sitting in Ebury Street talking to girlfriends on the telephone or meeting them for lunch than she had been working with her committees in the library at Broughton?

She turned away from Lancaster House and walked slowly towards the Victory Arch with Buckingham Palace on her left. The Royal Standard announcing the monarch's presence in London hung limply against its staff. Tourists hovered at the railings, peering in with rapt attention, as if they hoped to catch a glimpse of some Royal Highness strolling down a corridor or coming out for a breather. And again, as she walked, Edith considered the mystery of unearned greatness. She thought how Tigger and Googie and Charles would all be invited to the next court ball, an event of unimaginable glamour to these Japanese travellers with their clicking cameras, to these northerners in their hideous anoraks, blobs of bright, synthetic colour against the cold grey, neo-Georgian facade. Any one of these would have made an invitation to the Palace into a life-long story, sodden with repetition and yet she had turned away from her role in this fairy tale in order to be – to be what precisely? Happy?

The fact was that of late Edith had come to wonder just how much she could be fulfilled by 'personal happiness', if that was what Simon was offering her. Perhaps because she had never succeeded in disentangling her ambitions of fulfilment from her mother's values, she had already begun to hanker for that sweet sense of self-importance that her life at Broughton had brought with it. She understood that these feelings did her no credit but her defence was a pragmatic one. How else was she to enjoy the good things in life if she did not marry them? And her faith in Simon's eventual triumph was waning. She knew more about show business now than she had when they met and she sensed that the series he was in, with a couple more to follow, was probably the best he could hope for. Whatever they might pretend together, they would not be holding hands tightly, stiff with anticipation, at the Oscar ceremony. What was her life to be then? A vicarage in the Home Counties and the occasional interview for an evening newspaper? Was she really expected to provide vocal and emotional support through twenty years of semi-failure to prove she was a real person? Some might say it is only personal achievement that should lead on to glory but what of those who have no talent or special gift with which to achieve? Are they so blameworthy to want to live among the blessed? Poor Edith was aware that she could neither weave nor spin but was she therefore forbidden to covet a life of splendour? Was this so shameful? She shook her head in irritation. At the far corner of her brain, these thoughts were beginning to tell her that despite the reckless choice she had made, her own assessment of the world and her place in it had not really changed in the least. She felt herself resenting anew the accusations she heard from her parents and friends when she first made her run for it, that she could not settle to her new life because beneath the skin of a rebel beat the heart of Mrs Lavery's little girl. And she resented them because she was beginning to be horribly afraid they might be true.

Walking towards Victory Arch, watching the afternoon light glint against the windows of Apsley House, whither she and Charles had been summoned for a party the previous summer, one of the first engagements she had been obliged to cancel because of the split, she recalled with amazement (and it really had begun to seem almost unbelievably strange) that she had jettisoned a high place in the world of the worldly for the position of partner to an obscure man in a generally despised profession. And not for the first time she sat down to think about the extraordinary events of the last year of her life in more detail.

Simon was at the flat when she got back. He was drinking tea and watching an old film. When he was working he was at peace and so inclined to relax and take it easy. It was only when he was out of a job that he would go haring about London keeping lunch dates with people he disliked and telephoning his agent every four hours.

Edith left her coat in the hall. 'Is there a cup for me?'

He waved his mug in the air. 'I just made it with a bag. The water's still hot if you want some.' He had taken his trainers off and they lay, pigeon-toed on the hearth rug. His coat had been thrown across an armchair and books and scripts were littered about the room. Edith stood at the door, taking in the whole scene like a spectator from another country. *The Way We Live Now*. This was the way she lived now, with sixties sofas covered in stained, oatmeal tweed, with large nondescript flower prints in coloured mounts on the walls, with a Perspex coffee table and a gas-log fire. This was the way she was living now. She was acutely aware that she had no desire to enter the room.

Simon, sensing some strangeness between them, stood and approached her in the doorway. He slid an arm around her waist and squeezed her, pushing his mouth onto hers. They had been in an Indian restaurant the night before and she could still taste the spices on his breath. He pressed himself against her and she could feel that he was already aroused. 'Good lunch?' he said.

She nodded. 'Googie sent him. He and Adela were down in Sussex last weekend. They went over to Broughton and of course Googie dragged him off to her lair. The meeting was her idea.'

'And?'

'They want to hurry the divorce.' She paused, sensing his recoil. 'Googie wants to involve you.'

'Jesus!' Simon didn't know what to think. Part of him revelled in it. Visions of more picture spreads on page three in the *Daily Mail* flickered through his brain but with them came trailing streamers of a distant panic. He felt as if he was hurtling down some tube, weightless and powerless, into the unknown. 'Is she serious?'

'I think so but you can calm down. They're wrong. I'm fairly sure no one has to be cited any more. The point is they want to get on with it.'

'What did you say?'

Edith studied the pretty boy before her. He had abandoned his customary flirtatious, winking manner and, although he didn't realise, he looked the better for it. A little seriousness added charm to his bright blue eyes and the careless locks of shining hair that fell forward to veil them. 'I said I had to think about it.'

'Can you stop them?'

'If I want to.'

'How?'

'I'll tell Charles not to go ahead with it.'

Simon laughed. 'And that would do it?'

Edith observed him coolly. How provincial he was! How little he understood men like Charles! She was almost haughty in her defence of her discarded husband to her preferred lover. 'Yes. That would do it.' Simon had stopped laughing but suddenly there seemed to be something irredeemably irritating about him. She couldn't be bothered to embark on the usual chats about how bad everyone was in any film they were watching, how jealous his fellow actors were, how stupid the cameraman. 'I'm going to have a bath,' she said, disengaging herself from his embrace.

Simon threw himself back into the sofa, fixing his gaze once more upon the screen. 'You're very sulky,' he said. 'I shall be charitable and blame the time of the month.'

She didn't answer but went instead down to the basement bathroom that opened off their dark, little bedroom. An attempt had been made with a looking glass and a wallpaper of enormous poppies to brighten the two rooms up but it only deepened their lightless gloom. She ran the bath, undressed and climbed in. She was aware that since she had entered the park she had been in a kind of strange, unworldly mental state. She felt intensely aware of every movement of her limbs, of every ripple of the water against her skin. She felt spacey, almost drunk – although she certainly drank very little at lunch. A vague sense of apprehension seemed to bloat her stomach and her very nerve ends prickled individually the length of her body. But then, at last, she realised what it was that was catching at the edge of her attention.

Simon had said no more than he knew. It was her time of the month. She was as regular as clockwork.

And she was five days late.

TWENTY

~

The morning following my lunch with Edith our doorbell rang at not much later than a quarter past eight.

'Christ!' said Adela. 'Who on earth's that?' We were in our tiny bedroom, which overlooked the area. As the front door was just out of sight to the right, it wasn't possible to sneak a preview of our visitor but, in any case, at that time in the morning, I just assumed it was the postman so I was not particularly careful with my toilet as I shouted that I was coming. When I unlocked the door in my underpants with my hair unbrushed, I discovered it was not the postman, who must after all be accustomed to such sights, but Edith Broughton who stood on the mat.

'Hello,' I said with something of a tone of wonder.

Edith pushed past me into the room. 'I have to talk to you.' She threw herself down onto the sofa that divided the living bit from the eating bit of the flat's solitary 'reception room'.

'Can I dress first?' I asked.

She nodded and I hurried back into the bedroom to inform the amazed Adela, busy struggling into her clothes, of the identity of our early morning caller.

She was ready first and when I rejoined them Edith already had a cup of coffee in her hand and a piece of toast before her. 'So?' I said. There didn't seem to be much point in pretending that this was a normal way of carrying on. Edith glanced at Adela who jumped up.

'I'd better be off, hadn't I? Not to worry. I've a mass of paperwork to do . . .'

Edith waved her back to her seat. 'Stay. There's no secret. Anyway,' she glanced around at our minuscule accommodation, 'I imagine you'd be within earshot wherever you went.' Adela settled herself and we both waited.

'I want to see Charles.' Her voice was quite flat as she spoke but of course we were both most interested by what she said. I did not really understand why she had felt the need to come round and communicate this to us at dawn but I was fascinated nevertheless. I was soon to understand what my part was to be. 'I want you to arrange it.'

Adela caught my eye and faintly shook her head. She had all the horror of her kind for getting involved in this kind of thing. Whatever the outcome, somehow one is always blameworthy. She also, as she told me later, had no wish to incur Lady Uckfield's enmity and she suspected that this would be an inevitable by-product of the proposed plan of action. One must remember of course that Adela, from first to last, was entirely on Lady Uckfield's side and never on Edith's.

'Why do you need me?' I said rather wanly.

'I rang Broughton last night. I asked for Charles but I got Googie. She said he wasn't there but I'm sure he was. I rang London and Feltham and they said he was at Broughton. I know he was. She doesn't want me to speak to him.'

All this would only confirm Adela's suspicions that in some vague way we were being asked to take on Lady Uckfield. 'I don't really see what *I* can do.'

'They'll let you speak to him. Say you want to ask him to lunch or something and then, when he comes on the line, tell him I want to meet him.'

'I don't think I can do that,' I said. 'I don't mind telephoning,' which was a lie, 'but if Lady Uckfield asks me what I'm going to say, I'll tell her. She can't imagine she can prevent you meeting for ever.'

'Not for ever, no. Just long enough.'

'I don't believe that,' I said. Although I did.

In truth, I was pretty sure that I too was on Lady Uckfield's side when it came down to it. The facts were simple enough. Edith had married Charles without loving him in order to gain a position. She had then made a complete failure of that same position, abandoned it, broken her faith with Charles, made a great scandal and caused him a good deal of pain. Lady Uckfield now wished to be rid of her once and for all and, frankly, could anyone wonder at it?

'Do you think Charles will want to see you?' asked Adela. 'Perhaps it was he who refused to come to the telephone.' Which was certainly a point worth considering.

'If he doesn't, I want to hear it from him.'

The three of us sat in silence for a while. Adela crunched her toast and turned to Nigel Dempster.

'Anything?' I said.

'Sarah Carter's sister's married some painter and the Langwells are getting a divorce, which we knew last October.'

'Will you do it?' said Edith.

Adela and I looked at each other but I refused the message in her eyes. Ultimately, much as I would have liked to, it would have been wrong of me to have abandoned Edith to her fate and espoused the cause of the Broughtons. Whatever I might privately think about the wrongs and rights of the matter, this would have been a dishonourable course. First, and before everything else, I had been Edith's friend, as even Lady Uckfield had acknowledged.

'I will,' I said. 'But I won't do it either at this time of the morning or with you listening. Go home and I'll telephone you.'

Edith nodded and, after finishing her coffee, left.

'Something's up,' said Adela.

I rang at half past ten and asked for Charles. Despite what Edith had said I was quite surprised when Lady Uckfield came on the line.

'Hello,' she said. 'How are you?'

'I was trying to track down Charles.'

She was very smooth and clearly four steps ahead of me. 'I'm afraid he's not here. Can I give him a message?'

I toyed with the idea of bluffing but she was obviously well aware of why I was ringing and it seemed a foolish corner to paint myself into. 'I'm on an errand, I'm afraid. And I'm not at all sure you'll approve.'

'Try me.' Her voice had gone from reserved to glacial.

'It's Edith. She wants to see Charles.'

'Why?'

'I don't know why.' This was true.

'What's the point?'

'I don't know that there is any point but I do know that you won't get a straight answer out of her concerning your proposals re the divorce unless she sees him.'

'You've asked her then?'

'I've asked her and she says she wants to think about it. Part of that thinking, I take it, has to go on in Charles's presence.'

222

There was a pause for a moment and I could hear down the line that eerie echo of other conversations, other, strange anonymous bits of lives being lived, a thousand miles away. 'Are you free this afternoon? Can you meet me for tea?'

'There's nothing I would enjoy more but in this instance I don't know that I'll be able to add anything to what I've already told you.'

'I'll be at the Ritz. At four.'

I was interested that she did not want me to come to their flat in Cadogan Square.

'Perhaps Tigger's coming up with her. Perhaps Charles is there,' said Adela and for a moment I was tempted to walk round and ring the bell. I thought better of it, having decided that it might behove me to hear what Lady Uckfield had to say first.

I did, however, telephone Edith.

'What are you going to say to her?'

'I don't know. That she is wasting her time trying to keep you two apart, I suppose. If that's what she's doing.'

'Of course it's what she's doing.'

'I mean without Charles's knowledge.' Edith was silent. 'At any rate, I'll call you this evening.' I rang off.

I asked tentatively whether or not Lady Uckfield had arrived but the manager was not one to let such an opportunity slip by. 'Gentleman for the Marchioness of Uckfield,' he observed loudly to a passing waiter, who escorted me courteously past the turning heads to where she waited. She was sitting trimly at a table in the Marble Hall to the right of the great, gilded fountain. She smiled and waved a little hand as I approached, and stood to greet me with her neat, bird-like movements. The man brought the tea with a lot of milady'ing, all of it gently and serenely acknowledged. She laughed gaily. 'Isn't this a treat?'

'It is for me,' I said.

Her manner became not exactly more serious but at any rate more direct. She was a little less breathlessly urgent and remembering that scene in her sitting room at Broughton I understood that she was going to impart some real, as opposed to faked, intimacy. 'I want to be quite honest because I think you may be able to help.'

'I'm simultaneously flattered and dubious,' I said.

'I don't want Charles to have to see Edith.'

'So I gathered.'

'It's not that I'm being unkind. Truly. It's just that I think he's in the most tremendous muddle and I don't want him any more confused.'

'Lady Uckfield,' I said, 'I know very well why you think it a bad idea. So do I. You believe the marriage was a mistake and you had rather not prolong it. I quite agree. The fact remains that, at this moment, Edith is Charles's wife and if she wants to see him and if he, as I suspect, also wants to see her, then hadn't we better get out of the way?'

A momentary flicker of irritation shadowed her face. 'Why do you think he wants to see her?'

'Because he's still in love with her.'

She said nothing for a moment but poked among the sandwiches to find an egg one, which she nibbled with exaggerated delight. 'Aren't these *good!*' she whispered covertly, as if we must prevent anyone else hearing at all costs. She looked at me with her darting, cat-like eyes. 'You think I've been unfair to Edith.'

I shook my head. 'No. I think you don't like her but I don't think you've been particularly unfair to her.'

She nodded in acknowledgement of this. 'I don't like her. Much. However, that's not the point.'

'What is the point?'

'The point is that she cannot make Charles happy. Whether I like her or not is neither here nor there. I detested my mother-in-law and yet I was fully aware of what a success she had made of Broughton and of Tigger's wretched father. It took me twenty years to bury her memory. Do you think it would matter to me if I simply didn't like her? I'm not a schoolgirl.'

'No.' I sipped my tea. This was flattering indeed. For some reason Lady Uckfield had decided to draw aside the curtain that habitually clothed all her private thoughts and actually talk to me. She had not finished.

'Let me tell you about my son. Charles is a good, kind, uncompli-cated man. He's much nicer than I am, you know. But he is less . . .' She faltered, searching for a loyal adjective that would fit the need.

'Intelligent?' I ventured.

Since I had said it, she let it pass. 'He needs a wife who values not just him but who he is, what he does. What their life is. He is not one to be able to give weight to a different philosophy in his own home. He could not be married to a socialist opera singer and respect her for her different views. It is not in him.'

'I don't think it's in Edith either,' I said.

'Edith married an idea of a life that she had gleaned from novels and magazines. She thought it meant travel and fashion shows and meeting Mick Jagger. She saw herself throwing parties for Princess Michael in Mauritius . . .' She shrugged. I was quite impressed that she'd heard of Mick Jagger. 'I don't know if some people live like that. Maybe. What I do know is that will never be Charles's life. His whole existence is the farming calendar. For the next fifty years he will shoot and farm and farm and shoot and go abroad for three weeks in July. He will worry about the tenants and have fights with the vicar and try to get the government to contribute to rewiring the east wing. And his friends, with very few exceptions, will be other people reroofing their houses and farming and shooting and trying to get government grants and exemptions. That is his future.'

'And you're sure it could never be Edith's?'

'Aren't you?'

I could remember Edith sobbing with boredom on the shoot at Broughton and sulking through evening after evening of Tigger's stories and Googie's charm. But of course, what Lady Uckfield did not know and I suspected, was how bored and depressed Edith was with her new life. I thought of her at Fiona Grey's party being led around like a prize heifer. Lady Uckfield interpreted my silence as agreement and her manner warmed. 'It's not entirely her fault. Even I can see that. That terrible mother has stuffed her head with a lot of Barbara Cartland nonsense. What chance had she?'

'Poor old Mrs Lavery,' I said. Lady Uckfield shuddered with a tiny grimace. This was the woman Mrs Lavery had planned to share scrumptious lunches with and trips to the milliner.

'I'm not a snob,' started Lady Uckfield but this was really too much and I could not prevent at least one eyebrow rising. She attempted to rebuke me. 'I'm not! I know people can marry up and bring it off. I have lots of different sorts of friends. I do!' She was quite indignant. I suppose she believed she was telling the truth.

'Who?' I said.

She thought for a moment. 'Susan Curragh and Anne Melton. I like them both very much. I defy you to say that I don't.' She had named an immensely rich American heiress who was now the wife of a rather dull junior minister and the daughter of a clothing millionaire who had married an impoverished Irish earl thereby putting him on the social map. I knew neither woman but I trembled for Edith if Lady Uckfield thought them good examples of 'marrying up'. 'You don't believe me, I know, but I was brought up not to think in terms of "class".'

What interested me in this was that Lady Uckfield could have made that statement quite safely on a lie detector while the truth was, of course, that she had been brought up to think in terms of nothing else and she had largely (if not entirely) been true to her teaching. She continued. 'The important thing is not Edith's class, whatever that means, but that she simply doesn't enjoy the job. She and her frightful mother are "London Ladies". They want to lunch in Italian restaurants and go to charity balls and fly to the sun for the winter. Running a house like Broughton, or Feltham for that matter, is just slog once the gilt's worn off. It's paperwork and committees. It's arguing with English Heritage inspectors who all hate you for living there and want to make everything as difficult for you as they possibly can. It's pleading with government departments and economising on the heating. Those houses are fun to stay in. Even "London Ladies" like that. But they're hard, hard work to own. She could never take either pleasure or satisfaction in that life. I don't even blame her but she couldn't. And to be quite frank,' she paused, almost hesitating in case she was giving away too much ammunition, 'I'm not sure how much she likes Charles.'

I thought of that far away engagement dinner with Caroline Chase on my left. *It's frightfully dreary down here ... flower shows all summer, freezing pipes all winter.* I could hear the echo of her cold, hard voice. *I suppose Edith's ready for all that?* And how triumphant Edith had seemed. How she had swept the pool and gained the prize.

'If what you say is true then where's the danger of letting them meet?'

'Because I suspect that eight months with an out-of-work actor in Ebury Street has reminded her of why she found Charles attractive, or should I say an attractive proposition, in the first place. I think she may want him back.'

'And you're against that?' I felt a bit sorry for Simon to be described as an 'out-of-work actor' when he, poor soul, thought he was dazzling in his success. Still, it didn't seem the moment to cavil.

She spoke with statesmanlike clarity. 'I am against it with every fibre of my being.' I suppose in some part of me I was surprised at her honesty. I was used to the token revulsion for divorce that is one of the obligatory attitudes in Society. Although in truth they care little whether people are divorced or not, simply whom they are married to at the time. Even so, she was of the old school and I was fairly sure there was no such thing as a divorce in either her, or Tigger's, genealogy. She nodded. 'You're surprised I'd prefer the scandal to run its course. I admit it. I would rather have what little of this story is left than patch things up and risk a bigger smash in five years when Edith has either rediscovered how bored she is, or found someone as rich as Charles who bores her less. There may be children involved by that time and I prefer to see my grandchildren brought up at Broughton by both parents.'

'I do see,' I said. It was fruitless to deny that there was a good deal of logic in her reasoning.

'So can you help me?' She tucked busily into another sandwich and filled both our cups. She had been honest with me and I could not be less than honest with her.

'No, Lady Uckfield, I cannot help you.' She stopped pouring in her surprise. I suppose she felt that she had extended such an enormous privilege to me by revealing so much of her hand that I could not fail to be firmly attached to her interest. Seeing her disappointment, I clarified. 'It is not because I do not agree with you. As a matter of fact I do. It is because I do not believe any argument will turn Edith from her meeting. And I do not believe I have the smallest right to interfere.'

She nodded slightly, a sharp, jerky movement, which betrayed her terrible pain. 'I imagine you mean I have no right either.'

I shook my head. 'You're Charles's mother. You have the right to interfere. I am not sure you have any hope of success but you have the right to try.' I felt the interview had come to an end and I stood. As it was, I doubted that Lady Uckfield and I would be so easy in each other's company again. She'd abandoned too many of her customary defences to be able to forgive me quickly for witnessing her in this state. To make matters worse I could see that her eyes were beginning to moisten and before my horrified gaze a single tear, amazed to be released from a duct that must have held it prisoner for twenty years, started to make its tentative way down her carefully powdered cheek.

She stood and put her hand on my arm. 'Just don't help her.' Her voice was urgent, it is true, but not with that girlish, don't-tell-Father, pseudo-urgency that I had grown used to. This was a cry of desperation. 'Just don't encourage her. That's all I beg. For her sake as much as for his. They'll both be wretched.'

I nodded and gave what assurances I felt I could, thanked her for my tea and watched her pull herself together before my eyes so that, by the time I turned at the arch taking me towards the Arlington Street entrance, she could wave at me as composed as if she were in the Royal Box at Ascot. All I knew was that I could not have been less clear as to quite what I was going to say to Edith.

'You're right, of course. She doesn't want you to meet.'

'I told you.'

'Even so, I don't really see how she can prevent it.'

'She'll send him away again. To America. For horse sales or something. She'll fix it up with her friends. They're everywhere.'

'Sounds like Watergate.'

She gave a harsh little laugh. 'You think you're joking.'

'At any rate,' I said, 'he can't stay in America for ever. You'll just have to keep trying. I don't think he'll avoid you when you do run him to earth. Really I don't. You must just bide your time.'

'I haven't *got* time,' said Edith.

Something in the tone of her voice prevented my asking for clarification and, indeed, I confess that I deliberately put the remark out of my mind. I did not want to address it, I suppose, and I certainly did not want to share it with Adela, sensing perhaps that it could mean everything or nothing. If everything, why risk the release of that knowledge into the ether? If nothing, why not forget it?

We were silent a moment with Edith perhaps aware that she had said more than she'd intended. She may have been pondering how to contain the remark without referring to it again.

'What do you plan to do then?' I asked.

'I don't know,' she said.

TWENTY-ONE

~

She didn't know. It seemed crazy but she literally did not know how she could contact her own husband. It may surprise some people but for a time, Edith had assumed that either Sotheby's or Christie's would rescue her from this dilemma. The public is not aware of it but over the last decade the summer parties of those two great auction houses have become in many ways the high points of the London social calendar, a chance for the genuine *gratin*, as opposed to the ubiquitous Café Society, to meet and mingle before they disperse for the summer. Edith knew that Charles would attend both, as would Googie. Even Tigger was prepared to struggle up from the country in order to renew his acquaintance with most of his class. It was an annual, pleasurable duty cheerfully undertaken by a large proportion of the high aristocracy much as the opening day of the Summer Exhibition used to be. There Charles would be found and there Edith would buttonhole him. The only trouble was that the days went by and every morning the envelopes flopped down onto the mat but the requisite, white, pasteboard cards with their embossed, italic script were not among them. Whether to spare Charles from embarrassment or perhaps to shield Lady Uckfield from discomfort (nobody can have thought that Lord Uckfield would even notice Edith's presence), for whatever reason, the Countess Broughton's name had clearly been excised from the list. She was not invited to either gathering.

At last it became impossible for her not to accept that she had been passed over. It was time for an alternative plan. She sat hunched over her address book, leafing through the neatly pencilled names. This was a habit she had unconsciously adopted from her hated mother-in-law. It meant the entries could be more easily rubbed out when their owners moved or when their use was finished and done with. This morning she stared at page after page, trying to find one who would help. At last, *faute de mieux*, she dialled Tommy Wainwright's number. Arabella answered and Edith asked for Tommy, a request that was greeted with a cool silence at the other end before Arabella spoke.

'He's at the House, I'm afraid.'

'When will he be back?'

'The thing is, he's most frightfully busy at the moment. Can I help?'

No, thought Edith. You cannot and you would not. 'Not really,' she said lightly. 'I don't want to be a bother. Just say I telephoned.'

'Of course I will.' It was obvious from her flat tone of voice that Arabella intended to say nothing but, in the event, she felt discomfort at the thought of being discovered in a lie so she did pass on the message while predictably urging her husband to ignore it. Edith had already played out this scenario or something like it in her brain so it was quite a surprise that evening when she picked up the receiver to hear Tommy speaking.

'I want to see Charles and everyone's stopping me,' she said after the usual pleasantries.

'Why?'

'Because they're frightened of Googie, because they want to stay in with the family. I don't know why.'

There was a short silence. The request may not have been articulated but it had nevertheless been made. 'I don't want to land him in it.'

'Nor do I,' said Edith firmly. 'I just want to see him.'

Another silence. Then with something like a sigh, Tommy spoke. 'He's coming here for a drink on Wednesday at about seven. You could always drop in then.'

'I will never forget this.' Edith's voice was sonorous with significance and from it Tommy could easily gauge the treatment she had been receiving elsewhere from her erstwhile world.

'Don't get your hopes up too much,' he said. He was after all fully aware of the powers she was ranging herself against.

*　　*　　*

I was already in the Wainwright drawing room when Edith arrived. It wasn't a large party, roughly twenty or thirty souls who had nothing better to do. They had dutifully assembled in the cramped mews house near Queen Anne Street to start their evening with a few smoked salmon whirls from Marks & Spencer and some bottles of Majestic champagne. The gathering was already past its zenith and the guests had begun to peel away, heeding the call of dinner reservations and theatres and baby-sitters, when Edith came through the door. She was smiling with anticipation but I could see her face shrink with disappointment as she surveyed the room. I went up to her.

'Don't tell me Charles has gone. I got stuck in traffic and I left too late anyway.'

It was easy to see why. She had taken immense trouble with her appearance and I could not remember seeing her in better fettle, her lovely face flawless, her hair shining and an alluring evening outfit encasing her already desirable form.

'Stop worrying,' I murmured reassuringly. 'He hasn't arrived yet.'

'But he is coming?'

'I suppose so. Tommy said he was.'

'That's what he said to me but where is he?'

She bit her lip in annoyance as a couple of her former friends grudgingly decided to acknowledge her presence and draw her into conversation. Adela came up to me.

'What's she doing here?' she said. 'I thought this was the other camp.'

'Not really. I gather Tommy was trying to bring them together.'

'You amaze me. Two days ago, I ran into Arabella at Harvey Nicks and she was saying the break-up was the best thing that could have happened.'

'I don't doubt it but even married couples can on occasion disagree. Or don't you believe such a thing possible?'

'I believe it,' said Adela sourly, 'but I still don't see how Arabella could have allowed the invitation in the first place.'

The answer, of course, which I could not give then but I was able to supply later, was that Arabella had given no such agreement.

The party was on its last legs. A few of us had been invited to stay on for dinner and we were in that uncomfortable, if familiar, period when almost everyone who is not invited to remain has gone but there is always a couple who do not realise that they are delaying the launch of the next stage of the evening. Usually, the hostess weakens and says to the obdurate, 'Do stay for something to eat if you'd like to.' To the trained ear, this translates as, 'Please go. We are hungry and you are not invited.' The old hand on the cocktail party circuit will then look around, blush and scuttle away, muttering about having to be somewhere else. But there is always the risk that the stayer will be uninitiated in these rituals or stubborn or simply stupid – in which case they may accept the unmeant offer of hospitality. In this instance, Arabella Wainwright was clearly not prepared to take a chance on having to entertain Edith for the rest of the evening and so she said nothing. But still Edith would not leave. I strolled over to her.

'I suppose you're having dinner here?' she said.

'We are. And so I imagine is more or less everyone else in the room.'

She looked around. When she spoke her voice had a bleakness that almost brought tears to my eyes. 'I was all geared up. It didn't occur to me that he wouldn't come. His mother must have got wind of it and put him off somehow.'

'I don't see how. Tommy didn't tell me you were coming and I can't imagine he would have told anyone else.'

She didn't linger all that much longer. When Arabella brought a pile of plates out of the tiny kitchen and plonked them noisily onto the dining room table alongside an arrangement of sporting mats even Edith had to admit defeat.

'I must run,' she said to her detached and unbending hostess. 'Thank you. It's been lovely seeing you again.'

Arabella nodded silently, only too glad to be rid of her but Tommy took her to the door. 'I don't know what happened,' he said. 'I am sorry.'

Edith gave him a sad little smile. 'Oh well. Perhaps it's not meant to be.' Then she kissed him and left. But for all her pretended acceptance of fate, she continued to think someone had wrecked her chances. And she was right.

It was much later in the evening when, in a rare break with my personal tradition, I was helping to clear some plates away, that I overheard a short snatch of conversation coming from behind the kitchen door.

'What do you mean?' said an exasperated Tommy.

'Exactly what I say. I thought it was unfair to spring an ambush on him when we're supposed to be his friends.'

'If that was really what you thought then why didn't you tell Charles and let him make up his own mind?'

'I might ask you the same question.'

Tommy was clearly flustered. 'Because I'm not sure he knows his own mind.'

When Arabella spoke again, it was hard to discern the faintest traces of regret. 'Precisely. And that is why I told his mother.'

'Then you're a bitch.'

'Maybe. You can tell me I was wrong in six months time. Now take in the cream and don't spill it.'

Unable to pretend that I was arranging the dirty plates for much longer, I pushed the kitchen door open to find no sign of dispute within.

'How kind you are,' said Arabella, smoothly relieving me of my burden.

My wife was reluctant to be drawn into a moral position as we drove home. 'Just don't do anything of the sort to me,' she said, and I agreed. Not that I would criticise Tommy. Indeed I thought he had acted the part of a true friend but, rather feebly perhaps, it was not a position I was anxious to find myself in. I did not repeat what Arabella had said about the six-month interval probably because, even at that stage, I did not want to take it on board.

*   *   *

A few days later, Edith awoke to find herself vomiting into the lavatory bowl. She must have fumbled her way there in half-sleep and it was only the act of retching that finally brought her to her senses. When at last it seemed that even the very lining of her stomach must have been discharged into the pan, she stopped, gasped for air and sat back. Simon came to the door, with his hand over the portable telephone. He slept naked and normally the sight of his godly form cheered her into a sense of present good but this morning, his lightly muscled charms were wasted on her.

'Are you all right?' he asked superfluously.

'I think it must have been those prawns,' she said, knowing full well that he had chosen the soup.

'Poor you. Better out than in.' He smiled, holding up the receiver, and mimed, 'It's your mother,' with a comic grimace. Edith nodded and reached out her hand for the telephone. 'I'll make some coffee,' said Simon, and wandered off to the kitchen.

Edith wiped her mouth and settled her thoughts. 'Mummy? No, I was in the bathroom.'

'Was that you being sick?' said Mrs Lavery at the other end.

'Well, I don't know who else.'

'Are you all right?'

'Of course I'm all right. We went to a ghastly place in Earl's Court last night that's been opened by some failed actor Simon knows. I had shellfish. I must have been mad.'

'Only I thought you were looking rather green around the gills when I saw you.' Edith had accompanied her mother on a fruitless search for a hat the previous week. That was enough in itself to make most people fairly green but she said nothing. 'So you're not ill?'

'Certainly not.'

'You would tell me if there was ... something, wouldn't you?'

Edith knew very well that she would hesitate to trust her mother with the time of day but there was no point in going into that now. 'Of course I would,' she said. There was a pause.

'And I suppose there's no news. About ... everything ...'

'No.'

'Oh, darling.' However irritated, Edith did feel sorry for her mother. She was forced to concede that Mrs Lavery, shallow as her values might be, was experiencing some perfectly genuine emotions. Particularly regret. 'You won't take any ... step you might be sorry about, will you?'

'What step?'

'I mean ... you won't burn your bridges until you're sure ...'

Edith was used to her mother's seemingly limitless supply of clichés so she needed no translator to tell her what they were discussing. Oddly, despite the paucity of her mother's vocabulary, the question had succeeded in centring her thoughts on the matter. As she brought the conversation to an end and cleared the line, she knew the time had come for positive action.

It was a Saturday, a mild, pleasant day for them as a rule, involving newspapers, a lunch out somewhere, perhaps a cinema or possibly a dinner with some friends in a Wandsworth kitchen but as Edith dressed she knew that no such day lay ahead for her. She selected her outfit with considerable care, casual country clothes, well bred, unshowy, exactly the type of skirt and jersey that she had renounced with a religious fervour so short a time ago. Just as when she was choosing her clothes for the dress show, she was once more conscious that her two lives demanded two costumes. A duke's daughter might get away with wearing some streetwalker's outfit from Voyage at a dinner in Shropshire, indeed she would be praised for her aristocratic eccentricity but she, Edith, would never be given the same licence. Had she dared to wear London clothes in the country, to Charles's circle it would only have been a confirmation of her ill-breeding. When she entered the kitchen, Simon looked up in surprise. 'My word. You look as if you're auditioning for *Hay Fever.*'

'I feel such a fool. I promised to take my mother to a lunch party today and I completely forgot about it. That's why she rang. Can you forgive me?'

'Whose lunch party?'

'Just some country cousins.'

'You don't have any country cousins. Wasn't that the whole point?' In saying this, Simon showed one of his rare flashes of understanding. It was exactly the point.

'I do but I never talk about them. They're too boring to live.'

'Which means you don't want me to come.' Simon hated to be left out of anything. Or at least, if he was, it had to be his choice. He didn't mind being too busy to join in, in fact he quite enjoyed it, but the thought that people were not anxious for his company – even if it was for a journey to the post box – was anathema to him.

Edith smiled a wistful, wouldn't-that-be-nice smile. 'I wish. But she's been begging me for us to have some time on our own. I suppose she wants to talk about everything.' This was accompanied by a half-shrug that brooked no argument.

'Just be nice about me.'

She gave him a warm and supportive smile, knowing that in her heart she was plotting his fall, and set off downstairs to their bedroom to collect her coat. She did not want to tell Simon where she was going as that would have detonated a scene and she was by no means certain of the day's possible outcome. The last thing she wanted was for him to flounce back to his wife in a pet, leaving her to come home to an empty flat.

The truth was she had determined, in that morning moment of surveying her own floating sick, that she was not going to be put off for one day longer. She would drive that very morning to Broughton and beard the lion – or rather the lioness's cub – in his den. As she sped out down the A22, she couldn't really understand what had taken her so long to come to this decision. This was her husband and she was going to what was, after all, her marital home. No one could argue with that.

An unpleasant surprise was waiting for her, as she had forgotten that on a Saturday in summer the house would of course be open to the public. Somehow that had slipped through her calculations and she was now in the faintly ludicrous position of having to choose between parking her car in the courtyard and going in through the family's entrance or entering by the public door and travelling up into the body of the house surrounded by tourists and housewives from Brighton. She made the bold decision to go in by the latter route. She thought there would be plenty of time to block her path if she rang the family's doorbell and she was gambling on Charles being in his own study, which was next to the library. It would be the work of a moment to slip through the cordon and open the door and she correctly guessed that none of the guides would stop her. Indeed, she made a point of pausing to say hello to the pleasant woman in a stout, country suit who stood taking tickets. 'Hello, Mrs Curley, how are you? Can I creep in this way? Would you mind?' Edith had mastered this particular trick of her husband's people, that of asking as a favour something that cannot be refused. 'Oh, Mrs So-and-so, could you *bear* to wait up until we get home? Would that be a *terrible* bore for you?' Of course, the wretched woman being instructed in this way (as well as her employer) knows that this really means 'You are forbidden to go to bed until I have returned' but it is of course a more self-congratulatory way to deliver a command. It is all part of the aristocracy's consciously created image. They like to pride themselves on being 'marvellous with servants', which usually means making impossible demands in the friendliest voice imaginable.

Mrs Curley was clearly uncomfortable with the request but as Edith had predicted, there was nothing she could do about it. 'Of course, mi-lady,' she said with a cheerful nod, and dialled the family's private number the minute Edith had passed by.

*   *   *

Charles Broughton was indeed in his study or, as Lady Uckfield liked to call it, the Little Library, just as Edith suspected. He was answering letters in a vague sort of way, pretending to be, rather than actually being, busy. The house party was of his mother's choosing and, as always, those friends she had selected for him were not congenial to his wounded soul. Diana Bohun he found cold and too self-consciously grand to be of interest while her husband was very nearly mad. Clarissa was not among them. He had at least managed to persuade his mother that she was barking up the wrong tree there but . . . if not Clarissa then who?

He knew about Edith's appearance at Tommy Wainwright's. Indeed Tommy had told him the following day, perhaps not wanting to have someone else deliver the news. At first Charles had been extremely angry, not with Tommy but with his mother. On the evening in question she had suddenly made him take her to visit some ancient friend in hospital, a mission that was represented to him as crucial but was of course, as he could see now, the simplest ploy to keep him from the Wainwright party. But then, after he had calmed down a little, he wondered for the thousandth time what would have been achieved by their meeting. Whatever his friends might say about the strangeness of her actions, he did understand why Edith had left him. He was dull. He knew this was true because, alas for him, he was just clever enough to be aware of it. He knew he was no company for her once the joy of her advancement had worn off. Half the time, if he was honest, he didn't really know what his wife was talking about. When she questioned the policy of the Opposition or tried to evaluate the benefits and harm of intervening in the Middle East . . . Charles knew there were differing points of view on these subjects but he didn't see why he was called upon to have them. So long as he kept voting Conservative and saying how frightful he thought New Labour, wasn't that enough? It was all and more than most of his pals in White's expected of him. Well, clearly it wasn't enough for Edith. Now even he had begun to suspect that she might conceivably want him back – or at least that she wanted to talk about it – but had anything changed? Wouldn't she tire of him again within a matter of months, if not weeks? Wouldn't it better for her and for him if they knew when they were beaten? This in short was how he had begun to think of his marriage. A defeat certainly but a defeat that should now be faced up to and walked away from. Which was of course precisely what Lady Uckfield had intended. It is customary these days to suggest that all interference in the private lives of one's children invariably leads to disappointment but this is not true. Clever parents, who do not play their game too fast, can achieve their aims. And the Marchioness of Uckfield was cleverer than most.

He looked up as the door opened and the sedate figure of the Viscountess Bohun slid into the room. 'Charles?' she said with a despairing roll of her eyes. 'Thank God you're here.'

'Why? What is it?'

'I'm in the most frightful fix. Peter's gone for a walk and we haven't got the car with us. Anyway . . .' Charles waited patiently. 'The thing is . . .' Diana moistened her lip nervously. She was really quite a talented actress. 'I've made a sort of muddle of the dates and I've come without anything . . .'

Charles looked at her, puzzled. This made no sense at all, like a piece translated badly from a foreign tongue. 'I'm so sorry,' he said in answer to Diana's pseudo-blushes, 'I'm not sure I . . .'

Diana overcame her revulsion for this sort of tactic. Desperate times breed desperate measures and as her hostess had made clear, these were desperate times. 'I wasn't expecting it but . . . it's that time of the month and I've got to get to a chemist . . .'

'Oh, Lord.' Charles leaped to his feet in a frenzy of embarrassment. 'Of course. What can I do?'

Diana breathed more easily. She had reached her goal and wonderfully quickly. 'Could you bear to run me into Lewes, only everything in the country shuts at one and—'

'Certainly. Right away.'

'I've just got to tell your mother something.'

'Righto. I'll get the car. Be outside our entrance in five minutes. And don't worry.'

She rather loved him for telling her not to worry about an experience she had been going through once a month since she was twelve but she chose not to assuage his anxiety. With a weak smile, she watched him scuttle out of the room. In this choice of lie, Diana had judged correctly if she wanted instant action. As she calculated, Charles, like all men of his type, had the greatest possible distaste for any of the mechanics of womanhood. One hint of them and he neither needed nor wanted further explanation in order to make him act fast. As he thundered down the family staircase, she listened with the just pride of an efficient workman.

*   *   *

Edith had hardly reached the landing by the bronze of the slave before Lady Uckfield issued forth from a roped-off archway. 'Edith? Is that you? Why didn't you tell us you were coming?' Her mother-in-law slid her arm through hers and attempted to drag her towards the door into the family sitting room. Edith knew that the game was up, silently cursing herself for not pulling a scarf over her face and sliding in unnoticed, but even so she would not give in at once. She extricated herself from Googie's grip and started towards the library and Charles's study beyond.

'I thought I'd be a nuisance and I only want a quick word with Charles. It won't take a moment.' She was walking so fast that, to the delight of the public present, Lady Uckfield was forced to break into a sort of trot to keep up with her. They passed into the splendid library with its high mahogany and ormolu-mounted bookshelves. Above the chimneypiece, an early Broughton in a chestnut periwig gazed down, startled at the scene being played out below him. A few tourists had recognised one or other of them and since the marital split had been in half the newspapers in the country, they left off their bored examination of the thousands of gilded, leather spines and turned all their attention to the two women, thrilled by this unexpected entertainment opportunity.

'Are you staying for luncheon?' said Lady Uckfield, aware of being the cynosure of all eyes and anxious to normalise this very abnormal situation.

'Why? Would you like me to?' said Edith. She in contrast was thoroughly enjoying the exposure of her mother-in-law to the gaze of the common multitude.

'Of course,' said Lady Uckfield, grabbing and pulling at Edith's sleeve in a vain attempt to slow her progress across the gleaming floor.

'I don't think so,' said Edith. She was at the study door by now and her hand was almost on the knob when it opened to reveal the stately form of Lady Bohun. Imperceptibly, with a movement hardly visible to the naked eye, she nodded to her hostess. Edith saw it and at once knew she was too late. The bird had flown.

'Hello, Edith,' said Diana in her slowest and most mannered drawl. 'Will you excuse me? I'm just running into Lewes for something and I must get there before everything closes. Will you be here when we get back?'

'What do you think?' said Edith, and Diana had gone without further ado. Left alone with her daughter-in-law, Lady Uckfield drew her into the room and closed the door. 'Sit down for a moment,' she said, taking her own place behind Charles's desk and absent-mindedly tidying his scattered papers into neat piles.

'There's no need for this,' answered Edith. 'If Charles isn't here, I'll go.'

'Please sit down,' was the repeated request, and Edith did. 'I am sorry you see us as your enemies, my dear.'

'You may be sorry but you can hardly be surprised.'

Lady Uckfield gave her a hurt look. 'I wanted your marriage to work, you know. You have misjudged me if you think otherwise. I always wanted you to be happy.'

'You wanted us to make the best of a bad job.'

'But you didn't, did you?' said Lady Uckfield crisply, all trace of her customary gush and *vibrato* gone.

There was a measure of reason to this that took some of the wind out of Edith's sails as she was forced to admit. Was it rational of her to suggest that Lady Uckfield should have celebrated when she, Edith, came into their lives? Why should her mother-in-law want her back now that this unpleasant episode was almost over? Lady Uckfield was not finished. 'A year ago,' she said, 'you were sick of the sight of Charles. When he spoke you gritted your teeth, when he touched you, you shivered. I am his mother and I lived in the same house with you. Did you think I wouldn't notice these things?'

'It wasn't like that.'

'It was exactly like that. He bored you. He bored you to death. Worse than that, he irritated you to the point of distraction. He could not please you however hard he tried. Nothing he said or did was right. He set your nerves on edge by his very presence and yet now ... what am I to make of this sudden eagerness to see him? What has changed?'

Edith drew herself up and looked her opponent in the eye. She was determined somehow to try to gain the initiative. 'Has it occurred to you that I might have had some time for reflection? Or am I too stupid in your eyes to think of anything but money and social climbing?'

'My dear, I never thought you stupid.' Lady Uckfield held up her palm in protest. 'You must at least give me credit for that.' There was a noise on the gravel and the older woman walked over to the window but it was not, as she had feared, Charles coming back for something he'd forgotten. 'I have to ask myself why now, why suddenly, a meeting is so essential when in the first months away you exhibited no such wish. I am a mother and I have to say to myself, what could have changed that might make a reunion with my son so desirable now when it was so *un*desirable then?"'

'Perhaps I don't feel I've made a good choice. Is that hard to understand?'

'On the contrary. I find it easy to understand. Especially since I think you've made a very poor choice indeed. But...' She rested her fingertips against each other like an avuncular preacher making a point in a pulpit. 'Why *now*? Why such a change upon an instant?'

Edith stared at her. 'You can't stop me seeing him for ever,' she said.

Lady Uckfield nodded. 'No. I dare say I can't.'

'Well then.'

'I think I can stop you seeing him for a few months. Six perhaps, or even three. Let us see how we all feel then about this poor choice you have made.'

At that moment Edith realised that of course her mother-in-law, dear Googie with her mind as pure as snow, knew. They never talked about it, neither at that time nor in the ensuing years, but they were always aware from then on that, beyond a shadow of doubt, they both *knew*. Edith stood up. 'I'm going now.'

'Are you sure? Can I at least give you something to eat? Or what about a loo? You've come *such* a long way.' Once again the tone had settled back into its usual intimate pattern with the rhythm of shared midnight secrets in the dormitory.

At this moment, in some strange way, it was hard for Edith not to admire this woman, her sworn foe, who held onto the high ground in every argument against all-comers. It was hard but it was not impossible. 'You are a fucking cow,' she said. 'A fucking cow with a hide of leather and no heart.'

Lady Uckfield seemed to think over these words for a moment

before nodding. 'Probably there is some truth in your unflattering description,' she acknowledged. 'And it is perhaps for that reason, or something resembling it, expressed hopefully in more fragrant language, that I have made such a success of my opportunities and you have made such a failure of yours. Goodbye, my dear.'

~

You may ask yourself why Edith, outfoxed at every turn, did not travel the more modern route out of her dilemma and, released from embarrassment after a short stay in some discreet, rural nursing home, why she did not then wait the three or six months stipulated by Lady Uckfield and outface them all. I suspect that she hardly knew the reason herself but somehow she was determined not to go that way. She was not, so far as I am aware, particularly religious and, I would have thought, operated on the minimum of moral scruples generally but perhaps because she had seen a way in which she could spare a life, a life that depended on her and her alone, she could not now bring herself to sacrifice it. It was, I think, an essentially animal decision rather than a sentimental one – or else then every tigress in the jungle is sentimental. Women, I suspect, can understand better than most men why something that hardly existed notionally and legally did not yet exist at all should still have been able to command such loyalties.

In the end, help came from a most unlikely sector. She had told me the following morning about her brief sojourn at Broughton and I was naturally dreading the request that I should take a more proactive hand in the whole business when she surprised me by telling me that she was going to wait until Charles's next visit to Feltham. 'He goes every fortnight or so. I'll collar him there.'

'How will you know when he's visiting?'

'Caroline's going to tell me. She'll drive me down.'

This information was both relieving and astonishing. Relieving because of course it meant I could be dispensed with and astonishing because it would never have occurred to me that Caroline would work against her mother's interest. Even now I am not completely sure of her motives. The Chase marriage was looking rocky. It is possible that she did not want the issue of her own satisfactory divorce arrangements being swamped by the divorce of the heir. It may have been an act of rebellion against her mother whose values Caroline always thought (quite wrongly as it happens) she had rejected. It may have been simpler. She loved her brother and she must have hated seeing him unhappy. In the end, I suppose it was, as always, a mixture of all these elements.

'When did you get in touch with her?'

'She telephoned me this morning. She'd heard about my visit to Broughton. I suppose she feels sorry for me.'

'Well, I won't say I'm not surprised but I'm pleased for you. It's certainly a good deal more suitable that Charles's sister should help you than that I should. Will you let me know how you get on?'

'I will,' she said.

※　　※　　※

Despite her explanation, Edith herself was not really clear as to Caroline's motives. They had never been close since Edith's admission into the family. They were not enemies. Indeed, despite Eric's almost continual stream of snide comments directed at Edith, she and her sister-in-law had achieved a kind of guarded familiarity but 'friendship' would have been too strong a word for it and Caroline would never have been confused as to where her loyalties lay. For all her professed modernity, Caroline Chase, devoid of self-knowledge as she was, remained very much a chip off her mother's block. She might despise the taut-faced countesses and ministers' wives that made up Lady Uckfield's coterie but when it came down to it her own friends were generally these women's rebellious and oddly-dressed children.

At all events, whatever her motives, she was as good as her word. Two days later the telephone rang in the Ebury Street flat and when Edith picked it up Caroline was on the line. 'Charles is at Feltham now if you're serious. He went down last night and he's on his own there until tomorrow.'

Edith glanced over to where Simon was deep in the *Daily Mail*. He also had the *Independent* delivered every day but he never read it. She steadied herself for one of those faintly Chinese telephone conversations designed to conceal their subject from the witnesses present. 'That's kind of you,' she said.

'So do you want me to take you down?'

'If you can,' came the stilted reply.

'Can't you talk?'

'Not really.'

'I'll be at the top of lower Sloane Street by Coutts at ten o'clock.'

'Fine.' Edith replaced the receiver carefully. It was not, as she explained later, that she ever wavered in her desire to see Charles but, just as she kept silent about the Sussex visit, she was not a big one for bridge-burning. As it happened, Simon had hardly been aware of the telephone conversation at all. She smiled across at him. 'Aren't you working today?'

He looked up. 'In the afternoon. Why?'

'That was Caroline. Asking me to lunch.'

'You're keeping your options open, then.'

She didn't answer but he didn't care.

Once again, she chose her clothes with some deliberation. The easy option was to repeat herself and simply to don a country outfit from her Broughton days but that seemed somehow dishonourable after her humiliation at the hands of Lady Uckfield. It was also, as she now saw more clearly, obvious, which was worse. No, if Charles were to take her back it must be as herself and not because she could pass as Diana Bohun or any of the other cold-hearted bitches who enjoyed their loveless marriages at the heart of Charles's world. Eventually she selected a tight black skirt that showed her legs and a loose blue sweater interwoven with coloured ribbons. She brushed her hair and applied her make-up fairly heavily (that is, for Charles rather than for Caroline). She surveyed the results and was pleased. She looked pretty and bright and just Londony enough for it not to seem as if she was trying too hard.

'Very nice,' said Simon. 'Where are you off to now?'

'I thought I'd do some shopping. I've got to get a birthday present for my father.'

'I suppose I'm not included in the girls' lunch.'

'It's at Caroline's flat . . .' She shrugged sadly. 'Why not come with me now? If I can find something for Daddy, I'm going on to Harrods. See what they've got in for the summer.'

It may seem that there was a calculated risk in this cunning approach but there wasn't really. No man in his right mind would accept the job of trailing a woman through a series of departments when she isn't even looking for anything specific. Especially when there's no lunch at the end of it. He shook his head as she knew he must. 'Not really. If it's all right. I'll see you tonight.'

'What time will you be back?'

He shrugged. 'Seven. Eight.'

They kissed and Edith seized a coat and was gone. A minute later she was walking towards the antique shops at the Pimlico Road end of the street. She knew that Caroline would ask her what she was up to in the two hours on the road that lay ahead and she was trying to determine both what she would say and what was the truth – not that these two would necessarily correlate.

She knew by now, if only from Lady Uckfield's near-hysterical opposition, that there must be a chance she could get Charles back. For a while she had pretended to herself that she was still simply exploring the possibility but in her heart she had already gone a stage further than that. She was bound to acknowledge that she would not have been as anxious as she had been in her attempts to secure a meeting had this not been the case. The question remained, how much did she want him back? Did she want him at any cost? Would she try to exact concessions? Would their life return to precisely the same pattern? And then again, could she gain concessions anyway? Weren't all the cards in Charles's hand? Worst of all: suppose she was wrong and he *didn't* want her back? In these ruminations, she was conscious that she had pushed the *real* reason for her change of heart to the back of her mind but she reasoned that if she was successful then that was after all where it was going to stay and so why worry about it now? It seemed to present her with such a yawning chasm that there was no reason to negotiate it before she absolutely had to. To all intents and purposes, from the moment she had known that she was at last to be permitted to see Charles, her secret had ceased to be true.

She stopped outside the art gallery opposite the Poule Au Pot and glanced at some sketches in the window. As she stood there, a gleaming limousine drew to a halt and the chauffeur helped a woman of some indeterminate Middle Eastern aspect to alight from the vehicle and enter the shop. Looking at this heavily-rouged, sable-wrapped creature, diamond bracelets flashing in the sun, Edith suddenly thought of her mother-in-law. How well she knew that this would not be Lady Uckfield's way. She would arrive in a taxi with a minimum of fuss, in sensible clothes and excellent pearls, and rely on the recognition of the manager. And yet the fact remained that, should these women meet, this Levantine would be nervous of Lady Uckfield while Lady Uckfield would be politely indifferent to her.

Her clash in the Little Library at Broughton, far from lowering Lady Uckfield in Edith's eyes, had paradoxically resulted in a grudging respect for her code. She had always faintly despised those members of her, or Charles's, circle who had fawned over her mother-in-law, but over the last days she had come to re-examine her feelings. In the early stages of her marriage she had perhaps yearned for more of what this Eastern woman in her furs took for granted in her daily round, luxury, glamour, famous faces. All these things – at any rate an English version of them – the young Edith Lavery had wrongly perceived as being connected to the world of a 'Lady Broughton' and she had been taken aback when so much of her new life had proved mundane. She knew that Lady Uckfield thought she, Edith, had gleaned her ideas from novels and nineteenth-century biographies, she had even attempted to defend her own mother occasionally from the accusation of filling her head with bourgeois fantasy, but she realised there was justice in the charge. The reality of life with Charles had seemed so flat and changeless compared to those action-packed plots, the glittering, power-filled ballrooms, that dizzying Lady-Palmerston-like career that she had been anticipating.

And yet, that day at the dress show, when the crowd had broken before Lady Uckfield and her minor Royal Highness like the Red Sea before Moses, Edith had seen what she had thrown away, the key to every closed door in England and most of the rest of the world – at least among the superficial. A landed title might not secure an invitation to Camp David but, even in the twenty-first century, she need never be alone in Palm Beach. And Edith knew by now that the kind of people who *were* superficial, the snobs whose social life was based around collecting people to underpin their own status, outnumbered the rest by ten to one. This kind of power might not be worth much in the great scheme of things but it was something and what had she gained in exchange for it? Life at Broughton might be dull but what was life in Ebury Street? Which did she prefer, lack of noise or lack of muscle? She had walked out of the world of the worldly in a petulant pout of boredom and overnight she had transformed herself from a high court card in the Game of Society into a non-person that people were ashamed to be seen with.

With something akin to a shiver she resumed her walk. Then she thought of the two men. Her subconscious assumption, because she knew that she had married Charles for his name and his fortune, had always been that, stripped of these things, she would never have looked at him. In their two years together she had grown to resent him, absurd as that now seemed even to her, for luring her with his worldly possessions without having the personality to amuse her once she was caught. The truth was she had pursued him and yet, in her self-justifying and dishonest mind, by the time Simon had come along, Charles had assumed the moral status of a baited trap.

Now, strolling down Pimlico Road, admiring the antique window displays, she thought back to her ruminations in the Green Park and realised that separation had changed things. It was her unconscious habit these days to think of her husband more gently. Was he really so disagreeable as company? So much less attractive than Simon? After all, men far worse than Charles find wives all the time. Would the idea of Charles as a husband have seemed so bad in the old days before her marriage? If she had been introduced to Mr Charles Broughton as a schoolfriend's suitor would she have wanted to run out screaming into the night, dragging the doomed girl with her? Of course not. Certainly Simon was a good deal better looking, there could be no doubt of that, but over the months she had grown used to his looks and she had begun to be irritated by the perpetual twinkling that seemed to accompany his every social interchange. All those half-smiles and narrowed lids lavished on waitresses and air hostesses and girls at the check-out in Partridges, all that tossing back of the golden locks, had started to bore her.

More troubling than the comparison of appearance (Charles, after all, while no beauty, was perfectly respectable to look at) was the question of sex. She had to concede that Simon was much the better lover, an excellent lover indeed by any standards let alone poor Charles's, and this was harder to dismiss. She enjoyed going to bed with Simon. Very much. In fact, the thought of making love with him was still enough to tickle her innards, to make her slightly fidgety and uncomfortable, to make her want to cross and uncross her legs. Dear Charles could never be a competitor here with his fumbling, five-minute thrust and his *'thank you*, darling', which nearly drove her mad

But for the first time she acknowledged, predictably perhaps, that after a year, making love to Simon had lost its novelty. The sex, though less frequent than at first, was still excellent, no question, but it could no longer blind her to the life for which she had left her gilded cage. After all, how much time does one actually spend in bed making love? Was it really worth the rest of the bargain? Did a pleasurable half an hour two or three times a week compensate for those endless, terrible parties, those awful people with their flat accents, sitting around the flat smoking, or those frightful drama school pals discussing 'hair-dos' and gardening tips and bucket-shop holidays? And anyway, wasn't Charles rather sweet in his way? Wasn't he more decent than Simon? Wasn't he truer as a person?

So Edith continued up Sloane Street belabouring herself with her false values, all the while attempting to convince herself with a litany of Charles's essential worth until, in a rare moment of honesty, like the sun breaking through the clouds, she saw the irony of this inner conversation. She, Edith, was using these arguments as if the opposition to them would overwhelm her should she give it a hearing. She was forcing herself to the next step when any impartial observer, and of this she was suddenly quite sure, would have freely volunteered that of course Charles was more decent than Simon. In fact, in any real way, it was perfectly obvious that Simon wasn't decent at all. Unlike Charles he had no honour, only pragmatism. He could not be true because there was no truth in him. His morality was a tawdry bundle of received, fashionable causes that he believed would make him attractive to casting directors. Edith was talking herself into thinking that in some ways she preferred Charles to Simon when to anyone who knew them both there could be no comparison. Charles, dull as he might be, was infinitely the better man. Simon was a mass of nothing.

She saw then that people would not think ill of her for coming round to this opinion – something she dreaded – but, on the contrary, they were amazed she had ever walked out on her husband for such a hollow gourd. Even so, and at this moment she felt it behoved her to be honest for once in her life, it was not for Charles's virtues that she wanted him back nor even because of her secret. It was for the sense of protected importance that she missed and that now, in her unadmitted crisis, she needed more than ever. The truth was that her months away had only finally confirmed her mother's prejudices. Edith had gone for a walk and found it was cold outside.

'I think I'm leaving Eric,' said Caroline, as they nosed at last on to the M11. Edith nodded, raised her eyebrows slightly and said nothing. 'No comment?' asked Caroline. She was a terrifying driver, as she had never mastered the art of conducting a conversation without facing the other person.

Edith glanced nervously at a lorry that passed within inches and shook her head. 'Not really. I don't know that I'm in a position to make a comment. Anyway,' she stared out of the window, 'I never grasped why you married him. Leaving him seems much easier to understand.'

Caroline laughed. 'I've forgotten why I married him. That's the problem.'

'What luck there are no children.'

'Is it?' Caroline's face had assumed a hard Mount Rushmore look, which gave her the appearance of an Indian chief in some fifties western when one was still allowed to be on the side of the cowboys. 'I think it's rather a bore. It means if I want any I'll have to go through the whole bloody business again.' There was some truth in this. 'I can't help feeling sometimes that, within limits, it doesn't seem to make much odds whom one marries. One's bound to get a bit sick of them in the end.'

'Then why leave Eric?'

'I said "within limits",' answered Caroline with some asperity, taking her eyes completely off the road and narrowly avoiding a large transporter. 'In my old age, I have to concede that Lady Uckfield may have been right.' One of the most chilling comments on the private family life of the Broughtons was that Caroline and Charles, when talking to each other, would refer to their mother as 'Lady Uckfield'. It was sort of a joke and sort of a comment. Either way there was something troubling in it. Caroline continued. 'She told me it was a mistake to marry a man who was vulgar and had no money, which of course I went on to do. But she added that if I had to break these primary rules then I should be sure to marry a man who was polite and kind, rudeness and cruelty being the only two qualities that absolutely poison life.'

Edith nodded. 'I agree with her,' she said. She was perhaps surprised at the wisdom of her mother-in-law's injunction. She shouldn't have been. Lady Uckfield was far too intelligent not to realise that true misery stifles all endeavour. It was just that she was much more sensible than Edith about what constitutes true misery.

'Eric was so rude. Not just to me but to everyone. A dinner party at our house was a kind of survival course. The guests had to arrive armed and see how many brickbats they could avoid before escaping into the night. Looking back, I can't imagine why anyone ever came twice.'

'Then why did you marry him?'

'Partly to annoy my mother,' said Caroline, as if that was absolutely understood. 'Then partly because he was so good-looking. And finally, I suppose, because he tremendously wanted to marry me.'

'And now you don't think he was genuine.'

'No, he was genuine all right. He was desperate to marry me. But it was because I was a marquess's daughter. I didn't see that. Or I didn't see it was *only* that.'

Edith said nothing. The conversation was moving into a dangerous area. She heard the distant sound of cracking ice under her halting steps. 'Right,' she murmured.

But Caroline had not finished with her. 'Rather as you wanted to marry Charles,' she said. When Edith made no comment, she continued, 'Not that I blame you. There's much more point to it that way round. At least marrying Charles made you a countess. Even now, I can't see what Eric thought he'd get out of it.'

They drove on for a bit in silence. Then Edith re-opened. 'If that's what you think why are you driving me up here?'

Caroline thought for a moment, wrinkling her brows, as if the idea had only just occurred to her. She was almost hesitant when she spoke. 'Because Charles is so unhappy.'

'Is he?' said Edith, thrilled.

'Yes.' Caroline lit a cigarette and for a moment Edith thought they were going into the central divider. 'I know Lady Uckfield thinks it'll blow over. She has a fantasy that he will forget you and marry the daughter of some peer who'll give him four children, two of whom will inherit estates from relations of their mother's.' Caroline laughed wryly. This was of course a wonderfully accurate *résumé* of Lady Uckfield's dreams.

'Are you quite sure she's wrong?'

'How little you know my brother,' said Caroline, and lapsed again into silence. Edith naturally longed to hear more of this wretched and unhappy man, whose life was a misery without her and to whom, by some strange miracle, she was already married. She gave Caroline a quizzical look and the latter relented. 'In the first place I do not think that my mother's idea of your perfect successor is Charles's. To put it bluntly, if that was what he was looking for he could have found it with very little difficulty. But that is no longer the point. Charles is a simple man. He is capable of feelings but they are uncomplicated, straightforward and deep. He can hardly communicate and he cannot flirt at all.' Edith thought with wonder of her other love, who could only communicate and flirt. Simon's problem was the opposite of Charles's. He could not feel. Caroline was still talking. 'Charles has made his choice. You. You are his wife. In his heart that's it. Finish. I am not saying that if you did divorce him he wouldn't eventually settle for someone else as brood-mare but in his heart he would have failed and his real wife would be out there walking around with someone else. And that, my dear, would be you.'

The rest of the drive was accomplished in silence. It was almost as if they were waiting for the next event in the plot before they could continue their discussion. And so they wound their way through the flat Norfolk landscape until at last they turned into a well-kept but somewhat overshadowed drive, which in its turn, when they had been released from the high walls of rhododendron, brought them to the wide, gravelled forecourt of the main house.

Feltham Place had passed into the Broughton family in 1811 when the then Lord Broughton had married Anne Wykham, only child of Sir Marmaduke Wykham, sixth baronet and the last of his line. The house was Jacobean, more a gentleman's than a nobleman's residence, picturesque rather than magnificent with roofs bristling with barley sugar chimneys and possibly for this reason it had never managed to catch at the family's imagination. Like many houses of its period it was in a dip (before the pumping innovations of the late seventeenth century allowed those splendid, landscaped views), although the flatness of the county gave a certain openness at the bottom of its valley. It might have functioned as the Broughtons' Dower House or as a seat for the heir, but there were other houses nearer Uckfield that had served these turns at least until the Second World War and recently, as we know, the heir had chosen to live with his parents.

In the past, Feltham had been let but it was taken back for the shooting in the 1890s and had been farmed in hand ever since, despite the family's allowing the sport to lapse after the war. Charles had revived the shoot over the last few years and he was proud of the fact that he could now safely let two and three-hundred-bird days, secure in the knowledge that there would be no great disappointments. He and his keeper had worked hard. The covers and hedgerows had been replanted, the feeding pens reorganised, indeed the whole appearance of the countryside had been more or less restored to the condition of a century before. But despite this, he was not tempted to bring his own shooting guests to Feltham. They were offered the splendours of Broughton while businessmen, people with mobile telephones and gleaming sports wear, took the shooting at Feltham by the day. At a (considerable) extra cost they could even stay overnight, which may have accounted for the somewhat boarding-house quality within.

The Wykham who'd built the place had been a favourite of King James I and in those days it had been much larger but the king's beau had been improvident and his heir (a nephew since, unsurprisingly, the builder had never married) demolished two-thirds of it. This meant that the brickwork and carving on the façade and throughout the house was of a much higher standard than one would normally associate with the scale of building. Inside, all the first-rate furniture and pictures had long since been swallowed up by Broughton and most of what remained dated from its rehabilitation as a shooting-lodge at the end of the last century. Lumpy, leather-covered Chesterfields provided the seating and the walls were covered with second-rate portraits and enormous, indifferently painted scenes of hunting, shooting and all the other methods of country killing. Still, the rooms themselves were pleasant and the staircase, more or less the sole survivor from the days of the Jacobean favourite, was magnificent.

Edith hardly knew the place. In Charles's mind it was the nearest thing to an 'office' in his weekly round. He ran it as a business and apart from an occasional appearance at a village show and an annual cocktail party for all those neighbours who might be tiresome about the shoot were they not courted every so often, he had no social profile in the county at all. Quite frequently he stayed with the Cumnors at their infinitely larger and more luxurious house four miles down the road, rather than put the ancient care-taking couple to the trouble of opening a bedroom.

Caroline drew up by the front door and the two women made their way into the wide and gloomy hall that took up two-thirds of the entrance front. It was decorated by a frieze of slightly bogus armorial tributes to the Wykhams and the Broughtons but otherwise boasted no colour at all apart from the brown of the panelling and the less attractive brown of the leather furniture. 'Charles!' Caroline called out. It was a chilly day and the interior of the house was noticeably colder than the air outside. Edith pulled her coat tightly around her. 'Charles!' shouted Caroline again, and she set off through a doorway that led first to the staircase and then into the former morning room that operated as Charles's office. Edith followed her. Desks and filing cabinets stood about the room, the chill slightly alleviated by a three-bar electric fire in the grate that looked as if its very existence breached the entire safety code. They were still standing there when another door, facing them, opened and there all at once stood a flummoxed Charles. To her amazement, even to her delight, Edith suddenly realised that she was shocked at his appearance. Gone was that sleek country gentleman who always looked as if he was on the way to make an advertisement for Burberry's. She was astonished to see that her fastidious husband was looking scruffy and unkempt. He was almost dirty. Caught out by her stare, he pushed his fingers through his hair. 'Hello,' he said, with a watery smile. 'Fancy seeing you here.'

At this point Caroline took her leave. 'I'm going in to Norwich,' she said. 'I'll be back in a couple of hours.' It was a relief really that she didn't even try to normalise the situation or start any we-were-just-driving-past nonsense.

Charles nodded. 'I see,' he said.

Left alone, Edith was oddly blank as to quite what she was going to say next. She sat on the edge of a chair near the fire like a housemaid at an interview and leaned forward to warm her hands. 'I hope you're not cross. I did so want to talk to you. Properly. And I began to feel that I was never going to be allowed to. I'm afraid I thought I'd just chance it.'

He shook his head. 'I'm not a bit cross. Not at all.' He hesitated. 'I – I'm sorry about the telephone calls and all the rest of it. It wasn't my mother not telling me, you know. Well, it wasn't only that. I expect you thought it was. It was just that I didn't really know what to say. It seemed better to leave it all to the professionals. Of course now you're here . . .' He tailed off disconsolately.

Edith nodded. 'I had to know what you were thinking about everything. I understand your parents want you free straight away.'

'Oh that.' He looked sheepish. 'I don't mind. Honestly. Whatever suits you.' He stared at her in the unflattering light of an overhead bulb. 'How's Simon?'

'Fine. Very well. Loving his series.'

'Good. I'm glad.' He didn't sound it but he was trying to be courteous. Edith was struck anew by the decency and kindness of this man she had tossed aside. What had she been thinking of? Her own actions sometimes seemed to her so hard to understand. Like a foreign film. And yet these had been her choices. The conversation limped on.

'I don't think I ever came to Feltham at this time of year. I must have but I don't remember. It's rather lovely, isn't it?'

Charles smiled. 'Dear old Feltham,' he said.

'You ought to live here. Do it up. Get some of the stuff back.'

He half nodded. 'I think I'd be a bit lonely, stuck out here on my own. Don't you? Nice idea, though.'

'Oh, Charles.' In spite of the cynicism with which she had embarked on this mission Edith had become a victim of her own justifications. Like Deborah Kerr in *The King and I*, whistling her happy tune to make herself brave, Edith had succeeded in talking herself into believing that she was a romantic figure who had lost her love rather than a selfish girl who bitterly regretted her comforts. Her eyes began to moisten.

Oddly perhaps, it was only at this moment that Charles fully grasped she had definitely come to try to get him back. Up to this point he was still wondering if it might not just be for some financial or time-related scheme that she had made the journey. Despite his earlier suspicions, his non-existent vanity made him slow to reach the obvious conclusion and he thought she might want him to agree to something before his lawyers could talk him out of it. He was not offended by this but, if it should prove to be the case, he was anxious to conceal his wretchedness from her. Both out of consideration for her feelings and from a (perfectly justifiable) sense of pride. It now occurred to him, with a lurch in his stomach, that this was not what he was dealing with. She wanted to come back to him. He looked at her.

For all his simplicity, he was not an idiot. Thinking along the same lines as that night in his study at Broughton he knew that he was no more interesting than when she left him. He also suspected that the world of show business had not really appealed to her, not at any rate for 'every day'. Just as a year of sin had served to give Edith a clearer idea of what Simon consisted of, so two years of marriage and a year apart had made Edith comprehensible to Charles. He knew she was an *arriviste* and the child of an *arriviste*. He saw her vulgarities of spirit now as sharply as he saw her fine points, of which, despite Lady Uckfield's comments, he still believed there were many. He also knew that if he made a move towards her the thing was settled.

He stared at the hunched-up figure, trying to scoop warmth out of the electric bars. Her coat was a sort of camel colour and looked rather cheap. Was this sad little figure, this 'blonde piece' as his mother would say, to be the next Marchioness of Uckfield? To be painted by some indifferent chocolate box portraitist and hung alongside the Sargeants, Laszlos and Birleys of the preceding generations? Was it in her to make a go of it?

But as he watched her, the sense of how vulnerable she suddenly seemed to him, with her bright make-up and her chain store coat, trying to charm him and looking instead somehow pathetic, overwhelmed him with pity and, in the wake of pity, with love. Whatever her suitability, whatever the limitations of her feelings, whatever her motives, he knew that he, Charles Broughton, could not be responsible for her unhappiness. He was, in short, incapable of hurting her.

'Are you happy?' he said slowly, knowing as he did so that the words gave her permission to return to him and to his life.

At the sound of them Edith knew her pardon had come through. Despite the difficulties with Simon, with her mother-in-law, with the newspapers, with the sun, with the moon, she could now be Charles's wife again if she chose, which, not very surprisingly given all the circumstances, she did. For a second she felt almost sick with relief but then, since she did not wish to appear too desperate, she waited for a minute before she spoke, deliberately punctuating the moment with a pregnant pause. Once satisfied that her answer was anticipated by them both she carefully raised her tear-stained eyes to his.

'No,' she said.

EPILOGUE

~

Smorzando

It did not, so far as I remember, cause any great murmur when Edith was delivered of a daughter seven months or so after the reconciliation. Of course, there was a lot of talk, particularly from her mother, about their being taken by surprise as Edith was 'so frighteningly early'. In fact, Mrs Lavery rather over-egged her performance by insisting on sitting in the hospital throughout the night because of the 'risks of premature birth', which naturally gave rise to a few funny stories on the dinner circuit, but nobody minded. Versions of this sort of folderol are still rather touchingly employed in Society on such occasions. These things are rituals rather than untruths and cause no harm. The point was the baby was female, which took any future strain out of the situation. It meant everything could return to normal without a lingering after-taste.

Even Lady Uckfield, usually so careful, gave herself away in a rare unguarded moment when I telephoned to learn the news.

'Boy or girl?' I asked when she picked up the receiver.

'Girl,' said Lady Uckfield. 'Isn't it a *relief?*' Then, quickly but not quickly enough, she added, 'That they're both doing so well.'

'A great relief,' I answered, going along with this dishonesty. There was no point in blaming her for retaining the deepest prejudices of her kind. Now that the baby could not inherit the glories of Broughton, thanks to the arcane laws governing the peerage that even Mr Blair, for all his trumpeting of women's rights, has not seen fit to change, she would present no further danger and might be lived with in peace. Since all three 'parents' were fair there was not much chance of the baby having the wrong colouring and, at least to date, the girl does not seem particularly to favour Simon, always assuming of course that the infant is his – something of which one can, after all, never be entirely sure. Not at least without resorting to DNA testing, which no entrant in

258

Debrett's would ever risk for fear of what it might reveal. One foreign visitor at Broughton, ignorant of the excellent Edwardian maxim never to 'comment on a likeness in another's child' asked me if I did not think she took after Charles.

I may have imagined a momentary chill in the room but I nodded. 'I do,' I said. 'She's not like Edith at all.' Thereby earning an especially warm glance from my host. Amusingly enough, when I looked at the toddler properly, she did seem to resemble him a bit. But then again that may have been in expression rather than feature. It might seem strange but in later years Charles came to love the girl so much that his younger children would complain of his favouritism. Even less logically, she would eventually develop into the preferred grandchild of Lady Uckfield, which only goes to show that the old maxim is correct and there's nowt so queer as folk. At any rate, barely fourteen months later, Lady Broughton was once more brought to bed, this time of a boy. The new Viscount Nutley was welcomed with bonfires and bun fights in Sussex and Norfolk and, frankly, to be brutal and unmodernist about it, the exact paternity of little Lady Anne had ceased to matter much to anyone.

Caroline did divorce Eric. It was a quiet business without acrimony and with more style than I confess I thought Eric capable of. He was not single long. Within eighteen months he had married the daughter of an immensely rich Cheshire industrialist, Christine somebody or other. They were much better suited than he and Caroline had been. For one thing, she shared Eric's ambitions, which she pursued as relentlessly as if they had been her own and of course they soon were. I happened to meet them both at Ascot a few months after they married and I must say I liked her. She was full of energy and in many ways a good deal easier to rub along with than Caroline, even if she was already infected with Eric's nonsense. I remember her using the phrase 'our sort of people', meaning, I imagine, some sort of exclusive social group to which they belonged. It must have been a luxury for Eric who had spent his entire first marriage being reminded daily of an Inner Circle forever closed to him.

He growled at me by way of recognition but I was not offended. I had by this time forgiven Eric his earlier insults and anyway one of the freedoms of growing older is that one is no longer obliged to dislike someone simply because they dislike you. After all, he was entitled.

Lady Uckfield had made no secret of how little she relished his company and had, somewhat maliciously I suspect, used me at times to demonstrate this.

'I suppose you still see them all?' he said when his wife had stopped discussing her new Poggenpohl kitchen.

I nodded. 'We've got a baby now so a bit less than I did. But yes, I see them.'

'And is dear Edith happy in her work?' Of course, it was quite understandable that he should be irritated when he contemplated one who had survived the course that had brought him down.

'I think so.'

'I'll bet she is. And how is darling "Googie"?' He spat out the name just as I had once heard Edith do before her rehabilitation. Now, for her at least, the name had re-normalised. 'I wonder what my dear ex-mother-in-law thinks of all the recent developments.'

'Oh, I'd say she was pretty merry, one way and another,' I said, for all the world as if I thought he cared, and we nodded to each other and moved on.

As I strolled away to rejoin Adela for tea with Louisa in the Household Stand I pondered my answers and concluded that I had spoken no more than the truth. Of course, as everyone had predicted, the children had changed everything. One may be exhausted but there is little time to be bored with two children under four, particularly as Edith, to her mother-in-law's bemusement, had eschewed a proper Norland nanny and chosen instead to have a series of Portuguese and Australians. Charming girls, one and all (or nearly all), but not the type to take over the nursery as their province. I thought it a wise decision and so, I was pleased to note, did Charles.

But as to quite what Lady Uckfield really made of it all ... One would have to get up very early in the morning to know precisely what she thought about anything, earlier than I rise, certainly. We were not, as I had predicted, quite such friends after the reinstatement of Edith. Although I have not yet given up hope of regaining my former position of Court Favourite. Poor woman, she had allowed herself to dream a little during the interregnum and the imagined life she had woven for herself with dear Clarissa or one of her kind as junior chatelaine had filled her with happy prospects. Ironically her imaginings had not been all that unlike the despised Mrs Lavery's. Lady Uckfield, too, had seen herself as a special friend of her daughter-in-law's family. The two grandmothers would lunch together perhaps and take in an exhibition ... So it was hard to reconcile herself to the Return of Edith, not least because she had allowed herself the rare luxury of admitting what she really felt while Edith was away. Worse, she had confessed these secrets not only to herself and her husband, which was bad enough, but to me, a non-relation. In doing so she knew she had given me a weapon. From now on whenever she referred to 'our darling Edith' there was a risk that I might catch her eye if I so wished and in her heart expose her. I had no intention of doing this but the threat of it introduced a coldness between us nevertheless. I was and am sorry but there is nothing to be done about it. Meanwhile, Adela and I continue to stay at Broughton pretty regularly.

I remember once Lady Uckfield did let herself go a little. There had been a dinner party and the guests were spread out in knots over the drawing room and the Red Saloon next door. Edith was at the centre of an admiring group, for you will understand that a lot of people had a good deal of ground to make up having dropped her during her period of exile. One might have thought that those who had been loyal, Annette Watson for one, would have been rewarded with a shower of invitations but I don't believe they were. Perhaps this was predictable. Anyway, on this particular evening, surrounded as she was, Edith made some remark, I forget what, which was greeted with gales of sycophantic laughter. I was alone, having helped myself to some more coffee, so there was no one to overhear when Lady Uckfield drew level.

'Edith *Triumphans*,' she said. I nodded. But she would not let it go. 'To the victor the spoils.'

'And is Edith the victor?' I asked.

'Isn't she?'

'I don't know.' I shrugged. I imagine I was attempting to be philosophical and by an easy and familiar transition had become dishonest.

'Of course she is the victor,' said Lady Uckfield, quite truthfully. 'You have won.'

Now this was irritating. She was right about Edith, I do admit, but not about me. If anything I had always been a partisan of the Uckfields during the struggle for Charles's soul and she knew it. 'Don't blame me,' I said quite firmly. 'You asked me not to encourage her and I didn't. It was your own daughter who arranged it all, not me. The fact is Charles wanted her back. *Voilà tout.* He must know what's best for himself, I suppose.'

Lady Uckfield laughed. 'That, of course, is precisely what he does not know.' Her tone was a little bitter but more predominately sad. It was also, as I knew it must be, the tone of resignation. 'I told you I didn't believe they would be happy and I wait anxiously to be proved wrong. However,' she waved her little claws and the jewels in her rings flashed in the firelight, 'the thing is done. We must make the best of it. It is time to move on to the next square. Let us at least hope they will be no less happy than everybody else.' And she was gone.

Would they be less happy than everybody else? That was certainly the question. Although she had returned to him without treaty, Edith had nevertheless wrung some considerable concessions in the process. To start with she had grasped the folly of her earlier belief that it was safer to be bored in the country than entertained in London and she had persuaded Charles into a house in Fulham, which had been purchased for more or less what the little flat in Eaton Place had gone for. Now she allowed herself a day or two in London a week. She had also found some committees to sit on and had become involved, down in Sussex, in the actual day-to-day running of a hospice near Lewes. All in all, she had started to evolve the life she would be leading at sixty when she herself, never mind everyone else, would have forgotten that there had ever been a hiccough in her early married life. I thought, on reflection, that it all boded quite well.

We went down to Broughton two or three times a year as a rule. Adela and Edith were never much more than amiable with each other but Charles became very fond of my wife and so we were easy guests, I think. We enjoyed it as, apart from anything else, we had a baby in tow and the houses we could stay in without feeling that we had imported a miniature anarchist were few. Our son, Hugo, was about five months older than Anne and that ensured a measure of shared activity, accompanied by a good deal of merriment from both mothers. It is a truism but it is still true that the longer one knows people the less relevant it becomes whether or not one liked them initially. As I knew from my friendship with Isabel Easton, there is no substitute for shared history and it was clear that by the time ten years had passed, my wife and Lady Broughton would think of themselves as close friends without ever necessarily liking each other much more than they did to start with.

Needless to say, at an early stage after the great patch-up, Edith wished me to understand that she was not interested in pursuing long conversations about her choices, past or present. I quite agreed with her so she needn't have worried. I know only too well how tedious it is to have the recipient of earlier intimacies still hanging around when those intimacies have become irrelevant embarrassments. Anyway, so far as I was concerned, she had seen sense and I hadn't the slightest desire to shake her resolve.

She tested me a few times, waiting, when we happened to be alone, to see if I would bring up the subject of Simon or Charles or marriage or, worse, the baby, but I never did and I am happy to say she began to relax into our old intimacy.

In truth, even had she questioned me, I would have had little to report on the Simon front. I don't know how anxious his wife was to take him back when she had been given the surprising news that his Great Affair was over but, whatever her feelings, she had done it. I saw him once, some months later, at an audition and he told me he was planning to move to Los Angeles to 'try my luck'. I wasn't surprised since this is not an unusual reaction for a player after a disappointing career. As a rule the Hollywood pattern for English actors is simple. They are delighted to go, they are told there is a lot of work for them if they stick it out, they tell everyone how fabulous it is, they spend all their money – and then they come home. It seems to take from two to six years. However, there are always exceptions and I would not be surprised if Simon were one. He seemed to have all the qualities the natives of that city admire and none that they dislike.

Perhaps because he knew we would not be meeting for a while, he asked after Edith. I muttered that she was well and he nodded. 'I'm glad.'

'Good.'

He shook his head at me and raised his eyebrows. 'I don't know,' he said. 'Women!'

I nodded and gave him a sympathetic laugh so we parted friends. I suppose one might gauge the extent of his heartbreak from this subsequent reaction. I do not think Charles would have shaken his head to an acquaintance and said, 'Women!' like a character from a situation comedy had his wife chosen never to return. I think he would have curled up in the dark somewhere and never mentioned her name again, so I suppose we must all concede that Edith had ended up with the man who loved her most. Even so, there was no malice in Simon's eyes and I think one should remember this at least, that when all was said and done there really wasn't any harm in him. It is surely not so terrible a testimonial.

Nor did I ever betray to Edith the Eastons', or rather David's, anxiety to stay in with the family, if necessary at her expense. Gradually even that slightly uncomfortable connection was also resumed. All in all, things went back to normal surprisingly quickly. Even the papers only gave it a couple of squibs – in the *Standard*, I seem to remember, and in one of the tabloids – and then it was over.

Just once she did bring it up, perhaps because I never had. We were walking in the gardens on a Sunday in summer three or even four years after she had returned to the fold and we found ourselves down by the approach to the rose garden where they had set up our chairs for the filming, however long ago it was. The others were playing croquet and as we strolled along, the sound of balls being hit and people getting cross wafted gently over us. Suddenly I was struck by the image of Simon Russell, in his frilled shirt, stretched out on the ground in all his comeliness, as he gossiped that faraway day to a younger, sillier Edith. I said nothing of course and I was taken by surprise when she suddenly spoke into my imaginings.

'Do you ever see him now?' she said.

I shook my head. 'No. I don't think anyone does. He's gone off to California.'

'To make films?'

'Well, that's the idea. Or at least to make a television series.'

'And is he making one?'

'Not yet but you never know.'

'What about his wife?'

'She's gone with him.'

Edith nodded. We strolled on into the rose garden. Some heavily scented, dark red blooms, Papa Meilland maybe, filled the warm air with their sweet stench.

'Aren't you ever going to ask me if I'm happy?' said Edith with a provocative flick of her head.

'No.'

'Well, I'll tell you anyway.' She broke off a half-open bud and fed its stalk through the top buttonhole of my shirt. 'The fact is, I'm happy enough.'

I did not question her statement. I am glad she was and is happy enough. That is a good deal happier than a large proportion of my address book.